WHISKEY STORM

WHISKEY WITCHES PARA WARS BOOK 1

F.J. BLOODING

Whistling Book Press

Alaska

Printed in the United States of America

Published by Whistling Book Press

Whistling Book Press
Alaska
Visit our web site at:
www.whistlingbooks.com

Pre-order now at: https://www.fjblooding.com/preorder

Other Books in the Whiskey-Verse

Shifting Heart Romances

by Hattie Hunt & F.J. Blooding

Bear Moon

Grizzly Attraction

Here's the reading order to make it even easier to catch up!

https://www.fjblooding.com/reading-order

Other Books by F.J. Blooding

Devices of War Trilogy

Fall of Sky City

Sky Games

Whispers of the Skyborne

Discover more, sign up for updates and gifts, and join the forum discussions at www.fjblooding.com.

WHISKEY MAGICK & MENTAL HEALTH

S ign up to learn more about our books and receive this free e-zine about Whiskey Magick and Mental Health.
https://www.fjblooding.com/books-lp

To Sandi-Mom.
You really are appreciated.

A horrendous crash sounded in the living room followed by the screech of a baby owl and the yip of a baby—Paige didn't even know what. But she was learning fast as her two-day-old twins were quite good at shifting into any animal they thought of. And how they were able to think of all these animals was absolutely beyond her.

Paige stepped into the large living room in time to see one of the lamps fall over and smash onto the floor as a downy baby owl launched herself off the side table, shooting thunderbird electricity through the room in a single zinger.

A black and grey wolf pup struggled to walk as he yipped at her from the floor, his rajasi paws sparking with spurts of flames.

Dexx, the baby daddy, snored in the chair in the middle of all of it.

Paige pulled in a deep breath and barked with her alpha will, "Hey!"

The twins froze in midleap and yip, turning to look up

at her, Rai with her big electric blue eyes and Ember with his big, fiery amber ones.

Paige was looking forward to getting them past this point in their already short little lives. She should have known raising shifter witches was going to be a challenge, with everything they'd learned over the last year, and yet, each of these moments hit with an open-palm of surprise.

Bobby, her God's prophet toddler son, ran in on his three-year-old legs, a huge grin on his face. "Big noise!" Which was his way of saying trouble was afoot and he wanted to be a part of it.

Paige still had no idea if God was rolling over in His ethereal grave at the idea of His prophet being raised by witches or if He was laughing it up, dreaming of the day when it was revealed to His followers. She was rooting for the latter, though she doubted He was anywhere in the "caring-verse" anyway.

Bobby gravitated to the broken light bulb.

"Dexx," Paige barked, keeping the toddler away from the broken glass shards with one arm.

He startled awake, immediately wiping the drool from his five o'clock shadow, and sat up. "Huh? What did I miss?"

Paige daggered him with her gaze.

He ran a hand over his short dirty-blonde hair, his green eyes wide as he took in the room.

Two lamps were on the floor. One was salvageable. The other was completely destroyed. The green striped couch had a huge gouge in it where one of the twins had obviously been something with claws and had fallen *off* said couch. And the stuff that *had been* on the coffee table was now on the floor.

5

He looked up at her sheepishly, grabbing Bobby. "They were asleep. I swear."

Paige growled low in her throat and gathered the twins, one in each arm, and maneuvered around the solid burgundy couch, the brown comfy chair, and the other side table.

Ember was now a kitten, which made it immensely easier to carry him.

Rai had decided to shift back into a fully clothed human baby. Which, if Paige could just *talk* to her daughter, she'd have asked for a different shape. Humans were designed poorly for carrying. How had humans taken over the earth?

Leah hopped down the stairs, her blonde hair kind of "flat hair" bouncing behind her. She reached up and took Rai, giving her baby sister smooches. "How is the cutest baby girl in the whole wide world?"

Rai chose that moment to squirm out of Leah's arms and shift into a wolf pup.

Leah giggled and set her down before she crashed, then led the way to the back door to let her pup-sister into the back yard. "At least that one does her business outside already." She reached for Ember and goochy-gooochy-gooed his now human nose with hers. "If only Rai could teach this one."

He let out a screech-laugh that was only cute on babies and flailed his arms.

Leah whipped a diaper out of her back pocket and lightly thwapped him in the face with it.

He startled to a freeze position and then latched onto it with all the strength of a baby much older than him.

With Ember well in hand by Leah, Paige went to the kitchen to prepare bottles for them both.

Bobby came bumbling in and pushed one of the kitchen chairs, intent on toppling it.

"Bobby!" Paige didn't know whether to shake her head, scream, or pull out all her hair. "Stop. Breaking time is done."

He pulled a very pouty expression and clapped one hand to his face, his entire body slumping.

This kid was going to be a comedian one day.

Rai scratched at the door to be let in.

"Bobby," Paige pointed to the door.

The almost three-year-old's face lit with joy as he galloped to the door to let his sister in.

Dexx zombie-strolled to the coffee machine and went through the process of making Paige a cup. It wasn't for him. He liked a little coffee with his sugar and milk and preferred just to drink chocolate milk if given the choice.

Paige didn't *do* words first thing in the morning. She did grunts and growls and barks and bites and glares and hand gestures. But not words. Occasionally, there'd be a name thrown in there so people *understood* which person had drawn her wrath that time, but that was about it.

Her phone rang as she pulled the first bottle out of the boiling pot of water.

As a new mother, she should be breastfeeding. She knew that. But her milk jugs weren't working. They were producing. Kind of. They hurt. But there wasn't enough milk in there for one kid, much less two.

Oh, well.

She looked at her phone on the counter. Elder Yad.

"Doesn't he get that you should be on maternity leave?" Dexx asked, handing her the cup of steaming coffee like it was a sacrificial offering, moving the reusable straw toward her so she could sip out of it without dropping the bottles.

She hit ignore on the phone, grabbed the other bottle, and took a long, hot pull of the coffee cup as she carefully took it from her lover's hands. "Thank you," she whispered gratefully.

Dexx took one of the bottles from her and went to Rai. "Sorry," he whispered back.

Bringing twin shifter witches into the family had been hard on all of them. None of them had really had a chance to sleep. The twins were up at all hours, and there was no way to control what they'd even shift into.

Leslie sleep-stomped into the kitchen, her face blurry with the need to wake up. Her light brown, curly hair was a wild array of...well, wild. She went to the coffee machine and grabbed the cup Dexx had managed to make for her as well. "Those kids are from demons."

Paige knew for a fact they weren't. Paige could summon and send demons back to Hell, something her sister knew all too well. But she couldn't *produce* demon children.

But that brought another thought. A Hell gate had been seared into her bones years ago, making it a struggle for her to... well, be the demon summoner-exterminator. But ever since Sven Seven Tails had tried to destroy the world as they knew it and destroy the Hell gate itself, her bones had been quiet. Like, really quiet. The fight to stop him had put them all on international TV, but at least there weren't demons trying to possess her all the time. It was pleasantly quiet.

Her phone went off again.

Leslie grabbed it on her way to the dining table and handed it to her. "Danny Miller."

Crap. That was one phone call she should probably answer. With Ember guzzling down the bottle in her arm, she tucked the phone to her ear. "Hey. What's up?"

"I could ask the same." His tone told her he wasn't in the mood for small talk. "New babies treating you okay?"

She didn't do small talk either. She didn't understand it, but she did realize that some people needed it to feel like they were relating. "They're destroying my house one parent-nap at a time." Time to get to the point. "What's up, Danny?"

He sighed. "Have you watched the news lately?"

"Who watches that?" She had newborns tearing up her house.

He growled a little. Danny Miller prided himself on his news reporting abilities and didn't believe in this new era of news where the corporation that purchased the station or paper controlled the stories. "Just turn on the TV to Local Six."

Paige rose from the table, keeping Ember firmly in hand. The only TV in the house was in the living room, and it was rarely on. She fumbled with the remote, unfamiliar with the buttons. She never got much of a chance to watch it.

The president of the United States was addressing the nation.

"... in a state of emergency," she said, her blonde hair barely moving with the breeze. The lapel of her blue suit jacket jumped a little. "We now know of the paranormal presence and it must be addressed swiftly."

Wait. What?

"How many of them are there?" the president continued. "How great a threat are we facing?"

Dexx stepped beside her. "What's this?"

Paige didn't bother answering, her heart lurching to a stop. She knew just as much as he did at this moment and it didn't look good.

"We need the funding and the manpower to address this situation with the force and might it deserves." The president's normally distinguished face twisted in anger. "We can't allow another Troutdale situation to happen again or become the norm. How many lives were lost?"

That was a question Paige hadn't even asked, though, to be fair, she'd had a lot on her hands after that brutal battle. She'd lost her grandmother and had given birth to her twins on Main Street.

Images of the fight flashed across the TV screen. Sven towered over the street in a golden light as he pulled in the magickal energies from all around him. Demons swarmed the streets. Shifters and witches and all number of other paranormal creatures fought back, including more than a few humans.

They'd all united that day in order to fight back against Sven's demon army. Paige had felt like they'd done something amazing, and now it was being twisted?

"I'm issuing an Executive Order giving these paranormals four days to register with the government. They will be assessed and provided new homes in more secure areas. I'm—"

Dexx took the remote and turned off the TV, his face a boil of rage. "Relocated? Secure areas?"

Hadn't the U.S. tried this already? With the Japanese? And hadn't that ended badly?

Well, not for the government. For the Japanese Americans, it had.

Rai's fingertips buzzed with electricity as she suckled on her bottle, her eyes moving between her parents. Even her eyelashes danced with lightning.

Electricity and phones were a bad mix. Paige stepped

away from her daughter. "How far is she going to go with this?"

Danny was quiet for a long moment. "We've already received word she's got a few areas set up. They're prepped and ready."

"What kind of areas?" Resorts? Reservations? Prisons? "What do you mean?"

"Areas of 'relocation.' I don't know more yet, and my source has to be really careful so her cover isn't blown."

Paige understood that, but just hearing him repeat the word 'relocation' sent a chill of fear down her spine. "But no word on what they're planning?"

"No. But... tell me you're going to do something about this."

She really wanted to say no because this *shouldn't* be falling on her. She still didn't fully understand why people were looking to her to fix this. She was on maternity leave, trying to bond with her two little world destroyers. "Yeah." She offered a few more vagaries and hung up.

Dexx made movements to take Ember.

She moved away, the bottle propped up with her chin, and dialed Elder Yad. If she was going to save the world, she was going to do so *with* her kids beside her. Because...

Seriously. She couldn't *choose* anymore. She needed to be an adult and a mom and a responsible person in society all at the same time. She'd just have to figure out how to make it work.

Elder Yad answered quickly but said nothing.

She had no idea if he was having an issue with his Bluetooth headset or if he could even hear her, but she wasn't going to wait forever, either. "Gather those we need. My house. Lunch."

The line disconnected.

Well, that just left cleaning the house and preparing a meal for a small invading army. Both of which she hated.

Coming up with a plan to save the world?

She was getting better at that.

2

"Well, babe," Dexx said with a tired smile that was only half as sultry as it normally was. "As much I love just hanging out with you, I've gotta get some work done before everyone descends on this place."

Paige stared at him, a little poleaxed. Not because it was strange that he was working but because she realized she wasn't. Work had become such a normal thing to her. She'd *fought* to get more parenting time. She had. But now she was staring down the double barrels of parenthood and it was a little intimidating.

But that also meant it was time to get all the kids to school, too. She gave her husband a kiss and they and Leslie all worked to wrangle kids into cars.

The Whiskey siblings—Leslie, Paige, and Nick—all lived in the house along with their significant others *and* their kids. This meant that, when it was time to send kids to school, it took all of them, their cars, and no small amount of coordination to get it done efficiently. They'd accidentally left a kid at home alone before.

Paige had the twins strapped down in car seats only because they were currently sleeping in human form. It was her turn to take Leah and her tween niece, Mandy, to school. They were in the same grade, so they both went to the same school. Kate, her informally adopted elven niece, and Tyler, one of her nephews, were with Dexx, and Bobby and Kammy, her toddler nephew who had been born the same day as Bobby, were with Leslie. Car seats took a lot of freakin' space.

Leah and Mandy were having some sort of debate. Leah was wedged between her siblings in the back, and Mandy rode shotgun. Paige had no blasted idea what either of them was even talking about. They were speaking in some code she didn't get. They talked in texting short-hand, and the only thing she really got was LOL.

Was she getting *old*?

She pulled up to the high school—the mundanes' high school—and the two tweens spilled out. Rai woke and decided it was time to shift into a kitten and escape. Which was...great.

Paige held up the drop-off line to wrangle her kitten-kid back into the car. It wasn't a ton of cars, thankfully. The parents who were stuck behind her managed to hop the curb and go around. She waved apologetically. Most gave her tight looks in return.

However, a lot of the high schoolers drove. Paige didn't even want to think about that. Having Leah and Mandy the same age was like having another set of twins. Those two were going to be driving at the same time.

Wendy Green walked out of the high school as Paige wrangled Rai back into her seatbelt. Wendy waved, flagging Paige to wait.

Paige gave her daughter a stern alpha warning. "Stay in

human form until we get home." She still wasn't sure if Rai would obey because she was a baby. But Paige *hoped* her shifter spirit would provide a little guidance because when humans didn't obey, they still survived, but when animal babies didn't, they died.

Rai flapped her baby arms, slapping her hands against her bare thighs. Paige had barely gotten her into a diaper and a onesie before they'd left the house.

Ember was still out cold. Paige reached over and put her hand on his chest to make sure he was breathing. He was. He was just a good sleeper.

"Human," Paige said, putting her finger on Rai's little button nose and closing the door.

Wendy had made it to her by that point. "Paige." Her tone was pleasant, but her smile said she had something to say. "Can I have a word?"

Paige really wanted to say no. She wanted to tell the tall, black woman that she didn't have time. Not because she didn't like Wendy. She really did. That woman had the ability to control raging teens, which, in Paige's book, was a superpower. It was the fact that Wendy always brought problems Paige didn't know how to solve.

Respect won out. She pasted on a smile and leaned against the car. "What's up?"

Wendy bit the inside of her lip and leaned against the car as well. She pulled away quickly and glanced at Paige in askance.

She shook her head and gestured to the car with a shrug. "I'm not going to yell." Dexx might have if *anyone* had opted to lean against his 1970 Dodge Challenger, but Paige's car was just a sedan. Nothing special. It ran. It carted kids around. It took the bags to the airport. It got the groceries. It did its job.

Wendy scratched her eyebrow and leaned back on the rear door, glancing inside. Her expression melted a little. "They're adorable. They're getting so big so fast."

She wasn't lying. "They're shifter witches." Paige didn't know what that meant because this was new territory. "They can shift into anything, and my theory is *that's* the reason they're growing so fast."

Wendy pulled the corners of her lips down as she nodded. "I need to talk to you about clothes."

Oh. Since Sven had tried to destroy the world, humans and paranormals were now forced to coexist knowingly. And one of the things they'd done was to get the paranormals and humans together in the same schools. When a shifter witch—like Paige, Rai, Ember, or Leslie—shifted, they kept their clothes on because of their witch abilities. "Normal shifters lose their clothes when they shift, and they practice certain aspects of their shift at school."

Wendy raised her hand. "I get that. I do. But..."

Paige knew exactly what the "but" was. "Look, it took me a long time to get used to it too. So, we have cabinets stationed around our house for shifters to grab robes when they find themselves arriving unexpectedly. Because, trust me, they can stand in front of you completely naked and carry on a full conversation like it's nothing."

"But it *is* something."

Paige had been saying the same thing for about a year now, but hearing it come from Wendy made Paige realize that maybe the mundanes were wrong. "Maybe the issue isn't the shifters."

Wendy rolled her eyes.

"Listen to me." Because this conversation along with all the other things going on in the political news with the #MeToo movement was striking a chord in her that needed to be addressed. "The issue is that we've sexualized the body to the extent that little girls have to be careful of what they wear to class."

"Not *my* classes."

And that was reason one hundred and eighty-three why Paige respected the hell out of Wendy. "We can't teach our shifters that they need to be embarrassed with their bodies. That they need to be scared. What we're telling them is that others have more powers and more rights to their bodies than they do."

Wendy thought about that for a minute. "I get where you're coming from, but it doesn't work that way in the real world."

"Only because there are more people willing to sit around than there are those willing to make it a better place. This shit is hard. You've gotta make people uncomfortable, and we know how that goes."

Wendy bowed her head and then looked up at Paige briefly before pushing off the car and standing. She swung her arms a few times and then clapped her hands together. "Cabinets and robes."

Paige pushed off the car as well. "I see woodworking projects in class."

"Agreed. Okay. Have a good day." She gave the twins a sweeter smile and waved as she disappeared back into the school.

Well, at least this time was an easier issue.

With the older kids dropped off, she went to the grocery store—which was now more like a circus event with the twins in tow than a chore—and then went home. She was exhausted. She'd had to alpha-will both kids so many times just between the produce and the meat departments. And everyone had cooed at her kids like they were well-behaved

17

humans when they were, in fact, the most outrageously difficult—

She didn't even realize she'd fallen asleep until she was awakened by a loud noise.

Merry Eastwood stood beside her, a cool smile on her villainous face, her fingers perched on the rather large volume that was now resting on the side table beside Paige's head. "Nice nap?"

Paige wanted to throttle that woman until her dark hair turned grey. Two-hundred-year-old witches were a little hard to strangle, though. They had a lot of tricks hidden up their sleeves. So, she grimaced and got up instead, looking for the twins. One day, she'd get Merry Eastwood back in paranormal prison where she belonged. But for now, she was a needed ally.

The twins were in the dining room, tangling their tiny bodies around the feet of all the people invading their home.

She went to gather them, but Faith, their regional high female alpha, put her hand on Paige's arm and steered her to the kitchen instead. "We've all raised young ones before. We won't step on them."

Faith's soft tone was at war with the harsh scar over her eye. Faith had seen more battle damage than Paige—

Actually, by now, that probably wasn't even the case. But Paige was able to hide her scars because *hers* rested in her bones.

It was going to take Paige a long time to realize that she was an equal in this mix of high-ranking, powerful people.

She grabbed her coffee and went to the table. Their dining table was L-shaped and custom built. Families their size weren't the norm. Along with the Whiskey family, Dexx's pack lived out back, and they all sometimes shared the kitchen and dining room. Their family was a small community.

She stopped Elder Yad before everyone sat down. "Why is everyone in *my* home and why am *I* leading this charge?" The Elders, him especially, had been pushing her toward this since she arrived in Troutdale two years prior.

Elder Yad raised his bushy eyebrows and stared at her hard. "You're the one they saw on national news taking down Sven."

The unbelievably powerful demon who'd attacked her and the town just a few weeks ago. "Okay. That doesn't mean I should—"

"Who else do you think it *should* be?"

"I don't know. Someone who knows what the fuck they're doing?"

He shook his head, serious. "You're the best we have, and, in this time, you need to learn why. I could tell you it's because you're so powerful—and you are—and I could tell you it's because you're destined—because you are." He gripped her shoulders, his intensity high. "We're here because none of us *want* to be in your position, and you're taking this because this is who you are."

But was it? Really?

After getting the twins situated, Paige banged an empty sippy cup on the table and took her seat.

She'd at least seen most of the people there before. They were the high alphas and the most powerful elementals of their region. And she was one of them. At some point, that was going to have to stop surprising her.

It was time to get this party started. "Tell me you've all seen the news."

Elder Yad looked like that wizard from *Legend of the*

Seeker. He kinda sounded like him too. "We've been watching and the time to act is now."

"Great." But Paige was tired of hearing words and sentiment, which was usually what people brought to her because she was the person of action. "I think it's high time to hear what the Elder Council has in mind."

The Elder Council—for all that Paige had been able to gather—had been around since almost the time paranormals crossed over to the Americas. They "managed" the paranormals who swore fealty or whatever to them in Central and North America, but she was pretty certain their reach stopped there.

In all this time, though, Paige never knew or understood what their intent was. It wasn't to keep the paranormal secret. Or maybe it was. But that had been the job of the Shadow Sisterhood, who might work for them? She wasn't even certain at this point. But the council liked to gather information. They didn't' typically share it.

Yad rubbed his eye and nodded as if making a decision. "We need to gather our people and provide a united attack."

"On the government." Paige hoped he meant something else. They couldn't be talking about a revolution. There *had to be* a peaceful resolution in there somewhere. "You want the paranormals to rise up against the U.S. Government."

"I do."

Whoa. That'd been sarcasm.

Faith shifted in her chair, anxiety tinging her dark eyes. "Do you even know what this means?"

Yad took in a deep breath and laid his heavily age-spotted hands in front of him. "The president started this. We are merely reacting to her actions."

Merry just rubbed her finger against her lips, deep in

thought, her frown troubled. Leave it to the villain of the group to realize this was a bad idea.

Everyone else looked like they were working their way into accepting it.

"That's not good enough," Paige said because for fuck's sake! Seriously. "This would be an act of...treason?" She didn't even know. "It'd be civil war at the very least." That was huge and, frankly, inconceivable. This shouldn't be the *first* thought. It shouldn't be an *easy* conclusion. They needed to exhaust their efforts. "Has anyone talked to senators? Government representatives? Lawyers? People who understand this?"

"Yes," Elder Yad said, holding up his hand with a tired sigh. "But we've been informed that this isn't their matter."

"Not their—" Paige wasn't sure she could trust the Elders. "Maybe someone else should try who actually wants a solution instead of war."

Yad shook his head like he was biting off a nasty comment. "We already know how this is going to play out."

But did they? This wasn't history on replay. This was the twenty-first century. "We're U.S. citizens."

"They're not seeing it that way," Yad said, his tone equal parts patient and cutting, "and we all know it."

Leslie pressed her fist to her forehead as if trying to push her frustration back inside her skull. "What do we think the president will do next?"

No one answered.

"Let's look a' wha' was done in the bloody war, why don' we?"

Paige frowned at the red-headed man who looked like a really tall garden gnome. "Who are you?"

"Duglas Maclellan," he said in his—it could have been anything because Paige sucked at accents—accent.

"Lead water elemental for the region," Faith said softly to Paige. "Became a citizen after being here for a decade. Elder Council brought him in. He's the strongest water elemental we could get for the council, but his loyalties?" Faith shook her head with a sigh.

Water elementals were strange people. "Great. Thanks." Knowing names and people was seriously going to have to become a superpower Paige honed. "Which war?"

"The World War. Ya know the one. Where they killed off a bunch of people wha' got in their way of a perfect world view."

World War II and the Jews. "The president isn't a Nazi." She'd better not be. Paige'd voted for her.

"She isna?" Duglas clapped his lips into a thin line before speaking. "Ya really thin' we're not headed to that event? First, it's her tellin' the nation and the damned world that it's 'us against them,' makin' a right ruddy mess of it too. Turnin' neighbor against neighbor. Friend against friend. They're already forcin' us to register so they *know* who ta fear."

Paige frowned. The U.S. had racism. There was no hiding that fact. That didn't mean they were being run by Nazis. It just meant they had a lot of really loud assholes.

"Then, they'll start tellin' the humans tha' we're *diseased*. Start callin' us animals."

Paige could easily imagine that.

"After tha', they'll create special groups of people to 'handle' us lot."

They already had DoDO, an organization funded by the government to deal with the paranormals. Paige had already had run-ins with them that hadn't gone well.

"Then..." Duglas pointed to the living room where,

presumably, the TV was. "They tell the other side to be afraid o' us. They turn the mundanes against us."

Which was exactly what the president had just done.

"Next step? Relocation, which your ruddy fuckin' president just said she'd be doin'. Don't think they'll do it because they're no' bloody Nazis? Well, what about wha' they did to the bloody natives? The Japanese. Or the damned immigrants tryin' to just get into this fuckin' shit storm of an ass-swell country?"

The man was making entirely too much sense, and Paige didn't like where it was leading.

"Then, they'll start stealin' from us. Rapin' us. Killin' us. Mass massacres in the name of all that's 'safe.'"

A cold chill swept down Paige's spine. This *was* turning out to be a dark, dystopian novel. But this was her life. *Their* lives.

This was real.

"And then? What's to stop them from outrigh' killin' the lot of us? Stop the fear then and there. Kill us all to protect the mundanes and meanwhile, they'll tell the world they're big bloody heroes doin' only what needed to be done and that they did the best they bloody well could with the situation they'd been handed."

Paige couldn't believe they'd ever go *that* far. They lived in the United States of fucking America for crying out loud. "We can't act out of fear," Paige said quietly. "We can't escalate this too soon. What if they're just scared? We could inform them who we are."

"The president already knows," Yad said, his tone final.

"But the American people don't." Paige wouldn't entertain the idea of taking things this far this fast. "We teach them. We talk to them. Just look at Troutdale. Our kids are going to school with human kids. Right now."

Faith took in a deep breath, releasing it slowly as she looked over the faces of the people gathered around the table. "We can start—"

The front door banged open. "Paige!" Dexx came through the door, his eyes wide. "You weren't picking up your phone."

"DND." She always put her phone on do-not-disturb when she was in a meeting, especially now that she wasn't a detective. "What's wrong?"

Dexx's green eyes were wild. "DoDO has arrived and have put up roadblocks around the town."

They *what?*

"They're blockading us in."

Yad met Paige's gaze. "It has begun."

3

As much as Paige enjoyed the *Mortal Kombat* reference, she didn't enjoy how close fiction was to reality.

She needed to see just how bad this was.

Paige grabbed her keys but then thought differently. She and Leslie could just shift into whatever shape they chose and get to the location quickly. That would leave Dexx in a tight spot as he would either have to shift and lose all of his clothes or drive. However, the man drove like a maniac, so she was fairly certain he would get there quickly one way or the other.

Dexx seemed to have caught on to what she was thinking. He shook his head and gave her a look of warning. "Let's not make a scene."

She had no idea what that even meant, especially coming from him. She turned back to the council and realized that the people she needed to talk to about keeping her children safe weren't even there. "We'll assess the situation." Then, she headed for the back door.

She really didn't have time to walk at a leisurely human

pace, even if it was a quick human pace. So, she shifted into tiger form and ran.

The Whiskey lands were rather large. They had twenty-four acres and growing. They were still in negotiation with one of the farmers to the east who was looking to sell. Dexx and Paige's pack—really it was just Dexx's pack— lived in the woods around the main house in tree houses. Though, they were rather elaborate tree houses, she still had a hard time wrapping her head around the fact that wolves preferred to live so high above the ground.

There was a strategic advantage to this, of course. It was easier to hide from potential predators and they had the advantage. Even knowing all of that, Paige still struggled to see wanting to live up there.

Her brother did. He and his boyfriend had created a treehouse and lived in it part-time. Though, they also had a house on the ground and lived there just as often with their adopted elf child, Kate.

Paige followed her sense of smell.

She might state that the pack belonged mostly to Dexx. He certainly was the one who invested most of the time into their training, upkeep, and welfare. But she was their alpha's mate and an alpha in her own right.

So, she felt each member in a way that was hard to explain. It was as if each one of them had somehow become a part of her. She could tell when they were in a bad mood or a good one. And sometimes, their emotions would affect her own. She could tell when they were in danger or when they needed assistance. And more than once, she had risen to the occasion and swooped in to save the day.

She found Margo with Ripley, building a shed of some sort.

Paige shifted as soon as she saw the two of them and

walked up as a human. "Dexx and I have to leave to check out a situation." What *were* they building?

Margo rose to her feet with incredible grace. She was a fierce warrior who preferred going barefoot and wore many scars over her body. "Where do you need us?"

Ripley got to her feet with a little less grace and a lot more attitude. Her long dark hair cascaded over her shoulders as she pushed it back, revealing a T-shirt with a slogan that would probably upset people if anyone chose to actually read it. Too often, however, they were mesmerized by her voluptuous boobs. "Let me guess. Babysitting duty."

Paige rather enjoyed the fact that Ripley was so perceptive. She also had another gift Paige needed to utilize; her death omen ability. "Do you see anything?"

Ripley paused for a moment and then shook her head, her dark eyes slanted with worry. "Is something coming?"

If Ripley couldn't see anything looming on the horizon, they were safe.

For the moment. "Potentially." Paige turned around and prepared to shift and fly back to the man she loved. "Just be on the lookout for anything strange."

"What kind of strange?" Margo asked, her tone on edge. She had protected the Whiskey lands from a wide variety of infiltrators.

Paige turned and met Margo's vice-like gaze. "DoDO."

Margo's eyes widened.

Ripley's eyes narrowed. "We'll keep the kids safe."

Paige knew they would. She hated leaving her kids—especially her newborns—but knowing they'd be safe with these two women made her feel marginally better. One day, she *would* be a good mother to her children. One day, she would be able to be there for them, would be able to raise them.

That day was not this one.

She ran back to the house on four large paws and found Dexx already in his car.

Leslie was nowhere to be found.

Paige smoothly shifted back to human form and slipped into the Ranchero—which was really Leah's car—grabbing the lap buckle. It didn't work, but she still preferred to at least hold it in her hand. "When are you going to fix this?"

"It hasn't been much of a priority." He put the car in gear and spun around the circular driveway, gravel flying. "Besides, what are you complaining about? You can just shift and fly out of here."

He wasn't lying, but she could also tell that he was irritated. "What happened?"

He glanced at her and wrung the steering wheel as he brought them onto the paved road, the backend fishtailing. "I told her to wait."

He really didn't have to finish that statement. He was talking about Leslie, who was technically a part of his pack. She was a shifter witch, like Paige, except her spirit animal wasn't a cozy kitten like Paige's. It was a strong-willed, overpowered griffin that, when teamed up with Leslie's already strong personality, meant she was very hard to alpha-control.

Dexx didn't enjoy the struggle.

Paige turned and watched the scenery of farm fields and vineyards fly by as they raced toward town. "She can protect herself."

"I already know that. I wanted to try to curb tensions."

Oh, boy. Her man really *was* growing up. "When did you ever want to do that?"

He glared at her and said nothing more as he turned onto the street that would lead them downhill and straight into town. He maintained his silence as he went under the overpass and turned toward Walmart.

Why did trouble always seem to visit them in the Walmart parking lot?

He went around to the back and parked the Ranchero with a screeching halt.

Paige put her hand out in order to brace herself against the dashboard. "Jerk."

He grunted and got out.

Leslie stood along the back wall of the store, her arms crossed over her chest.

The wards Paige and the rest of the townspeople had put up around Troutdale glimmered with a slight rainbow hue, rippling away each time it was touched.

Men and women in black tactical uniforms fanned out around the town. They stood just outside of the protections of their wards.

Dexx walked over to Leslie and said something in a low tone Paige couldn't hear.

She didn't need to. Whatever that conversation was, it was between her sister—who could take care of herself—and their alpha—who could take care of himself.

Paige needed to handle this situation.

She walked to the ward's edge and called out to the men and women in black. "I assume you have a leader over there. How about he comes forward?"

The line parted and a man stepped through, only he was dressed in a grey business suit with a steel-blue tie. He had pale hair, nearly invisible eyebrows, and piercingly blue eyes.

Of course *he'd* be here. "Mario. Wish I could say I was surprised to see you." But she wasn't.

He smiled and straightened the front of his suit jacket.

"I only wish we were meeting yet again under better circumstances." His voice rang with a soft English accent she knew would deepen as he grew emotional.

"When are you going back across the water?" Paige didn't ask that question to be a jack-hole. She asked because he was on loan from England. As far as she had been able to determine, Europe had their own Department of Delicate Affairs and he was a part of *that* branch. Why they decided to team up with the U.S. was completely beyond Paige. But she severely hoped they didn't decide to create a home office on American soil.

That was the question she was really asking. DoDO was bad news.

"Really, Ms. Whiskey. With the current state of affairs? I really don't think we're going anywhere."

That made Paige's warm and fuzzies turn cold and prickly. "What can I do for you? And why are you blockading the town? Again."

Mario shrugged. "President's orders. You made quite a fuss last week. The president just wants to ensure that the situation remains... contained."

Contained. This certainly wasn't going to end well. "We're still recovering from saving the world." Which they had. If DoDO had saved the world, they'd be getting awards. But Troutdale was just getting blockaded. Again.

"You really didn't *save the world*, Ms. Whiskey. You just made a mess of it." His smile was smug.

She wanted to punch it off his face. She knew they needed to fight this, but how? With peace? That was anti-fists. "We will need supplies."

"I'm sure you will. Which is why we will keep them back until you are ready to register."

That was a pretty heavy threat. They were going to

hold the entire town hostage until the paranormals were registered? Because that'd worked so well in the Marvel universe. "We're talking now. So, you don't have to hold the town hostage anymore."

He tipped his head to the side. "Mmm."

"Why don't we just stop beating around the bush?"

"Such a curious turn of phrase."

"Not really." Especially when that was exactly what they were doing. "Just tell me your terms and then we can be done here. You never know. We might actually accept them."

His smile was cold. "I sincerely hope you do." He clasped his hands behind his back and hopped up on his toes. Then, he walked across the ward and up to Paige.

The wards simply made those who were magically evil a bit uncomfortable. It wasn't as if those wards really protected the town against anything physical.

Not yet, anyway.

Mario was of average height, and usually, he looked down at Paige.

But Paige was a witch shifter and that meant she could alter her own height, which she had actually done without realizing it, forcing him to look up at her ever so slightly.

A flicker of uncertainty entered into those pale blue eyes.

She wasn't about to shift herself shorter. She rather enjoyed having him look up to her.

"Each paranormal *shall* register with the federal government," he said succinctly. "They *will* be put under careful supervision, and we *will* assess their danger level."

Paige knew there were many different ways his words could be interpreted.

He could mean that the paranormals would register and then they would be hauled off to internment camps and jail.

Or it could mean they would register and then they would be treated like sex offenders.

Or it could mean that they would register and then DoDO would sweep through, placing cameras everywhere, keeping the community contained, and allowing the president to watch this grand experiment like rats in a lab.

Paige didn't really enjoy any of those options. "Details."

Mario's expression lightened with muted delight. "Well, Ms. Whiskey, I really hadn't anticipated a willing ear. Motherhood really does change a person."

He knew she had already been a mother. So, she wasn't going to take the bait. Her twins were a valuable resource, and it was quite possible that Mario had his sights set on obtaining them and their shifter witch powers.

"Where are the twins?" His pale eyes roved the parking lot. "I had rather hoped to see them."

That only made Paige more suspicious. "They're napping. Now, details." She ended with a growl.

Mario clamped his lips shut in a tight smile as he pondered his next words. "The registration process will be rather painless. A simple form to fill out, allowing us to know which type of paranormal each person is and what type of danger they might present."

"You do realize we've been living in peace for hundreds of years. I don't know how much of a danger we are."

"On the contrary, Ms. Whiskey. We caught the danger on video. The world is aware of just how brutally dangerous your kind can be." His eyes shone with a note of victory.

Your kind? "Are we forgetting that you're also a witch?"

He raised an eyebrow. "There is so much you do not know." He raised his chin and continued. "After the registration process, each paranormal will be equipped with a collar that will assist them in repressing their more dangerous aspects. And they will be surveyed."

Paige knew about those collars. She'd experienced the effects in Alaska. DoDO had been handing them out to paranormals for a while. And the only thing they really succeeded in doing was to push the shifter animal to the background until the shifter spirit was forced to power through. The experience had been rather explosive.

DoDO had no intent on keeping the population safe. They were working to create a much bigger situation. She was almost certain that if Sven hadn't forced her hand to make a big international TV situation, DoDO would have. And she was pretty confident they'd been the reason the TV crews had been there in the first place.

Once the shifter—or paranormal—overwhelmed the collar, the "threat" would be blasted out on world news for everyone to see.

Justification for the president to do something even worse, she was sure.

Paige wanted to say no immediately, but she needed more information. "And our supplies would come in?"

"Life would continue per normal. Everyone could get back to their jobs and their lives." He licked his lips and looked at her in surprise. "We have even changed the look of the collars. They are quite stylish now."

She was sure. "But they're still collars."

"Honestly, Ms. Whiskey. Don't you put them on your pets?"

He was baiting her again. "And how long would this go on for? When would this end?"

His left eye twitched, and his gaze darted away before he righted his expression. "As soon as the president can assure the nation they are no longer in danger, then we can alter the arrangement."

Which meant they would be living this way for an eternity. Or until they got a new president. Perhaps. "And what about our rights as citizens?"

A frown flickered across his brow. "You would still pay your taxes and serve your country."

But they would lose their rights. They would lose the right to vote. They might lose their ability to receive medical treatment and more. Paige could read between the lines. However, she could not give him the answer then and there. She wasn't the spokesperson for the entire paranormal community. If she said the wrong thing at this particular moment, she could send the nation into war.

Before they were ready for it.

She was starting to realize there might not *be* a peaceful solution to this after all. But there had to be. Right? This was the United States of freakin' America. "I will take this information to the council."

That gained his interest. "Council?"

Paige gave him a smile of her own, beating down her fear that she'd just given him information he shouldn't have. "Did you expect us to be wild heathens? If there are any other terms, now's the time to set them."

Several emotions shifted across his features. Doubt. Intrigue.

And uncertainty.

The last emotion was quickly replaced by confidence. "No. That really is everything."

She was sure it wasn't. She'd bought a house once. It'd seemed simple enough until they got into the details of the agreement, and then things had become rather complicated. She was certain this would be no different but on a much grander scale. "Sounds simple enough. I have your number. I'll call you when we have an answer."

Mario smiled. "I wouldn't take too long, Ms. Whiskey. You only have four days. The president is not a patient woman."

Paige gave him a smile of her own and leaned forward. "Neither am I."

Mario's smile warmed. "Aw, there she is. I was wondering when you would grace us with your presence."

Paige calmed herself. He and the president had counted on her rising to the occasion and handling the situation the way... well, the way she handled things. With magick, power, and finality.

She took a step back and gave him a cool gaze. "I'll call you. Until then, please get out of my town."

He smiled tightly and returned to his side.

Things weren't going to be this easy for much longer. They needed a better game plan.

Fast.

4

Dexx was *still* having a conversation with Leslie by the time Paige made it back to the car. They both turned to her when she approached, neither of them looking overly pissed.

That was a good sign, right?

Right. Yeah. Of course. Right.

No. It wasn't. Those two were getting really good at hiding things from her, and she was starting to get the feeling that it wasn't a good thing.

"What did he have to say?" Leslie asked before Paige could mention anything.

Another not good sign. "Nothing good. We're being forced to register."

Leslie rubbed her brow, her brown eyes closed momentarily before they opened with an orange flare to them. That was her inner griffin raising his head, threatening to spill out. But the orange receded back to brown as Leslie let her hand drop. "That's not going to happen."

"I know." But it might. What other course did they have? They couldn't afford to have a stand-off like this against the United States *government*. Demons from Hell? Sure. But the government? No. "But until then, they're blockading us in."

"Supplies?"

They'd really just been through this last week. "We'll have to get the supply chains up again."

Dexx took in a deep breath. "I'll have Kate—"

"No." If things really were about to get bad, she needed Dexx on his A Game and not relying on an elvin tween to open illegal passages through Underhill. "People are going to get scared."

"More scared than when they were facing demons?"

"Probably. This is a bit more real. Demons are..." Paige shrugged, having a hard time finding words. "They're superstition and religion."

"People were hit real hard by that 'superstition.'"

Agreed. "But a lot of us voted for this president."

Dexx pulled a twisted face. "Did you?"

"Yes. I thought she was a great candidate." And she'd never thought *anything* would go this far. "But that doesn't matter. Right now, I need you being the face of trust."

He screwed on a smug smile.

But it was thin. He was tired. He was scared.

He understood what was going on here. She could see it around the edges of his eyes and lips.

"People could see you as the enemy." This was something she'd been forced to face in Denver once. "You're the cops, and cops are the bad guys when the government gets involved."

"Good thing I don't work for the government."

That wasn't quite true. "Remember how we answer to Tuck? The elected sheriff? Well, *he* works for the government. So, technically, you do too."

He narrowed his eyes.

That wasn't what he wanted to hear, but she didn't care. Paige really had no idea the level of decisions that would end up in her lap, but she needed her partner to keep the peace for her.

He just wasn't terribly good at that.

They all piled into the car, with Leslie giving Dexx a hard time about a few things. Which was cute, but Paige wasn't paying any attention.

She couldn't get it out of her mind that this was escalating quite quickly. And if she didn't watch it, things were going to get out of control. Things were already past what she'd ever thought she'd experience in her lifetime.

And it terrified her. Weren't they over locking people up based on race or differences?

No. Obviously. All she had to do was to look at the reports—as few as there were—about how the illegal aliens were being treated. The government was *actively creating* their next generation of war criminals.

But how had it become the citizens of the United States being treated like that?

But wasn't that what black families asked every week? How was this happening in the United States? Or brown families. Or trans families.

This was her now. Being paranormal was the new black.

That stark reality hit her in the gut like someone punching her. How had she been so... ignorant to reality before? Because it wasn't happening to her? Around her? Was that an excuse?

Dexx stopped at the light, and someone pounded on the window.

Paige startled. She hadn't even seen the person run up. She didn't know the woman by name, but she'd made some trouble the last time they'd been on lockdown. Frankly, Paige thought the woman would disappear, go somewhere easier. But she hadn't. It was her "God-given right" to be there, in her home—which Paige couldn't disagree with, except maybe the god part—and she was staying—which Paige kinda respected her for. But it would be a lot easier and better for everyone if the woman actually *helped* instead of just made things worse.

Dexx shook his head. "Babe, ignore her. Let's go home."

Leslie squished between them both.

Paige released her grip on the seat belt and reached for the door handle. "If I don't deal with her now, we'll have a riot on our hands. You know that. I'll see you at the house."

Dexx grunted as she opened the door and got out but then turned toward town instead of home.

Hopefully that meant he was headed toward work. Good.

Paige guided the hefty woman back to the street corner and out of the road. "What can I do for you?"

"I'm Cheryl Doumsbury." She ran a hand over her short, blonde hair. "You may remember me."

"You're hard to forget."

Cheryl gave a tight smile as if accepting the barb as a compliment. "We're being blockaded again, aren't we?"

Paige released a sigh. How had Cheryl even heard about that? Frustration created a tight knot in Paige's neck as she debated quickly the best way to handle this situation. Talking directly to the town's negative-gossip—the person who *only* shared news if it was bad—wasn't the best way to handle this. She needed to talk to the mayor, who was better at dealing with things like this. "Before I share anything with you, let me figure out the plan. I'll—" No. "—*we'll* have answers as soon as we can."

Cheryl opened her mouth to spew a few more questions and to probably insult Paige while she was at it.

But Paige shifted into an owl and flew away on silent wings before the woman had the chance.

The mayor's building was downtown. If it were up to Mayor Suzanne Briggs, her building would be quite grand. She liked everything big and gleaming, something Paige would have been okay without knowing. However, Paige's new position as paranormal spokesperson meant she got to know the sometimes self-centered woman more than she'd ever hoped.

She shifted into human form at the doors. Suzanne didn't like it when Paige flew in unexpectedly. So, she showed her respect by walking into the building. Though, sometimes, she did so on four feet instead of two just for spite.

Suzanne met her at the door to her second-floor office. "I can't do this anymore."

Paige held her eyeroll to herself, realizing she was in for a fantastic tantrum, but she wasn't really great at taming those. "You're being overdramatic."

"I assure you, I am *never* overdramatic," Suzanne said as her thick heels clunked on the tiled floor on the way back to her desk.

Okay. That was probably like telling a woman to calm down. Not a great tactic.

"We're being blockaded. Again." Suzanne took her seat in her stylish leather office chair and stabbed Paige with her blue eyes. "We haven't recovered from the last time."

They *had*. They just weren't back to the old normal. "I know."

"The innovations you've put through so far are..." Suzanne raised her shoulders, then licked her lips, her gaze drifting elsewhere. "Well, they're rather unique. But just how will *unique* keep us alive?"

Paige bit down on what she really wanted to say. "You know how to survive this because you've done it before. Use the protocols we established the first time. Use the people who stepped up the last time."

"You need to handle this. This is on you."

"No. I've got to handle *other* things."

"Like the war on our town?"

"Like that." But when it was said so bluntly, it felt more like a slap to the face. Like a wake-up call. "You know what to do. Make it happen, and tell the town that you're taking care of them as the best mayor they've got."

Suzanne shook her head and lowered it slightly. "How are we going to get our supplies? You said we can't use the elf girl."

"No. We can't." Paige didn't want to have that conversation with the mayor again, reminding her that putting children in harm's way *wasn't* the right answer. The woman wasn't evil. She just had a hard time seeing around her inconvenience. "But, just like last time, I need to know what we need. We're going to need money because we're not stealing."

Suzanne slumped her shoulders with a petulant sigh. "But we simply don't have the money for supplies. We're a town, not a kingdom."

Well, that was something Paige hadn't thought of. "Okay. So, figure out how you're going to get that money in. If things need to restructure, then that's what you need to do. How would a queen do it? Be a queen." But with less attitude.

The mayor gave her an exasperated expression.

"Look," Paige said, slashing her hand because she *seri-*

41

ously had no idea how to get this woman to do what was needed faster. "I don't know how long this is going to go on for. They're demanding we do something that—" Paige couldn't believe she was actually going to say this out loud. It made it terrifying and that much more real. "We're on the brink of something terrible."

"I know what they're demanding." Suzanne looked balefully up at Paige. "It won't go that far. We're civilized."

Easy for her to say. Suzanne wasn't paranormal. "I'm pretty sure that's what the LGBTQ or the trans or the people of color or the poor or women say. Take your pick. Muslims? Did I mention those?"

Suzanne opened her mouth to say something flippant, but then, something flashed in those brilliantly blue eyes, and her expression sobered.

Yeah. This situation was making a lot of people rethink their lives and just how easy they'd had it *before* the existence of paranormals was revealed. "I'll figure out *how* to get supplies. You figure out how we're going to pay for what we need."

"Fine." The mayor released a short breath and sank into her chair. "I'll let you know when I have something."

"Ditto." Paige turned and pulled her phone out of her pocket. "Text me," she said as she walked out the door. "Don't send your man to pester me this time."

"You're no fun!"

Something thudded against the wall beside the door.

Paige glanced down. Suzanne had thrown her shoe.

Paige turned back around with a frown of did-you-just-seriously-do-that?

Suzanne blinked rapidly and smiled angelically as if to say she had no idea what Paige was upset about.

Leaving and glad Suzanne was a poor aim, Paige pulled up a contact she never thought she'd use. Eldora Blackman.

"Hello?" Eldora seemed as confused about the phone call as Paige was.

"Where are you?"

Eldora paused. "At the grocery store."

"I'll be right there." Paige hung up, stashed her phone, and shifted into an owl again.

She *preferred* walking on four legs. She didn't have the best balance in the world and flying really futzed with that. It was something with the bird head, the way it worked. Transitioning from "flying" brain to "walking" brain felt like she was stumbling in an earthquake.

But she did it because it was the fastest way to travel and speed was imperative.

Technically, there was more than one grocery store in Troutdale. Paige knew this all too well because of the last time the town had been blockaded and on lockdown. But she also knew that Eldora Blackman only went to the one closest to her family home, even though it didn't necessarily have the best prices. It did, however, carry her produce, so maybe she got a better discount. Paige just didn't know.

She flew in, shifting into a sparrow to do her flyover because she'd already discovered that people freaked out seeing an owl or an eagle in the store.

She spotted Eldora by the frozen vegetables and came in for her landing, shifting to a fully clothed human as she stepped out. She appreciated being a witch for the simple fact she didn't have to worry about showing up naked when she shifted.

Eldora closed the freezer case door, leaving whatever she'd been looking at inside, and frowned at Paige with a look that asked what in the world she was thinking.

Paige held up a hand to wave that line of questions off and took a step back, her head still woozy. Flying—while flying—was great. But this part wasn't getting any easier. "We have a situation." A slight pain shot through her left eyeball for a split second, and then the world went still. Finally.

"So I heard."

Eldora had ears everywhere, something Paige didn't quite understand. Well, she did, but it was the fact that Eldora lived the life of the Amish—not really. A true Amish person didn't own a car, but she certainly appreciated living off the grid. The Blackman Compound resembled a small farming community of ultra-strict religious folk.

Which was okay as long as that ultra-strictness didn't creep into Paige's front yard, which it sometimes did.

"We're being cut off again and need supplies."

Eldora narrowed her dark eyes and folded her arms over her ample chest.

Paige was pretty certain the woman knew where she was going with this. "The elves cut us off from Underhill."

"I could have told you they would."

A few startled cries went out at the front of the store, accompanied by a few screeches and a couple of coos.

Paige used her keen hearing to detect what was going on.

Only to hear a tiny roar and a bird-like squawk.

Her twins had arrived. She was going to murder Margo for not keeping a better eye on them.

Paige sent out an alpha-mom flare with her emotions that basically told her twins where she was but didn't look away from Eldora. "I need to know if we can use door magick to get supplies."

44

Derrick came up to his mother, tall, dark, and bearded. He smiled at her. "Hey, sis."

"Hey." She hadn't grown up even knowing about him. *He'd* known about *her,* which explained why *he* was so much easier calling her that. But he didn't feel like a brother, just a stranger.

A younger woman came and stood next to him, her black eyes studying Paige with interest.

A fledgling bird came crashing out of the air.

Eldora's eyes widened with alarm.

Paige just held up a hand, her lips clamped shut, and shook her head to tell Eldora the girl was okay.

Rai tumbled to the ground and shifted into a bear cub, rolling as she came to a stop on her butt, blinking eyes that danced with lightning.

Ember tripped on his long tiger tail, taking down a display of ice cream sauces, shifted into a fox to run a few steps, tripped again, and shifted into a wolf pup to make it all the way to his sister.

Paige turned to Eldora with her kids frolicking at her feet, shifting into different animals every time they blinked almost. "Door magick? Supplies? Possible? Yes?"

Eldora studied the twins intently. "Yes."

"Willing?"

"No."

Crap. They hadn't been on the best of terms ever since Eldora had kidnapped Leslie, Leah, and Mandy to get Paige's attention back in Texas. Paige wasn't going to say she was the type who held grudges but...

Yeah. She held grudges. For ages.

She couldn't afford that at the moment, though. "What do I need to do?"

Eldora took in a deep breath and released it.

The young woman stepped up. She wasn't dressed in normal Blackman female attire with the black dress and the white cap holding back her hair. She dressed like a normal person. Jeans, T-shirt, flip flops. Maybe she was from another area? "I'll teach Leah."

Eldora had already tried that approach, trying to get Leah into the Blackman school. The problem with all of that was that the Blackman Coven came off as a cult, and Paige wasn't into that. "No."

The young woman tipped her head forward and to the side, looking up at Paige through narrowed eyes. "It's what she needs." She snorted. "Frankly, so do you. You come. I'll teach you too."

It frankly wasn't a bad idea. She got her door magick from her father—Eldora's cheating now-dead husband. She'd never learned how to use it. Well, she kinda had. She sent demons back to Hell using her door magick.

But... the Blackman cult had to be dealt with. Not because cults were bad—because... right. No. Yeah. They were bad. But because things were getting dangerous, and if the town was cut off yet again, they needed everyone on Team Troutdale, not Team Trout-Black... whatever. Okay. That sounded so much better in her head.

She was shutting up her inside voice now. "Your kids join ours in school."

"With the others?" Eldora asked, but this time, her tone wasn't derogative.

That was a change. Since the Whiskeys had come into town, Eldora had preached about how her witches would never join the other paranormals in classes. "Yes." She drew out the word, mostly because she couldn't quite believe she *might* get a—

"Okay."

Someone could have hit her with a stick in that moment. "Great. When do we—"

A loud crash sounded at the front of the store. Men shouted, telling everyone to stay down.

The civilians were quiet. A few shouts, nothing more.

This was the drill the American people had practiced for—and the people of Troutdale most of all.

A threat. A live one.

Paige took a step to shift and see what was going on.

A man in DoDO utility black cleared the aisle with a fully automatic assault rifle sighted on them.

Eldora took a step forward, her arms out, shielding Derrick and the other woman.

"Don't move," the lead man shouted.

Rai cried out in puppy fear.

The barrel of the rifle dropped to sight on her.

Paige's power coiled along her hands, and the world went red. In her head, she knew he'd only followed the sound. She had to be *careful*. She didn't speak for everyone.

But the mother in her didn't care. A man with an assault rifle had entered the grocery store and was pointing it at her baby.

She pulled her head back and released a guttural roar.

The man took a step back and sighted his rifle on her.

The magick took over. Paige didn't have a conscious thought. Rage. Protective... rage.

In her mind, she saw each of the rifles. Over a dozen DoDO men and women had filed into the grocery store, endangering the lives of the people—her people.

Mario stepped into Paige's view, unruffled. He fixed his shirt sleeve with a smug smile. "We're here to register you."

Paige's world swirled with emotion-charged magick. She barely heard him.

He smiled at her. "Please. Make this difficult."

Oh. She would.

Not fully knowing what she was doing, she clapped her hands together, and an arc of energy flew outward.

Her magick, inky black hands that manifested her door magick, also clapped. Doors opened behind each DoDO man and woman, and the gale force of her energy pushed each through.

But she wasn't done.

On Mario's way out, she collected a hair from him. Several, actually. Then, taking that hair, she pressed it into the magickal ward protecting the town, whispering her intent. *No one from DoDO comes or goes.*

Her wards sang out a clear bell-tone.

Then her magick released her.

And she fell to the ground, spent.

Eldora sighed and stood next to her, looking down. "And this is why you need to learn how to control your abilities."

Paige wasn't going to naysay her.

She was just going to take a nap.

Clean up on aisle fourteen.

5

Paige was actually pretty much out of it for quite a while. She remembered her brother carrying her around like a damn damsel. She wasn't so out of it that she was knocked out. She could see, speak a few words, but not much more than that. Derrick loaded her into his vehicle, Eldora and the other woman taking the twins, who had decided to remain in one animal form for a bit.

Eldora doted on Rai and Ember, which should have made Paige concerned since she didn't trust Eldora in the slightest, but... she just couldn't get herself to give a shit. She was exhausted. The only thing she'd managed to get across to Derrick and Eldora was that they were absolutely *not* going to the Blackman complex.

Derrick pulled up to the Whiskey house and winced. "When are you going to let up on your wards?" He rubbed the back of his neck. "We're not the enemy here."

She grunted and made a mental note to think about that later. She made it to the living room and passed out on a chair, Margo apologizing profusely for letting the twins escape.

She woke with a start when the front door slammed. "Paige," Dexx roared.

She was starting to feel a little better. She pushed the blanket off but didn't get to her feet. "In here."

He looked around as he stepped into the room and then went to her in two long strides. "What happened?"

She quickly filled him in.

His hands balled into fists. His mouth opened and closed, then opened again as his eyes closed. Dark emotions rolled off him.

Margo growled low in the other room.

Joe's bear pelt pushed at his shirt.

Paige didn't think she'd ever seen him quite this pissed. She put a calming hand on his arm. "Babe." She didn't get a response. "Babe."

He finally opened his eyes, a seething rage turning his green eyes molten.

"We're safe."

"This time."

"You're not wrong."

Merry walked in with a steaming cup. "Drink this."

Who was this woman?

"Everyone's here," the ancient witch said. "Might want to get in there."

"Who showed up?" Paige took a sip of the tea. It was really good and did help. She pushed herself out of the chair and stood.

"When you pushed DoDO out," Merry said, her tone ringing with respect, "you let us all know that something was wrong. So, we came here to see what had happened. Eldora filled us in."

"Then what do you need me for?" Paige might be feeling better, but she wasn't in the mood for a meeting.

Merry raised an eyebrow. "We need to figure out our next actions." She licked her lips with a catty expression. "I thought you were the one who didn't wanted to go to war."

"I don't."

"You should have thought of that before you punched first."

She hadn't, though. However, everyone? Paige stepped into the dining room and saw the leaders of the paranormal region. "Remind me why I need to be here?"

Merry ground out a long sigh, then grabbed Paige's arm and pushed her into the living room.

Dexx growled low and moved to stop her.

But Merry flicked her fingers on her way by, a drop of blood oozing from her wrist, and he was unable to move.

"Merry," Paige warned as she continued to walk backward into and around the furniture.

"He'll be fine." Merry stopped when they made it to the large window and then got in Paige's face. "You're the most powerful witch in our region." She clamped her lips tight and tipped her head to the side.

Paige shook her head. "That's you."

"It *was* me but is no longer. As much as it pains me to admit, you're the one we need on this panel. But because you're such an idiot, I'm remaining to make sure you don't screw things up even more than you already have."

"I don't understand." That wasn't exactly true. Paige understood the need for the panel—council, group, whatever. She was struggling to wrap her head around the fact that *she* was the most powerful witch in the region. She'd known she was getting powerful—powerful enough for paranormals to be concerned, but they'd been concerned because she was a shifter witch, not just because she was powerful magickally.

If she did anything just a smidge wrong—forgot what she was doing and hit a wolf a little too hard with wind, or misjudged and—

Attacked sanctioned officials, sealing them out of town during a president-backed mission?

It finally hit Paige just how bad she'd made the situation. She'd played right into DoDO's hands. She'd reacted exactly the way they'd wanted.

And she hadn't even thought about it.

She walked back to the dining room table, but Merry stopped at Dexx, releasing him from whatever hold she'd had on him.

The last time they'd had a meeting—mere hours ago—the room had been loud enough she'd had to bang a sippy cup on the table to get their attention.

This time, silence surrounded her.

Paige had no idea what she was supposed to say. Yeah, she was getting experienced with these types of situations, but why were the situations she was handling getting bigger? She wished whatever god was writing the script of her life would *stop*. "I'm sorry," she said to the quiet room.

Elder Yad raised his bushy white eyebrows, his lips pursed. "Well, it is what it is now and not undeserved."

The others around the room nodded in various ways. Some nods were open and vigorous. Some hesitant.

But no one was berating her about what she'd done.

Because this was what they'd wanted as well.

A few hours ago, she'd only heard from Yad and Duglas. Faith and Leslie had offered concern but no real direction. Paige needed direction. "Do any of you have..." Paige didn't even know how to start this conversation or just how *big* it really was. All of her experience was as a police detective and as a fighter of evil demons who wanted to take over the world or whatever. She was inexperienced for this. "...any idea how in over our heads we are?"

No one answered. The top-most powerful leaders of the regional paranormals didn't have an answer.

Not out loud, anyway. Their faces did, though.

Chuck, her regional high alpha of the shifters, looked at her, his lips set, a bright light in his blue eyes.

Daenys, the elf queen—yes, a literal elf queen—released a long breath and settled back in her chair, her long white hair pulled over her shoulder.

Brack, the lead dragon in the area, breathed, smoke steaming out of his nose, but his amber eyes leapt with the promise of war.

Duglas clamped his lips shut, as if saying he wasn't going to do much to help her.

Ryo, the air elemental of the region, just twirled his fingers, creating a small air current.

Merry tapped her chin with her manicured fingers, her dark eyes distant.

Dexx just stared at one person and then the next as if wondering how to extricate himself from the room. Sure, he was upset. Paige knew that. But she also knew he didn't like being the one in charge. He liked being the one busting heads.

These were the most powerful people of the region.

Paige ran her fingernails over the line of her top lip, resting her elbow on the table and looking into the back yard. The one thing they'd all hoped wouldn't come to pass was upon them; the fear of the humans was directed at them. History told her what would happen if she did nothing. Hell, it told her what would happen if she fought back.

But "fighting back" wasn't just about taking out a group of demons. This time, it was going up against a nation she'd

53

sworn since childhood to honor and protect, even if it was under one god she didn't believe in.

They were delving into crazy territory. This entire thing was insane. Likely just a misunderstanding. Her head told her she could go to whoever was in charge, apologize for overreacting, and try to find a peaceful solution.

But the person in charge was Mario, and he'd been pushing for this ever since Paige had known him. She wasn't talking about people she didn't know in Alaska. This time, he'd targeted her kids. In the grocery store. Who'd be next? Where? Would they be attacked in their homes? Be dragged from their beds?

How were they going to win this war? She couldn't just seek out the biggest demon and kick its ass. Even if she managed to somehow get to the president, she couldn't kick *her* ass. Paige would be arrested and would never see the light of day. But—just for kicks—if she *did* manage to kick the president's ass and win and not end up in jail or worse, there'd just be another person to rise up. And then another. Because humans had bigger numbers than demons.

And when the fear started rolling in the ranks of mankind, it infected at an easy rate.

Her anxiety reared its ugly head, making her think dark thoughts. This was an impossible situation. She glared at Merry, who *should* be leading this discussion.

Oh, right. Yes. A serial-killing witch should definitely be leading *this* conversation. Damn it! Paige needed to pull her head out of her ass.

Solutions. What were they? "We have to get in front of this," Paige said into the quiet room. "We have to change the story." Who was the real enemy? The president? DoDO? Or neighbors, friends, and family?

"How?" Chuck asked, equally quiet.

Maybe this *was* just a misunderstanding. This nation *prided* itself on its Christianity and *not* its freedom of religion. The ultra-right base liked to think of themselves as the purifiers of the nation, the people who kept everyone clean and good.

Being a witch was bad, which was why witches hid themselves from the "good people," who would burn them or hang them.

Being a different religion was bad. Being a different sexual orientation was bad. People couldn't even have different colored skin, so why would a person who shifted into a wolf feel safe?

Understanding the power of *fear,* the paranormal society had hidden themselves, making themselves secret.

That gave the power of the story to the people who wanted to paint them as monsters.

So, if paranormals just "educated" people, got them to see that they had a lot of similarities with everyone...

If Paige could *diffuse* the bomb of American fear, she might be able to take the power away from the president and DoDO. "Okay. Look." Paige felt a little bolstered by this plan. "We need to find a way to inspire people to..." She was at a loss for words.

"Rise up?" Faith asked, the scar along her cheek twitching in frustrated anger.

"Be better?" It was too easy to see only two sides of an argument when, in reality, most people fell solidly in the middle. They just wanted life to not suck. "If we can get people to talk about this? To get real information out there? Real day to day stuff?"

"Like they did for Black Lives Matter?" Ryo twirled his fingers as air played around him. "We need a better plan."

Except... "Racism has been trained in us for generations. *We're* in fairytale books." Not history books. That had to matter, make things easier.

Daenys chuckled and steepled her fingers. "What is your plan? As you are out there spreading 'tales of normalcy,' your government will be strangling your towns, your communities. You already have no supplies." The pale elf pointed a long finger at Paige. "And you are not using Underhill."

"I already knew that." The queen did bring up a good point, though. "While you're worried about Underhill, we've got entire villages and towns—maybe even other cities —who might be under the same attack." Though, they hadn't really been *attacked*.

But hadn't they? She might be struggling to *believe* this was her reality, but a man had pointed a *rifle* at her *baby*.

"And you think we do not?" Daenys said indignantly. "I am a queen, not merely a tribal leader of pack animals."

Dexx puffed out his cheeks and pulled back, his eyes widening mockingly. "Oh."

"Dexx," Paige said low in warning.

He sighed petulantly. "Our cities have alphas. Maybe some bigger groups. That makes them easier to hunt for people like me. They don't have what we built here." He held up a finger. "And they don't have a witch like you."

What was the best way of handling that? Bringing everyone together? But wouldn't that just make it easier for DoDO to strike them? The Department of Delicate Operations was like a mix between an army of specialized soldiers and hunters. Maybe her first instincts weren't the right ones. "Agreed. They're not being blockaded. They're being *hunted*."

"Or they are living their lives in beautiful quiet," the

earth elemental said, her dark skin gleaming in the soft sunlight streaming through the windows.

Paige couldn't remember her name. Karen, maybe? Or Carn? It started with a "k" and ended with an "n," and that about all she could remember. The woman rarely spoke. "DoDO has been studying us for years. They were developing a collar to suppress the shifter animal so it can explode out publicly, and they're using it. What other things do they have to make this situation worse? How much are you willing to bet that others are safe? That they're doing better?"

Yad licked his wrinkled lips and looked at her. "Let's hear your plan."

She didn't have one yet, but it didn't matter. This was how she worked. All of her experience had been like this, where she was handed an impossible situation and told to find a solution. This was her superpower.

And maybe *that* was the real reason she was on this council.

"We need the media." If their real threat was normal humans, then that's where they needed to hit first. Give them information. "We can't be silenced. This *has* to get out."

Brack pulled out his phone, the steam coming out of his nose cooling for a moment. "I can handle this. I own a couple of news stations and know several others who should be willing to air you."

Paige wasn't stupid, though. Their real enemy right now was the government. They were the ones attacking the paranormal people. They could get the word out to the world, get them to understand who and what they were, but someone high in the chain of command had issued an order stating it was okay to point a gun at a baby. "I'm going to need to talk to someone high up in government."

Yad shook his head with a worried expression. "I have a few contacts."

"The president," Merry said in challenge. "You need to talk to the president."

"Of the United States." There was no way Paige was going to get in to see her. Even *with* everything going on.

"Yes." Merry's tone was dark and laced with don't-be-an-idiot-ness. If that was a thing. "I can make that happen. But in order to do that, you're going to need to drop the wards."

"Absolutely not," Dexx said, his alpha will surging forward.

Merry lifted a shoulder in a shrug. "Then she's not getting into the White House."

First off, Paige couldn't believe she'd actually be going to see the most important person in the country. Secondly, the thought that, in order to do that, she'd have to endanger the lives of the people of her town, her kids, other people's kids, other people's *people,* made her feel a little ill. Thirdly, would going to see the president actually help them?

"How badly do you want this?" Merry asked.

Paige *had* said she needed to talk to someone high in the chain of command and this certainly was that. She had to try, didn't she? If she didn't, their only *real* choice was to lower the wards and allow everyone there to be registered. It would be peaceful, sure, but they'd be slaves or worse. Or they could go to war. Which would be better? It seemed like a long shot, but it was one she had to take. Right?

And it had to be her because she was the one with the experience in making tough choices and finding good solutions when there were none. That's where her true powers lay. "When can you get the flight ready?"

Merry just gave her a tight smile and turned to Eldora. "I trust we can get a door to the airport?"

The room exploded in conversation finally, but Paige wasn't listening. She stared at her sleeping baby girl, nestled in the corner of the green striped couch.

She had to make the world a safe place.

And she would.

6

P aige had to do a few things first, though. Merry was right. She had to give the president a peace-offering before she went there, but she wasn't going to just open the floodgates to terrorists without setting a few things in motion first.

It was time to see if there was something Merry could add to the wards that she hadn't yet. Something that would set limitations to what could be done inside the wards.

"Blood magick is powerful," Merry agreed. "But it is still limited to blood."

"There has to be a way to make the wards safe to take down." Paige wasn't going to entertain the idea of inviting danger to the town she'd fought so hard to protect.

Merry sighed and stared up into the branches of the ward tree in the Whiskey front lawn.

The Alaskan wood witches had taught Paige how to use the power of trees to combine the elements for protection. With Paige's witch sight, she could see the different colored tendrils of power the people of the town had infused the ward tree with as they rose from the branch tips to meet and create the dome that surrounded the town.

There were three of these ward trees. One at the Whiskey house, one in downtown, and the third stood in front of the entrance to the Vaada Bhoomi, the land of the shifter spirits.

The wards themselves were good and strong, taking a little bit of each person's soul into the protections.

But Paige had instilled her own magick into them.

What would happen if Merry did as well?

The blood witch glared again but took a small, curved blade from the sheath on her necklace and made a thin slice along the length of her left forearm. "Hands are a terrible place to make incisions," Merry said, as if instructing youth. She stepped toward the tree as she resheathed her blade and tucked the necklace into her shirt. "Power comes from the hands, which is why everyone wants to go there. But we do not heal as easily as shifters do, and so the cuts can fester."

Paige glanced at Leah, realizing that Merry wasn't teaching *her* anything. She was instructing Leah, her granddaughter.

The girl narrowed her blue eyes and nodded.

When Merry touched the ward tree with her blood, a force hit Paige. It was...less of a force and more of a deep sense of knowing. But what?

Paige waded through the information, the voices and sounds, the memories and emotions. Blood magic was to the soul what a tree was to the elements. A tree *used* the earth, water, air, and the fire from the sun in order to survive.

Blood used the earth of the body, the air in the lungs, the water of life, and the fire of the heart to keep the body alive.

Paige pressed her palm to the tree's trunk. It wasn't solid. Not to her hand.

It was warm and supple.

It bumped.

Paige's eyes shot open, and she stared at Merry.

The blood witch raised a black eyebrow and frowned.

The bark jumped again, stuttered, and found a rhythm.

Like a heartbeat. Merry had given the ward tree life.

Life. No. Paige's magick was life magick.

Merry had tied Paige's life magick to the earth and gave it form.

Paige stepped away. "I think it worked."

Merry took a couple of steps back as well. "Something worked, anyway."

Merry wasn't Paige's only stop. There was another powerful witch family Paige needed to bring in to assist the town as well: the Blackmans with their door magick.

Eldora arrived with several of her witches. Derrick showed up, along with the new girl.

"I have a few ideas," Eldora said as she met Paige and Merry beneath the branches of the ward tree. "Phoebe calls them trip portals."

Paige felt like she'd just stepped into the middle of a conversation. "What?"

Eldora didn't expound. "Follow me." She turned and walked toward the Whiskey ward surrounding the house.

It was secondary to the one surrounding the town. It was like a dome within the dome. The Troutdale wards were far supreme to the Whiskey wards, and technically, Paige probably didn't need them anymore. But they'd been attacked so many times, she wasn't risking it.

Eldora bent down and set up two rocks about a door's

width apart. She touched them with her hands, and a door opened, inky black and undulating with darkness.

That looked like any old portal. "I don't get it."

"It's a booby trap." Eldora grunted as she straightened. "Anyone who trips this ward will be pulled to this portal."

Neat. "Where does it go?"

"Hong Kong. Lovely restaurant." Eldora rubbed the dirt off her hands. "One of my favorite places."

"You've been to Hong Kong?" Paige couldn't get past the idea that Eldora lived the life of the Amish. She sometimes forgot that the woman had her own private plane.

Eldora gave Paige a tight smile and turned away.

"Okay. So, this door is just going to stay here? Like this?" Paige struggled to see how this was a good booby trap. "Everyone can see it."

"Exactly." Eldora walked out to the left, placing down other rocks, drawing a line along the ground connecting each one.

Between this and what Merry had done, Paige was almost certain their wards would work better.

Each person of their town had offered a piece of themselves into the wards. If she looked at her wards like they were a living creature, the pieces of soul each person had offered created a type of brain, while the trees offered the body. Merry had just given the tree a pulse, and Eldora had provided it with courage and a way to fight back.

All it needed now was guidance.

Paige looked at Merry and then Eldora. "The wards are a—" When she thought about saying what she was about to, she felt like a mad scientist or a god. "They're alive. Somehow, we've created a living thing with what we've done with our magick so far. Can we..." She looked at the other two coven leaders, wondering if she was out of her mind. "Can

63

we tell them what we want, giving them—our wards—our magick again but with the intent of giving them the ability to decide?"

Merry frowned but blinked, looking over at Eldora.

The door magick witch shook her head, her brow crinkling. Licking her lips, her dark eyes met Paige's. "We can try."

Paige sucked up her courage and smiled. She might not like either woman, might think they both had ulterior motives Paige struggled to see around, but she probably did too.

Together, they combined their magick, which was getting easier with the continued practice, and reached up to touch the wards.

They answered in a thousand voices. They spoke through visions and a mash of memories.

Talking to the wards was like trying to talk to bees or an entire classroom of overzealous children. But Paige needed to get through to them, to the wards. So, she balled her inky magick fists and pushed through.

Merry made another slice in her arm, allowing her blood to leach into the Whiskey ward tree, her lips moving silently.

The wards went quiet and listened.

Paige dipped into her alpha will and mentally shouted her intent: *Keep the town safe.*

Eldora touched the ward tree with her door magick, and the wards rippled and shivered.

But then the voices leapt with excitement and, like children, they zipped along the surface of the wards in silvery lines of energy, touching each of the doors Eldora had set up. Paige could almost hear the giggles of excitement she felt.

Protect the town.

The wards went still and the tree quivered, a face appearing in the bark.

Eldora let out a surprised screech and took a step back before placing her hand over her chest and glaring.

Suppressing her chuckle, Paige waited for the face to speak.

It sent her a barrage of images of men and women attacking in various ways; rape, thievery, murder, abuse.

Paige went through each of them, pulling the wards away from the common ones, the ones the wards could misinterpret. She didn't trust the wards to know the difference between abuse and a parent getting her child's attention. Paige was known to rap her knuckles against Leah's head a time or two. That wasn't abuse, though she was certain there were some who would think it was.

She was concerned with people coming into their town with rifles, people who looked like they were military.

People intent on harming those the wards were bonded to.

The wards hummed, the sound growing louder and more intense. Paige's eyes watered, but she remained firm, hoping the wards would stop soon.

With a final, silvery shudder, the hum ceased and the presence of the wards' "intelligence" fluttered away, seeking, watching, protecting.

Releasing her magick, Paige turned to Merry and Eldora. "I think we did it." Paige tried to keep the surprise out of her tone. She was actually kind of impressed.

Merry smiled at Paige, looking pleased with herself. "I'll have the plane ready by the evening." She turned to Eldora. "I don't have a car."

Eldora gave Paige a surly look. "You can use conventional means sometimes." Then, she used her inky black magick to cut open a door.

Merry stepped through the door, and it flashed with a black light again.

Eldora sent out a magick pinging sound Paige had never heard before. "We need to work on your door magick."

"I agree." But, unfortunately, there were a lot of things she needed to do first. "When I get back?"

Derrick and the other woman appeared around the corner of the Whiskey house, in deep discussion.

Eldora smiled, pleased. "And Leah?"

"You enrolling your kids in our schools?"

"Phoebe is working on that as we speak."

"Excellent." Who was Phoebe to Eldora anyway? No. No. She didn't need to know. She had a town—all the para-normals to save and she needed to check in with Red Star, something she'd meant to do earlier and had forgotten. She turned around to shift and fly out of there. "Coordinate with Leah to see what times she has free, and I'll make sure she knows to make it happen."

"Thank you."

Except that Paige really didn't trust Eldora just yet. "If you try anything..."

Eldora nodded, her dark eyes clear but free of malice. "I will not."

Paige hoped so. She shifted into bird form and headed toward Red Star Headquarters.

Paige wondered if she would ever be able to step foot inside this building and not feel like she'd been booted, like someone had pushed her out—her husband, even though they weren't officially married yet—and had taken her place.

But Dexx was doing a *good job* at keeping the order.

He'd fought it. He'd wanted to just be the guy who

chased after demons and had refused to do his paperwork. And Paige had *tried* to give him that life.

But he'd quickly discovered that the Red Star Division was more than just a job. It was more than just a thing to do to help pay the rent.

She'd brought the people together, but he'd made them into a team dedicated to protecting the paranormals and enforcing the laws on them to ensure peace within their town.

The cubicle walls were still lined with greenery, making it feel less like a police bullpen and a little more inviting. Of the people on the Red Star team, only one was a legit police detective.

But they were all busy, and she didn't have the twins with her, so they looked up and said hello with their faces, but they didn't get up and greet her.

Which was okay.

Dexx was in the office—in what *had been* her office. But it was most definitely Dexx's now. There were shelves up with... things. She didn't know. A lot of cars and car parts. The man obsessed over those. Well, cars and guns. And knives. And swords. Okay. So, he had a little depth.

He saw her coming and got up, meeting her at the door and wrapping her in his arms.

Those arms could put her soul back together.

"You feeling better?" he muttered into her hair.

"Yeah."

He pulled away and studied her with his green eyes, Hattie—his spirit animal—flashing through a little. "Really?"

"Yes." She pulled away from him and took a seat. "I need to talk to you about a few things."

Dexx usually took the seat next to her, but this time, he

took the chair behind the desk. Power move. "You're not letting them in, are you?"

"I am."

He clenched his jaw and bared his teeth.

"But I've taken precautions."

He looked around, pissed. "Really."

"Yes. This isn't just me. There's an entire council."

"Oh, I know, but I also know how you get things the way you want."

Ouch. But she let that pass for the moment because it was a loaded can of worms. She walked him through what she and Eldora and Merry had done and then took in a deep breath for the next leg of this conversation. "I'm flying to D.C. tonight."

Dexx licked his lips angrily as he fell back into his chair. "I'll take care of the kids, I guess."

"I, um..." This next part was going to be the fight. "I'm taking them with me."

He sat forward, folding his hands over his desk. "Over my dead body."

"Don't be dramatic." But she thought she understood where he was coming from. He was the dad and she was endangering them.

"Dramatic?" His eyebrows shot up, and the hand on his desk flexed with cat claws. "You're trying to tell me that you're taking *our* kids out of the *safety* of our town, and I'm the one being dramatic? You're being stupid."

"It's Washington D.C., Dexx. What the hell's going to happen there?"

"Anything!" He slammed his non-clawed hand onto the desk. "They're the fucking government. They can do whatever the fuck they *want* to there."

This wasn't the time to get into a debate on government.

"I'll be okay. The kids'll be fine. If we get into trouble, I'll get us out of it like I always do."

"No. They want to ki—"

"We need to *show* them that they're safe with us around!"

"So, you're going to masquerade our *babies* around the media like *circus pets?*" His left eye twitched. "Is that it?"

When he said it like that... "No." Yes, but maybe not like circus pets. "We need to educate these people, to let them see that we're normal... people."

"They don't care," he growled.

Paige didn't want to admit it out loud, but she knew he was right. How many other groups had tried the same thing, appealing to the human nature and the hearts and souls of others? Sharing pictures of *their* babies who had been shot or killed while in their own yards or while watching TV on their own couches?

People struggled to remain empathetic. The over-whelming weight of the stories had made it easier to turn that off, though, like a switch. They might care. They might not. They could invest in others. Or they could save their energy stores and invest in themselves. "I have to try."

He gave her a cool glare, working his jaw. "Do I have *any* say?"

Paige swallowed. The right answer here was yes, but she'd already made up her mind. She wasn't going on a mission without her babies. The same babies she'd literally just pushed out of her frelling body not even a week ago. She'd already sacrificed too much of being a mom so she could have a job. "I love you."

Dexx growled and glared at his desk. "Yeah."

The conversation was done.

Paige *hated* leaving it like this, but she *knew* they'd be okay. And maybe she wasn't right. Maybe he was.

But she was done leaving her kids behind in order to save the world. At some point, she was going to have to stop sacrificing her mom time.

She just wished the world had waited to explode for another month. Or year. Or... ever.

But the world didn't care about her at the moment.

7

Dexx made it really hard to stick with her plans. His bad mood was rather pervasive, and he wasn't giving it up.

The mayor had decided to call a town hall meeting before Paige left so she'd have a "better understanding" of the town's need before she went to Washington D.C. and messed everything all up. Paige still didn't believe she might actually meet the president, but Merry informed her not to worry. She had that under control.

It was easy for Merry to say. She wasn't the one about to meet the president of the United States and issue the demands of the entire paranormal nation.

Which... what the hell was she thinking? Who did she think she was? She was a *nobody*. Okay. A powerful nobody, but still. She was a police detective from Texas. She didn't *know* everyone.

It was difficult to remember that she was what the paranormals needed because, as a nobody, she'd won against some pretty powerful foes. That meant something, especially now. Perhaps this was exactly what the Elders had been grooming her for when they'd been sending her across the United States to deal with the paranormals when issues arose.

While the town was busy with their meeting, a few key people were already at work getting the town the supplies Mayor Suzanne West had said they needed. Paige didn't have to be a part of that, which felt really weird. She was used to being the person who did the things.

And now she was the person who came up with the ideas and delegated.

What had her life become?

Late to pick up the kids, again, she didn't speed. The kids were used to this by now, and the twins were once again asleep in the back seat. Paige wanted to cry on the way to the high school. She wanted to rail at the world for making Dexx angry with her or for being forced to choose her kids over the world again or at the danger she was inflicting on this town.

But she didn't. She pulled up to the curb and smiled as Mandy and Leah piled into her silver sedan.

Leah called navigator, but Mandy already had the back door open.

They left the school in search of Danny Miller, the reporter who'd kind of been following her since Denver. He was at his new office, which had been abandoned after the battle with Sven. He almost immediately volunteered to hold one of the twins, so she gave him Ember, who could sleep through anything.

Danny smiled down at Ember's furry form. "I'll do what I can to help, but I usually give news. I don't build news channels."

"I understand, but silence is the best way to keep us in line, and we can't afford that." Paige stared down at Rai, who was sleeping curled up in her car seat in the form of a kitten. "We need to get to the word out. We need to make sure that the real news is getting out there."

He nodded, his dark-rimmed glasses sliding down his nose a little. "They offered you a position in government?"

As if government positions were like royal titles that could just be handed out—not that they were done that way in reality. Were they? Did people have to be voted into *all* of them? "No. I don't know the first thing about politics, and it hasn't been offered."

"Then why are you the one leading the charge?" He pulled out his phone with his free hand.

She sighed as he scrolled through his apps. "Is this an interview?"

"Maybe."

She wasn't ready for this. What if she said the wrong thing? Which she did on a semi-regular basis. "Look, I'm just a normal person trying to do what's right."

"So why you?"

"Because everyone else said no." She probably shouldn't have said it like that. But she'd *tried* giving it to others. "They have people they're responsible for. I... I mean. I don't have a coven. I don't have a pack. I don't have a police force." Anymore. "I have a family, so I have the time."

His brown eyes didn't hold any judgement. "Even though you should be on maternity leave."

She snorted a laugh. "We pride ourselves on our slavery of service. Who gets maternity leave? Canadians. *Canadians* get maternity leave."

He chuckled and ducked his head. "Are you taking them with you, then?"

She released a long breath. "Yes, but can you keep that

to yourself for now? I—" She shook her head. "Dexx is a bit pissed about that."

"Does he have good reason?"

"Yup."

Danny's face twisted with concern. "But you're doing it anyway."

She didn't say she was being rational. "Yup." The momma bear in her wasn't going to allow her to leave her darling little terrors behind.

She finished up the rest of the conversation with Danny, which involved him talking to Mandy, who thought she wanted to be a reporter when she grew up. Paige wasn't done making the rounds, though, so she piled the kids into the car and went to the Walmart parking lot, where she told the DoDO agents on the other side to get their fearless leader.

Mario came to the ward and gave Paige a guarded smile. "I'm hoping you're ready to see reason."

Paige hooked her thumb in her belt loop. "Your people are free to come in."

"That's excellent news, Paige," Mario said, his voice warm. "We'll begin registering everyone immediately. Things *will* go back to normal again very soon. You have my word."

"We're not registering."

His expression cooled around his eyes while his smile grew slightly. "I see."

Paige didn't like that look. "There's a town hall. You can come. Speak your piece. But registering will be a choice."

He nodded, narrowing his eyes. "That seems fair."

She gestured for him to step through the wards. "I'll give you a ride." Which was probably a bad idea, but she didn't want him bringing his escort with tanks and

Humvees into town. She decided she wasn't going to warn him about their wards. She'd let him figure that out on his own.

The twins were still in animal form. They napped for long periods of time, which was good for her because that gave her time to do things. She shoved Mandy and Leah to the backseat with the twins riding in their laps, the car seats stashed in the trunk.

Mario looked around the small car. "Cozy."

Paige grunted and drove him into town.

The "town hall" was actually out on the street. There were too many people who wanted to be a part of it, similar to the last time they'd had a meeting like this to discuss how the town was going to handle Sven. The mayor had a microphone set up by the museum at the far end of the street. The shops had little tables out on the sidewalks. It wasn't that they were trying to make money, but they offered things the townspeople needed.

Like coffee and donuts.

And spells in bottles and soaps.

The basics.

Suzanne greeted Paige on the flatbed she'd had set up. It was very impromptu and well-thought out. Maybe just very workable. It was amazingly very workable. "I hope we can calm the crowd. They're very nervous. Don't forget that a lot of humans stayed behind to create a life living with your kind."

No pressure. "I won't." She stopped herself midway to the podium. What the hell was she doing? She didn't have what it took to lead these people. All of them. They looked to her—well, they were mostly facing her, but looking just about everywhere except for *at* her, which was okay—but they were expecting her to know how to answer the threat against them.

And she just didn't.

She composed herself and stepped to the podium, confident on the outside.

She glanced at Mario, who looked rather pleased with himself. She wanted to hear what he had to say, so she introduced herself quickly before moving to the important stuff. "Look, guys, I know we're all scared. But we've got someone from the agency who started this. Let's hear what he has to say."

Mario looked a little surprised and then he climbed up on the flatbed and smiled down at everyone. "Good evening, everyone," he said in his slight English accent. "I just have a few words for you."

Half an hour later, his few words were still going. The president had issued a warning to all paranormals throughout the nation. They needed to register with the government—like sex offenders—so they could be monitored. They'd be given a device to keep their paranormal powers oppressed to keep their neighbors safe.

The more he spoke, the more uncomfortable the people in the town got. And it wasn't just the paranormals who were showing concern.

Paige gave the crowd a tight smile and gently pushed Mario out of the way. "He's certainly given us something to think about, hasn't he?"

"What are you doing about this?" a woman shouted at her.

"I'm going to D.C. to talk to the president." Mario's speech had managed to push Paige's fear aside, so at least there was that. She knew she was the right person for this job, not because she was skilled or good at it but because she had experience with terrible situations. "I'm hoping this is just a simple misunderstanding. That once she realizes we're not horrible people, things will settle down again."

"And what if they don't?" a man shouted from the front. "What if they decide shooting is easier?"

Paige didn't want to have *that* discussion in front of Mario, but she had no way of politely getting him out of there.

Luckily, Eldora did. She took Mario's arm, opened a door to ink-black nowhere, and pushed him through.

Good enough. Paige just had to hope he didn't have any other ears there, even though she knew there would be. There had to be. That was just the law of averages.

"Then we'll face it like we have everything else."

The man looked more irritated.

She could understand that. "There's something you don't know. My family have been fighting bad guys for generations. My grandma—the woman who died saving all of us just—" She couldn't continue past the lump in her throat. It had only been two weeks since Alma had died fighting Sven. It was too soon to be this flippant about it. "She fought evil during the World War. My sister and I have been fighting evil since we were in high school. My kids? Her kids? Since they were in grade school."

A couple people she could focus on directly in front of her looked worried, turning toward each other or putting their hands to their heads.

"Can I promise you things are going to get better, that we'll be able to return to normal? No."

A couple of people raised their faces to her.

A few turned away.

"They're not going to stop hunting you," someone shouted from somewhere in the middle of the street.

He wasn't wrong. "I know, and none of us wanted to drag *any* of you into this fight with us. We just want to live normal lives."

"What if we can't?" Dexx demanded loudly. "What if they come in here and take us, our kids? What if they try to force us to submit?"

She heard the underlying of previous conversations. He hated big government, and he wanted to simply overthrow it. "Dexx."

He looked at her, his green gaze solid and unmoving. "This is our chance to fight back."

She shook her head. "We have to try peace first."

"And when that doesn't work?"

She looked out over the crowd, not wanting to utter the next words out loud. "Then we may have to fight." She took in a shaky, scared-to-Hell-and-back breath. "Go to war."

He shook his head. "You *know* we're going to war. It's what they want."

A few people in the crowd cheered this. A few of those were human, though, and it didn't *feel* like they were cheering the *idea* of war but were showing their support of his idea, that this was the only play.

"We don't have to *give* them what they want." She had to find a way to end this peacefully.

"So, then, we surrender." Dexx gestured to the crowd, his rising anger charging his words and dropping his tone. "And the nation follows our lead. Then all the paranormals will be tagged and rounded up, herded into jails and detention facilities. Tested on. Beaten. Tortured."

She hated him sometimes.

"Our kids."

She knew he was right, but she *had* to believe in people. "We're trying peace first."

"And when it fails?" he asked again.

"We're going to war," she growled.

The crowd joined her, their voices rising and filling the street.

This thing could go so badly, and everyone knew it.

8

Paige raised her hands for calm. "Okay. Some of you are worried about the wards. They're designed to prevent anyone coming in from violence, and if they try, well, let's just say they shouldn't."

She didn't want to go into great detail to explain *what* would happen to people who tried something harmful, only that they wouldn't appreciate the outcome.

She watched a few relax. Maybe a few felt safer. Maybe.

Until Paige explained that those living under the ward couldn't do anything harmful either. They could discipline their kids, but they couldn't beat their husbands.

"Is this for everyone?" one woman shouted. "Or just those who didn't add to the wards? I couldn't do that. I can now, if that helps."

Paige didn't understand the reasoning behind that. Did the woman *want* the freedom to beat her husband or kid?

No. That woman down there was an American who prided herself on not having her freedoms stripped, and unfortunately, they lived in a time when more and more of those freedoms were lost in order to protect the growing public.

"Are you trying to force your moral intentions on us?" another man yelled.

"No." Her voice didn't carry far over the growing din of voices.

With Suzanne's help, they *did* manage to get everyone calmed down.

A woman stepped up and volunteered to take down the names of all the people who wanted to add themselves to the wards, people who'd opted not to before. "Willow Matthews," she said, introducing herself during a small break in the crowd. "I want to offer myself as your personal assistant."

Paige wasn't going to say she didn't need one, but she'd never had anyone come up to her and just volunteer to be hired either. "I'm not sure I'm looking."

"You are," Willow said, her eyebrows high as she turned back to the crowd. She fished something out of her pocket and handed it to Paige. "That's my contact information. I'll get these names to you after everyone leaves."

Paige didn't even have a chance to say thanks or okay or bye. Willow just met the people and bought Paige some space.

Paige tried talking to Dexx afterward, but the crowd swelled in around Willow, asking questions and pushing Dexx away. Her first instinct was to push them back so she could have some of *her* space. Instead, she texted Dexx and listened to the people around her.

This was her new job. She just hoped she figured out what to do with it soon.

Retirees who couldn't move to a safer place because they couldn't afford to and had no one to take them were worried they were now in the war zone. They had an entire retirement community she'd never known about. And they were all gloriously human. Not a lick of magick in them. They wanted their medications—which they each had a laundry list of—and internet. Not so they could do a lot on it, but so they could video call. And they wanted the cable TV turned back on so they could watch the news. It was the only way they could keep their finger on the pulse.

And a lot of them loved the more biased cable news stations. A few even knew that it was false reporting, but it was like watching a soap opera called *News*, and they loved that. It made them feel like they were part of the action.

She was letting the irritation of Dexx not texting her back get the better of her. So, she texted him a long string of grenade emojis to get his attention.

At the house with the twins, he finally texted back.

There were no emojis. Yeah. The man was still mad.

She found Willow as the crowd dwindled. "I need to get home."

Willow nodded, her dark, curly hair pulled back in a full braid. She handed Paige a few pages out of her notebook, her dark skin a little ashy around the knuckles. "Here's the list of who would like to add themselves to the trees."

That was just a weird statement. "I'll show someone what to do and have them..." This was weird. Who was she going to get to do this? Leah. She'd get Leah to do this. "Should I have my daughter just call you when she's ready?"

Willow nodded. "There are other things they had concerns about too," she offered.

Maybe Paige *did* need an assistant. "Organize them so we can attack them better."

"I'll offer a few solutions, too, if you think that would help."

"I would." Someone offering solutions? What a treat. "And go see Leslie about your hands and drink water."

Willow frowned.

"Your knuckles." Paige searched the crowd for any of her family. "Your skin looks like it hurts right now."

"Yeah, well." Willow shrugged and turned away. "Call me."

Paige would. She really, *really* would. That woman might be the answer to a wish she hadn't even known to ask for.

She couldn't spot any of her family still there. If she left a kid behind, she'd have to go find them again later or hope that they could make their own way. This was going to add a whole new element to their already crazy family life.

She found Dexx at the house like he'd said. The twins were both sleeping, and Dexx was absolutely silent. No jokes. No attempts to make the situation lighter.

Which only made it worse.

She went up to Dexx, trying to kiss him.

He accepted her lips. He didn't give his in return.

Ouch. "I'm sorry, Dexx. I just can't leave them behind."

He nodded, his lips pursed and quirked down.

She could almost hear his words as if he'd spoken them out loud. She'd gone into dangerous situations when she'd been pregnant, but she'd always left the kids at home where they were safe.

Except they weren't always safer at home away from her protection. "Do you remember the time DoDO came and shot up the house, not even knowing where the kids were?"

He gave her a cold stare. "Do you remember how I

handled that situation?"

"Do you remember the time you invited our enemy to a BBQ and he nearly killed us?"

His gaze dropped a few chilly degrees. "He didn't even come close."

No. That'd been later, like the next day. "They're in danger no matter where they are because they're *our* kids."

"Yeah." He finally looked at her, stabbing her soul with those brilliant green eyes, his lips so temptingly close to hers. "*Our* kids. But I never purposely tossed them into the lion's cage."

"Hey, Mom," Leah said as she bounced down the stairs. "I'm packed."

Dexx's hackles rose. Technically, Leah wasn't his daughter, but he treated her like she was and that mattered more. "Veto. Put your stuff away." He more growled than spoke.

She *knew* he was right. She *was* being irrational but saying that mind-loud wasn't enough. She had to *teach* Leah the ways of the world because she was going to be an adult before any of them were ready. And Paige wasn't leaving the two lives she'd just spat out into the world for a few days.

Leah froze, not sure who to listen to, her blue eyes flicking from one parent to the other.

Dexx shook his head, seeing the answer on her face. "And Bobby?"

That was their other adopted son, a little older than the twins. "Staying." But only because the Whiskey wards truly were the only thing protecting him from the angels and demons hunting him. Well, and the fact that the Heaven and Hell gates were almost impossible to open now. D.C. was *not* a safe place for their prophet child.

"Why? Because he's the one you don't care as much about?"

Oh, spicy. "Because I only have two arms."

"Leah brings another two."

"Those are the two I was talking about." He needed to understand that she wasn't *stupid*. The mother in her just wasn't allowing her to consider leaving her babies behind. That was all. And, besides, she didn't care who she was talking to—their little hearts would melt at the sight of babies. And their babies were *adorable*.

Did it make her better or worse to take them as political weapons versus taking them because her inner mother refused to leave them behind? She couldn't tell.

But she had a terrible feeling in her gut. It might be that she had to poop. Her hormones were still wildly out of whack. She *knew* things weren't going to be good. She just hoped she could figure it out.

He licked his lips and gave her a hug, his body stiff with anger still. "I love you."

She hugged him back with everything she had. It was all she could do. "I know."

"I hate you." He pulled back, shaking his head.

"I know." She cupped his big, brick head in her hands and stabbed as much love as she could into his green eyes. "I love you... *so* damned much. Please know that."

He flicked a blond eyebrow and stepped back. "I'll get the twins ready to go."

Merry and Eldora showed up not long afterward. The babies were strapped in their car seats. The diaper bag was fully loaded. Paige's computer was ready, along with her go bag—a backpack she had at the ready for when she had to leave on unexpected trips.

Dexx hugged Leah tight and whispered something in

her ear. She whispered something back and hugged him harder.

Eldora cut a door open, a dark void staring back at them.

Dexx refused to look at Paige as they stepped through the door.

Damn! That was like a knife to the soul. "How did the supply run go?" Paige asked Eldora in order to get her mind back to the matters at hand.

"Well." Eldora held out a silver coin that had what looked like a family crest on one side and a pentacle on the other. "Take this. When you're ready to come back, we'll get you out. Do not open your own door until you've been trained."

Paige took the coin and shoved it into her pocket. "Thanks."

Eldora handed one to Leah as well.

Merry took Ember from Leah. "I'm not getting your bags," she told the teen.

Leah smiled up at her and grabbed the rolling suitcase. "You're coming too?"

Merry raised her nose in the air and stepped through Eldora's door and disappeared.

Paige let Leah go first, then followed her daughter through and stepped onto a noisy tarmac directly beside a plane.

"I'm not going with you." Merry handed Ember off to one of the waiting flight attendants and booped his sleeping nose before he was taken away. "At least, not this time. I'm staying behind in case you need help." She met Paige's gaze squarely. "You are walking into a trap."

Hearing Merry utter those words out loud only made Paige feel worse. "I should leave the kids."

"No." Merry sighed heavily, folding her hands in front

of her black business dress. "You parade those darlings around every camera you can find. You make people see you as a concerned mother. You're white, you're clean, and you're an upstanding citizen of the U.S. Use *those* weapons to their fullest."

How had things gotten so screwed up?

Reality was that they hadn't. Not really. They were just twisted enough so *she* and those like her fell on the to-be-hated radar. The hate had always been there, like a sleeping giant in a tiny room.

Well, if she could figure out how to break through for her kind, she'd find a way for everyone else too.

Baby steps.

Make people fall in love with her adorable children. *Then* world domination and free love for everyone.

Fuck love. Just an even playing field would be nice.

The flight attendants had already strapped her sleeping circus onto the plane. Paige loved using the Eastwood jet. It even had onboard Wi-Fi, so she was able to catch up on the news and research the area for places to take Leah.

But what she saw concerned her. There was *no* news about the paranormals aside from the president's address.

No one knew what was going on.

Like the bombing of the black neighborhood a hundred years ago hadn't been on the news. Could Paige *trust* that everyone was okay? That it was really this good? Or were the horrors being covered up?

She hoped Brack, the dragon, really was on top of this. If there was something else going on here, the world needed to see it. The press really *was* a powerful tool and one the people couldn't afford to lose.

She managed to get a slight nap in on the flight. She wasn't stupid. She was a new mother and not nearly as

87

young as she should have been to bring two new lives into the world. She also had zero idea what she was walking into.

Though, the reality was that she wasn't going to see the president, even with Merry's political strings. She'd make it some senator's office. Maybe even Oregon's senator. She had no idea how the government even worked.

That thought spawned an entire research session that lasted a good five minutes. It could have been closer to three. It was really boring and put her to sleep faster than Dexx talking to her about car parts.

When she woke, they were landing. The flight attendant was super nice and made sure that the babies were okay. Which, surprisingly, they were. They'd slept through it all. Paige'd thought for sure they'd wake up for at least the landing, but no. Rai pulled on her ear as they descended, but she didn't stir.

Once the plane came to a complete stop, Paige gathered Ember.

Rai woke up and shifted into a wolf pup.

"No." Paige scowled at her youngest daughter. "We're going in public. I need you to be human."

Rai gave her a dejected look and whined.

Leah chuckled and scooped up her baby sister. "I'll carry her in whatever form."

That wasn't the point. "We're about to go into a city of humans. We *need* to appear as normal as we possibly can."

Perhaps taking her untrained children into Washington D.C. had been a worse idea then she first thought.

She invoked her alpha will on her twins, calling on their spirit animals to show a little more experience. "That means no shifting unless we are alone and safe. You are to remain as humans while we are out and about."

Rai was not easily subdued. She was a fighter, true to her Whiskey heart, but she did eventually return to human form, though...was that onesie fitting a little tighter now?

Leah's eyes gleamed with concern, but she said nothing.

Paige was ever so grateful for the flight attendants. They made getting off the plane with the babies and the suitcase and her computer bag and the diaper bag and Leah's backpack easy.

She spotted the car waiting for them and headed toward it.

A motorcade came through the airport gate.

Paige looked around to see if another plane had landed, maybe with some visiting dignitary or something.

However, the motorcade seemed to be headed toward her and her kids.

She stopped, her heart pounding, her magick restless. She had just told her *kids* they had to be human. That meant her as well. Crap.

A small army of men and women in black suits, ties, and sunglasses, spilled out of the vehicles, and two of them approached Paige. The man never stopped swiveling his head, scoping out the area.

The woman smiled tightly. "Ma'am," she said, her voice clipped. "You'll have to come with us. We're here to escort you to the White House."

That was unexpected.

Leah looked up at Paige and grinned. "See? This isn't bad."

This probably wasn't going to turn out as well as Leah hoped. A chill of fear rippled down Paige's spine as two other men took her bags from the flight attendants. There were senators at the White House, right? Or was it only the president?

The woman turned and gestured toward the motorcade. "If you and your kids will just get inside?"

Paige didn't want to get in that SUV, and she certainly didn't want to take her kids into it. Were they really going to the White House? Or would they be taken to a prison? "I actually have a rental car waiting for me. With room for the car seats."

The woman's smile grew tighter. "Your rental has been taken care of. There's ample room for your car seats."

One of the men went to Leah to take Ember from her.

Leah frowned, confused. "These are the good guys. Right?"

Paige hoped so. "Yeah, Lee Bean. They are." She shuffled her children into the SUV and got both Rai and Ember into their seats. As soon as everyone was strapped in, they were off.

Leah asked a million questions.

None of the security personnel answered her questions.

That didn't bode well for them at all.

Paige's nerves ratcheted up the closer they got to the White House.

Leah had finally gotten the clue that no one was going to answer her questions, so she kept them to herself and just stared out the window.

That twisted Paige's heart. Hard.

Somewhere along the way, Rai had dozed off, and Ember had decided to wake up. He was hungry. And screaming.

Paige wasn't about to pull him out of his car seat to feed him. So, she had Leah make up a bottle for him and give it to him. She had brought the travel heater. It worked okay. It probably wasn't safe. None of the conveniences of the modern day were. But it would at least stop the screaming and probably keep them from dying. Ember's screams were certainly starting to get on the driver's nerves.

They pulled through the White House gate and into a small media circus. Cameras snapped nonstop.

The security team assisted Paige in dragging her kids through the throng of people. They threw question after question at her, but there were so many of them, she couldn't really make one out from another.

As soon as they made it into the White House foyer, they were shuffled into another room. This one was blessedly quiet. The door was closed, and Paige finished feeding Ember and then burped him.

Her nerves went on high alert.

I don't like this. Cawli's voice was like a soft blanket inside her head.

She was so glad he'd chosen *this* moment to show himself again. Her spirit animal wasn't like everyone else's, constantly riding shotgun. Cawli was often gone, leaving only his ability to shift. *I don't either. I'm really thinking this entire thing was a bad idea.*

Whatever happens, I am here.

That reassured her.

The door opened, and a woman in a blue pencil skirted business suit walked through. She had four assistants with her, each carrying a box. She smiled as the door closed behind her. "Ms. Whiskey, we are deeply honored to have you here."

Paige didn't think that was strictly true, and she was afraid to ask what was in the boxes.

"I hope you will understand our need for security. While you are in the Washington D.C. area, you and your children will have to wear these."

The four people carrying the boxes opened them to reveal silver, metal collars.

She had actually been expecting this in the quiet recesses of her mind. "You've got to be kidding me." But maybe this would work to her advantage. She already knew the collars were defective. She'd only *guessed* they'd been designed that way.

The woman smiled and tipped her head to the side. "We have no true idea of your full power potential. But we do need to make sure that our president is safe while in your presence."

Wow. She really *was* going to get to see the president. She wished she'd prepared for that instead of thinking she'd be off the hook by talking to a senator instead. "How about I just promise not to use my powers on the president and then we just go with that?"

The woman smiled but didn't say anything further.

Paige knew that if she fought now, she would just make the situation worse.

She nodded once to Leah, who frowned.

The people with the boxes stepped forward and clicked the collars into place.

As soon as the collar snapped around Paige's neck, she lost her connection to Cawli. She hadn't realized that, even when he was elsewhere, she could still feel an echo of him.

Something else filled the void, though.

Voices from the now unraveling Hell's gate embedded in her bones.

With Cawli suppressed, his ability to seal that gate was gone.

The woman smiled. "The president will see you now."

9

P aige was told how to address the president on their way to the Oval Office. There were so many rules that had to be followed to show respect, Paige was fairly certain she was going to slip up in some weird way. Like, she would burp at the wrong time or fart inappropriately or something.

She'd never come into contact with anyone with presidential political clout before. It felt a little like meeting a king or queen. Well, it kinda was like that. In this country, the queen was called Madame President.

Paige was shown into the Oval Office, and the door closed behind her. No one was there yet, and the other door was still open. Paige wasn't certain what to do, so she just kind of stood there, waiting.

She trailed a finger along the back of the couch. No stains. How long had it been since her own couch had been stain-free?

The collar chafed at her skin. It wasn't comfortable in the least little bit, but it was irritating. The voices of the demons whispered against her mind. If she was forced to wear this much longer, they'd all be in a lot of danger. They'd managed to push Hell's gate further away from Earth, but this one?

It didn't seem to be having any issues. Crap.

Paige pulled out the silver necklace she never took off and looked at the tiny, silver sea turtle, remembering when Dexx had given it to her for Christmas. It was their inside joke. Paige was secretly hoping that, in her next lifetime, she would be allowed to come back as a sea turtle. She wanted to take a hundred-year vacation, just surfing the tides in the ocean. Just swimming around and seeing the wild blue wonders.

She felt separated from Dexx in a way she'd never felt before. She'd gone on missions before. They'd been separated by miles.

His anger worried her. He'd never been *that* angry with her since before Louisiana.

He'd been right about the kids. She knew that. She'd known that at the time too. But the mother in her wouldn't *budge*.

There was movement at the other door, and she quickly shoved her necklace back into her shirt.

The president of the United States stepped into the room and closed the door behind her. She looked over at Paige and smiled, her blonde hair in a perfect poof, her blue pant suit immaculate. She gestured to one of the two sofas. "Ms. Whiskey, please have a seat."

Paige wasn't entirely certain that sitting at this moment was what she wanted to do. However, if the president of the United States told her to sit, then she was going to sit.

"I was glad to hear you decided to come."

Decided to come. That was a funny way of putting it, as

if there'd been an invitation sent. Paige fingered her collar and grimaced. "You have a funny way of showing that."

"This is just for the safety of everyone. We all saw how powerful you are. What we don't know is what you want."

"What *I* want? It's not like we're aliens from another planet." Paige leaned back on the couch but didn't get comfortable. "I was born here. I was raised here. What do you think I want?"

The president smiled and folded her hands in her lap. "It's my job to make sure Americans are safe."

Paige narrowed her eyes, reminding herself yet again she needed to show respect. "Last time I checked, I'm American too. And I believe you know exactly how safe you are, Madame President. Based on the collars, I'd have to say you and your people have been researching us for a very long time." Something she already had intimate knowledge of. "Long enough to know how to mute our abilities, and that doesn't make *me* feel safe."

The president flicked her eyebrows up and relaxed on the couch opposite Paige. She let her head fall back slightly as she assessed Paige. "What I mean to say is that I don't know if I can trust you."

That seemed reasonable. "I don't know if I can trust you either."

The president took in a deep breath and tapped her leg. "You threw my team out of your town."

"They came into the grocery store and pointed a gun at my baby. My *baby*. How was I supposed to react?"

The president grimaced. "That was, perhaps, an over-step on our part."

Paige didn't buy that for a moment. Now that she was in the same room as the woman, she was getting a much different feel for her than she had through the campaign trail. The president was colder, more calculated.

The president had a certain confidence that emanated from her, and she didn't react like someone who was "new" to this paranormals-exist situation. She wasn't stupid. She didn't seem like the type of person who made an error of judgement.

The only thing the president didn't know was just who Paige was. "If you truly want peace with our kind, then make sure that it *looks* like you want peace with our kind."

"And what would that look like?"

"Perhaps fewer guns." Why would she even have to say that out loud?

"And when you bring out your abilities? You can do things with your mind. Our people only have guns."

That was a lie. "So, you don't know that DoDO are witches?"

The president smiled and bit her bottom lip. "They are not, but I do appreciate you trying to undermine them."

She wasn't stupid, was she? "I assure you they are."

"They do have abilities, which is something they need in order to hunt your kind, but they most certainly are *not* witches."

So, what did they tell the president they were? Wizards? Because that was so much better? "Do you even know who you've gone to bed with?"

"Your enemy. Your natural predator."

That was rich. "Did you employ any background research when you deployed them to hunt the people of your country? People you swore to protect?"

"But you aren't, are you?"

Wait. What?

"People, I mean. You're something *different*."

The president was treading a dangerous path. As soon as people stopped seeing others as *people*, as soon as they started seeing them as *things* to be feared, then the rules of propriety were thrown out the window. It didn't matter what was done to those who weren't *people*. They could be as ugly and as cruel as they wanted. "I think you'll find we are, indeed, people. We just have different skill sets."

"That's the reason you brought your children? Smart move, actually."

"I brought them because I just gave birth to them last week." Paige was starting to get a bit pissed and needed to tone that down. "I'm on this thing called maternity leave? I know it's not a thing here, but I'm on it."

"Yes. Well." The president stood and walked to her desk. "Bringing them won't save you. This isn't going to make you look sympathetic to anyone, no matter how hard you try. You're a terrorist living in our back yard. You and your kind must be eradicated."

Eradicated? Terrorist? People could shoot schools without being named a terrorist. They could shoot churches, malls, grocery stores. But Paige had saved the world from a demon and *she* was being named a terrorist? People who binge-watched Netflix like normal humans but could shift into animals at will were being called terrorists? "You can't really believe that."

"Yes, I do."

This was her chance. Fuck, she couldn't blow it. She scooted to perch on the edge of the couch, not wanting to stand and face off with her, even with the desk between them. "Look, Madame President, we're normal. Okay? We're just... we're normal shape shifters and witches and..." She couldn't keep going on with the list because she wasn't certain how much the president knew. If she blew it, then people would start burning down forests to kill dryads. "We grow up the same. We fall in love the same. We mourn the same when we lose people."

The president pressed her fingertips into the desk and stared at her, listening.

"I—" What could she say? Why hadn't she been practicing *this* instead of looking at places to take her kids? Her kids! That was it. "Leah's so excited to be here, to learn her history. To meet *you*." She released a ghost of a chuckle, only now realizing that she wasn't certain she even *wanted* her daughter to meet this woman. "She is becoming a woman, discovering what she's passionate about, making..." Paige rolled her eyes, recalling some of the dumb things that had come out of her daughter's mouth. "...hilarious mistakes in assumptions."

The president opened her red lips to say something, then clamped them shut and looked down at her desk for a moment. She raised her gaze, and it was like the door had closed. "I had a daughter once."

Oh, crap. Paige hadn't even realized that was a mine field. "I *lost* my daughter once."

"I heard." The president rolled her head slightly to the left, stretching a muscle, her expression filled with irritation. "I'm not certain you should have gotten your daughter back."

Paige swallowed. "Neither was Rachel. Who was also a witch."

"And who took custody of your daughter because you used your powers for ill intent, if I'm not mistaken."

That woman wasn't going to use that one decision to her advantage. "I was young and grieving, and I made a mistake."

"How many more of you are able to do that? To use grief as an acceptable excuse?"

Paige didn't know how to respond.

The president went to the phone and put one hand on the receiver. "You are a power I can't control. I have no idea what you truly want."

"Then maybe you should ask."

"I can't trust you will tell me the truth. You work outside any laws we have in place. If you truly want to be a part of our society, then there need to be laws that govern you and your kind. And that, Ms. Whiskey, is why I allowed you to be here."

That pissed Paige off, her alpha anger rising.

"If we cannot come to an agreement, then you and your people will be treated like the terrorists I know you are." She picked up the phone and pressed a button. "We're done."

The door Paige had walked through opened, and a security person filled the frame.

The president gave Paige a tight smile. "I look forward to our further conversations."

"Somehow, I don't believe that." Paige didn't believe the president had any intention of *having* any further conversations.

Paige followed the security guard to the room her kids were being held in. She gathered them to her and hugged them close for a long moment, sharing in their fear. But she had to shoulder it if they were going to make it through this.

"It's time these come off," Paige told security.

"The president has ordered these remain on as long as you're in the city, ma'am," one them said.

Paige wanted to lash out, but she remained calm. She

shoved her own fear down deep, smiling into Leah's face. "Let's get out of here."

They were shuffled out the door and into another throng of voracious media people. However, now the reporters were interested in their collars.

Paige might have been able to push down her fear, but that only raised her anger. Merry had told her to parade her kids in front of the cameras? Well, this was her opportunity to do so. She stopped, holding Rai close to her.

The reporters didn't pause. They continued throwing out questions she had to ignore in order to get her statement out there. But what would she say that would get people stirred enough to care?

"I just met with the president." Paige released her emotions and hoped to the goddess the *right* words would come out.

The reporters quieted.

"The collars she has forced us to wear mute our abilities... for a *time*. She's scared of us. And she's treating us as though we're not *people*. She's treating us as though we are *things*. She called us *terrorists*. So, the only thing I really can say for certain is that we had *every* reason to hide for centuries. And—" The fear and the anger running rampant inside, Paige pushed for release. "Apparently, we should have just let the demons and angels take your world. We should have remained in hiding and let you burn."

That was probably not the right thing to say. However, her kids were wearing collars as though they were dogs and the property of the president.

Which... they chose to be canines only about a quarter of the time anyway.

She let the security personnel shuffle her and the kids into the motorcade.

She didn't get to ride in the front this time. She was forced to ride in the back with the kids.

But there was another woman there this time. She introduced herself as Naomi Wright. She, apparently, was from the Office of Faith-based and Neighborhood Partnerships and had been assigned to Paige and her family to ensure that they were properly taken care of while they were in the city.

Paige's emotions were running too high for her to really hear anything the woman had to say. Her ears buzzed with rage. She felt lucky to have gotten Naomi's name.

But as her emotions burned hot, her magick danced along her fingertips.

Interesting. So, the collars suppressed Cawli, but not her magick.

That could be something she could use to her advantage.

The motorcade stopped, and they were shuffled from the vehicles and into a rather large townhome.

It was quite spacious and furnished. And the security people helped bring in their bags.

Naomi went to the kitchen and put water in a kettle. "I'll make us some tea."

Paige set Rai on the floor next to Ember. They both sat there on the floor, touching their collars and frowning. Shocks of electricity shuffled across the surfaces of their collars but didn't seem to hurt the kids. They were probably trying to shift, but they couldn't.

They started to scream their upset.

Paige knelt next to them and reached for her alpha will. It, at least, hadn't disappeared. She projected onto her children, sending a gentle command. "Stop. Don't use your abilities. Stay in human form."

Ember looked up at her, and flames danced in his dark eyes. He was angry. An angry baby boy with a very powerful shifter spirit buried inside of him.

When Rai looked up at her, there was an answering dance of blue lightning in her eyes. She was just as angry.

However, Paige got the affirmation from both of her children that neither of them were going to attempt to shift anymore.

Paige stood and turned to Leah. "Make sure they don't try anything... baby."

The girl nodded, fingering her own collar. "I don't like this, Mom. I want to go home now."

"I know, Bean." Paige went to the small kitchen.

Naomi shook her head, staring at the babies. "It's so hard to believe they're only a week old. They're already so big and sitting up?"

Right. Maybe people *wouldn't* be falling in love with her cute babies. "We think it's because they're shifter witches."

Naomi made a humming sound.

Leah entered the kitchen, looking small and scared.

Paige wrapped her in her arms and tucked Leah's head to her chest. "I'm sorry, Lee Bean."

Leah just shook her head and held onto Paige tightly. "You don't have to be sorry. *She* does." Leah leaned back and looked up at her. "They're so dumb."

Paige wished she had the answers. "They're just people and they're scared." She tucked Leah's head back against her shoulder and looked at Naomi. "And people react like this every time they're scared. America's superpower is its ability to react to fear like a bunch of rabid animals." That was taking things a bit too far.

Except was it? The paranormal communities had lived

in secret out of justified fear. So...*was* it going too far? Really?

Naomi licked her lips and turned away from the counter, three mugs waiting. "My daughter's about your age."

Paige knew she needed to stifle her rage. She needed to get to know people, to show she too was a person. So, she swallowed hard and gritted her teeth. "Oh, really?"

Naomi gave Paige a hesitant smile. "Yeah. My son's three years younger. He's the quiet one. She's the handful."

Paige really didn't want to have this conversation. She wanted to tell Naomi to pack up her shit, stuff the tea, and to get the hell out of her apartment. However, she needed allies. "Where are they now?"

"With their father." Naomi grimaced. "We divorced and he has them most of the time. His job gives him a bit more free time than mine does."

What kind of world did they live in when a parent had to allot their kids as "free" time? "When do you have visitation?"

"I'm supposed to have them tonight, but I told Roger he needed to keep the kids."

Paige frowned. "Why?"

"Because I'm supposed to be here." Naomi raised her brown eyebrows at her cup. "With you."

"Keeping a watch on us? Keeping us out of trouble? Or spying on us?"

Naomi sighed as the tea kettle whistled. She turned toward it and poured the boiling water into the three mugs. "I'm here to make sure you feel safe. That you don't—" She stopped herself and focused on the act of making tea.

Paige knew what she was going to say. "Retaliate?"

Naomi's lips thinned as she handed Paige a cup. She

put her hand on Leah's shoulder hesitantly, drawing the girl's attention. "Would you like honey in yours?"

"It depends," Leah said petulantly. "Is it supposed to mask the flavor of the poison you put in there?"

The look on Naomi's face was hilarious. She looked at the cup in Paige's hand and then at the other two. And then she looked back at Leah. "There's no poison unless there's something that reacts to your—oh, no. You can't have choco —*can* you have things like chocolate?"

Okay. This made Paige feel a little better. They weren't dogs, but this was a *little* funny.

Naomi hastily grabbed one of the mugs, put it to her lips, and sipped, jerking a little from the heat. "It's just chamomile. Only trying to settle your nerves." Her eyes rounded as she set her cup down. "Unless chamomile is bad for you somehow?"

Paige chuckled and stepped away from Leah. She took a sip of her own water because it hadn't steeped enough to be tea yet. "See? We're safe." She looked over at Naomi. "I doubt she'll drink tea straight, but honey would probably be good. Also sugar and all the bad things. Maybe Tang. Maybe just throw some Tang in there."

Naomi stared wide-eyed at Paige, and then the light dawned on her face and a smile slid into place. "Right." She disappeared as she rummaged in the lower cabinets.

Paige really did need to make a concerted effort into making allies. Naomi sincerely looked like she was just trying to be a halfway decent human being. She couldn't let that go to waste.

Naomi reappeared with a canister of some sugar-based drink mix and grabbed honey from an overhead cabinet. "I stopped by the store and picked some up when I heard you were bringing your kids." She turned and glanced at Paige. "That was really a smart move."

The president had said that as well. That didn't make Paige feel any better.

Naomi looked at Leah. "This is the honey that Ginny likes. It's wildflower and it's local. We went and visited the place where it's made. It was really neat. Perhaps I could take you there."

Leah glared. "I don't want to go anywhere with you."

Paige took in a deep breath, working hard to push her anger further down. "Why don't you invite your kids over for visitation tonight?"

Naomi frowned and then glanced at Leah's collar before hurriedly turning back to the counter. She stashed the honey and then handed Leah her cup again. "It's probably not a good idea."

"Naomi, we have our collars on. We have no powers. We really can't hurt you." Which was a lie. Paige could definitely still hurt her. "We brought UNO cards and Munchkin."

"And Magic the Gathering," Leah added with a grumble.

Paige widened her eyes in mock horror. "And that." She had really been hoping *not* to play that one because she didn't quite understand it. She had a deck Leah had specifically built for her, but she didn't play it very well. "Let's just do game night."

Naomi pondered it for a moment.

"It's what all of us terribly *scary* paranormals do."

Naomi chuckled and then ducked her head. She glanced up at Leah, still a little uncertain. "Okay. I'll call Roger." She swallowed hard and walked away, pulling her phone out.

This particular battle wasn't going to be won on the field, and Paige doubted it was going to be won like this.

But it had to start somewhere.

Paige was going to win. Nobody put her babies in collars and walked away the victor.

10

A ll in all, game night went rather well.

Paige relaxed and accidentally had fun.

That led to Naomi and her kids relaxing as they all stuffed themselves on some of the best pizza Paige had ever had.

They traded war stories—literal war stories. Naomi had been stationed in the Middle East when she'd served, and then, when she'd come back to the civilian sector, she'd served on the streets of New York.

Her insights were a chilling reminder that, no matter how much a few people might care, it was still easier to hate and to allow the haters to have the stronger voice. Because there would always be someone *else* to clean up the mess.

Society didn't even realize it, but they had societal wives, men and women who cleaned up the mess, who made sure the kids were fed and clothed, and who made sure the system was generally working so that the societal husbands could work without having to worry.

And Paige understood that *she* was one of those societal husbands, as was Naomi.

In order for their society to grow, they would have to change their views on a lot of things. She wasn't certain they were ready for that.

The next morning, however, Naomi wasn't there, and the two guards stationed at their door informed them they should stay inside. They had no need to be out in public. Call it a staycation.

She needed to call Dexx, to apologize to him, to tell him he was right and she was wrong. The twins were getting *really* upset about having to remain in human form. Human babies were useless for a good year. Well, okay. They could scoot around sometimes sooner, but these two were used to *flying*—something they *shouldn't* have been able to do in the first place because baby birds were born with down and not feathers—and running around on four legs. Also, she and Leah were used to them taking themselves outside to do their business. They hadn't brought enough diapers.

Her breasts were the only things really happy with the twins being there. That was something few women talked about because, seriously, the milk bags were supposed to be sexy and life was about women being sexy and if some random man were to pass by and see her feeding her kids from Mother Nature's devices, he might feel overwhelmed by the urge to force her into having consensual sex with him.

They were milk bags. And they hurt. And they were disgusting. And they leaked. And they made a mess.

And she was over this entire feeding babies from her chest thing.

Except for the small moments when it was just her and baby—one at a time. She wasn't supermom. And those little eyes would stare up at her with this... light. As if the whole world had dialed down to just the two of them.

And, in that moment, everything in the world was right and good and filled with hope.

But she was ready to turn off the milk producing process.

She still hadn't gotten a call from Dexx. She'd tried Leslie and Michelle. Neither of them answered. So, she left text messages for both of them. She gave Leslie a bunch of emojis. There was a clown and the poop, which never got old, and the angry devil emoji. The last one was the crossbones.

What if they'd been cut off from communicating with the outside world?

Finally, she got a call from Suzanne. "Paige, thank goodness."

"What's going on?"

"We need—well, first. How are things?"

Paige needed information. "Have you seen anything on the news?"

"I have. Are you and the kids all right?"

Well, at least there was that. "Yes. We're fine."

"When are you coming home?"

It was strange to hear the mayor asking her that. "I don't know. I need to figure out what *I'm* doing and what needs to be done."

"Did you actually talk to the president?"

Paige filled Suzanne in on the conversation.

"I see," was all Suzanne had to say.

"Yeah. I have no idea what to do."

Suzanne paused, squeaked, paused again, and then blasted, "Are you asking *me* for advice?"

Paige had no idea why Suzanne would think that was a dumb idea. She was the freakin' *mayor* of Troutdale. Paige was a mother of a small circus and a detective who hadn't actually worked a case in two years. Three? It'd been a while. No. Two. Bobby wasn't *that* big yet.

"Well, um." Suzanne took in a deep breath and then let it out. "I would get some publicity. This is all about what the people are thinking and what they're feeling, and that means you have to be seen."

"But there are guards on my doors."

"Are you under arrest?"

"No."

"Then, by rights, you're free to go. You're an American citizen. They can make you *feel* like you're not allowed to go anywhere, but they really can't arrest you."

Which Paige *knew*. She was in law enforcement, but she was bordering on something new here. The people of the U.S. saw her and her family as terrorists. For saving the world.

But didn't most terrorists think they were saving the world?

That was a terrifying thought she couldn't take back.

The difference was she didn't kill people to save the world.

Suzanne gave her a few more insights on how to get the media to show up where she wanted. How to ask for interviews. What stunts would work better than others.

She needed to get in front of the camera.

Right. Okay. "Thanks!"

"You're—I mean, no problem."

Almost as soon as they hung up, Leslie called. "Yeah?"

Paige almost sagged with relief just hearing her sister's voice. "I haven't been able to get a hold of anyone. Is everything okay?"

"Yes. I mean, the supply run went well. Is it weird that

we're workin' so close with Eldora? I mean, she *is* creepy. Am I right? It's not just me?"

Paige chuckled. "It's not just you." But Leslie's tone said there was something else going on. Actually, it was her accent. Her Texan drawl always got deeper when she was upset. "Anything else?"

"Well, people are tryin' to buy m' damned soap without any money. That's a problem because I can't order supplies without cash money."

"You're able to get shipments?"

"Well, no. But I *might* be able to get it delivered to a post office and then have Eldora get me a door there."

She had a point, but if anything, her drawl was getting even deeper. "Out with it."

Leslie sighed. "Fine. Dexx is missin'."

"What do you mean missing?"

"I mean he disappeared. Was at work. Then he wasn't."

"At work?" The world fell out of Paige's stomach.

"That's what I said."

"Did you check the vide—" She was talking to the wrong person. "I love you."

"Be safe."

They hung up, and she called Michelle, who didn't pick up until the third call. "I did check the video surveillance," Michelle said without saying hello. "I have no information. As soon as I do, I'll let you know."

"What do we know?"

"Nothing."

"But the wards..." This shouldn't be possible.

Michelle paused. "Did you and Dexx have a fight before you left?"

"Yes, but..." Understanding flooded through her. The wards prevented anyone from coming and taking Dexx. If he left, he did so willingly. "No. You know him. Even if we were fighting, he wouldn't just leave."

"I don't... know." Michelle paused. "He was pretty upset."

Paige couldn't even begin to imagine Dexx just leaving like that. He'd been there through all the shit she'd dealt for the last few years. He hadn't run once. He wasn't a quitter. "I want you to treat this like it's a kidnapping."

"Kidnapping?" Michelle's voice was clipped. "Even with the wards?"

She didn't know *how*, but she *had* told the town about the wards, and if word had gotten back to Mario... he may have found a way around them. "DoDO has more to gain by holding him hostage."

"Because of the way things are going?"

"Yes."

"And you're becoming a bigger player."

Apparently so. "Yes."

"Okay." That one word was light, as if spoken with a small swarm of relief. "I'll have everyone continue to dig. Not that they would stop if I told them to."

"How's crime?" Because Paige needed the distraction.

"Down. People are scared. They're working together. It's good. The wards are working—or the threat of them are. I don't know."

"Good." There were other questions she wanted to ask, but again, those were questions for someone else. "Keep me apprised."

"Will do."

They disconnected and Paige's *next* call was to Merry freakin' Eastwood.

She knew that if she tried to do a spell of any sort, it

wouldn't work. It wasn't the collar. She still had access to her magick.

It was the fact that she sucked at spell work. She needed the best.

Normally, that would be Leslie, but her tone had said she was elbows to eyebrows deep with stuff. Leslie was the Whiskey wife. She handled everything so that everyone else could handle every*thing* else. Paige wasn't going to burden her with more.

That left Merry Eastwood who was the best, most powerful spell caster she knew.

Merry answered on the first ring. "This is a surprise. You're quitting already?"

"No." Paige couldn't think past Dexx being missing. "I need your help."

"My help?" Merry seemed bored, as if she already knew what Paige was going to ask.

"I need you to tell me where Dexx is."

Merry paused. "Isn't he at work or playing house cat?"

The cat jokes were funny, something Paige didn't want to admit, but she didn't have time for that at the moment. "He's gone."

"Did you two have a fight?"

Why did everyone—she didn't finish that thought. She knew why everyone asked that question. It was the right one to ask. "Yes. But he wouldn't leave right now."

"Is he chasing a lead or whatever it is that he does?"

"He didn't check in with his team." And Paige had finally gotten him—no. His *team* had finally gotten him trained to do that.

"The wards would prevent any harm from happening to him."

"I know."

Merry didn't answer right away. "What do you *think* happened?"

She had no idea. "I *think* DoDO somehow got in and that they have him."

"Why?" Merry clicked her tongue in a sophisticated tongue-click which was soft and light, instead of the harsh tongue-click Leslie typically used. "Never mind. I'll be right there."

Paige had no idea what she meant by that, but Merry didn't provide further details, and when she looked at her phone, she realized she'd been cut off.

She had enough time to fix her and Leah some lunch. The twins were being fussy in the living room. Rai *really* hated being in puny human form. She was trying to pull herself up so she could at least stand on her wobbly baby legs, and it was taking a lot more effort than the girl wanted. Shoots of baby lightning danced around the room.

A jagged black line of magic appeared in the middle of the living room right before a door opened, and Eldora and Merry stepped through.

Merry assessed the room with a cool eye and walked to the kitchen island, dropping a rather large bag on the grey marble counter. She curled a lip at the collar for a moment and then pointed at it, one eye narrowed more than the other as she raised an eyebrow.

"Represses the spirit animal," Paige said shortly.

Merry nodded, her lips still clamped tight. "Not your magick?"

Paige shook her head. "But the demon door is opening."

"The—" Light dawned on Merry's face. "Right." She turned to her bag and started pulling things out. "Would you like to help?" she asked Leah.

Leah was interested and repulsed at the same time. She licked her lips and glanced at Paige. "Yes?"

Eldora went for the stove and turned the burner on for hot water.

Paige kept forgetting or overlooking the fact that Leah was Merry's descendant, thanks to the fact that Paige had married her son. She hadn't *known* it at the time because he hadn't said. She still secretly believed Merry was the one responsible for Mark's death, but she couldn't prove anything.

But if Paige was going to allow Leah to learn her door magick from Eldora Blackman, then she had to allow her daughter to also learn blood magick from Merry Eastwood. Paige had been very lucky growing up with Balnore by her side. But there weren't enough demigods to teach all the Whiskey kids on their various forms of magick.

Paige kept the twins busy while Leah and Merry talked quietly about the objects she set on the counter.

It was like Hermione's magick bag that held everything. Paige was a little disappointed when a tent didn't come out. The only thing she could think of was what Harry Potter had said. Magick really *was* cool.

The twins seemed happy to self-entertain for the moment, so she joined Merry and Leah at the counter.

With the countertop prepped, Merry looked up at Paige. "I need something of his."

Eldora finished making tea. She placed a mug in front of Merry and another in front of Paige. She turned to Leah. "Cocoa?"

Leah frowned at her grandmother and grudgingly nodded.

Paige could almost feel for the girl. She'd grown up thinking Rachel was her *only* grandmother. Then she'd come to live with Paige and realized that Alma was *another* grandmother.

And then they moved to Oregon and discovered that the wicked witches of the east and west were *also* her grand-mothers.

And they were both currently helping her locate her unofficially adopted dad.

That kid was the poster child for the new "nuclear" family.

Merry sipped her tea and gestured for Paige to do the same.

She picked the cup up and sniffed it. It smelled good. She took a sip. It tasted like water. "What is it with you and tea?"

Merry's black eyebrow twitched as she lowered her cup. "There are many herbs that assist in many ways with magick, something your sister knows well. But you both could do with a few lessons on real magick."

"From a blood witch." Paige *had* been instructed by one of the most powerful witches she knew—Alma.

"Our magicks require a lot more structure than yours."

Paige knew she wasn't wrong. Her magick was... life? She still didn't quite know how to peg it into a bucket. It was nature magick. That's what it felt like, and nature *had* rules. Not just the kinds that humans seemed to require.

Merry drank a bit more, Paige following her lead.

And then the wicked witch of the west got to business.

Being on the outside of the spell was a little like watching air move, which was possible when the sun streamed through the window to highlight all the little dust particles. She pulled the turtle necklace Dexx had given her off.

Merry handed it to Leah. "Place it in the center, girl.

Good. Now, one hand up, the other down. Feel your core and draw from your blood." She took out her curved blade and pricked her thumb before handing that to Leah as well.

Leah sighed, but took it, pricking her finger with a wincing frown. She and her grandmother allowed their blood to drop on the sand and then chanted the words Eldora had given them to repeat.

Nothing happened for a few seconds. Leah glanced at Paige but calmed and settled into the spell.

The charm wiggled and rose.

The charm glowed a brilliant orange, like a hearth fire, and floated above the dust circle she and Leah had drawn using red and black colored sand.

Merry's head fell back as she continued to chant, and black smoke sizzled around her as if the very air was alive.

Paige's heart leapt, hoping for good information, for good word, or for Merry to just provide her with a location or procure him right then and there.

The air stopped sizzling, and the charm fell to the counter with a clank, all the magick disappearing from the room.

Merry pressed her hands to the countertop, palms down, until her fingertips went white.

Eldora swapped out her mugs for another one.

Merry took a long drink from it, glaring for a moment at the other witch.

Leah looked at Paige and shook her head, her lips open, her blue eyes filled with concern.

Paige held out a hand to quiet her. They needed to give Merry time to speak.

She did finally. "He's alive. He's safe."

That was good. "Where?"

Merry shook her head, looking fatigued. "His location is

protected by something very powerful. You are right. He is being held."

Paige had to get him. "Where?"

Eldora thumped her lightly on the arm. "Didn't she just say she didn't know?"

Paige ignored the fact that she actually had a ping of comfort from that small action. She missed having Alma around, someone older and wiser. For that one brief moment, she forgot that Eldora Blackman was the enemy. "A general area maybe? Near? Far? Anything?"

Merry's expression sagged. "He's facing something from his past."

His past? He'd already faced the demon who'd taken his brother. There was nothing left for him to *deal* with in his past. "What past? He's dealt with his past. The demon that—"

"A past life," Merry said simply. "He needs to follow this through, and it doesn't concern us. Concentrate on the here and now."

"I don't understand."

Eldora started gathering Merry's things.

"It's connected." Merry lifted one shoulder, not looking like the powerful witch she always presented herself to be. She looked vulnerable. "It's all connected."

Paige didn't know what that meant.

With their stuff gathered, Eldora opened another door and walked through.

Merry paused and touched her chest, pointing to the amulet she'd given Paige. "Next time, use that. It can't be traced." She walked through the door and it closed behind them.

Paige stood in the silence, staring at Leah, "Did you see anything?

"I— I'm not sure. I might have seen Hattie? I don't know what that has to do with his past. Do you?"

"No." Paige whispered a swift prayer.

The goddess didn't reply. She never did.

What in the world had they gotten themselves mixed up in this time?

P aige itched to do something. Anxiety pressed at her to take her kids and go home, but would that solve things or make them worse? Her love for Dexx drove her to *find* a damned location and rescue his damned damsel ass. But doing that with the kids in tow was a bad idea wrapped in a bad idea topped with a bad idea all while *carrying* a bad idea.

What should she do? The mayor's advice came back.

She started making phone calls. She called Danny and got a few media contacts. He didn't know *everyone,* but he knew people who knew people, and he knew who she should ask for.

She told the guards they were going sightseeing. They didn't like it, but they let her go. So, over the next couple of days, she and the kids went around the town, eating at different restaurants and visiting the places on Paige's tourist list. They almost forgot about the collars.

But not about the reporters. They followed her and the kids everywhere.

She was caught on video nursing. Well, she'd already

been caught giving birth on international news, so why not? Nature mom, doing nature things.

The reporters were filled with questions. She answered as best she could and spun her answers to build up the paranormal community.

The tone of the questions changed as the days progressed. She even got the reporters to help with the kids. To be fair, they were still shifters and had a bit more energy than normal human babies.

That was something the reporters noticed almost immediately. The braver ones were a little concerned with the lightning and the fire that would dance in the babies' eyes when they were angry. So, she had to talk them through that and what to do if they were caught by a rogue spark. You know, stop, drop, roll, and say, "Bad baby!"

There was a lot of laughter through these impromptu, nearly constant interviews. Everyone wanted to know what it was like raising powered kids because raising normal kids was tough enough.

The collars didn't stop chafing as the days wore on. By the end of the third evening, all of the kids were starting to get a little bit punchy and irritable. Luckily, by this time, the newness of them had worn off so they were able to go to the family favorite hamburger place and have a great burger and endless fries, something Paige was almost certain they'd stop offering due to her and her kids. Shifters had two extra empty legs to fill.

Naomi's kids, Ginny and Todd, took an instant shining to Leah, so they were almost always around. Rai was also a fan favorite, leaving Ember to his own devices. Paige didn't understand how even babies could be separated from the herd. However, it appeared as though Rai was going to be the socializer while Ember remained on the outside. It

F.J. BLOODING

wasn't that Ember was horrible for any reason. He was probably just an introvert and it was already showing that people overwhelmed him.

Naomi and her kids walked Paige and hers up to their townhome door. "Hey, I wanted to ask— um, we could show you some places you missed. Interested?"

Leah looked about ready to refuse out of hand.

Paige took the invitation and ran with it. "Sure. We got some of the touristy places out of the way, but maybe we could go someplace full of history but doesn't cost a lot?"

Todd had a list of several places.

Paige wasn't certain that Todd's interests were necessarily the same as Leah's, but it was still nice to have Leah treated like she was a human being instead of a zoo exhibit.

The next morning, Paige got the twins ready with Leah's help before Naomi arrived.

Leah gave her mother a small glare. "I hate the reporters. This isn't anything like I thought it would be."

Same with Paige. "I think it's working, though, and if we can make it easier for the other paranormals, then I'm willing to be inconvenienced a bit longer."

Leah's expression said she didn't appreciate that statement at all. "Collared like dogs. Why do they hate us so much?"

"Fear." Paige hated to be forced to open her daughter's eyes quite like this, but she knew she had to. "People fear what they don't know."

"But they don't even want to know."

"It's easier to fear that way. But the reporters have learned a lot, and you've seen the news. You've read it. People are taking notice."

"And others are twisting it. They make fun of us. If *one more* asks which house I'm in, I'm going to call a horde of zombies. Either that or calls me a Fillory reject. I'm not in a fiction novel. This sucks."

Leah wasn't wrong. There were several news channels that were taking every little thing—like Paige breastfeeding in a restaurant to keep Rai from exploding—and making it horrible.

It didn't take Paige and Leah long to get the twins ready. Naomi had decided to take Ginny and Todd out of school for the day. That way, they wouldn't have to fight bigger crowds.

Paige was all for it. She didn't want to have to wrangle her kids and fight crowds and watch for those who were too scared to react well. That would be too much, especially since she didn't have full access to her magick.

A small voice in the back of her mind said the demons might actually be able to help against the humans.

She couldn't allow any situation to descend to that level.

She wasn't sure how much longer they would stay in Washington D.C. She'd requested another conversation with the president, hoping this one would go better, but so far, she'd been declined. These collars needed to come off and soon, but she'd stay as long as she could manage. In that time, though, she would build relations for as long as she could.

Naomi showed up right on time. Ginny and Todd burst through the door with wild excitement. They clambered around Leah and babbled about some of the things they were going to see that day. Todd assured Leah that he had planned everything so they only saw the interesting stuff and that they wouldn't waste their time on everything else.

Apparently, statues were boring because the Lincoln Memorial was nowhere on Todd's list.

Naomi gave Paige an apologetic smile. "I feel as though we're kind of taking over."

Paige chuckled but shook her head. "I feel the same way every time the Whiskey tribe goes anywhere. Imagine this at the store, but there are more kids and more adults."

She bent to retrieve Ember.

Ginny rushed in and batted her hands away. "I have Ember today." She lifted Ember and set him on her hip. Ginny seemed to take responsibility well, which was good and bad. Good for the adults in her life. Bad because when she grew up, she'd probably find people to use her to get by.

Paige chuckled. "Okay. Let me know if you need anything."

Ginny smiled and turned away, talking to Ember and tickling him.

Todd gathered Rai, all the while talking nonstop to Leah.

Naomi piled diapers on the counter. "It was a contest to babysit. Rock scissors paper. I still don't know who won."

Paige found wipes and blankets for the diaper bag. "Well, at least your kids are at the age where babies are a novelty. I'm pretty sure the Whiskey kids are totally over them by this point."

"How many do you have?" Naomi opened the door to their townhouse and waited for everyone to file out.

Paige stepped through the door and found their security detail ready for them. "Four. Bobby and Kammy are the same age, mine and Leslie's. And then the twins."

One of the security personnel placed his hand to his ear and muttered something as he led the way down the steps.

"And then you have all the kids."

"Yup."

"It must feel like a zoo sometimes."

"Sometimes?" Paige didn't want to admit the fact that having the security detail actually made her feel a little safer, even though she knew they might turn on her rather than save her. "Try most of the time."

They made it to the SUVs on the curb and got in with very little fanfare. It wasn't until they got to the Smithsonian Museum that they were assaulted by the media, many of whom Paige knew by name now.

Naomi put her hand on the door handle and paused. She turned to Paige. "Be careful what you say to the media. The president is aware of what you're doing, and she's concerned."

"Tyrants usually are when the oppressed are allowed to be heard." Paige grabbed her door handle and stepped out. She wasn't going to be silenced in a nation that prized the freedom of speech and held it prisoner in the same breath.

The kids did a really great job of handling Rai and Ember. Paige now realized that the best way to travel with children, especially the tiny kind, was to have a small army of older children. The Mormons seriously had this fact *understood*.

A couple reporters tried to get through the security guards in place. Naomi sure had *planned* this out. "Guys," Paige told the reporters, "from a distance today. Okay?"

They weren't too happy about that, but they didn't leave either.

There were strollers for the twins waiting for them at the museum door and, apparently, their tickets had already been taken care of. She felt a little like a celebrity.

The museum was also oddly quiet. "Did you clear the place?"

"No." Naomi grimaced. "But we are keeping the

number of people allowed in today to a minimum. For your safety. And for the safety of your kids."

No. That didn't work for her. "I'm not impacting people. If they want to be at the museum, they aren't *banished* just because the 'monsters' are here."

Naomi didn't move to change the situation.

Paige loved museums. Denver had the best one she had ever seen, the Museum of Nature and Science.

But this one? This one knocked the one in Denver out of the ballpark.

Paige could easily have spent the entire day there. But she didn't want to be a bother. She could see the people being cordoned off. The security personnel were doing a very good job of making sure very few civilians were anywhere near Paige and her family.

This wasn't going to work, though. This could be used to tear down the bridges she'd worked so hard to build.

Paige slipped away from Naomi and went to the nearest door. She pushed past the upset security officer to greet the first person she came into contact with. There were several plastered at the doorway, trying to get a glimpse of them on their phone.

Paige just had to hope that whoever she offered the olive branch to wasn't going to be one of the fear-filled enemies.

The man she chose seemed nice. He was tall, black, and had a great smile. He also had his young daughter with him, and they seemed to be bonding rather well.

Paige felt a kinship to him through the connection he had with his daughter. She made eye contact with him and smiled, her heart racing. There were so many ways this could go badly. "Would you like to join us? It's kind of lonely going through the museum by ourselves, and the more the merrier. The kids would love to share this experience with others."

"Ma'am," the security officer behind her said. "I can't allow that."

"Yes, you can." Paige turned and smiled harshly at him. "Last I checked, this wasn't a prison state, and my children and I weren't prisoners. Besides, I can't *smite* anyone because you've got a collar on me that protects everyone. So, what kind of harm can this nice gentleman really get into?" She beamed up at the guard. "You are not protecting me."

The security officer was unruffled and unmoved.

The man she had extended the invitation to just smiled and held his daughter a little closer. "We really can wait. We don't want to cause any trouble."

"I *do*. Because I feel as though this is one of those situations where something needs to be done." She could understand if he didn't want to be the one to cause the ripples, though. So, she turned to the woman next to him.

She was white, shorter, and heavyset. She had a look about her, as though she was searching for some way to stand out from the rest. She had obviously fake lashes and her face was painted beautifully. The woman was gorgeous.

"How about you? You like to be a rebel with me?"

The woman beamed a lit-up smile and raised both of her shoulders in a nonverbal squee of excitement. "I would love to."

Paige nodded once. She would take what she could get. "Anyone else who wants to join us certainly can. We're not contagious. We can't hurt you. And the worst thing that could happen is that one of the babies will bite you." She paused for dramatic effect. "But they don't have any teeth. So, I doubt it'll hurt."

The black man chuckled.

His daughter looked at him with a plea. "Come on, Daddy. I want to go in." She bounced on her toes.

Paige turned to the security guard and gave him a tight look. "How about we let a few people in? They paid good money for their tickets." And then Paige just went back into the exhibit room.

The first woman she had talked to went to Leah and started chatting her up. Paige was going to keep an eagle eye on her. It wasn't that she thought the woman was going to do anything crazy. But Leah was her *daughter*. She'd *invested* a lot of resources into that girl, like patience. A lot of patience.

The young father she had first approached came in and stood beside her as his daughter went to Todd and Ginny, exclaiming over the twins. "I'm sorry. About earlier."

Paige waved them off. "Don't be. It's difficult for everyone." She took in a deep breath and looked up at him. The man was very tall. "I just want to show people that we're not something to be scared of. We're the same people we were before."

"Is it true that your kind live among us?"

That sounded like a line from the X-Files. Paige tipped her head to the side and nodded. "Yeah. And look at how many of you are still alive and kicking and had no idea we were even there."

He smiled, but his brow furrowed as he shook his head and offered his hand. "Jerry. That's my daughter, Gretchen."

Paige smiled and shook his hand. "It's a pleasure to meet you."

He opened his mouth to say something but then something drew his attention away.

Paige turned to see what was going on, and her mouth nearly fell open.

Rai was buzzing with a lot of electricity, obviously done with the collar. She was pulling on her shifter abilities harder and more insistently, and her collar was zapping her.

That collar was hurting her kid.

But then Paige realized that the situation could get even worse. Because she had just invited several people into the exhibit hall with them.

If Rai didn't stop, some of that electricity could spill out onto the people nearest her.

It wasn't just about her daughter. It was about *all* of their kids.

Naomi turned to Paige in alarm. "What do we do?"

"Get that collar off my baby." That seemed pretty common sense to Paige. She rushed over to Rai's stroller, trying to figure out what to do.

"But that collar is the only thing protecting us."

How could she still think that? "That collar is hurting *my baby*."

But then, it hit Paige. It really wasn't hurting Rai. Rai was a thunderbird. She was lightning.

Paige was focused on the wrong things. Again. She was here to change opinion, so she needed to start now, to stop freaking out over her daughter, who was fine. Frustrated and upset but fine.

Naomi gave her a completely flummoxed look, taking note of the cell phones as people videoed what was going on.

Paige reached out with her alpha will to see if Rai was in trouble, but the only thing she got was that Rai was frustrated and was going to find a way to shift, one way or another.

That could be explosive. How would people see that? That *babies* were now a danger? Crap. Paige took Gretchen's shoulder and tugged her backward.

The girl looked up at Paige, her dark eyes wide.

"It's going to be okay." Rai was *just* a *baby*. "I think."

Jerry came to rescue his daughter from Paige. "Are we in danger?"

Gretchen refused to leave. "Is your baby going to be okay?"

Leave it a *kid* to realize the most important question. "I think so? I hope so." She should probably sound more confident.

Gretchen turned her attention back to Rai.

So did everyone else. People were now jockeying for a better view for their video and several of them were commentating.

What the hell had their lives become?

She had to take control of this. Paige turned toward the crowd. "Ladies and gentlemen," she called out, getting everyone's attention. "My daughter, Rai, has bonded with the thunderbird. Her spirit animal controls lightning. What you're seeing is my daughter being very frustrated with the fact that she's been a human for nearly a week."

The gathered people divided their attention between her and Rai.

"Imagine being a person just brought into this world days ago—because it really has been just days ago—and being unable to walk in human form. These two have been able to shift since almost the day they were born, and in practically any other shape, they are very mobile. But as humans, little Rai has to rely on others to get her where she wants to go. And she hates that."

That elicited a few oohs and ahs.

"What's it like having animals as children?" one man shouted.

"You could ask any pet owner that same question." Because she felt the edge of the dagger that question was meant as, and she wasn't going to take the bait. "As a parent, I can tell you I much prefer it when they do their business outside versus in the diaper."

"Outside—what?" Jerry stared at her, his expression slack. He closed his mouth and glanced at the top of Gretchen's head. "They're how old?"

"Just over two weeks now." Paige felt like a tour guide in a zoo. Not what she wanted. "Rai likes flying. So, if she manages to break out of the collar—"

A few startled screeches filled the air. But phones never wavered. The video was probably already viral.

Paige raised a hand to silence them. "Remember—she's just a *baby*. She's a little over two weeks old. The worst thing she does, really, is poop on the lamp shade and eat your favorite shoes."

A couple of people chuckled almost unwillingly.

Naomi was stuck in horrified silence.

Todd danced with excitement as he watched, his hands fisted up, a wild grin on his face. He kept glancing at Leah and back at Rai.

Leah stood there, her lips sucked in, her brow furrowed. She blinked her gaze to her mom, giving a judgy look to the crowd, and then went back to watching Rai.

Ginny kept reaching out to Rai, to hold her or comfort her or... Paige didn't know what, and then she'd take a half step back when the snap of electricity got a bit too much for her.

To her credit, though, she was gaining ground.

With one final burst and a loud pop of electricity, the

collar fell, and Rai got up, shifting into an owl in front of everyone.

Some people gasped.

A few clapped.

One whooped loudly.

The pretty woman with the amazing yet fake eyelashes —Paige needed to seriously invest in some of those because they really *were* amazing—shrieked.

Ginny leapt, her arms forward as she shielded Rai from everyone, including her mother.

Rai wasn't about that. She took to the air, made a circle, and then perched beside her brother.

Paige pushed down the fear clogging her throat. She had to make this just a normal day in the Whiskey family. "One of the things that has plagued us," Paige said, trying to keep her voice normal, "is that Rai seems to have developed the ability to shift into birds with full flight feathers. When we discovered we were having shifter babies, I had hoped their shift would be delayed or they'd shift into downy baby birds. At least they'd be easier to control until I taught them rules and, you know, other stuff. How to be people. That kind of thing."

Jerry snorted. "I hadn't even thought of that."

"Poop. On the lampshade. I'm seriously not even kidding. It's a thing, and it's gross, and she's not big enough to clean up after herself yet."

Lightning shot from Rai's beak and hit Ember's collar squarely.

Paige raised her hands to stop Rai, but it was too late.

The collar fell and then Ember was up and crawling out of his stroller as a monkey until his feet found the floor, and then he shifted into an elephant. Thank the goddess his elephant was baby-sized.

Paige released a tired sigh. This could really turn against them. "Because they're half witch and half shifter, they can choose any shape they want." How much information was too much? Well, she wanted to inform the public, so... "While Rai likes to fly, Ember likes walking on four feet. And lately, that's been as an elephant. Though, they haven't been able to shift for almost a week, so you guys are probably in for a treat. They'll probably cycle through several animals in a few minutes."

"Like," one woman asked, her voice breathy, "is this normal?"

Nope. "Yup."

Rai chose that moment to find the floor and shift into a tiger cub.

Paige narrowed her eyes at her daughter and asked her to choose creatures that weren't so terrifying.

Rai looked up at her and then shifted into a kitten. Just a regular kitten.

The people clapped and exclaimed.

Gretchen looked up at Paige. "Are they dangerous?"

Paige wasn't going to say they weren't. "They're about as dangerous as any babies. If they choose to become a bear, just remember they have teeth."

The mood of the crowd around them was starting to shift, to relax, which was good.

"How about we make this a game? Let's take bets on what they're going to shift into next."

That seemed to loosen people up considerably. A few shouted what they'd like to see.

The woman with the amazing lashes took a step forward. "Are you able to communicate with them?"

"I used to. In a primitive way." Paige tapped the collar around her neck. Yes. She was lying. She was going to use any opportunity she could to spin this. "But with this blocking my abilities, I can't. They don't understand English. They're *literally* two weeks old."

That brought another round of exclamations as people closed in to get closer to her children.

Security personnel burst through and tried to keep people away.

As much as Paige appreciated that, it was the wrong move. She put her hand on one of their shoulders and nonverbally told him to back off, inserting a bit of her alpha will to ensure her order was followed.

The security guard backed away but stayed close. He, however, was visibly pissed. Keeping them safe was his *fucking job,* and his face told her that. Loudly. In a look.

Right. Yup. Okay. "Just remember they *are* babies. They don't know the rules. They might piddle on your foot. And if they choose a shape that has teeth, they *will* gnaw on you. Ember really likes your favorite shoes, so I hope you didn't wear those today."

Dexx was going to be so mad when he saw these videos.

She hoped he was okay.

One of the people on the other side of the room looked at Leah. "What can she do?"

Leah didn't look like she wanted to answer any questions. She hid behind Todd and Ginny, who were doing a fantastic job of keeping people away from her.

Kids really could be good.

Paige turned to the man in question. "She is a necromancer. She can communicate with and revive the dead."

A few people pulled away.

But a few people just looked at Leah like she was that much more interesting.

How to make that seem less terrifying? "Imagine being

eleven and freaking out because you're being attacked by angels and all of a sudden conjuring ghosts."

"You were attacked by angels?" the young woman to Paige's left asked.

All Paige had to do was say the wrong thing once. In *her* life, angels were assholes. In the Christian world, they were subjects of worship. "It's not nearly as amazing as it sounds. Angels are just another kind of butthead."

"So, they're real too?" the young woman asked.

"What did you do wrong?" another man shouted out.

Why did it always go that way? "In the Bible—the *actual* Bible—angels were put on this earth as warriors. They're not guardians. They're not nice. Well, most of them. They're soldiers and people aren't."

"And?" the man baited.

Right. Well, that one wasn't going away. "And I'm a demon..." Uh. "...exorcist and they wanted my full and undivided loyalty." Kind of.

"You were thinking of not helping? You some sort of demon *familiar* or something?"

Oh, funny man. "No. I'm a mom and wanted to spend some time *being* a mom." She turned to the crowd. "Because, apparently, I can't even have a couple of days with my *babies* whom I birthed on the street in the middle of saving the world from a *powerful* demon *two weeks ago*." She smiled to soften that blow, but she was really very angry over this little fact.

The man opened his mouth to say something else, his face filled with hate.

The woman beside him took his arm, blinking as the reality of Paige's statement hit her in a familiar place. It was evident from the light in her eyes.

Paige took in a deep breath, realizing she needed to

invest more on *this* and *less* on making people angry. She needed to make people like this man understand they were just people. She wouldn't do that by sparring with him. "We came here to see the museum. Mind if we walk and talk?" She didn't wait for an answer and started on her way.

Leah and Ginny scooped the kids up and went toward the next exhibit.

Paige strolled along through the exhibits, explaining a few things about her family and paranormal people in general.

She exclaimed over certain exhibits—especially the dinosaurs. She *loved* dinosaurs—and listened as a few offered their own stories. It was a fantastic bonding moment. But Paige wasn't certain if it was going to be enough.

One thing was for certain. Everyone loved playing with her babies. Two legs, four legs, or wings.

The currency for the "next shift" wagers was anywhere from a stick of gum to a quarter. One person wagered an eraser that everyone seemed to be vying for. She doubted it was the eraser, though it *was* a poop emoji. It was the act of wagering *for* an eraser that made them feel less like monsters...

...and more like people.

Before they reached the aeronautical exhibit, security personnel informed Paige that the president had requested her presence and they would have to leave the museum.

Her heart raced with her nervousness. This was the audience she'd asked for, and she'd managed to make that happen.

Naomi's phone rang before they reached the motorcade.

Paige continued to keep up appearances and talk to as

many people as she could, answering questions as they went.

Hopefully, the videos had hit the web and created a weapon she could use.

As they exited the doors, Paige sent a command to her twins, telling them to shift back into human and allow Todd and Ginny to collect them.

Leah had even seemed to make a few new friends, including Gretchen.

Jerry shook her hand as the kids piled into the SUV. "I'm really glad I got to meet you. I have to admit I was more than a little scared."

At least he was being decent. "So are we."

His dark eyes met hers with an acknowledgement of the fear of fear.

She was glad she was able to relate more to people. She just wished she didn't have a dire reason for it. "Paranormals are just like any other people. Some are great. Some are not. And most are somewhere in between."

He gathered his daughter. "Maybe we'll meet again."

"Maybe." Probably not but talking to him had been one of the upbeats of the museum experience.

Leah, Todd, and Ginny were a bubble of excitement on the way to the White House. Todd and Ginny couldn't stop talking about how that was the best experience at the museum *ever*. Todd even bemoaned that Leah had now ruined the museum for him. He was joking. Kind of.

When they got to the White House, Naomi told Paige she would watch the kids and not to worry because she would protect them as if they were her own.

As if she could. But Paige knew Naomi was under orders, and she couldn't disobey them.

Paige walked through the media circus with her security detail keeping most of the reporters back. This time, she was guided directly to the Oval Office.

The president stood and walked over to the two couches, offering her hand. "Please have a seat." She gestured toward the striped couch.

Paige sat after shaking hands, feeling just how different it was to be in this room the second time around.

"I have to say, Ms. Whiskey, you played that very well."

Paige wanted to take that as a compliment, but it felt like the threat level had just gone up a notch.

The president picked up the remote and turned on the TV. The volume was muted but Paige and her kids were all over the screen. As she watched, Ember shifted from a kitten into a floppy eared puppy. Several of the kids around them clapped. Shortly afterward, Rai turned into an eagle chick.

She heard herself repeat, "Remember, they're babies and that one has teeth." She didn't remember how many times she'd repeated that.

The president set the remote down and gave Paige her full attention. "You did much better than I would have thought. But I'm afraid you have lured the people into a false sense of security."

Paige refrained from rolling her eyes. "Is that so?" What was her agenda?

"Indeed." The president leaned forward and folded her hands primly in her lap. "Let me be perfectly clear here, Ms. Whiskey."

It was about time. She leaned forward and folded her hands in her lap, mimicking the president's stance.

"The paranormals in our community *are* dangerous. I happen to know how many paranormal attacks there are each year because I have been forced to clean up your mess before."

"And are you going to be sharing these numbers with the public? Are you going to reveal to the world that you've known about us all this time? And..." Because she wasn't done. "...are you going to share how many non-paranormal attacks there are each year? Because there are still fewer paranormal attacks than there is gun violence."

The president didn't immediately respond.

The president could still save face.

Paige went forward to nip it in the bud. "What you don't realize is how the paranormal community works together to ensure that there are very few of those occurrences. We work just as hard, if not harder, to protect your mundane citizens as you do. The only difference is we're not trying to get media coverage or poll numbers for it. *We're* not trying to win future elections off this platform. We're just trying to make sure our friends and neighbors are safe and taken care of. Why? Not because they're voters. Not because we can make money off them. But because they are our *friends* and *neighbors*."

The president's eyes cooled. "Here's what I want you to do, Ms. Whiskey."

Paige licked her lips and remained quiet, listening.

"You are going to take yourself and your children out of my city. And when you get home, you were going to take those wards down. You are going to allow my agents *full* access to your town."

Not likely. "And if I don't?"

"Then I will see that as an act of war."

A chill ran down Paige's neck. "And what are your people going to do once I take those wards down? Are they going to come back into my town with guns blazing? Are they going to endanger the lives of my children and the children of my friends and family?"

The president raised one regal eyebrow. "Do I need to?"

Paige leaned forward and released her alpha will just a little. It was time for the president to understand who she was dealing with. "If you do, be assured *I* will see that as an act of war."

The president stared at her in surprise, though her mask was firmly in place and the surprise only showed at the corners of her eyes and mouth.

Paige got the distinct impression that very few people had the balls to stand up to her quite like this. "Try to remember that my people have infiltrated your entire nation. You may know who some of us are, but you don't know all of us. It isn't like we're an invading nation. We're already here. This is our country just as much it is yours." Paige stood. This wasn't how she'd planned this meeting to go.

The president stood as well.

"I had really hoped that we could leave on a more peaceful front. My kind doesn't want to wage war on yours. We don't want to send our great nation into civil war. We don't want to pit friend against friend, neighbor against neighbor. But if that is what you want because you would rather live in fear—ignorant fear—then we shall answer in kind."

The president didn't react. Not so much as a twitch.

Paige offered her hand. "But if you wish to learn about us so we can figure out a way to live together in peace, then my door is always open."

One eyelid twitched.

"You make your decision. I will follow your lead, Madame President."

The president didn't respond for a long moment. Then, she took one step forward and clasped Paige's hand. "You're not how I imagined you to be."

Paige didn't know how to take that. "Neither are you."

But it was past time for Paige to get out of D.C. She was going to get on that plane.

And this collar was coming off.

She turned and headed for the door. "I look forward to more conversations." She stopped at the door. "And next time? Perhaps we could start by not insulting each other with collars. Let's show the world that we can play as adults instead of as kindergartners."

Paige didn't wait for the president to respond. She opened the door and left.

Paige checked her phone as soon as she could and saw she had a new message and four missed calls from Michelle.

The text message was very brief.

DoDO has Dexx. He's working for them. He just took Rainbow.

What in the hell was going on?

13

Paige used the plane's internet to get to the bottom of what was going on with Dexx and DoDO on the flight back, but she didn't learn much at all.

Until they made an unplanned stop in Kansas. "What's going on?" she asked one of the attendants.

"Everything is fine." The flight attendant smiled as she checked on Rai and Ember. "There's nothing to worry over. Just an unplanned stop."

Said every serial killer everywhere.

Well, no. Maybe not, but the statement didn't give her the warm fuzzies.

The twins ran around in bear form. Paige had absolutely forbidden Rai to fly... anywhere. She still had no idea how bad that stunt would affect everything she'd worked so hard to build. She had a magickal fight on the White House lawn. Frankly, Paige was surprised she'd been allowed to leave at all after she'd had a chance to think about it. And crap her pants a little.

This shit was real. Really fucking real. The realest

fucking crap she'd been in since her powers had been forced awake in St. Francisville.

She was scared.

When she got out, she was greeted by a single black SUV and a familiar face—FBI Director Stef Lovejoy. She was a fire fox spirit—uh... something. Honestly? Paige had no real idea *what* Lovejoy was. She wasn't *quite* a shifter and she embodied a fiery looking fox. Anything more than that and Paige was clueless.

But she was also a trusted and valued ally who kept her paranormal presence a secret at all costs.

"Where are those adorable babies?" Lovejoy demanded.

"On the plane. Am I in trouble?"

Lovejoy shook her head and headed to the plane with a tired smile. "Nice wheels."

"Perks of making friends with Merry Eastwood."

Lovejoy winced, pulling a subtle face that said she didn't agree with releasing that murderer on the streets, even if it did mean they'd defeated Sven. Fact of the matter was that Sven was taken care of and Merry was still walking the streets.

But without Merry Serial-Killer Eastwood, Paige would be stuck in Troutdale without a voice and the people wouldn't have had a chance to interact with her shifter children.

That might be the reason Paige wasn't in a hurry to put the woman back behind bars.

And the tick around Lovejoy's eyes said she recognized why as well.

"Let's get inside. My ears are ringing." It was loud, even without any planes immediately around them with their engines going. As soon as the door was closed, though,

Lovejoy sat down and cooed at the babies, who chose to shift into fox kits.

Those two. Seriously.

Lovejoy sighed as Rai chewed on her fingers. "How are you going to handle DoDO when you get back? Are you dropping the wards?"

Paige sat in her seat and gave Leah a look that said she could listen and form opinions, but she couldn't speak. She had no voice in this discussion.

Leah nodded, her lips clamped shut.

Lovejoy smiled at the girl.

One day, if they survived this, Paige hoped Leah would be a force for good in their world. Not just their home or their town. "The wards are already down."

Alarm crashed over Lovejoy's expression. "Do they know that?"

Maybe. "It's possible. Dexx was *taken*. I know I don't have evidence to back that, but he wouldn't leave."

The FBI director shook her head with a frown, inviting details.

"I set up the wards so that all violence will be met with... well, an open door to, I think, North Korea."

"You're inviting a war with North Korea?"

She hadn't thought of that. "Well, if the president is busy fighting them, it might be harder to fight her own people."

"Hmm." Lovejoy's expression said that wasn't a terrible idea. "Pick another location."

Paige added that to the rather long list of things she needed to handle.

"How was Dexx taken, then?" Lovejoy picked Ember up and cuddled his fox face to hers. As soon as her nose touched his, fire lit his tail.

"No fire inside this plane," Paige barked.

Lovejoy raised a blonde eyebrow at him with a grin.

The fire went out, but he remained a fox.

"I don't know." Paige chewed on her lips, just now working out the details and how preposterous it all seemed. "If they'd come by force, then the wards would have shipped them all out. But if they came in and invited him to leave?"

"Invited by..." Lovejoy looked up at her with a look of confusion. "Drugs?"

"How many things on this world can change a person's mind?" There were a lot. Demons, djinn, angels, empaths. And that was the short list. Some of those things didn't apply to Dexx, though. Demons couldn't possess him, and angels set him off for the most part

Lovejoy tipped her head to the side and booped noses with Rai. "I'll look into it. You've got your hands full, and we need you focused on this." She waved one hand to encompass her new situation. "I'll handle Dexx."

That made Paige feel a little better. "Michelle is working the case, too."

"I'll coordinate."

"Thank you." But that wasn't the reason the director of the Oregon branch of the FBI was meeting her in Kansas. "Why are we really here?"

Lovejoy set Rai and Ember both on the floor and gave Paige her full but not undivided attention. "The world is following you. Whatever you do will set the precedent for everyone else."

Nothing like a little pressure. "What's going on every-where else? We've heard nothing."

"They're repressing the news." Lovejoy growled at Rai who must have nipped a little too hard.

Rai yipped and came back in for another leaping attack that wasn't quite as vicious.

"They're taking people," Lovejoy said, battling Rai with one hand. "We don't know where. But our people are disappearing. Mostly civilians right now but no communities."

A lava flow of emotions swept down Paige's spine. It *was* as she'd feared. "You think DoDO doesn't know about them?"

Lovejoy shook her head and pushed Rai to the ground again.

Rai bounded back up like she had a spring in her tail. Almost. It was a spring made of legs.

"DoDO has been studying us for a while," Lovejoy continued. "The information you provided from Alaska was invaluable and sent us on a whole new search. From what we've been able to gather, their database on us is extensive."

So much so that they'd managed to capture Dexx. She needed to talk to him, to see what was going on, to make sure he was okay.

And to see if he could gain some inside information. "When you locate Dexx, see if you can get him a message."

Lovejoy met her gaze with an expression that said she was thinking along the same lines and got up. "I just wanted to caution you on how things are handled in Troutdale. The world is watching, and if you give in, paranormals across the nation will be put in a worse situation."

"Give me information on the areas that are being targeted. The Blackmans and I will coordinate efforts to retrieve them."

Lovejoy narrowed her eyes in question.

"Door magick."

The director shook her head, still not fully caught up.

"We can go pretty much anywhere."

Lovejoy paused and turned toward Paige, fully facing her. "Do you think..." She tipped her head to the side, her gaze unfocused. A light dawned as she straightened. "That's how they're doing it."

"Doing what?" Paige had no idea what was going on behind the director's skull.

"DoDO has doors, too."

Huh?

"It makes total sense now. We've had reports of their agents being in one location and then appearing on the other side of the world within an hour. And it would make sense as to how they were able to slip through your wards undetected."

Well, that and the fact that DoDO *had* to have heard how to maneuver around the wards somehow. A person? A spell? A device? They'd known how to retrieve Dexx without tripping the failsafe.

Shit. She needed to figure out a way to get these wards —plus a few failsafes of their own—up around the other paranormal communities. Like Nederland. Shit.

She needed to call Billie Black again. She needed a small army of wood witches in order to pull this off.

Lovejoy handed Paige a flip phone—probably a burner —and headed toward the door again. "I'll send word."

"I'll keep you in my loop."

The flight to Troutdale was then filled with a whole other kind of worry. The world was watching her. If she fucked up, she could make things worse for paranormals everywhere.

But Lovejoy hadn't mention that the stunt at the White House had made things worse, so maybe... maybe it hadn't.

Yet. All she needed was to give people time to spin it, and they would.

Paige landed at the airport, prepared to use another door to get home, but was met yet again by another motorcade. This time, it was DoDO. Mario greeted her with a smile and offered to help her get the kids into the SUV.

"I was really okay with Leslie coming to pick us up." Paige wanted to go for the man's throat. He had Dexx and he knew it, and she had to dance around him?

"Orders from the president," he said in his slight English accent. "She wanted to make sure you got home."

"Are we actually going home? Or are you shipping us off to some hidden cell?" Like Dexx? And should she tip her hand to the knowledge that they had him or keep that to herself? Could she get information from Mario?

Probably not.

So, she'd keep that knowledge to herself. For the moment.

Mario gave her a tight smile and opened the back door. "I assure you we're only going home."

Had he offered the same assurance to Dexx? She got the kids buckled in with Leah's help—who didn't like this situation—and got in the front seat.

Mario pulled away from the airport and got them into Portland traffic.

Leah and Ember were asleep within moments, before they'd even hit the highway. But little Rai was bright-eyed and bushytailed. That girl hadn't fallen asleep the entire way here.

"Your flight was delayed."

That was an obvious question. Fine. She'd answer. "Mechanical issues? I don't know. We weren't down long."

"Well, I'm glad you made it back safely." Mario looked over at her and gave her a genuine smile. "I almost wanted to see the look on the president's face as she was watching the news, though. You're still trending."

Okay. Now Paige was just confused. "You don't like the president?"

"She's a rather simpleminded woman. She lumps people into few buckets."

"And you are simply not to be lumped in with the lot of us," Paige said in her best English accent interpretation.

He chuckled. "To be blunt, no. We're in a *special* bucket."

Since she had him trapped in the same car as her, she wanted information. "So, do you feel you're so much better than the rest of us? You *royal* witch blood or something?"

Mario frowned at her, taken a bit by surprise. "You really don't know?"

Paige really didn't want to admit that out loud. But she would. If there was one thing that could be said about Paige Whiskey, it was that she didn't have an overinflated ego. "No, I don't. Enlighten me."

Mario blinked and merged onto the highway that would take them east and home. "Well, suffice it to say that there are various types of magick users and they're not all witches. Honestly, witches are probably the least powerful of all."

Paige had a really hard time believing that just looking at her family. "Well, you and your people weren't a big help against Sven."

"Indeed." He grimaced and tapped his thumbs against the steering wheel. "You, though. *You* are an exception, to be sure. That causes some I know considerable stress."

That was neat and it actually made her feel a little bit better about herself, but it wasn't answering her questions. "So, what are you? You disdain witches. So, I'm guessing you're not?"

"No. I am not."

Silence filled the car as he refused to continue.

Paige wasn't going to let that happen, though. She had him. She pushed a little with her alpha will. "What are you?"

He smiled and flicked his eyebrows at her. But then he did something that surprised her.

He pushed back.

Okay. So, did that mean that he had an alpha spirit too? Was he a shifter witch? If so, then why hadn't he shifted to fight her and Leslie back in Alaska? Why did he allow them to win?

He let her think about that for quite some time but then he finally answered, "Mage."

Paige had heard the term many times. In fiction. She just didn't know what it meant. "So, what is it that you do?"

He lifted one shoulder in a shrug. "You know of ley lines?"

Of course she did. Every witch did. Some felt the rivers of magic, some resonated with them, but none of them really connected with them. "Sure."

"Well, we use them. We tap into the network, and that's the energy we use in our spells."

That would explain why their magick was different and sometimes more powerful in limited ways.

The exits leading into town were blocked. He drove past the roadblocks, waving to the highway patrols.

It was time to bait him. "The wards have been released to allow you and your people in." But she was going to figure out a way to disrupt their surveillance. Somehow.

"I heard."

"So, that means the blockade can come down."

"No. We need *full*, unfettered access."

She smiled at his acknowledgement that he *knew* of the traps. "Paint a picture for me. What's it going to look like if I do? What's your plan? Collar us? Collect us? Take us to restricted locations that aren't even on the map?"

He pulled to the side of the road and put the SUV in park. He took off his seatbelt so he could twist around to face her. "We are going to register every single paranormal in that town. Man, woman, child. No matter how young. We are going to document what each person is capable of doing. And then you are going to be chipped."

Oh, hell no. "Are you chipped?"

"Of course not. The nature of our magic would simply fry the device. If you will notice, there's nothing electronic inside this car. The reason for that is because we simply ruin all things electrical."

Oh, how very Harry Dresden of him.

"Also, most of us aren't citizens of the United States of America, and therefore, we do not have to abide by its most stringent laws."

"Except this isn't a law."

Leslie's car pulled up on the other side of road. She put the car in park and got out.

Someone must have told her they were on the way.

"Not yet. But soon." He gave her a smug look. "Very soon."

She wanted to wipe it off his face with the pavement. "And then? Are you going to enforce this around the world?"

He chuckled. "There are very few places like the United States. So very few people who are contagiously fearful the way you lot are. So, no. It is highly unlikely anyone else will follow in your lead. Well, a few places, I'm sure. But not the first world countries."

Which meant that if she could find someone in some other country, someone with political pull, she might be able to... she didn't even know what. But maybe she could get some help or some guidance or some political pull or push or the political fist. Anything. Something. "It's a good thing you've got doors."

He went still and glanced at her. "What do you mean?"

She smiled at him, not really interested in playing cat and mouse. "I know you have Dexx, and I know you used a door to breach the wards."

He narrowed his bright blue eyes. "I had wondered how long this would take. Can I expect retaliation, then?"

Paige chuckled. "You'd be silly not to."

"Oh, Ms. Whiskey," Mario said, turning his gaze to the ceiling. "This won't en—"

"But not from me."

He stopped, listening.

"I don't know what you've done to Dexx—" But she really wanted to punch him in his smug-ass fucking face for it. The fear and worry pounded at her chest, willing her to *do* something. Anything. "—but he's going to tear you up from the inside. And I'm—well, frankly, I'm just really pleased you took him and brought him in." Anger raged inside her, and she fought to keep it in check. "Because now my man's inside." Her lips turned up at one corner. "By invitation."

Mario made an uncomfortable sound while smiling. "He will never break through."

Paige chuckled, keeping it calm and cold. Oh, he'd break through. And if he didn't, then, yes, Mario could expect *retaliation* from her. "Okey-dokey."

Mario got out and opened the passenger door, pulling

Ember out of his car seat. He tucked the baby close to his chest.

Paige collected Rai, watching him, confused. This man gave her so many different mixed signals. It was kind of infuriating a little bit.

Leslie walked up to them and took Rai from her. "You good?"

Paige nodded and shook Leah awake. She came to, but her eyes were droopy, and her personality wasn't fully charged.

Paige then went to the back and grabbed all of their bags, allowing Leah to just stumble her way to the other car like a zombie.

Leslie put Rai in the car seat, but before Rai could get buckled in, she shifted into a bird and flew to the top of the car.

Paige got a sense that she was antsy and needed to burn off excess energy. Paige could understand that. "Rai and I will fly home."

Leslie nodded, her eyes only on Mario, who had safely installed Ember in his car seat.

Paige put the bags in the trunk and then closed it. "See you at home?"

Leslie nodded and then disappeared into the car.

Paige stared at Mario for a long moment. She wanted to punch him, to demand he release Dexx, release the town, and pull his head out of his ass.

But she knew that she and her children and the people of this town weren't going to be chipped. If she allowed that...

Then what would she be inviting to the rest of the nation?

Without another thought, she shifted into an owl and took off.

Rai took to the air as Leslie pulled back into the street. Rai wasn't nearly as fast. She was a baby bird. But she was doing pretty well for being a little over two weeks old.

As they got further away from Mario, Paige's nerves unknotted a little. She hated so much about Mario and everything he stood for. She wanted to take him down and kick him out of her country.

As she expected, Rai tired about halfway. She did pretty well and better than expected, really. They landed and then Paige shifted into a gorilla. Rai followed suit and climbed up on her back, holding tight to Paige's long fur as they traveled along the roads and through the wooded areas and farmland.

This was what Paige needed—to be home with her kids, to show them the world was safe.

And it was, for that small moment.

However, when she and Rai got home, Paige's phone buzzed almost as soon as she'd shifted. Michelle had texted her a message.

Dexx took Tarik and Frey.

The moment was gone.

14

Paige was, to put it lightly, done.

But she was in a bit of a tough place. From what she'd gathered from Mario, Dexx *hadn't* broken free of whatever they'd done to him. Also, with the fact that Dexx'd just taken three of his team members...

Was this Dexx trying to get his team back? Or was DoDO seriously in control? Mario had seemed a little too confident for it to be anything other than a DoDO plan. She needed to get her partner back.

It wasn't like she could just walk into a DoDO facility and demand her not-quite-husband, though. Mostly because she had no idea where they were headquartered.

No. Damn it. He was her partner for a reason. He was her equal in so many ways. She had to bet on the fact that Dexx could figure this out.

But she really needed him, needed his arms and the hard time he always gave her and... she needed him to do the damned laundry even if he couldn't match socks right.

She sat on the edge of the bed with a matched set of socks in her hand and cried, hating the fact that both socks were white and frustrated that her man wasn't there for her to be mad at his face for it.

Was he still angry with her?

What if he'd gone willingly because he felt like his voice wasn't being heard? He was a strong man who *refused* to bend to the wills of women, to the extent that he sincerely thought she'd be changing her last name to Colt once they were married. He wouldn't even *think* about changing his last name or of her keeping her own.

What if she'd missed something? What if she'd been so busy being her that she'd overlooked the fact that he was unhappy, that he needed to be more of a *man* in a house of women? Had she overrun him?

On this one matter, sure. Yes. She'd known that. She'd known it as she was doing it and he'd told her no and she hadn't listened and she'd taken the kids—his kids, including Leah—and—

She curled in a ball, hugging his pillow tight to her, and wept into it.

Eventually, though, she had to drag her tired ass out of bed. She didn't have time to be upset about her mate when there were hundreds of thousands of other people out there looking to her to fix something else.

She needed to test the wards, to see if they truly did work. If they didn't, she and Merry and Eldora needed to fix them. So, over the next day, she set everyone to attack the wards or to do bad things in town. Eldora moved the door's exit location to a holding area in Utah and had a Blackman witch on the other side so that, when the wards kicked their people through the door, they could be retrieved easily.

The wards worked pretty well. At first, they didn't quite know how to understand what was a threat unless the wards themselves were being attacked. But as they were introduced to more and more scenarios, they became quite adept.

It was a little like teaching an AI, she thought.

During that time, Paige got together with Willow and a few of the other witches—not Leslie who was *busy,* thank you—to add everyone to the tree who wished it.

The wards were strong and ready to be distributed to other communities.

She also needed to figure out how to get rid of the surveillance devices or whatever was installed around the town.

So, she put Michelle and Ethel—the only two remaining members of the Red Star team—on lockdown and then deployed her rather large team of local witches to locating all the surveillance apparatuses around the town while she was testing and working on the wards.

She hadn't even *realized* just how *powerful* an asset that really was—an army of witches. She'd spent the past two years virtually ignoring them, only working with her own family—who wasn't even a coven. Not really. They were a group of solitary witches. Kinda. They didn't perform magick together very often. She sometimes forgot how powerful coven witches were.

In her defense, the Whiskeys *did* have other things to deal with.

Also, she had access to the greatest library anywhere. She couldn't even say it was anywhere in this world because it was in the spirit animal dimension.

Together with the librarian and the witches, she figured they'd located most—if not all—the devices around the town.

And there were a lot.

They were a mix of electrical devices and magical ones.

After what she discovered about the mages, she was a little surprised.

Merry reminded her that she shouldn't be. It was the best way to evade detection. So, they did one more sweep and discovered a completely different set of devices that had been installed around the town. This set was old school, almost mechanical in nature, with touches of magick applied to them.

After the second set of surveillance devices was rounded up, Paige contacted Danny Miller. She needed to know if there was a way to shield their recording devices against electrical surges.

She had an idea to invite the media in and didn't want Mario to short circuit the equipment—she was a huge fan of Harry Dresden books and fully understood the whole electricity versus electronics thing—thereby cutting them off. She worked to ensure that what was about to happen would actually get out to the people.

Paige called for a press conference through Danny's contacts. It was time to get in front of the media again. She'd talked to everyone on the paranormal committee who was still in the area.

The elves had left, as had two of the elementals. The rest had agreed it was time for the news to get an in-depth view of what they were doing in Troutdale. She'd set up for outside news crews to be there for a week if anyone wanted to take them up on the offer.

A few had returned a hearty yes, and then had called to let her know they'd been denied access.

So, she told them to report that to the world.

The mayor took matters into her own hands. She and several other people in the community decided to take a different stand. They were shooting videos of just about everything. They still had access to social media, so they were going to use it. They shared their stories with friends, and through them, the world.

There were stories from the schools and the social dinners and the distributing of their supplies.

The mayor had even hired her own videographer. It was her son. She hired her son. But he and his team followed Paige through just about everything for the next two days. Not the secret meetings. But through most of her days.

Including home life.

It felt invasive. She didn't appreciate it, but she had to get the story out.

Lovejoy contacted her on the burner phone and told her to keep doing what she was doing. It was helping, and the number of people being abducted had significantly reduced.

That was all good. Very good.

But this wasn't a solution.

Paige called Mario and personally invited him to Trout-dale and asked him to bring the media.

"I don't think that's a good idea, Ms. Whiskey."

"Why?" Paige was feeling good about herself. She'd *seen* the media coverage. They were trending and doing it while sending out a positive message. *We can work together.* "Because the president is running scared?"

"You baited her, and you continue to do so every time you mention the media."

"Being able to come in and cover this news story that will affect people all over the nation? You're right. That's very irresponsible of me. I should remember that, when tyrants want me to be silent, I should surrender my voice and do as I'm told."

He didn't respond.

"Bring the news." She disconnected.

It was time to show the people who they were fighting and give the power back to the paranormals.

Leah had to get back to school. She couldn't stay out any longer, even though Paige really could have used the help. Her education was more important. Paige kept the twins close. They were growing so fast. And, frankly, so was Bobby. That worried her. She appreciated the fact that they were getting easier to manage, but were they growing too fast?

She still didn't want to bring Bobby out into the spotlight. He was a prophet and was wanted by Heaven and Hell. So, she wasn't going to put a neon sign over his head and invite *that* trouble. They already had enough.

Leslie was no help on the twin front. She had her hands full with a mystery of new people showing up. It was— Paige really didn't know what was going on, only that she didn't want to get involved and Leslie didn't want her help. Great. Excellent. Moving on.

The upcoming news conference was giving her hives. Literally. It'd been a great idea two days prior, but now, with everyone gathering on Main Street and the big moment nearly around the corner, she realized she'd needed more practice. She couldn't mess this up. How many people were there? Why would the town show up for this?

Then she realized this wasn't the town. DoDO had done more than just let the media in. They'd let *everyone* in.

What were they planning?

The anxiety she *had been* feeling turned to panic.

Chuck took her by the arms as she headed toward the museum at the end of the street and exerted his alpha will on her, his blue eyes framed by black lashes. "Calm down."

"I am calm." She wasn't even a *little* calm. She felt like a kindergartner on the backlines of a major war, proclaiming to be a general.

He tipped his head to the side and gave her a frank look. "You are not. And why isn't your pack helping you with the twins?"

Because she kept forgetting about them? Also, the last time Margo'd been set to watch the twins, they escaped her to find Paige anyway. "They're busy. We've got security issues, and I'm not saddling any of them with babysitting duty."

He sighed, giving her a look that said he knew the real reason.

That man always did, which was probably why he was the *regional* high alpha.

"Fine. I'll ask."

He nodded and stepped away. "Do you know what you're going to say?"

Yeah. She'd written and rewritten her speech a few dozen times and had practiced it in every mirror she could find. She turned to the crowd milling in the street and released a long breath she'd puffed into her right cheek. Her speech now had absolutely nothing to do with how it'd started. Was it right? Should she have stayed with the original? What had that even been in the first place? "Yeah."

Chuck licked his lips, looked down, and then grabbed her arm, bringing her back around to face him.

She really just needed someone bigger and smarter and wiser than her to tell her she could do this.

He looked her in the eye. "There is a reason," he said, his slight accent softening his words, "we put you in this position."

"Because I'm the only one without a job?"

He gave her a look that told her to shut up.

Right.

"You're the most powerful witch in this region."

Being powerful didn't mean she was the right person for the job.

"You are also most capable of handling trying situations."

Cawli growled low in the back of Paige's head in appreciation.

"We haven't had a person like you in our worlds in a very long time, and you are the only one who can bridge our gap right now."

She realized he wasn't just talking about the gap between witches and shifters, which was wide. Or the gap between the other paranormals and witches and shifters.

No. It was the chasm between paranormals and humans. She'd invested a large portion of her career—nearly twenty years, which made her feel *old*—working with and protecting humans *from* paranormals. Too few could say that.

He nodded slowly, sucking in his bottom lip as he saw that understanding somewhere in her expression. At least, that's what she assumed.

Right. Right.

She turned to the podium on the flatbed trailer.

Right.

Wiping her sweaty palms on her jeans, she stepped up to the podium and raised her hands for the crowd to quiet.

Which version of this speech was she going with? The anxiety flooding her wiped out her memory. Almost.

Thank the goddess she'd practiced it *so* many times.

"Ladies and gentlemen, media, and all outlets of the world." She worked her feet, getting her "speech legs" under her. She felt like she was on a boat and the water was choppy. She wasn't going to focus on the fact that all these people were looking up to her, relying on her, waiting for her to mess up.

She focused on all these people who were searching for answers.

"We've had some pretty interesting days, haven't we?" She knew they wouldn't answer her, but they did respond. Some nodded. Others looked at each other.

She'd learned a lot over the course of the last week. It wasn't just about getting the message out there. She had to engage.

But this wasn't like being in D.C., where she actually got to talk to people. This was an actual speech.

"Many of you have come to Troutdale for your own reasons." She had no idea what any of those even were. "But you need to understand one thing. Being here has put you in danger."

A few people muttered around the crowd.

"What you don't know is that the Department of Delicate Operations, DoDO for short, let you in. For a reason. But what is that reason? They also allowed in the media. For a reason. But for *what* reason?" She had a guess. "I believe they plan on attacking us. Or inviting an attack."

A few people raised their voices in alarm.

She raised her hands for silence. She didn't get complete silence, but with the help of the microphone, she was confident she could be heard. "What you need to also understand is that Troutdale has been the center of several attacks, DoDO being one of them. So, we have protections in place. Protections that can be used and installed just about everywhere. And I'd like to walk you through them now."

She invested the next few minutes into showing the

people where the wards were. She set them off so they could see. Before this example could be made, Paige had ensured Eldora set the doors for somewhere *other* than North Korea and that a Blackwood witch was there to retrieve them.

She then had Margo attack her on stage in front of everyone. A rip appeared in the air, and Margo disappeared.

"They're being sent to a detention facility in Utah." After Margo went through, Phoebe, the Blackwood witch sent to bring Margo back, would leave that location and return home. "So, if there is an uprising or if we *are* attacked within the protections of our wards, then DoDO, or whoever the aggressor is, will be sent to jail. Of course, the president will bail them out, but that isn't the point. The point is that we're safe. Here."

Kinda.

"But the president wants us in cages. It will start with a forced registration. I've been informed that we'll then be chipped, and the more dangerous ones will be forced to wear collars. And I'm sure that makes many of you feel safer. But there are creatures in this world who are not answerable to the president; demons and angels and demigods. Yes, demigods. Thor is real."

That elicited quite a few chuckles.

She'd had to check the library records on that one. He *was* real. He just wasn't really on this planet.

She gripped the podium and whispered, "Bal, I need you."

A cloud of black smoke appeared beside her, and Balnore stepped out with Bastet by his side in her full regalia.

Paige sent him a thank you with her eyes, hoping he caught it.

He nodded a greeting to her but kept familiarity out of his expression.

"Try collaring the gods. See how that works for the president. She—"

An explosion interrupted her.

Mario looked at her with a frown of confusion.

Paige had set this up as well. If DoDO was going to play it safe—which was something they *could* do, especially when she'd so publicly called him out about it—then she'd force it to happen. But she had to make a good show of it.

She stepped back, her hands raised, her magick out.

Bal and Bastet reacted as well as only they could as demigods, ready for anything.

Nothing further happened, per the plan. The explosion was just to get people's attention, nothing more. This was a *show,* not the real deal. She didn't want to *actually* put these people in danger. She wanted to force DoDO's hand in doing *nothing*.

Paige stepped up to the podium again, not releasing her magick as she continued to scan the area. The gamble might not work. DoDO might step up and still do whatever they'd originally planned. This whole thing was one big gamble. It could blow up in her face. It could set Mario into *actually* responding in kind.

A demon walked toward them, the crowd parting for him. "I received your invitation."

Had Mario summoned a demon? Seriously? What was he planning?

Mario smiled and nodded, but his brow furrowed as if he were still confused.

So, the demonwasn't a part of his plan.

The demon shook his head at Paige. "You really think

you stand against them, against any of us? We've been on this earth a lot longer than any of you."

"Gerriel," Bal said. "What are you doing here?"

"Teaching these people a lesson. The paranormals are *very* dangerous." He smiled wickedly, and then a chuckle bubbled out of him, exploding into a rolling laugh. "Oh, I do so enjoy this president." He sobered and launched a fireball into the air.

The people screamed.

Paige reached out with her witch hand to grab his demon soul and shove it through the hell gate embedded in her bones.

But before she could, a door opened in front of demon and swallowed him up, closing with a whoosh.

The fireball went straight into the sky and was dissolved by the wards.

The street was quiet.

She turned to Mario, wondering if that'd gone to plan.

He raised two surprised eyebrows at her and shrugged.

So, someone was playing him as well. Who had summoned that demon?

She swallowed hard and released her magick. "We're living in a new era," she said, her voice a little hoarse. She cleared her throat and tried again. "One where we can't blindly believe that our government is trying to protect us. They're vilifying us and creating a war in our back yards, in our homes. Our families and friends."

Mario shook his head, staring daggers into her.

"It starts with chips and collars," she said, staring daggers right back at him. "But where will it end? In prison camps? Laboratories? Death camps?" She turned her attention back to the crowd. "We don't want war, but it certainly feels as though the president of the United States of

America does." Fear thrummed through her, wondering what in the hell she'd just said and why and what the consequences would be. "And we will not go quietly into the night."

And that was all she had to say.

Mario, however, looked like he was ready to explode.

Chalk one up for their team.

15

I t took hours to get the media circus to filter out of Troutdale. A few news crew had decided to put down stakes and take up residence.

DoDO blockaded the roads again, so it might be forever or *never* to regain access to the town.

Several people wondered if she'd been the one to summon the demon. If the president of the United States could create fake news, it made sense that she would too.

That irritated Paige beyond measure because doubts entered into everything at that point. No one would know what was real or not because it was so easy to make up the truth.

Bal approached her after the crowd dispersed and mingled on the streets. "That demon *was* summoned by DoDO."

Paige wasn't surprised he knew that. "But Mario looked surprised."

"Yes, he did, didn't he? He wasn't the one they wanted or expected."

Paige frowned up at him. She was still getting used to

the fact that her father figure was a demigod. He'd always been a demon, and that big reveal was still a little startling to her. "Coincidental?"

"Not really." Bal stopped her and gave her a very dark look.

"Thanks for... playing your part."

"Of course." Bal nodded, gave her a kiss on the forehead, then placed Ember on his shoulders and disappeared into the crowd.

Mario took Bal's place. He scanned the crowd once before speaking. "That was one hell of a stunt."

It was. It really was. "What were you really planning by letting all these people in?"

"I have no idea what you mean."

"Your people summoned that demon."

A frown furrowed his brow. "Come now. There's no need to pretend with me. There are no cameras."

"You might want to figure out who's pulling your strings," she told him. "Because for all the big talk, you're not the guy on top."

"I assure you, Ms. Whiskey, you do not know what you're talking about."

"Okay. Well, someone in your organization *did*. You're out of the loop, Mario."

He narrowed his blue eyes, his platinum blond eyelashes invisible.

"Maybe you should get out of my town while I'm still being friendly."

He tipped his head to the side and quirked his lips. "How very American."

She smiled at him. "Be blessed."

That was the highlight of the after-party, if that's even what she could call it.

The streets were festive enough. People milled around, gawking at the famous surroundings. Outsiders asked questions, requested tours. There were places they'd seen on social media or people they'd seen, and they wanted up close and personals.

Michelle pulled Paige aside as the party died down. "Any word on Dexx?"

Paige shook her head. "How's the investigation?" Even though Lovejoy said she was on it.

"You're not going to believe it."

Oh, she was almost certain she would.

"He's in fucking Europe." Michelle's body shivered. Her skin resembled bark for an instant.

Right. Of course he was.

Paige's body sagged with the overwhelming feeling of everything going on. Yeah. Of course he was on the other side of the planet.

Well, she didn't have time to have a meltdown. She'd save that for bedtime. Or after she was in bed. She had shit to do first and wondering why the hell Dexx was in Europe wasn't it.

She mentioned Dexx's whereabouts to Merry, who got this look on her face, said nothing, and just left.

Whatever that meant.

When the sun hit the treetops and the party wound down, Merry came to Paige again. "Are you ready?"

"For?"

Merry simply spun on her heel and led the way to the parking lot behind downtown, which was this weird, little diagonal thing that was ridiculous to park in with anything bigger than a mini Cooper.

Eldora was there with a door open. The blackness shimmered. "They're waiting."

Who was waiting?

Merry disappeared through to the other side.

Paige didn't wait. She followed.

Eldora closed the door behind them.

Paige stood in a rather large room with several people she knew and a few she didn't.

The room could only be called grand. The vaulted ceiling had an immense chandelier of crystal, and polished wood gleamed everywhere. The floors were white marble, and the table in the center of it all had the feel of something King Arthur might have commissioned.

All four of the elementals were back—earth, air, water, and fire already sat along one curve of the table. Showing solidarity?

Another fae-looking woman stood off to the side with a small retinue who—well, they looked fae only because of their unique features, if that made sense. It was like looking at creatures from a Jim Henson movie.

Brack, the dragon from earlier, was there with another two men who looked remarkably like him. Other dragons, she assumed. He took one of the three seats along the end of the table. She assumed he either owned the place or his family did.

Chuck sat next to two other power people, alphas she didn't know, a mated pair with matching scars.

Cawli squirmed in her head.

Dammit, Dexx. He needed to be at this meeting so Hattie could push back. Everyone here was an alpha in their own way.

Bal and Bastet were even there, regal and commanding from where they stood near the corner.

It appeared as though many of the paranormal races were gathered.

Time to get this party started. "What are we discussing now? Are we hoping to accomplish something today?"

The older version of Brack sank into a green chair. He had salt-and-pepper hair that was mostly salt. He rested his ankle on his knee and draped one arm over his leg. "We're here because Merry gathered us."

That didn't help. "And your reason for showing up?"

He put both feet on the floor and leaned on the table. "She pulled a favor."

He talked like the kind of person who knew what power was. Real power. Not this fly-by-night, oh-we-have-unbreakable-wards-and-a-pack. He didn't seem like the kind of guy who needed his ego constantly inflated. So, she didn't buy it. "So, you're telling me you came all the way out here just because Merry-Merry-Quite-Contradictory—" Which she wasn't, but Paige was certain Dexx would approve of her attempt at snarky humor. "—snapped her fingers? You don't look like a lap dog to me."

He raised an eyebrow.

The scarred mated pair who had been talking with Chuck by the baby grand piano turned toward her, interest lighting their eyes with a distant amber glow.

Chuck raised an eyebrow as if trying to tell her to calm her jets.

There was entirely too much going on to *calm her jets*. "You're not here out of charity or favors. You're here because DoDO and the government pushed us into a situation. So, let's stop posturing and get to business."

"The situation you put us in," Ryo said, his dark hair moving with a breeze Paige didn't feel. His silver business jacket pulled away from his slim hips as if the air itself was having a love affair with him right there on the spot.

Paige couldn't refute his statement, so she shrugged. "I

could have just let Sven destroy the world, I guess. That's what he was intent on doing."

"What happened to the days of caution?" the curvaceous, dark-haired earth elemental asked. Her dark skin gave a whole new meaning to the term healthy glow.

"You try hiding someone intent on separating the Earth from the gates of both Heaven and Hell."

Duglas tipped his red head to the side as he took a seat in one of the uncomfortable looking grey-blue chairs. "I *did* wonder what they were doin'."

Paige didn't know if any of them knew why they were even there besides the brewing war. So, maybe filling them in on how it'd started wouldn't be a horrible idea. "Sven Seven tails was a demon who sought power, a lot of it. He got it and found a way to tear the gates from Earth. He would have made a kingdom all his own with absolute control over everything."

"Which would have destroyed everything," the earth elemental said, her voice low. It sounded like seductive pillow talk, even though there was nothing hot or sexy about what she said.

"Exactly." Now if only Paige remembered the woman's name, but honestly when she thought of the earth elemental, names were the *last* thing on her mind. "As it stands, he nearly succeeded. The gates are..." She didn't even know how to explain what they had been able to do. "Tethered, I guess? It's temporary. How temporary? I don't know. But it's handled for now."

"For now?" a woman demanded, walking toward her, her bright red hair rising and cascading from her in flames.

It wasn't hard to guess that she was the fire elemental. "I don't know if it's done."

The older dragon stood and went to a table along the

side wall, pouring himself a drink. "We are here to decide as a nation instead of as a region if we are going to war?" He took a sip and sat down in his spot.

Oh. National high alphas and leaders. That made sense. "What options do we have? I'm tired of fighting."

A tall, lithe fairy woman stepped into the room. "Daenys said you would try a path of peace. How is this working?"

Realistically? "It's too early to tell, but we're putting a good face out there. Popular opinion is shifting. That can only be a good thing."

"You do not win a war with opinions."

"You obviously don't know the American people," Paige shot back, feeling the woman's power rise within her. Paige didn't feel the need to call on her own. "Opinions are our greatest strength."

The fairy queen frowned slightly and raised her chin. "We can't all flee like the elves. We don't all have places to hide where the humans won't find us."

Would they want to if they could? "True. We can't hide like them. So, we have to deal with this head-on. DoDO has been spying on us for a long time." Paige told them about the recovered surveillance cameras throughout the town. "We don't know what they do or do not know."

The older dragon steepled his fingers and shook his head. "Tell us about your wards."

Paige filled them in about those as well. "As far as we can tell, they are sentient. I'll draw up a plan to see if we can get enough of these set up around all or most of the paranormal communities."

The female half of the power shifter couple strode toward them with the look and feel of a lioness. She stood beside the older dragon.

Didn't his name also start with a "k"? Paige needed to get better at this.

"That would paint a target on each of them," the lioness said.

She wasn't wrong. "But if we—"

The woman slashed her hand and shook her head violently. "You think too small, something Chuck tried to warn us about."

Paige gave Chuck a what-the-fuck look.

His expression read, *What did you want me to do? Lie?* and he shrugged.

She is our High Alpha, Cawli said inside her head. *She and her husband are a mated pair. They govern the North American continent. So, tread carefully.*

Oh. Well... she swallowed. Shit. Dexx *really* needed to be there instead of her.

Kat and Hadwin Wilcher, Cawli added.

Oh. Finally, names. "I hate to disappoint, Kat." Paige smiled tightly. "But those wards are the only things keeping DoDO from running around and kidnapping people off the street. Let's say we create wards in random locations, on private land that we have access to."

"Like the Whiskey property," Chuck offered.

Okay, maybe this wasn't a great idea. She suddenly pictured people invading the sanctuary of her home. But they couldn't use federal property unless they went to really remote federal property. They still paid taxes, registered or not. "Yeah. Like that. But we put the wards up and invite paranormals to come to us."

"Create our own concentration camps, you mean," the earth elemental said, stroking her own leg with dark seduction.

Paige hadn't thought of that. And why was that so damned sexy?

Neither had Kat. It looked like she'd been slapped in the face.

"This is not a bad idea," Hadwin said, coming to stand beside his mate. "Small, but not bad." He raised his blond eyebrows at his mate and silenced her with a wide-eyed look. "We claim a territory and then rule it."

"The government did that with the natives," Kat said, her blonde hair almost rising as it darkened.

Was her shifter spirit a *male lion?*

No. She is a lioness, but there are times when she chooses to invoke a mane when in half-form to subdue the wills of others.

Interesting. Paige focused on what he said. A territory they could rule? "Where are you going to go? Canada? There is no unclaimed land in the U.S." Was there in Canada either?

"Nor in the world," Hadwin said, turning toward her. "But were we to secede, we would no longer need to worry about the federal government. We'd have a country of our own."

"Sece—" What? Paige's brain just...stopped.

The older dragon—

Ken Waugh. Cawli filled in information as she looked at the gathering. *He's a dragon shifter and leader of the mythos.*

Mythos? One day, he was going to have to tell her the difference between mythos and ancients. But now wasn't the time.

Brack nodded. "Many of us would lose investments. Properties."

"We'd gain new ones," Kat said.

"What of the dryads?" Paige asked. They *were* entire forests. Uprooting was hard on the grove.

"Or the fae?" the fairy queen asked, nodding with respect in Paige's direction.

"Or anyone bloody else?" Duglas demanded. "This is our home."

Kat stared him in the eye and shook her head. "Not any longer. The only question you have to ask yourselves is how you wish to live?"

Secession wasn't a light topic. It would invite civil war—

Maybe not.

Other states had tried to secede, and there'd been no war.

But they'd also failed. "Who do we have who can research the reality of this?"

Brack opened his mouth to speak, but the door crashed open, and Daenys stumbled through, blue blood trickling down her front.

Ken's butler came into the room, calmly stating, "The elf queen has arrived, sir."

A dozen other elves, equally bleeding and battered, filled the room.

The butler looked over at Ken, his hands folded in front of him. "Should I start a pot of tea?"

These people were ridiculous.

16

P aige went to Daenys and helped her to one of the couches.

Brack didn't even complain about the blood. He nodded to his butler, who disappeared, and then watched the elf queen settle herself. She recovered *way* faster than Paige would have.

She is very old, Cawli said.

Whatever that meant.

Paige went to the couch too, getting a better look at the queen. Elves were powerful. Very powerful. And hidden in Underhill.

Eldora went to one of the other elves. Merry went to another and the two of them helped the wounded.

Which, okay, Paige could be doing too. But it felt like her other skills were needed here. "What happened?"

"We were attacked," Daenys said harshly, blue spittle flying.

"What did you think would happen when you ran like cowards?" the fairy queen demanded, stepping into view, her hands fisted on either side of her.

"I was trying to protect my people. What would you know of that, Llyntomi?"

Well, that certainly sounded like a raging cat fight of entertainment, but they didn't have time for popcorn. "Where are your people?"

"Our fortress," Daenys said, expelling a long breath.

"Who did this?" Paige was hoping she'd get particulars on *where* the fortress was later.

"DoDO."

"*How?*" Llyntomi asked derisively. "You hide Underhill."

Daenys stared up at the other queen, her green eyes filled with sorrow. "Not as hidden as we thought. They came with doors."

Eldora whipped her head around. "What?"

Right. Paige hadn't gotten to that part yet. "They have door magick of some kind."

"How?" Eldora demanded.

Paige shrugged. "I don't know all the particulars, but they're mages. They use ley lines?"

A dark realization crashed over Ken's features. He rose to his feet as the butler came in with tea. "Gather everyone."

The butler set down the tea calmly. "What should I say is the reason?"

"Mages," Ken growled.

The butler blinked, but no other real emotion flitted across his face. "Drink your tea, sir." And then he left.

"I take it you've had run-ins with their kind before," Paige said dryly.

Ken glanced at his sons briefly and nodded. "You and I are going to have a discussion about your wards because if they truly *are* mages, then they aren't enough."

Well, that was mildly interesting.

The next few minutes was all about getting information from Daenys with the help of her enemy, Llyntomi. Those two mixed worse than oil and water.

It didn't look or sound good.

Daenys no longer had control of the door leading to Underhill. Somehow, DoDO mages had cut her off. She'd barely been able to get a door open here, and the only way she'd managed that was with the help of one of Eldora's pendants.

Paige fingered the pendant Merry had given her. There was a wealth of information both those old witches had that could come in handy.

She'd have to send Leah to learn. And try to learn herself.

Chuck came to stand next to Paige. "You're the face of this. What do you want to do?"

Paige didn't know exactly. If this wasn't so huge, with so many implications, she'd— "I want to get over there, open a few doors, get as many people out of the immediate danger zone as we can, and root DoDO out like they're termites."

Chuck nodded. "How?"

Paige turned to Eldora. "How many doors can we open?"

"If you can open one, then we have two."

"And the amulet that Daenys has?"

"Was good for one door."

That was unfortunate. "What about—"

Eldora shook her head. "I am not sacrificing my family to save deserters."

Paige wanted to be upset with that, but it was a fair statement. She turned to Daenys. "Underhill is massive."

The elf queen nodded.

181

Paige also kinda remembered stories of other kingdoms and a big wooded area or something? "Are there places your people can hide until you return?"

She nodded again.

They couldn't extract. They didn't have those kinds of resources. But maybe—just maybe—they could relocate. She turned to Eldora and Merry. "We set up doors around the area to the wildlands of Underhill, protect them with wards—no matter what Ken says—and then leave instructions for them to lay low until their queen returns with something better."

Merry quirked her brow. "That's your plan?"

"In a nutshell, yes." Why did Merry make her feel like a stupid little girl?

Daenys clamped her pink lips shut tight, her green eyes narrowed. "Thank you," she whispered.

Paige didn't know anything about elves. They looked a lot like people to her. "Thank me when we've done something. Good intentions don't save lives."

Maybe she'd be learning *before* Leah. "Eldora, teach me door magick?"

The Blackman witch rose to her considerable short stature. "If you had come to me sooner–" She shook herself. "No matter. You're here now."

Eldora taught Paige to open a door.

Paige *tried* to pick it up quickly. Really, she did. She was a terrible student. Alma had said the same thing. Repeatedly and with a lot more curse words. Eldora was short, but she still managed to pack a punch with her tongue, even without cursing.

Door magick was a lot like sending demons back, except she had to open a door to *somewhere else* and that was tripping Paige up.

"It's *location*. It's fighting me." She just couldn't figure it out in her head what that *felt* like. When she cast a location spell, she could usually get a general sense of location—if the spell even worked, which it didn't always. But this time... "It's like there's something interfering. Like a static of some sort."

"See if you can hear it *through* the static." Though, Eldora wasn't succeeding either.

Paige fought through the static, pulling and twisting at the interference. The earth rumbled.

Eldora shot her a look. "What, *exactly,* do you think you're doing?"

The earth elemental rose and sashayed toward Paige, her dark eyes scoring her.

"Um." Paige hadn't *called* on earth or on fire, so she didn't know. "Sorry?"

"*Feel* the land," the earth elemental said, her silk voice caressing her like a lover. "The plants, the trees, the animals, the sky, earth. *All of it. Listen.*"

Paige closed her eyes to the chill of desire running through her and found her center. She stopped fighting the static and just tried to *listen* better. She eventually caught a very pale glimmer of what Eldora said she needed.

Opening the door wasn't anything special. She'd done this a hundred times when sending demons back to Hell. She just hadn't realized this was what she'd been doing.

Stepping through her own door, though. That was a trip that made her dizzy. For a brief moment, she was literally in two places at once—maybe three if she counted the doorway as a third?

When she stepped through, though, it was...

War. Elves ran, fought, and died.

DoDO surged forward.

This place didn't have sun, but there was light. Vines were everywhere—on the ground, in the trees, overhead. They writhed with lives of their own, defending the elves as best they could. The buildings were built out of the vines and living trees and were immense. They made the downtowns of the human world pale in comparison.

Paige wasn't sure what she was supposed to do, exactly. Well, no. She had the plan. She realized now that it was a mildly crappy plan that didn't take into account the fact that they'd be stepping into a *war zone*.

"Mom!" Leah shouted behind her.

What the fuck? Paige spun on her heel and stared at her daughter and Tyler in horror. "What the hell are you doing here?"

Eldora waved her off as she turned to her small army of Blackman witches and started giving them orders.

Leah had the audacity to ignore Paige and head over to listen to Eldora instead.

No. Nonononono. That was unacceptable.

Something exploded behind her, and more people screamed.

Paige ignored it and marched to her daughter, grabbing her arm and spinning her around to tell her to go home.

The girl turned to her, her face full of gritty resolve and just stared her down like an alpha would.

There was no alpha push, though. It was a hundred percent Whiskey stubbornness, and it hit Paige right in the gut.

She swallowed, realizing that her kid was starting to become an adult. She didn't want her to, not here. But where? They were heading into war and shielding her from that wouldn't do any of them any good. "Tell me the twins didn't follow."

Leah smiled. "Tyler did, but we made everyone else stay at home."

Well, at least there was that.

Something else exploded behind them.

Things were getting serious, and it was time to put on her war face. Paige turned to Tyler. "You make sure Lee is safe while she's focusing on the door. Help as many as you can, but when you're pushed—and you will be—" Blessed Mother, she was a terrible aunt and mother. "—you protect Lee. She's the least experienced out here."

Eldora sighed after sending the others off. "Not the least, but certainly one of them. Come. You're with me," she told the Whiskey kids before looking at Paige. "Go do your —" she waved her hand around. "—thing."

Right. Time to bring the war back to DoDO.

With a single person. What in the glorious hell?

She reached for her magick, her hands zipping out like arrows with lines of dark energy attached to them. She grabbed two DoDO agents. Before she realized what she was doing, a door opened and they were pushed through.

To Hell.

Yeah. She'd just sent them to Hell. It was like dialing the Stargate with the only address she really knew.

Eldora was right. She needed to practice this.

But not now.

The noise overwhelmed and focused her. That was something a lot of people didn't talk about. The fact that, in all that noise, a person struggled to hear things and could hear a pin drop next to them at the same time. The outside noise was so overwhelming, but something inside the brain flipped and made it easier to remain alive somehow.

People screamed and shouted and roared and generally made a lot of noise.

Bullets flew everywhere. The DoDO agents really didn't have a problem using semi-automatics.

On people who only had clouds and air to defend themselves with.

There were a lot of dead elves of all ages lying on the ground. Many more who were wounded and not dead and in a worse state, their faces twisted as they tried to figure out how they were going to remain alive or as they reached toward someone they obviously cared about.

Paige had to tune all of that out. She couldn't afford to become emotionally invested in anyone, no matter how hard it was to step over the form of a toddler wounded and crying in the street. If she stopped to help that toddler—and he wasn't alone—then others would be much worse off.

That one act was going to haunt her. But she pushed it aside for later.

Her witch hands pulled DoDO agents through the Hell gates she created. She didn't *need* to send them through the one embedded in her chest, though if her door magick started to get tough, she would.

While she did that, she called on the elements, using them to push other agents back, sending them toppling, giving the people being mowed down by the bullet spray a chance to recover, to gather their people and flee.

It focused the attention of the agents on her.

Good for the elves.

Bad for her.

She wasn't alone for long. She'd barely had a chance to throw a few tornadoes—yes. She was throwing *tornadoes* at these guys—when a few dozen elves scrambled to fight beside her, throwing their own magicks into the fight.

Their magicks were different as well. They were combinations of elements, much like the tornadoes, which were a mix of water and air and fire. The elves didn't simply use air. They used air and fire, or water and earth.

The tides were turning.

One DoDO agent stepped out from the rest and held up his hand, telling his agents to stop. He stared at Paige as both sides entered into the temporary cease fire. "Ms. Whiskey. What a surprise."

Paige didn't know the agent. They all looked alike with the riot gear on. The only person she'd ever known in the DoDO was Mario, and she was starting to get the impression that he wasn't that high on the totem pole.

The man smiled a sick smile. "You shouldn't have come, though."

"That's what all the bullies say." She was a little surprised he didn't ask where his people were being sent.

She hoped it didn't mean they had ways of just opening new doors and coming back, but she didn't know why she would hope that. They had door magick too. But their doors worked differently. If their magick was tied to ley lines, that might trap them in Hell because Earth's ley lines weren't Hell's.

"This isn't a war you can win." He looked around as doors opened all over and more DoDO agents poured through.

Oh, shit. Time to get out of there.

"We have the advantage," he said, with his cold, sickly smile. "And the president will be so pleased when I hand her your head on a platter."

It looked pretty likely he'd get that chance.

"Retreat," she said in a low growl. She just had to hope they'd managed to install enough doors and wards.

The elves with her didn't balk. They retreated, shouting in their own language as they moved.

Paige stepped over the toddlers again, but this time—she couldn't help it—she opened a door underneath them with the location of *home* and let them fall through. She didn't know if it would work. She didn't know if they would make it. Others fell through with them in the short span the door was open. She just had to hope she hadn't sent them to Hell or somewhere worse.

And while she'd been focused on that, she'd let a few agents slip past their lines.

Their bullets flew.

At least one of them hit her. She was too focused on the battle to really know where, but she was losing energy. She reached to create a door in front of one of the agents and it faltered. She tried again, feeding it more of her energy.

Finally, the door flared to life just as the agent dropped his rifle to hang in front of him and drew his knife. He disappeared with a shout before he could hit her with it.

Too close.

She focused harder, drawing on her magick, on her will. She opened doors to Hell, each one harder than the first. She didn't use the door inside her bones. These weren't souls. These were men and women with rifles and knives.

She stumbled, her leg nearly giving out. She needed to get out of there.

But there was too much space for her to cross between her and the gate home. With her own door magick not working super well, she didn't want to chance sending herself to Hell... or worse.

Where'd she send those kids?

Somewhere better than here, she hoped.

She wasn't going to make it home. That was clear.

There were too many dead. Too many wounded. Too

many DoDO agents. The original plan would have been okay if she hadn't forced DoDO to call in reinforcements.

Paige had just handed DoDO the elven fortress.

And the one person standing against them.

Her.

17

P aige sent out a hurricane gale force wind, sending DoDO agents flying backward. Some crashed into the walls of vines and toppled through. She'd never wished so hard for concrete in her life. With concrete, their bodies would have broken at least a little.

More elves joined them.

Eldora came behind her and shouted in her ear, "Move back. We're spread too thin."

"Retreat and close the doors behind you," Paige shouted back.

Eldora disappeared, hopefully to spread the word.

Paige needed to keep the main focus there on her. She was buying time for the elves, for Leah and Tyler, and for the other Blackman witches who were risking their lives to help this city.

Elves who had fallen in the field, who had been stuck in the city, who had been hiding the forest *were* fleeing. They *were* escaping

Underhill was massive. They could get into the woods. They could hide in other areas. But this city *was* lost.

Super Douche, which was what she was calling the DoDO leader, was getting upset. Each time he advanced with his bullets and his artillery, thinking he'd get the advantage, he lost ground.

That surprised her too.

Until his mages put their semi-automatics down—or let them hang from slings—and took up their magick instead.

This was the first time Paige got to experience mage magick.

And it wasn't awesome.

Their magick punched through her nature magick powered line—well, hers and the elves'—like a battering ram. She tasted copper in her mouth. Blood.

Tyler's voice pierced the air, sending several of the mages to the ground, clamping their hands over their ears.

That was nice, but the boy's lungs were only so big for a tiny kid. And shouldn't that kid be through the gods-be-damned door?

One mage didn't drop to the ground, but his mouth didn't move either. Was he deaf?

Paige didn't give DoDO or the lone mage a chance to react. She combined her witch hands, called up all the elements she could, whispered a prayer to the All Mother to give her the boost she needed, and shoved as many of those dressed-in-black sons of bitches into the biggest portal to Hell she'd ever made.

That certainly cleared the field a little.

It didn't escape her notice, though, that a few of the wounded and dead elves had fallen through with them.

She'd feel bad about that another time. She didn't have time for that emotional shit right then.

Super Douche rose to his feet as Tyler took in a gulp of air. His eyes landed on the boy.

Shit. Shitshitshitshit.

Paige gave him a sick smile of her own and punched him in the face with her witch hand.

Super Douche staggered back, putting his hand to his bleeding nose. He bleeding-finger-flicked a salute her way.

Yeah, okay. It might not have been her greatest move ever, but she was getting tired. Like...tired. She'd *hoped* her hand would at the very least transport his *head* to another realm, but a door hadn't even thought about opening.

Tyler went to sing again, but his voice cracked.

"Get out of here," she shouted at him. Well, at Leah, but who knew if that girl was even going to listen to her?

Super Douche frowned at the kids but returned his attention to Paige as he advanced. "You're going to regret this."

She sincerely knew she would.

She didn't know how much longer she could withstand this. Her ability to call up the big things was dwindling. No more hurricane winds for her. No more tornadoes. No more doors.

Just her normal magick.

She shifted into a massive gorilla and charged at him, releasing her alpha roar.

Two of the remaining DoDO agents cowered.

But the rest of them raised their damned guns.

What a bunch of fucking assholes, bringing semi-automatics to a magick fight.

The elves who still fought beside her sent another blast of wind, trying to send the rain of bullets away.

But *wind* was no match for the power of fast-flying lead.

Paige morphed into an armadillo, focusing on the shift, slowing it down so that for a brief moment, she was a massive gorilla with armadillo armor.

Those bullets bounced back at them. Hard.

Three fell. Two more staggered.

But as an armadillo, she was a tiny target and a slow one.

So, as soon as the best effect wore off and the elves were again the main target, she rose back up again.

As a t-rex.

Because why the fuck not? This shit was fun.

But her roar was like the alpha roar of a sick chicken.

Not nearly as cool as in *Jurassic Park.*

Choose another one, Cawli growled and took over.

Paige knew quite a bit about dinosaurs. She loved them. They were her favorite part of the museum. Well, that and the space exhibit, and never once had she ever thought she'd be able to *be* any of those dinos.

The first thing she learned was that they weren't impervious to bullets.

That blew.

But she also discovered that there were other dinosaurs with much scarier roars. Like the triceratops. She'd already discovered that being a hippo was really impressive. Seriously, never piss off a hippo. But being a triceratops was even better.

And their battle cry was terrifying.

She used those DoDO agents as bowling pins, not quite knocking them down faster than they could throw bullets at her.

But they did realize that bullets weren't their best answer. A few retreated, put down their rifles, and drew on their mage magick again.

A white and blue mage ball hit her in the right flank.

The energy sent her sideways. She slid and rolled over

bodies she hoped were dead and slammed into a rock. Goddess bless, she was tired.

However, her flank and her leg took that mage energy in. Her wound from earlier healed—even faster than shifter healing.

That was...weird. Right? That was weird.

How many mage blows had she taken?

Too many to count, really.

She should have petered out a long time ago. She should have just died, completely spent, protecting her kids.

She'd somehow managed to absorb the energy of their mage magick to keep fighting.

Not with the big stuff. But she was still fighting.

Okay. Well, that certainly changed things. She could take their mage hits. Just not bullets. So, she just had to push them to put their rifles down and use magick instead.

So, she got up and charged at them in varying arrays of dinosaurs, the biggest creatures she could think of.

Her favorite was quickly becoming the flying kronosaurus. Basically, the flying dinosaur crocodile. And, yes, she realized that those things swam.

But... with her ability to leap high as a gorilla, she transformed midleap into the kronosaurus—and all of those teeth. Seriously, there were a lot of teeth. And the fins? She used those like the wings of a small plane—as she plowed into the men and women fighting on the ground, biting some of them almost in half.

Not really. She wasn't that strong. But she had eaten pieces of them. She could tell that for sure. And it was gross.

She wasn't going to think about it.

Super Douche caught on that their magick was somehow powering her up, and he called a stop to all the magick throwing.

And, as luck would have it, they were finally out of bullets.

Paige settled on the ground as a gorilla, releasing one more alpha roar, which still had the mages unsettled. Then, she shifted into her human form. "Are you done?" she called out, using her failing witch abilities and her alpha will to make her words go further. She didn't want to admit it, but she was tired. Really, really, really tired.

He stared at her, his expression full of fury. "Where are my men?"

Thank the blessed goddess. Paige just smiled and blinked. "I'm going to let you rub two braincells together and figure that out. Okey-dokey?"

He narrowed his eyes and raised his chin. "Hell. You sent them to Hell."

"Did I?" Paige lost her grip on up and down and almost stumbled where she stood. She kept it together, though. She couldn't *afford* to show weakness. Not now. Not when her forces—she. *She* was her forces. The elves had fallen and there were only two left—were so beyond tired. Not when the elven people still had people to get out of there.

But there weren't too many of those left. Well, none that she could see. Bodies. There were still a lot of bodies, both elven and human alike.

But not her kids. Well, not in front of her.

There'd better not be bodies of her kids.

What were the elves going to think as they were mourning *their* kids?

Had the toddlers made it through? Shouldn't she have fought harder to save more?

How much harder *could* she have fought?

She was too tired. Time for her to retreat. "I'm leaving now."

He nodded slightly, refusing to take his eyes off her. "And if I say no? If I try to stop you?"

She didn't know if she had it in her. She hoped to the goddess she did. She called on her witch hands and pushed, trying to open a door.

That didn't work.

Well, there was one door that was always open. She hadn't used it before because...these still weren't souls. They still had weapons, and as they got closer to her door, to her, they *could* kill her. They could kill her as they went through her. She didn't *know*.

But she needed a threat strong enough to buy her a retreat.

If she survived it.

So, she grabbed Super Douche's gaze and held it in a vice as she dragged the one agent forward.

It was a young woman. Fear filled her eyes as she was pulled toward Paige. She raised her gun.

It was empty. Thank goodness because Paige would have been dead otherwise.

She pulled out a knife.

Okay. That wasn't going to be good.

Cawli growled and unraveled the door embedded in her bones.

The woman disappeared before her knife could find a place to slice.

Cawli growled again and sealed the door shut. He was pissed.

She could understand, but she didn't have time to care. "Do you really want to? I mean *really*?"

Super Douche's eyes widened with alarm.

He had to know Paige was pretty close to falling the

fuck over. She'd taken on his entire army while he'd stood around and pulled a fucking trigger.

Something shifted on his face. "We have your husband."

They weren't married yet. "I know."

He raised his eyebrow in surprise, a slow smile slithering into place. "Aren't you going to ask where he is?"

"Nope." Because she didn't have the resources to go save his ass right then.

"You're not..." He chuckled a little, shifting his weight to one foot. "Concerned?"

Oh, she was. She was raving mad inside the tiny room of her tiny heart she allowed herself to *be* mad in. "*You* should be."

His smile blossomed. "Because he's so powerful?"

She shrugged. "You can underestimate him if you want to, but he walks beside me as *my* equal." She gestured to the battlefield.

His expression clouded a little around the edges. "We both know he's not..." He sighed and looked out over the battlefield that had once been homes. "This."

Maybe not, but he *was* Dexx Fuckin' Colt. "Do you? Do you really?"

His eyes narrowed. "You will return my people."

Not likely. Oh, wait. Yes. Yes, she would. "When you return ours."

"What do you mean? Your *what?*"

She let a pained smile flash across her face. Well, she didn't *let* it. It just flashed and fell away as she thought about throttling his stupid, muscle-head neck. "The people you've been taking. The paranormals who have been disappearing."

"If anyone's disappeared, they ran away."

"Okay. Well, when they're returned, I'll return your people."

"That's not going to happen."

She sucked her head into her shoulders in a deep what-the-fuck-you-want-me-to-do shrug. "I guess they'll enjoy Hell, then." And hopefully not take it over.

"You're going to regret this."

Yeah. Probably. "I already do. And *you* will regret starting this war." Paige turned around, her body sagging with exhaustion as she limped back to the one remaining door. "I assume you can find your own way out."

Super Douche raised his voice to bark, "Move out."

She heard another door open and each body made a slight "whoosh" sound as it slipped through.

Eldora waited for Paige at the door. She pulled the corners of her aged lips down and nodded approvingly. "That was something."

It certainly had been. "Do we have the doors open?"

"Like you said."

"And the wards up to protect them?"

"As best we could. The elves helped."

Good because Paige knew DoDO would be back, and the elves would need places for refugees.

But before she left, she had one more thing she needed to do.

She turned, surveying the field of the dead. Super Douche was leaving through his own doors, and when the last of the DoDO agents she could see had left, she reached down and dipped her left hand in the blood of a dead elf.

She didn't know blood magick. That wasn't her thing. Leah had inherited it from *her* father. Paige had, however, learned a thing or two from working with Merry Eastwood and her blood witches.

And Paige had life magick.

With the blood of the elf on one hand, she reached to one of her several wounds and dipped into her own blood.

Then, she walked to the door. She didn't understand how, but the door connected to this plane, this dimension. It was the only thing she *could* touch, physically touch.

She closed her eyes and prayed.

Blessed Mother, help me find a way to protect the people here, to seal them away where they can remain safe until such time as we can unlock their realm and return their world to them. Help me keep DoDO out.

Paige rarely got an answer in return in the form of words. The answers or replies were almost always in the form of feelings and images. This time was no different, but the emotional response that came back was in the form of a question.

Are you sure?

Paige knew that with the All Mother, there were a million different ways this could go wrong, a million different ways it could be interpreted, but Paige just didn't have anything more to *give*.

I don't know what else to do, Mother. If you have a better idea, please give it.

The All Mother smiled—not with a face and lips. She smiled with warmth, understanding, and a sense that things would work out. *Of course.*

A power far greater than Paige, greater than all the witches and other paranormals she knew, reached into her, through her, pulled on the life energy of the blood on her hands, pulled it through her skin, her hands, her arms.

The power ripped out of her back in a way that was painful and with-standable at the same time.

A loud crack sounded over the land. The trees swayed with the force of it. The vines crackled and twitched.

Then they rose toward the sky, growing and talking and chittering.

And devouring the bodies of the fallen, taking the sustenance they needed to grow.

Eldora touched Paige's shoulder. "Come on. Let's get you home."

Paige was spent. She let Eldora guide her, her eyes barely working. Her ears barely registered what was going on.

When they stepped through the doorway, she was greeted with chaos.

Reporters. Refugees.

And Leslie.

A fully pissed-off Leslie.

"I just won one bloody battle," Paige muttered, holding out a bloody hand. "Can we not do this right now?"

Leslie's eyes widened with alarm.

The last thing Paige felt was Leslie's arms—and a few other arms. She didn't know where they'd come from—surrounding her as she fell, fell, fell into darkness.

18

The next day, Paige felt like she'd been hit by a truck. She hurt in so many places, and when she went to sit up, she discovered a sharp pain in her abdomen.

She looked down and saw a bandage. She'd been shot?

Right. She'd probably been shot so many times, but the mage magick. It'd healed her.

Well, not quite as much as she'd hoped. There were bandages on her legs, her left arm, and one on her foot.

Okay. Wait. Even with the mage magick helping, wasn't she a shifter? She should be fully healed by now.

Well, after questioning a few shifters—Margo. She'd questioned Margo—she discovered that they *did* heal faster but that they still needed *time* to heal. It wasn't magick.

It was. It really was, but Paige got the hint that she needed to cool her jets.

She'd spend quality time with her kids. Jet cooling couldn't be any better than that.

The twins were ready to nurse—thank the goddess

because so was she. Boobs sucked, and then Bobby was ready to play.

Of course, Paige wasn't. She was ready to lie down and take a nap because getting up, having one conversation, drinking one cup of coffee—after having made it herself because Dexx wasn't there to save her—and sitting on the couch to nurse had worn her out.

Which, seriously, was about right. Right? She'd just nearly single-handedly defeated a DoDO army.

Not quite, but yeah. Pretty much. There'd been a lot of magick slinging.

She invested a few more hours into sleep. She watched a few episodes of *Into the Badlands* because it was a good visual show that didn't require a lot of brainpower, though, there *was* something going on with the storyline and she was beginning to realize that maybe she should have been paying attention longer.

The next day, she felt a bit more like herself.

Venturing into town, though, was still a chore. She didn't want to shift shape. She was tired. She hadn't even realized that there'd be a "doing it too much" tax put on shifting, but it made sense. Like anything else, it required energy, and she had certainly expended that.

But it also meant driving, and she hadn't filled up her tank in a while.

Also, when *she* was tired of shifting, the twins were too.

They remained human, which was nice because it was easier to keep track of them. It was also harder because that meant she had to *carry* them and their fifty-pound car seats as well.

She pulled up to the mayor's office and began pulling the kids out. A random stranger walked down the sidewalk in front of the mayor's building and offered a hand with the twins. Just some random stranger, which... yeah. By the end of the siege, there would probably be a lot fewer random strangers.

"Thanks." Normally, Paige might have been a little more hesitant, a little more Mighty Mom about it, but not that day. "These things weigh a *ton*."

The dark woman carried Ember's car seat to the mayor's building and set it on the floor inside the door. "It's not a problem. We all got to stick together right now, don't we?" She smiled back at Paige and then continued on her day.

Once inside, it was a matter of pushing Ember's seat with one foot while she carried Rai with two hands.

For about two seconds. Then the receptionist—whose name Paige was really going to have to remember—came in and saved her, taking both the sleeping twins and stashing them by her desk. "She's just about ready for you."

Suzanne *knew* she was coming because Paige'd forgotten to call ahead.

The receptionist looked up from the sleeping babies. "How are you doing? I've been watching you on the news."

Did she even want to see what was being said about her on the news?

Yes. She did. She probably should have been watching that instead of *Badlands*. "I seem to be getting some airtime lately, don't I?"

The receptionist shook her head. "You look great for having kicked so much butt out there." She glanced at her desk and then back up at Paige. "She's ready for you now."

Paige was going to put that down as one of the classiest compliments ever.

But when she got into the mayor's office, Suzanne was in a snit. "Can you believe these a-holes?" She pointed to the TV, which was playing one of the news stations at a low level.

Paige could barely hear it. Something must have knocked out some of her hearing. She didn't even remember what it might have been. "I'm sure I can." Believe the reporters would say whatever they were paid to say? Yes. "What's going on?"

"The president is stating that you *attacked* her agents."

Right. Well, she *would* say that, wouldn't she? In a different world. *"We* attacked? Nothing about *how* they were causing a ruckus on a different plane?"

"We had no cameras going that entire time," Suzanne said, turning on Paige. "You can't ever do that again."

Paige was confused. "Go out and help people?"

Suzanne looked at her like she'd lost her damned mind, her blazing blue eyes daggering Paige with intensity. "Go in there, be the hero, and then forget your cameraman."

"Well," to be fair, "I hadn't realized we were *going* to be saving people."

Suzanne gave Paige a frank look. "Since we have no idea what's going to happen for the next few days or weeks or whatever, I'm assigning cameramen on you at all times."

That was a bad idea. "I can't promise to keep them safe."

"They're scrappy."

"They still die when they're scrappy." Because that was a word often thrown around in fiction novels to describe characters who were armed with nothing more than sass and a mouth. "We'll figure something else out."

"No." Suzanne pointed to the TV. "They're murdering us out there and you were sleeping for two days and we had no story. We tried. We really did. But that woman—Eldora isn't good for TV. And Merry is a convicted murderer, so we can't even *think* about putting her on the screen. And your sister?" Suzanne's dark eyebrows shot up, disappearing behind her bangs as her hand fluttered to her chest. "That mouth. We can't put *that* mouth on TV."

The mayor was a good person, but there was only so much *dramatic* Paige could take on this much sleep. "Talk to me about the refugees."

Suzanne settled down after that and filled Paige in on the town situation.

Quite a few elves *had* made it to their town for sanctuary and more were coming, though fewer now than there had been. The toddlers had made it through, but there were a lot of casualties and several of their bodies were being taken back to the elven plane for death rites.

Basically, what Paige had seen right before she'd left—he plants taking from the bodies what they needed to grow? That was death rites.

Paige tried not to imagine their tiny bodies—

Enough. She couldn't go there. Not when she was still this damned tired.

Things were running smoothly for all the fuss. Seriously, the mayor was doing a fantastic job.

During the battle with Sven, a lot of people had cleared out, leaving their homes abandoned. Granted, those homes still belonged to those people, but they weren't being "lived in" at the moment, so the mayor was assigning people to live in them. The proviso required them to respect the previous owners and box up things that didn't belong to them. If they broke something, they had to fix it, or they were kicked out to live on the street.

"How is the issue with the supplies going?"

"Glad you brought that up. I actually managed to get funds to help offset the costs. Different organizations and

F.J. BLOODING

corporations are contacting me to set up supply deliveries and donations of goods." She half sat on the corner of her desk.

"That's all pretty great. Things seem to be coming together." Paige took in a deep breath as she sat in the chair, looking up at the mayor, almost ready for yet another nap.

"I even have a drug company donating insulin because we have three Type I diabetics." Suzanne preened, pleased with herself. "That would be beyond terrifying if the supply was cut off."

Paige didn't know much about diabetes, but she did know it was scary bad. How? No clue. But it was bad. Suzanne *should* be pleased with herself. She'd done a... "Good job, Madame Mayor."

The town was being taken care of. That was the bottom line.

However, the president was winning, and Paige needed to get the word out. On her Twitter, Instagram, Facebook. Whatever. Pinterest. Paige was *really* good at Pinterest but had no idea how to get the word *out there*. She *could*, however, pin a thousand posts on craft projects she'd never do.

But also on YouTube. She could start a channel there.

So, she collected her kids, grabbed a sandwich from the deli—which... how amazing was it to go to the store and *not* have to use money? Everyone's accounts were frozen. F-R-O-Z-E-N. And not in the Disney way where they could sing a song about a snowman and feel good about themselves. No. They didn't have any money.

But they were still functioning as a collective of prisoners in the comforts of their own homes.

Then she took the twins to the park bench beside the downtown ward tree and pulled out her phone.

She clicked the live stream option, which seemed really dumb. She didn't understand how people could just turn a camera on themselves and talk like what they said actually mattered.

But what she had to say *did* actually matter.

She started the stream and began showing the park and retelling how they fought against the demon horde. That led to other things and she divulged information the elves would prefer remained secret, but the time for secrets had passed. They didn't have that luxury anymore.

She told the people watching—and there were a lot. It started off as a couple. And then there were more hearts flying across her video and likes and mad faces and... it was distracting. She told them what happened. What really happened in the elven city. She couldn't really read the comments.

She told them about the kids on the battlefield. About the pile of toddlers she'd tried to save, about the bodies being sent back.

And she cried. On her live stream. She tried not to but staring up at her ward tree—*their* ward tree, she couldn't hold back the tears. She did, however, keep the words going. People needed to hear them.

It was finally time to wrap it up, though. She looked into the camera. "You guys need to keep your heads down. DoDO and the president are serious. And they don't have barriers of morality to stand behind. They're killing kids— toddlers, babies. They don't care. They only care about repressing us, containing us, and keeping us out of their society. We're not safe."

She blinked as more hugging heart emojis flowed across her screen.

"There *are* paranormal leaders and we *are* discussing

what needs to be done to *make* you and *keep* you safe. But until then, find refuge."

That wasn't what she'd *wanted* to tell them.

Someone walked past and shouted a hello at her.

Paige smiled and waved back before returning to the live stream. "And to all of you who are human and afraid, remember that you've *been* safe for generations, for *thousands* of years, from us. *We* hid because of our fear of you and what I'm seeing now is that we were right to do so. The only way you're *not* safe now is if you attack paras. If *anyone* is attacked, *people* will defend themselves. That's the way the world works."

This had to be done. Geez. "Okay. Signing off for now. Sorry I didn't fill you in earlier but..." She paused and licked her lips. "Yeah. Okay. Be safe. *Everyone* be safe. And... could we show the world what it means to be amazing? Please?"

She hit stop on the feed and glanced down to see a ton of emojis and comments.

Not all of them were good.

The twins were awake and fussy. They didn't *like* being human, but she appreciated the fact that they were remaining so.

Chuck and Faith came up to help calm the babies.

But Chuck looked rattled. Paige had never *seen* the regional high alpha look *rattled* before. "What happened?"

He put Ember to his shoulder and bounced him. "Dexx."

Seriously? "What did he do now?"

"He—" Chuck's eyes widened, then narrowed as he sucked in his lips and bit down on them. "He attacked me, and I could not feel Hattie. It was as if she was being repressed."

A cold bucket of holy-shit poured over her. She'd had a *chance* to get him back. Super Douche had *offered* it.

"He did let me go."

That was a good sign. Right? "Do you think he was on orders to attack you? Kill you? Capture?"

"I don't know, but the way he looked at me?" Chuck shook his head as Rai nursed. "He didn't know me."

Rai went limp with food coma as the news hit Paige in the gut. Hard. She was weary, so the emotions were stronger. She knew that, but to hear that the man she loved didn't recognize his alpha? There was no way he would remember or recognize her. Or Leah. Or Bobby. Or Rai and Ember?

She shouldn't have taken the kids to Washington D.C. Granted, they were a huge pain in the butt a lot of the time, but it was possible that they could have helped. Leah could have, for sure. "This situation got a lot bigger really fast," Paige said, swapping twins for nursing.

Faith grunted as she took Rai. "This situation was *always* bigger."

"To some." Who could *grasp* just how big this was?

Chuck nodded, his tongue on the roof of his mouth making his lips look weird as he dropped his jaw. "How do we respond?"

Paige shook her head, giving Ember the other milk bag. "I don't know. Where are all the leaders? The big alphas. Kat and the other one. Can't they step up and help out here?"

Chuck shook his head and shrugged, shoving his hands in his pockets. "They're looking out for their own."

"Okay." Why were they even leaders, then? "What about the elf queen? Where is she?"

"She returned to Underhill to help the resistance there.

She's leading the fight, but she wanted me to tell you that she is very grateful and that she will allow Kate to remain with your family without question."

That was really gracious of her. For an elf.

But that wasn't what Paige was getting at. "Why is it falling on me?"

Chuck was quiet for a long moment and then he took a seat beside her on the bench. "Do you know what you did in the elven city?"

What she always did? "I fought DoDO."

He shook his head. "You showed us all that you are the strongest of us. You are the most versatile. You can tap into everything we can but as one person. You are a shifter. You control the elements and magick. You can talk to the plants and animals. You can tap into the other dimensions."

She knew all of that—it was like telling her she knew how to put pants on.

Not... well, not *really* like that. She *knew* she could do all that, but it wasn't that big of a deal because she was just *doing* it.

"And you're tapping into something else, something none of us have seen and we don't understand yet."

Was he talking about what the mage magick did?

He took her free hand. "I talked to Eldora and the elves who were there. I'm trying to find someone who can help you."

The look he gave her was so much different than the one he'd given her a mere six months ago. He was no longer her alpha in that moment. He was no longer able to be the one who told her what needed to be done. He was an advisor now, and that scared her. "Help me with what?"

Chuck met her gaze and kept his alpha will to himself for the first time since she'd met him. He didn't try to rise to answer her alpha will. He didn't rise to be her equal or better. He just looked her in the eyes.

That was a humbling moment because she *needed* Chuck to *be* her alpha. She needed him to know what to do when she didn't. She didn't *want* to outgrow him.

He didn't seem to care.

"When I have answers, I'll share them. When I have someone you can use as a mentor, I will introduce you. But until then, do not push yourself too far. Do not overextend yourself like you did in battle."

"What do you mean?"

He released a long breath. "You shouldn't have been able to withstand that fight for that long on your own. And you should not have had access to the animals you shifted into. And you should not have been able to combine them the way you did."

"But..."

There was a hint of fear in his gaze.

That stopped her cold.

She blinked and sat back, Ember releasing his claim on Paige's boob. She focused on tucking everything back in and getting him back into his car seat, while she worked through the maelstrom of emotions overwhelming her. With Rai and Ember both strapped into their seats, she stood, tears in her eyes. "When you have someone I can talk to, please let me know."

He nodded and rose with her. He offered his hand. "I will always be here for you, Paige."

But their roles were changing, and she didn't like it. It was like stepping out onto a tightrope without a safety net.

Without saying anything further, Chuck and Faith turned and left.

Paige stood in the park with her babies for a long moment, her emotions crushing her. She was so alone.

And so overwhelmed.

But *really* alone.

She'd make it. She would.

She just didn't know how.

19

Paige went home and walked into an empty house.

That was rare. Really, really rare.

She put the twins to bed and then she went to the living room with a steaming cup of hot cocoa and watched Netflix.

But then a wave of dread washed over her. She didn't know why. She just knew that something horrible was taking place right then.

She switched over to the news and nothing was on. She tried a few different channels. She even had CNN.

But there was nothing.

Then she pulled out her phone and went to her social media platforms.

That's where she saw it.

The president sat at her desk in the Oval Office, surrounded by reporters and other people. She signed something and held it up for people to see. "This is the Executive Order mandating the Paranormal Registration Act."

No.

The president smiled. "And as you can see, things can go very, very peacefully."

The video cut over to a group of people in what looked like a city. The DoDO agents walked in without guns. They did wear their normal black utility uniforms and they did have other weapons on them. But they walked into the town and the people who were already there weren't fighting back.

There were several tables lined up along the sides of the street. Civilians walked up to the table, gave their information, and were handed a collar that they then put on themselves. The cameras even cut over to a woman putting it on her child, telling him that everything would be okay and that this would be better because he "wouldn't have to fight it" anymore.

Why wasn't this on the TV? Why did she have to go to the internet to find this?

The first person she called was Chuck. She told him about it and asked him to spread the word.

But then she called Danny Miller.

She knew he was just an average reporter, but he was the *only* reporter she knew who could tell her how the president had been able to do this.

It took him a minute to catch up, though, but once he did, he was pissed. "I'll call you back."

The twins were still sleeping when she went to check on them. She didn't understand why they were still sleeping when the two rarely slept at all. It was convenient, though. The world was falling apart, and Mommy needed to go fix it. She'd worry later. For now, she'd hope one thing went right because that's what she desperately needed.

But they were sleeping... a lot. Convenient or not, it *might* be a bad sign.

She really needed it *not* to be. She took her "win" and ran with it.

She called Margo, but she was busy with patrols.

Leslie wasn't even answering her phone. Which... okay. That woman was busier than crap. Paige understood that. She sincerely did.

So, she called her brother, Nick. He said he and Mark would be right over. They talked briefly when they came in through the back door. She wasn't going to say she was close to her brother. They might never be, but he was a good guy and his boyfriend was too. They made great dads. Well, most of the time. Paige still thought they went a little too easy on the kids, allowing them too much leeway on *everything*.

With the twins taken care of, she prepared to head over to the mayor's office. That was a *much* better place to use than *her* house. She enjoyed the comfort of being able to stay in her own home for meetings, but she didn't necessarily want everyone there all the time, either. It was supposed to be a home. Not a conference center.

She tried a shift, but something inside said *no*. Her animal spirit energies were tapped out.

You're not tapped out, Cawli said in her mind.

Then, what is this? Because if she couldn't shift anymore then she was in some serious trouble if it came to a fight. She was still a seriously powerful witch, but she had gotten really used to being able to shift to fight.

I do not know, Cawli said, his voice dark. *But something has changed inside you and I do not understand it. I will be back. Do not attempt to shift again until I am back.*

She tried to ask him more questions, but he'd left. Where? No one ever knew because her spirit animal was the only one who just periodically—okay, most of the time—

left her alone to go wander around as a spirit. Everyone else bonded to their spirit and stayed stuck together.

But most people were either born together or had been bitten. She'd been neither.

So, she searched for her car keys, something she'd gotten out of the habit of doing. She'd just had them, so she retraced her steps.

They were in the refrigerator.

Of course, they were.

She drove down to the mayor's office quickly, her mind and heart working through the issues plaguing her, but nothing concrete came of it.

Chuck, Sheriff Tuck, Suzanne, and Duglas met her at the mayor's office.

"What is going on?" Paige demanded.

Chuck shook his head. "My contacts outside say that this is streaming on all the news channels."

"And it's interrupting already scheduled programs," Danny said, barging in, holding his phone aloft. "But they're running a shadow TV service for areas like ours."

Wait. "Areas?" Plural? "Is there someplace we can all see?"

"This way. The conference room." Suzanne led the way through the small maze to a room with a table large enough to seat ten.

Danny went to the laptop and started typing.

Suzanne didn't question it. She just reached over and jacked the HDMI cable to it and turned on the projector.

Danny looked exuberant. "They've got these shadow networks over eighteen different areas across the U.S."

"Why are you so happy?"

"Because," he said, looking at her with a grin, "we now

know what they know. These are the areas *we* need to target because these are the areas *they're* targeting."

She hadn't thought of it quite like that.

Leslie burst in. "We've got a problem."

Really? "We've already got one."

"Well, then you have two." Leslie gave Paige a fuck-me-running look and reached behind her, pulling a young woman through the door. "Tell them what you told me."

The young woman broke down in tears immediately, but she painted a pretty horrible picture of the cities that *weren't* being shown. The ones being hidden by the shadow TV network.

War.

DoDO had come into her home with guns drawn, had taken her entire family. Her dad had resisted and was dead. Her mother had been taken somewhere else for "war crimes." She and her brother had been herded away with a truckload of others.

They'd taken their names down, fingerprinted them, DNA swabbed them, and installed chips in them. She'd watched it happen to her brother.

And then she'd just blipped here and appeared in Leslie's shop.

Leslie gave Paige a what-the-fuck-do-I-do-with-this-shit look. "She's not the only one. She's the second one, but the first one was wounded and Barn's taking care of him."

They had a location. Lawrence, Kansas.

Paige rose. "I'll go take care of this." But how had this girl gotten here? "Prepare for more refugees." Because Paige had no idea *how* these were even getting here.

"At some point," Suzanne said firmly, "we're going to have to stop taking them in."

"I'll let you tell me when we're at the point we need to let people die rather than protect them." Because Paige could only handle so many of those kinds of decisions.

"That's not fair."

Paige gave the usually bubbly mayor a look of steel. "I know."

She left but Chuck followed. "I'll gather the pack. We'll be ready to go with you."

That would be helpful, especially since she had no real idea what was even going on with her.

Leslie joined her on the sidewalk. "Am I going or staying?"

"Which would you rather?"

"Go."

Paige nodded and held up her phone. "I'm calling Eldora for doors."

"Meet you where?"

Paige pointed to the end of the street at the train museum. The parking lot was big enough to hold a crowd, and the park bordered the side.

Leslie disappeared.

Paige called Eldora. She made the arrangements with her to get some Blackman witches there.

Eldora arrived with Leah. Mandy was with her this time because Tyler was still recovering. Mandy was great with fire, but she looked terrified.

Duglas came and stood beside Mandy and nudged her arm. "We'll protect the door keepers together," he said.

Mandy's smile didn't say she was reassured by that.

Paige still didn't know what she could even do without her full powers.

They were joined, of course, by Suzanne's son, who was

their new cameraman. He had a full crew, and they all looked like newbs ready for their first time in the field. Paige pulled in a breath and released it slowly. "I don't have time to save your asses. So, you follow these two rules. Number one, stay out of the way. Number two, *stay out of the way*. Okey-dokey?"

They nodded eagerly.

Eldora, her witches, and Leah began to open doors. Shifters rushed through, and it was time to get busy.

Paige stepped through into a war zone.

Fires burned everywhere. Ash fell from the sky. Debris and pieces of building crumbled to the street. Car alarms raised an echoing cacophony.

Without her powers, the best thing she could do was get the word out.

"Are you recording? Are we live?" Paige rubbed her nose at the acrid smoke.

Suzanne's son, Mark—yeah, she had so many men named Mark in her life—nodded.

She looked into the camera as her people fanned out around the street, collecting survivors.

Chuck's pack gathered information.

The Blackmans set up doors.

Mandy created a circle of fire around the hot zone.

"We're in Lawrence, Kansas. The president is giving you her false image of peace. She's lying to you."

Something crashed behind her.

Paige spun to see what it was. It'd been close, but both Mandy and Leah were safe. Clearing her throat and pushing down her fear and disbelief, Paige turned back to the camera. "She has several communities like this one on broadcast lockdown. They're not getting the news. No warnings. We don't even know if they knew about the

Registration Act in the first place, but this is the face of her *actual* war."

Several men with guns ran down the street in the opposite direction, away from her.

Paige walked down the street and found a body. She went to check on it, to see if the person was alive.

The woman wasn't.

The kid under her *was*.

Paige pulled him to his feet. Tears made a muddy trail on his cheeks. "Are you a shifter?" She tried to put as much mom-concern in her voice as possible.

He nodded. "Mommy won't wake up. I'm scared."

"Can you walk? Nod if you can."

He nodded.

"Okay, I want you to get to those people over there. That's the way to safety." She let the cameras see his face, let them see the reality of their situation before setting him free.

He ran toward the Blackman witches and their doors.

She turned to the camera again. "*This* is America, people. *This* is your president. Wake up. We're under attack. Our government has gone above and beyond atrocity. Those men out there aren't Homeland or the military. *That* is a foreign and private militia."

She gestured to the street and then turned back to the camera. "This is an entire *city*. It's a little harder to hide from that."

She got up and headed toward the sound of violence. Even without her magick, she had to do something. "This is what happens when a government gets too powerful," she said, recalling the words her conservative husband had repeated too often. She still didn't think he was a hundred percent right. Society needed government. They needed guidance. Just not a helicopter mom for a government.

"This is what happens when there are no check and balance systems in place, when the president doesn't have to obey the same laws as everyone else. Because this?" She pointed to a man and an elder who had been gunned down on the street corner. "This is murder."

She found a group of DoDO agents. She pulled on her powers, reaching deep, pulling up the fire through the earth until the ground rocked with the force of it. Thank the goddess she still had that.

They stopped shooting down the cratered street and turned to her.

"You're probably going to want to get out of here," she told Mark, the camera guy.

The others who had been terrorized by DoDO also got up and scrambled out of there with the help of Chuck's pack.

Super Douche came out of the crowd of agents and tipped his head to the side. "We're really going to have to stop meeting like this."

"Well, you stop tearing cities down, and I won't have to stop you. Problem solved."

He narrowed his eyes at her and grimaced. "I'm afraid I came a bit more prepared this time."

And here *she'd* come *under*prepared this time. "Well, let's see what you've got."

He raised his gun with a look that said he regretted the need. "I really wish you'd have stayed at home."

Shit. Yeah. So did she.

She didn't have time to scramble, though she tried. She also knew that reaching for any shape wouldn't work for her this time. She dove to the ground, only to watch in horror as a bullet spray peppered the asphalt in a line toward her. She pushed with her magick, not sure what she was hoping for, what she thought she could do. *Mother, I need you!*

The ground rose and fire shot skyward, hotter than any fire she'd ever felt in her life. It speared straight into the quickly darkening sky.

Clouds rolled in as an unnaturally fast and massive storm built overhead, the roiling underbelly of the clouds dark and green.

Super Douche's eyes widened as he stared skyward.

Paige could *feel* the flow of energy running through her, wild and unchecked. This was *her*.

Somehow.

She had a flicker of thought of watching Super Douche dance in lightning but pulled it back.

The sky lit electricity, the ground ripping with the impact.

Super Douche pulled a rod from his vest and lightning deflected around him like a human Tesla coil.

She had him, though. She didn't know how. She just *had* him.

She advanced, calling the lightning, feeling it resonate from the ground and meet in the air. It lanced the entire intersection, catching several of the DoDO agents.

One of them signaled a retreat. Magick doors of white light flashed open, and they disappeared.

Paige wanted to get to Super Douche, but she also wanted to let him live to tell the tale.

A part of her wanted to capture him and get information out of him.

A bolt of lightning launched from her hand and sizzled the air as it raced toward him.

He caught it in his hand, his expression dark.

The ball of lightning coiled around his arm like an adder. It didn't hurt, didn't harm him.

And then she knew why.

He sent his own magick toward her. Mage energy, mage magick.

And it was...

It was like hearing the Lady Mother, speaking to her when she called fire. But louder. With words and feelings and thought.

She let it fill her, reeling in the deeper connection to Lady Earth. Paige'd always been fearfully respectful of her fire. She'd never truly called *fire* like everyone else did. She'd always pulled it from the bowels of the earth. It had a different voice, a different feel. It was wilder and tamed at the same time. It was forceful and quiet.

Super Douche's eyes widened as he realized his mistake.

A moment before he burst into flames. The agony roaring from the flames lasted only as long as it took for a single breath to leave Super Douche's lungs.

Not enough, and too good a death for him.

Damn.

"Mom," Leah said carefully beside her. "Let's go home."

Paige released her magick, wondering what in the hell had just happened there.

And wondering if she was going to regret the fact that it had been captured on video—live video. Had she just given the president the ammunition she needed to take this war and make it public?

Paige took her daughter's hand and walked through the door.

She stepped onto a full and bustling Main Street, her ears ringing with the quiet, knowing the street was loud with everyone talking. There simply weren't the sounds of battle.

Paige needed to figure out what was going on with her powers. Now. Before things got worse.

And she got out of control.

The only problem with Paige learning to control her powers was that she had no idea where to even start. What was going on, and who would know?

Alma would. She had seemed to know a lot more than she ever said. But Paige didn't have access to Alma anymore.

She decided to go to Elder Yad.

Well, no. She called and asked if he'd come to her because Nick had a meeting with a client and Mark was working on a court case. Just because they were locked down in Troutdale didn't mean they weren't working. They couldn't get *paid*, but they were still doing their jobs defending people. She'd ask them how, but her plate was filled with too much information, so their answer wasn't retained in her memory. They were doing well and didn't need her help. That's what she remembered, and, at the end of the day, that was all that mattered.

When she got home, though, she was greeted by a surprise.

Bobby.

He had grown nearly a foot since the last time she'd seen him. Like... since that morning. Yes, he'd been complaining about things hurting and stuff, which kinda normal. Bones hurt when they grew. That was something she'd learned with Leah. She'd always known when that kid was headed toward a growth spurt. She'd eat them out of house and home—or cookies. That was all she was after, really—and then she'd complain that her left leg hurt. And then she'd be an inch taller in one day.

Not like this though.

He ran around naked because none of his clothes fit him anymore and he was "done" with diapers because he was a big kid now. He had dumped the trash on the floor to use the trashcan as a stool so he could pee on the floor while aiming at the toilet.

He *was* such a big boy!

No, really. She was quite proud of him for trying, but she was going to have to help him with his aim. If she'd taught a little girl how to wipe her hoohah separate from her butt, she could teach a little boy how to aim his pee-pee.

On one hand, she was glad that, while the world was falling down around her, she was dealing with pee pees and lost socks.

But on the other hand...

What the hell was wrong with her son?

She called Roxxie, the local angel guardian, but she didn't pop in like she normally did. Instead, there was the sound of a car door closing and Roxxie walked through the front door, looking a little more fragile than normal.

Paige really hadn't talked to her since Roxxie'd helped the angels kidnap her while she'd been pregnant with the twins. She'd felt as though Roxxie had broken her trust.

Roxxie had eventually freed her from Heaven, but that trust had never quite been rebuilt. Roxxie'd worked with Dexx since then, and she'd had a place in the battle against Sven, but...

Paige hadn't realized just how bad off Roxxie was now that the gate to Heaven was further away. Angels pulled power *from* Heaven in much the same way Superman pulled energy from the sun. If it was a cloudy day, he had a harder time healing from Kryptonite. Same with the angels, and Roxxie'd had a lot of cloudy days with the Heaven gate moved away.

Paige had known that but seeing the results and knowing were two different things.

"Hey," she said, letting her newly awakened realization hit her tone. Well, she hoped so, anyway. She needed to work on building more bridges. Not destroying them all.

Roxxie acknowledged it with a half-smile and a sigh as she closed the door behind her. Her blonde hair was pulled into a serviceable braid, which wasn't normal for her. And the angel wore jeans and a T-shirt. Also not normal. "What's wrong with Bobby?"

Paige vaguely remembered when they'd had a slightly different relationship. Roxxie had been a helper in the fight against demons, but Paige was realizing now that she'd used the angel.

What a wonderful human being she was. "Tea? Coffee?"

"Coffee." Roxxie frowned as she followed Paige to the back. "Is there something wrong with Bobby?"

"Maybe. But I've been taking you for granted, and I don't know how to fix that. So, let me get you coffee and *then* I'll hit you with what's potentially wrong with my son."

Paige revved up the coffee maker and flashed a cup of pre-packaged grounds at Roxxie.

"That would be excellent, thanks." The angel leaned against the counter as the coffee maker started dribbling coffee.

"What are you up to these days?"

"I have an apartment down by the *good* grocery store." She smiled at Paige with good humor. "I have a job too. I don't know if I'll keep that, though. Fuel may be an issue soon."

Oh, crap. Right. Gas. She hoped Suzanne was on top of that because Paige had no idea what to do if the gas wasn't flowing.

How many horses did they have in Troutdale? They might be going back to horse and buggy. Maybe Eldora had been on to something there.

Paige also discovered that Roxxie liked a little coffee with her milk and sugar. A lot like Dexx.

"As much as I appreciate this," Roxxie said, putting her empty cup on the counter, "what's the problem?"

Paige made a mental note to be less of an asshole later and called for Bobby.

He came screaming down the stairs and hurled himself into Roxxie's arms.

She caught him and staggered backward in surprise. She looked over at Paige in shock and then back at Bobby.

It was more than just the fact that he was taller. His speech was better too. He was talking in full and complete —okay, mostly complete sentences. He was still a full-blooded American taught by a large group of people who *spoke* in broken sentences. So, his grammar wasn't *that* good. But it was better than it should be for his age.

"Should I be concerned?"

Roxxie just studied him with color-shifting wide eyes.

"I'm gonna play now," Bobby said, pointing at Roxxie and winking with both eyes. That was a total Dexx move. "'Kay?"

Paige nodded, still not sure what to do. "'Kay. Don't die."

"You too," he said as he ran out the back door in nothing but Superman underwear.

Paige took in a deep breath and turned to Roxxie. "Is this related to the gate?"

The angel looked away finally, her mouth still agape. "Perhaps, but he seems fine."

"Okay. Well." Good. "That was the main concern." Because she *needed* one more thing to be worried about.

That was sarcasm. She really didn't.

"I can..." Roxxie cut herself off and shook her head.

Paige bit her lip, realizing that Roxxie had been about to offer her help. That was just what Roxxie did. It was who she was, and it was high time Paige remembered that. "Only if you *want* to. 'Kay?" She said that last word, mocking Bobby.

Roxxie nodded, with a ghost of a chuckle. "Does this mean you forgive me?"

"It means I'm finally pulling my head out of my ass." Because life was forcing her to, and she no longer had the leisure to be mad at allies. "You were doing what you thought was right. You didn't think I'd be in any real danger. And I need to stop being mad at you for being you. Just you being you is what saved my ass more than a few times."

Roxxie raised her chin and blinked quickly, diverting her gaze. Finally, she licked her lips and moved to follow Bobby. "I'll find him some clothes. What are you doing?"

"Trying to figure out what's wrong with my magick."

"What do you mean?" Roxxie stopped and frowned at her.

Paige took in a deep breath and shrugged. "Honestly? I don't know. But I've got access to more power, power that's... it's really big."

"More than you already had?" Roxxie asked incredulously.

Kinda what Paige had been thinking. "It's like it's always been there, but... I don't know. I don't *know*. I'm afraid I'm becoming exactly what the president is fighting so hard to protect people from."

Roxxie turned away from her but then turned back, studying her with the *angel eyes* which was the only way Paige could even describe it. "You don't seem wrong."

"That's something, right?" She hoped so. "But then, I have to meet with a bunch of people to see how bad I fucked up this situation with the president. To see how people are responding to how I handled the situation in Lawrence."

"Huh?"

Paige filled Roxxie in as quickly as she could.

"Oh. Well." Roxxie rinsed out her cup and stashed it in the dishwasher. "I'll see what I can find out about Bobby."

"Thank you," Paige said with real relief.

The front door opened and Elder Yad walked in, Merry Eastwood hot on his heels.

Paige had to go through the entire story again, from the elven city to what had happened in Lawrence, Kansas and her concerns that she was getting too powerful. She also wanted to know what the blowback was from the video that had been taken in Lawrence.

"Well, that," Merry said with a snarl, "is actually taken care of thanks to the president, I believe."

"What do you mean?"

"It means that all of our communication has been stopped."

"What?" No. That was bad. That was really, really bad.

Merry nodded. "None of us have access to social media or the internet or the news. Our phones are now dead."

Paige pulled out her phone. It said she had no signal.

Merry closed her lips, clasping her hands in her lap. "Electricity will go next. Water will follow. The blockade was nice while it lasted, but the president is quite serious."

"How much of what she did got out? Did anyone see?"

Merry nodded. "People saw quite a bit of it, but all the videos are being taken down. The posts we've all been sharing are being deleted. The news is being erased."

That couldn't happen. If they went that far, then...

If people weren't reminded of this, of the atrocities that were happening—

Would they care? Even with the reminders?

Some would.

But would enough of them?

It was time for Paige to face reality. There wasn't going to be a peaceful situation that would come from any of this. The president didn't want one. She was doing everything in her power to lie to the public. She was abducting families and killing them when they tried to flee or defend themselves.

She wasn't protecting the American people anymore.

But, at least, Paige didn't have to worry about the fallout from people seeing she might be the monster the president claimed they all were.

She just needed to figure out what kind of monster she *was* becoming.

Elder Yad brought out two ancient books.

Paige groaned. Not more ancient books.

He tapped one of them. "These might help."

Paige was really over books in dead languages that would give her the answers to the universe if she just had a year's worth of downtime to read them. "Cliff notes?"

Elder Yad shrugged with a smile. "No one's been able to read them."

So, they were paper weights. "I'm really glad you brought them over, then. This lamp's been a little low. I can use them to raise it up."

Merry gave her a dry look and pulled one of the books toward her, opening it. "There's a spell."

"But he just said that—"

"It's a spell that gives a person the ability to read it," Elder Yad said carefully. "We haven't had anyone who *needed* the information who could also use it."

"And you believe that's me?"

"I do," Merry said firmly.

Elder Yad gave her a frumpled look that said he didn't.

Merry closed the book on her lap with a loud thump and looked at Paige hard. "There's a reason we've been trying to hone our three bloodlines."

Which was the reason Paige had married her step-brother unknowingly, so Leah could be produced, an heir of all three covens. When she'd discovered that, she'd felt a little like Leia Skywalker after kissing Luke even though Paige and Mark-the-Leah-Daddy didn't share any blood relations.

But the family trees really did wind around each other a little too close for comfort. "And what reason is that?"

Merry bowed her head for a moment and looked her in the eye. "Back before the old witch families departed the old world, there were two different types of magick: wild magick of the witches and the war magick of the mages. Wild magick came from the elements. War magick came from earth's veins, the ley lines."

Paige was following so far.

"But as the families intermarried, those magicks became tainted and blended. Then, a witch was born with the ability to tap into the ley lines. She called her abilities life magick."

Had Alma known this? She'd kept a lot to herself. Paige loved the old woman deeply, but damn. She could have shared more.

"But shortly after she rose to her power," Merry continued, "she and the other witch families were pushed out of the old world and into the new. That one witch created the divided family we now had: the Whiskeys, Eastwoods, and Blackmans. Life magick, blood magick, and door magick."

They all shared the same, singular ancestor? "Fuck me." Why did she have to be related to Merry Eastwood?

Merry raised a brow. "You're the closest we've been able to come to having a witch who could tap into the same magick as the mages." Merry shook her head with a dry expression on her face. "You're our only real defense against DoDO."

Paige just stared at her for a long, withering moment.

Merry handed her the book. "If you don't believe me, open the book." She handed Paige a piece of paper with an incantation and her blood knife. "I want the knife back."

Paige muttered the spell Merry gave her, pricking her finger to bleed on the first page.

Nothing happened at first. Just as relief crept in it, was dashed as the scribbles turned to words.

A chill swept down Paige's spine. "No," she whispered. "This is too much."

Elder Yad set his book down on the table beside her, frowning at the book in Paige's hand. "Be that as it may, it is what it is. And you can either choose to wail about it or stand up to the tide."

Paige just stared up at him like he was a crazy person. What the hell did that even mean? Like she would stand around and wail.

For longer than fifteen minutes. Every once in a while, that's exactly what the situation called for. Wailing.

In private.

In the shower.

Where no one could hear her or see her cry.

The front door slammed open and Leah stumbled through. "Mom," she said, collapsing onto the green couch. "They have the Blackmans."

"What do you mean?" They who? How? When?

Leah took in a deep breath. "DoDO. They came and grabbed the Blackmans." She swallowed, her blue eyes wide. "They're gone."

As if on cue, the electricity went out.

Right. No communication. Power was gone.

And now they had no way to open doors to get supplies.

The war had truly begun.

21

Merry and Elder Yad rose to leave. "I'll have a location for you shortly." Merry held her hand out for the knife.

For her? What was she supposed to do? She wanted to stab the knife in the blood witch's heart.

Of course. *She* had to find a way to open a door.

She had herself and Leah, but neither of them were exceptionally good at that magick yet. Granted, she knew they were still Plan A, but she needed to find a good Plan B.

Just as soon as she wrangled the kids.

Cyn and her portal to the spirit animal plane might be the Plan B they needed, but Paige was going to have to talk to her about how possible it was to use it this way. The portal Cyn had led to *one* location; the library and the museum of magickally dangerous objects hidden in the spirit animal realm. It was kind of like their own Warehouse 13, only less cool because the entrance was a closet door and they didn't have a magick football.

Leah wasn't leaving her side.

Roxxie had disappeared somewhere, hopefully looking for a reason for Bobby's rapid growth, so Paige decided to just keep Bobby with her.

Leslie and Nick and Mark and the entire pack were busy doing their things, so Paige's kids were with her. Paige gave her siblings the heads up on what was going on and told them to keep their kids close.

Ember and Rai were awake finally and shifting into as many animals as they could, as if sleeping had cheated them on all their fun and they were making up for it. It was almost like a contest between them now.

On the rare occasion they chose human, Paige got to see their own growth. They were now the size of toddlers, standing on their own.

And Bobby had grown more just since earlier that morning.

That couldn't be good, right?

Okay. *This* was the red alert. The war could wait. She needed to handle *this* right now. Her babies were in trouble.

She piled all her kids into her car, telling the twins they needed to be human while she drove. No shifting in the car. They both gave her sad baby faces in every shape they could. They even managed to make a sad baby snake face, which she hadn't thought was possible.

However, Rai and Ember were now to the point where she had to readjust the belts on their car seats. Like, she had to take them out of the slots in the back and raise them up. How'd they grown *this* fast?

This was taking *forever*, but Leah helped it go a bit faster. There really *wasn't* room in a standard backseat for *three* baby seats. But if she slammed the door real hard and *leaned* against the door, Paige could *just* make it happen.

· · ·

Paige finally managed to strap *everyone* into their respective seats, and Leah was getting herself buckled.

Paige really appreciated older kids who could take care of themselves.

Roxxie appeared beside her just as she was about to slide into the driver's seat of the car.

Roxxie didn't look great. "What's wrong?" Paige got out and closed the door, catching Roxxie.

The angel closed her eyes and staggered a little. "The— it's just really hard to travel this way."

"Okay. Then maybe rethink that. Like, walk like a human for a bit." Which... Paige looked in the car. There was no way she could squish one more human into her car. Well, she could. But it would be like riding in a sardine can on wheels.

Roxxie leaned against the car, looking beyond exhausted. Her eyes were sunk in, as were her cheeks.

Yeah. Okay. Paige needed to hear what Roxxie had to say, but she also needed to talk to Cyn and she might also need to talk to Merry. She just didn't know. So, Paige opened the car door, assessing the kid situation. "Okay. We need to get rid of one car seat. So, Rai or Ember, I need you to shift into something small."

Rai responded first, shifting into a leopard kitten.

But Ember wasn't to be outdone. He shifted into a baby bird.

"No birds!" Paige opened the back door and took out Ember's car seat, popping the trunk to shove it inside.

Roxxie raised one hand and nearly fell over. "I'm fine."

"No, you're not." With Ember's seat in the trunk—that had been a lot of time wasted on readjusting their belts if she wasn't even going to use them—Paige went to the other passenger door. "Leah, you're in the back."

The girl grumbled but got out of the front passenger seat and wedged herself between the door and Bobby's car seat.

Rai had shifted into a ferret.

Ember shifted into a rat.

Rai then shifted into a small mouse.

Ember just disappeared.

Paige rolled her eyes and took the other car seat out, undoing the belt that held Bobby's seat, then put it in the actual seat, giving Leah more room.

Bobby glared the entire time.

Her toddler wasn't a toddler anymore. He was a small kid now. Geez. That should scare the crap out of her, and it did. A little. But not nearly as much as it made her feel relieved. She was going to be fighting yet another battle, a war, really. She didn't need to be saddled with tiny tots.

Roxxie maneuvered around the hood of the car to get herself into the front passenger seat.

With everyone belted in except for her two wild children, who were now both insects of some kind, Paige put the car in motion—with all the windows closed because insects could get sucked out— and headed toward Cyn's house. "You've gotta change the way you live and interact, Rox. You're not a full-fledged angel anymore."

"I know. I just..." She trailed off, gripping the dashboard, her fingertips going white. "I sometimes forget."

Paige sighed deeply. "Tell me you at least put yourself through this for a reason?"

Roxxie glanced over her shoulder. "Honestly, no. There's no precedent."

"Do you think it has something to do with the gates?"

Roxxie nodded. "But how? I don't know. I had gone to our library—"

"I'm taking you to another one."

The angel grunted. "—thinking that there might be some connection to the gates, but there's no information on them. At all."

Hmm. Because it wasn't something that needed to be shared or written down? Or because someone was hiding it? "You're losing power."

"And he's gaining it." Roxxie looked over her shoulder. "His height isn't the only thing he's getting."

"What?"

Roxxie nodded. "I don't know why. Prophets aren't usually powerful. They don't usually need it, but there were a few who did. Those eras did not end well."

"What do you mean? Like Biblical bad?"

Roxxie nodded, her eyebrows raised.

"Does this have anything to do with the twins?" Paige didn't meet with a lot of traffic as she crossed town to get to Cyn's house. Most people understood that, without gas, driving was a bad idea. There were, however, a lot of people on bicycles. "There was a reason the angels wanted the twins dead. Do you know why?"

Roxxie just lifted two tired shoulders. "I just know they're scared."

"Great. But there aren't a lot of angels here." So, it was unlikely she'd have a two-front war. Maybe. Hopefully.

"No. Most of the angels who *had* been here are gone. They're in Heaven. Staying here is a drain to our systems."

That didn't seem to be the case for the demons. "That's good for us." Except—Paige just had another thing whack her in her head. A thought. A memory. A fact she shouldn't have misplaced. "You're the anchor to the Heaven gate. Is that draining you?"

"If anything, it's making me better. I think?" Roxxie gave her a pained smile. "You should see the other angels."

Not *all* the other angels. She'd been attacked by one at the White House who'd seemed pretty okay. "Okay. Well, um." If angels weren't hunting Bobby, then the threat level was down. "Do you think Bobby will be okay?"

"I hope so? We just have to watch."

Paige pulled up in front of Cyn's house. "Well, then, Bobby isn't the main priority for you now. You are. So, take care of you."

"I'll take care of me and keep looking for information on him."

Paige smiled her thanks, shut off the car, and turned her attention to the twins. "Be something big enough that I can see you."

Ember and Rai shifted into baby elephants, which would have been cute except they were *big* and they squished Leah and Bobby.

Bobby zapped them both with some golden angel light.

Ember released an elephant trumpet that turned into a bear roar.

Rai screeched as an owl and flew out Paige's door.

Being a bear was still a bad idea because the kid was getting *big*.

Leah scolded him and she shoved Bobby out of the car to save his life from suffocation by baby bear fur.

Paige just got out and let them deal with themselves and turned toward the small mansion.

Cyn stepped out of the door, one hand on her hip, her blue eyes narrowed. Her streak of blue hair was brighter than it had been the last time Paige had seen it. Which was good. Someone had to have time for that.

As much as Paige wanted to do the fantasy hair colors

because they really did look neat, they were a lot of work, too. She'd be boring brown for a while longer. "Hey. I'd love to small talk with you, but, first, I suck at it and, second, I just don't have time."

Cyn clamped her teeth shut and crossed her arms over her chest. "What do you need?"

Paige glanced over at the rather large tree that dominated the front lawn. Cyn's parents had sacrificed their bodies to become the grounding stone for the base of that tree, their bodies permanently entwined in the tree's heart. They were on the other side of the portal, their souls inhabiting the library. Paige didn't understand all the particulars, but they weren't dead. That's what she really understood. "We need to see if we can use the Banga Boomy to get people from one town to another."

"The Vaada Bhoomi," Cyn corrected with a shake of her head. "It doesn't work like that."

Paige'd been afraid of that. "Well, I need to see if maybe there's something in your museum of fantastical things that might be able to help." She held up a hand to stall whatever was about to come out of Cyn's mouth. That woman could put up more roadblocks of what-if's and why-nots than Paige had ever seen. "We've got paras trapped all over the damned U.S. and we need to get them relocated to somewhere else that's safe."

Lynx stepped out, looking good. He'd been a cat just a few weeks earlier. He'd been trapped in the Vaada Bhoomi as Bastet's temple cat for over two hundred years. Or two thousand. Something like that. A really long time. He'd been trapped as a temple cat for a really long time, but he was back to human and mated to Cyn and he looked good. Even with his cat ears. "We'll do what we can."

"Great. Thank you." Paige should probably stay and

talk a little more. She got the feeling that Cyn was a person who appreciated being talked to. An extrovert. Paige didn't have time for that. One day, hopefully, the two of them could sit down and get to know one another. Now wasn't that time.

"While they're at it," Paige said softly, "could your mom look to see if there's some reason my kids are growing so fast?"

Cyn looked confused.

"I just need to know if they're going to be okay."

"Yeah." Cyn didn't look confident.

But Paige'd done what she could *for the moment*. It wasn't like she could take the three kids to the doctor. They wouldn't know what they were looking at.

Time to deal with the impending war. She really *had* to get the Blackmans back. Without them, Troutdale, and everyone else, were doomed.

She got back in the car and shouted, "Let me know what you find out."

Cyn glared.

Lynx waved.

The kids piled in with screams and screeches.

Paige didn't wait for the seatbelt check this time. Next stop, Merry's.

Before she left, though, she shot Leslie a text. *Grab Mandy and/or Ty and meet me at Merry's. Problem. Need [bomb emojo].*

The Eastwood "house" was even more of a mansion than Cyn's family home. But Paige was becoming a frequent flyer now, kinda. She rang the doorbell and opened the door, letting herself in. Rai and Ember were now puppies, making a bunch of noise.

Bobby chased after them but not in a toddler way. It was more of a younger Tyler way, if that made any sense. He was trying to get them to calm down.

"Guys," Paige barked in her best Mom voice, letting her alpha will slip through a little. "Cut it out." There were things more valuable than Paige and all of her kids combined, even if they were sold on the slave market.

Ollie appeared from one of the rooms to Paige's right with a warm smile. "Hey, sis."

This family line stuff was for the birds. They shared the same father, a Blackman, while Paige had married Ollie's brother. Ollie was only related to Leah through Merry. Weirdest family tree ever, and it made Paige feel more than a little redneck, but...Paige liked Ollie. For an Eastwood blood witch, he was pretty decent.

Wait. He was an Eastwood blood witch with Blackman door magick. He might be helpful. "Hey, brother."

He frowned at her, pulling back a little as he came in for a hug. "You're planning to use me."

She hugged Ollie back. "You're damned straight."

"Any word on Dexx?" Ollie muttered into her hair.

Paige shook her head and took a step back, her darker emotions pushed into a box sealed so tight her heart didn't even twinge at the sound of his name. "How are you with door magick?"

"Not that again." Ollie groaned as he led the way back. "Eldora hasn't let up on me since all of this blew up, so I've practiced a little."

"Well, good, because you, me, and half-pint are the A Game."

He tipped his head giving her a *greeeeaaaat* look and opened a door. "We have a location."

The room he led her into was obviously a magick work room but of the blood witch kind. There were a lot of darker witch elements like skulls and ravens that were probably real taxidermized ravens and a few other animals that were probably also taxidermized. If that wasn't a real word, Paige was going to make it one.

Paige refused to ask about the elements here. She didn't want to question them. She had to make alliances, and that meant accepting them.

Besides that, she had to acknowledge just how helpful Merry had been. Paige wouldn't have made it this far without her. So, it might be time to put her judgements aside.

There were about a dozen other witches in the room, lining the walls, standing with their hands folded in front of them, wearing dark robes that obscured their faces and bodies.

Merry stood at the table in the middle of the room. She raised an eyebrow at the kids, then looked at Paige again. "So, we're taking kids?"

Leslie and Mandy walked in.

Paige met Leslie's gaze, grateful she'd shown up. "You have your strengths. We have ours."

Leslie released a slight growl as she stalked past Paige and stepped up to the table. "Where are we going?"

Merry shook her head. "Portland. *If* you have the ability to open a door."

Right. Paige glanced at Leah and Ollie.

If this didn't work, they'd have to go with Plan B, and Cyn had already said it wouldn't happen.

Leah raised her chin and stepped up to the table, meeting Paige's gaze. She nodded once.

Ollie joined them, with a shake of his head and an expression that said he thought this was a bad idea.

Great. Well, if they were going to be learning on the fly, they'd better get started. They needed the Blackwood witches. The paranormal world was counting on them not to fail.

So, that's exactly what they *weren't* going to do. Fail.

22

The first thing Paige needed to do was to figure out how to lock in on the location Merry and her witches provided. It was one thing to see it on the map. It was a whole different animal to reach out with that pinpoint of information and open a doorway to it. Her mind, heart, soul, and rooted body had to comprehend what that pinpoint *meant* magickally.

Location spells with Leslie had helped her learn bare essentials. She wished for a moment that she'd had a little more time, like years, with Eldora honing this particular gift. Procrastinating, it turned out, was a terrible idea.

Leah didn't seem to be as bothered by the lack of training. Youth had advantages. She stepped up to the table, took a look at the map, and oriented herself with the sun and the cardinal directions. She closed her eyes and went to work. Her magick spun away in black wispy smoke tendrils.

Huh. What if her witch hands were actually doors? What if she wasn't just reaching out with her magick? What if she also was opening doors to other dimensions at the same time she called them up?

Ollie was working through his magick at the same time, a frown of concentration on his face. His magick was a dark red that was, frankly, quite beautiful to look at.

Paige reached inside and touched on her own magick. It felt like an old and treasured friend. She wouldn't say it had a personality. Not exactly. But it had a life. It wasn't some inanimate object like a blanket or a favorite sweatshirt. It was an uncoiled, wild thing that seemed to understand her in ways no one else did or could.

She pulled up her hands, watching as the inky black energy extended from her. She could make those arms as long as she needed. She could make her hands as big as was necessary and could lift things her body could not.

Her magick turned to her with a hint of question, as if that living thing inside of her was trying to have a conversation with her.

So, she focused the question toward her magick without using words. Words were thought-limiters that animals and elementals didn't understand. Every other creature on the planet spoke in broader concepts and thought forms instead of forcing those broad-stroke thoughts into tiny boxes of "understanding." She focused her question in visions and emotions and thoughts.

Thinking without words was a lot harder than it should've been. But that's what happened when you were raised in a society where words mattered more than actions, where what a person said or what words they chose were more important than the things they actually did.

Her magick answered back. Yes. This was within her power of *doing*.

But what did she need to provide? What did she need to give her magick in order to make this happen?

She needed a better understanding of how *she* worked.

A location. But not information. Not numbers or an address. Her magick needed to know the feel of the place. It needed to know the location based off how the earth would see it in this time.

And that was a completely different thought form. The earth spoke in life, decay, and change that didn't make sense because, with the earth, there was this alien sense of time. Time was different for the earth than it was for smaller people like Paige, and that was something she didn't know how to translate. Or could she?

She opened her eyes and looked at Leah. "I think I found a way, but I have no idea how to feed that to you."

Leah beamed a grin. "I've figured *that* out. I just didn't know how to take it to the next step."

Ollie shrugged. "Just get it started and I can take it from there because..." He shook his head at her, his expression dry, "this isn't my bag of Oreos."

Nice reference.

Great. Paige wished, not for the first time, that she could telepathically connect with her daughter, but the only one capable of doing that was Kammy.

Leslie raised an eyebrow. "Are we gonna be able to do this or not?"

The reality was that they might *not* be able to. They *needed* the Blackmans. "We'll get it done, but they might be bringing us back."

Leslie shrugged. "It don't have to be pretty."

Thank goodness for small things.

Paige and Leah couldn't connect telepathically, but maybe Leah and Paige could connect through their magick.

Paige closed her eyes and reached toward her daughter with her witch hands. That was something she'd never thought to do before. Her witch hands had always been "tainted" before, being demon magick which shouldn't touch anything living.

But the more she learned about it, the more she realized that Alma'd had no idea how to help Paige. Not really.

Leah reached out with her physical hand, but it was bathed in her door magick, with red veins shooting through it.

When Leah touched her hand to Paige's, she connected with a sense of where they needed to be. Paige had no idea how Leah had managed to figure that out, but she suddenly understood what "location" meant in a reference of time and space.

Other ideas hit her. If location dealt with time and if they had the ability to open portals to other locations, then was it possible to open doors to other times as well?

Could they go back in time? Could they do something different? Could they fix events?

Interesting, maybe they could—

Stop. Focus on the location, here and now.

She tucked the time travel idea away for future exploration. Like when she had time, and the world wasn't crumbling around her

With the location from Leah, she set an anchor. *This* was her place.

Anchor set, Paige focused on the instructions she received from her own magick and what Eldora had taught her. She reached out with her hands, and instead of searching for a soul to rip from a body, she focused on simply tearing a hole in the air.

It wasn't nearly as easy as a simple tear. Her hands—her magick—was able to tear a hole in space, but it was small and too high to reach. Paige was used to sending souls through, not making doors for people to *walk* through.

There was no way a human could fit through it, even if they could get to it.

But it also wasn't a hole to the location they needed.

No. Instead, it was a hole elsewhere. *Very* elsewhere.

Screams filled the large room.

Merry frowned. "What are they doing to them?"

"That's not the right place." Though, Paige had no idea where the door had opened. It wasn't the location Leah had given her.

Ollie laced his magick to theirs and the door dipped down to the floor, though it was still too small to fit through.

Merry released a long sigh and uncovered a rather large mirror. An ornate gothic piece that pivoted up and down. "Try this." She positioned it to perfectly level, making the room twice as large from a perfect position.

Paige really had no idea what she was supposed to *do* with that, but the three of them moved their rather small door toward the mirror.

It flashed and opened, revealing a lush yet foreign landscape. Where were the screams coming from?

A demon's face filled the opening, his maw open, his horns curled. It wasn't often Paige got to see them in their physical form. Most demons visited via souls. She didn't know why or how.

His large, black eyes widened. "What are you doing here, summoner?" He spoke in the harsh demon tongue.

"I'm trying to open a portal to Portland," she answered back in English.

His skin furrowed in a way that could have been a frown, but with the rough bark-like skin, it was hard to tell. "This isn't Portland."

"I see that." Paige tried to see around him. What was going on with the agents she'd sent there? What about the elves who had inadvertently fallen through? Were they okay? "Hard at work?"

He came into full view and then pointed the door to the right. The vision blurred slightly as the view changed.

DoDO agents huddled together in the middle of a full, healthy valley of wheat or wild grass.

As she watched, an agent dropped from above and landed in a heap among the others.

"I'm dealing with the trash you left behind. They do not belong here." The demon came back into full view, obviously not happy. "We do not want them."

Oops. "Sorry about that. I hadn't intended on dumping them there." Or not following up, but she'd actually never thought about what the demons would want. She just assumed they'd *want* the humans there to torture or whatever.

The demon growled. "Have you come to claim them?"

Nope. "Sure? I don't know where I'm going to put them."

"Not here, preferably." He let his head fall back and a mighty roar ripped through the room.

Demons moved, herding the agents toward the portal.

The demon turned to Paige. "Keep them out of my kingdom. They are a plague destroying your world. They will not destroy mine."

Huh. "Okay. Were there any elves?"

"*They* are being cared for."

Interesting. "Well, their queen might want them back."

"And when she is ready for them and they are healed, *she* will have them back."

What was going on? "Okay. Thanks."

"Do *not* send more here. I will hold you personally responsible for the damage they do."

Whatever. *Her* world was already imploding.

Okay. She *knew* she couldn't be that flippant about it, but...seriously. She wanted to.

The line of agents was long. What the hell was she going to do with them?

Merry crooked her finger at one of her witches and told them to take the agents to "the pens."

The upside to having the bad guys on her side was that they *had* plans for situations like this, she guessed.

Paige told them to tend the wounded, and they'd figure out what to do with them later.

There were a lot of wounded.

And a lot of glares.

Well, she'd just sent them all to Hell during a battle, so... yeah.

Though, Hell looked pretty damned nice. Where was all the brimstone?

After the last DoDO agent was through, the portal snapped closed.

Paige and Ollie shared a look.

Leah beamed with excitement.

No. No excitement. The door hadn't gone where it was supposed to.

Merry set a fist on her hip. "Well, that was... informative. Let's see if we can get to Eldora this time."

"*You're* welcome to try it." Paige smiled. Well, she showed teeth. She put Merry on ignore and tried again.

The portal reformed and opened to the inside of a fairly large warehouse. The Blackman family sat in a circle.

They weren't surrounded by cages. They weren't surrounded by guards, but they *were* strapped to chairs.

"Trap?" Not really a question but she should at least ask.

Leslie blinked, resolve making her cheekbones sharper. "Trap."

Great.

Merry just looked over at Paige and lifted one shoulder in a condescending shrug. "Do we need them or not?"

The Blackmans? Of course they did. They were their best offense against the president and DoDO because Paige had just proven that she wasn't really great at this. And neither was Ollie. Leah? Maybe.

Merry released a small sigh and turned toward her witches.

Leslie turned to Paige, looking unhappy. "Children with?"

Paige knew what she *should* say. She had no idea how bad this was going to get. She should leave all the kids there in the uncertain safety of the Eastwood home.

Safety of a murder's home with a bunch of DoDO agents "in pens" not far away?

"If we can't free the Blackmans, we might need Leah." Also, she just felt safer with Leah beside her in the dragon's den than in a house with murderers of two kinds. "You can leave Mandy here."

The firestarter gave Paige her best determined teenager look and shook her head. "If Leah's going, I'm definitely going. I'll protect her." And to emphasize her point, Mandy flared her fists with fire.

For the longest time, Paige had thought Mandy would be the strongest of Leslie's children with her pyrotechnic abilities. However, they'd discovered Tyler had the strongest abilities as a bard. "Tyler sitting this one out?"

Leslie answered with a growl.

Merry turned her attention to Paige. "These details should have been worked out previously."

Paige swallowed, not certain she had it in her. But she was starting to feel the strain of keeping the portal open for so long. She hadn't made a huge tear in the fabric of space and time, but it was enough to make her realize that she couldn't keep it open forever, even with Ollie's help.

She turned her concentration inward again, back on her magick. She flexed her witch hands and held the door open. It wanted to rise into the air. She didn't know why except that, for whatever reason, she got the sense that the door was lighter when it was higher. But it wasn't as though people could just leap through. Not one of them had wings or the ability to fly.

She dragged the door back toward the ground, with Ollie grunting beside her. It was like trying to put up a tent in a hurricane.

Leah reached out with her red-veined door magick and grabbed hold of both sides of the door, pulling it down. The door locked into place on the mirror. It stopped fighting Paige, but it was still draining energy from her.

Merry looked over at Paige and then nodded to her witches. "On the other side, we are to assist Eldora's people. If you encounter resistance, use any force necessary."

Paige opened her mouth to negate that command.

Merry stopped her with a look. "Our magick is stronger when blood is spilled."

Paige really hadn't thought that one through. In a battle or a war, Merry and her coven might just be the ultimate weapon. The more blood spilled, the stronger they became.

That wasn't entirely a comforting thought.

Merry was the first one to walk through the portal, followed by her small army.

Leslie and Mandy followed.

Then Leah looked over at Paige. "Should we go?"

"Yup." Paige wasn't entirely certain that was true. They were probably going to free the Blackmans and *they* could certainly create doors. But what happened if they were unable to free them? What if the trap was too strong? Too capable?

Her magick was calm. She had to trust in that.

Leah stepped through first and let out a startled squeak. That warned Paige that there was something she should prepare for.

When she stepped through, it was like walking through a cold shower. Not just a cold shower but a freezing one. Then, there was this sense of dizziness that slammed into her, knocking her every which way except forward. She seemed almost to get stuck.

But then, her magick came through and pushed her forward.

Her feet found ground on the other side.

Ollie followed with a grunt.

Merry and the other Eastwoods were gone. Leslie had disappeared as well. The sound of fighting was all around them.

But Mandy stayed close to Leah.

Eldora remained in her chair, but those black eyes followed Paige everywhere she went. The rest of the Black-mans remained seated as well. Why?

Paige went over to them, scanning the area with her witch vision. "What's wrong? Why aren't you getting up?"

Eldora narrowed her eyes. "What are you doing here?"

"I thought that was obvious. We're rescuing you."

Eldora looked in the direction of the portal Paige had stepped through. It was now closed, even though Paige had no idea how it closed. "You opened the door."

"Just like you taught us." Paige had the sense that something else was being said here, but she just didn't quite understand what it was. It was as if Eldora was trying to say something else, but she wasn't using her words. It was as if she was...

Was using that unspoken language of the elements and the rest of the world.

So, Paige stepped out of herself a little bit. She went to the space where her magick resided and listened to Eldora without using her ears. She listened instead with her soul.

The chairs were rigged with bombs. If any of the Blackmans left their seats for any reason, the bombs would go off and take the entire area with them. Eldora could open a portal and take the bombs away, but those bombs would go with her. Paige would need to get everyone else out of there.

Paige agreed.

"Protect Phoebe like she is your own." Eldora's voice was old and defiant.

Like she was a Whiskey? That was a rather tall order.

But it was time for Paige to grow up. The Blackmans *were* family and it was time to start acting like it.

"You will need her and she you. We are as one, and we *must* be if we are to win."

Eldora knew she wasn't coming back. She had the calmness that came with certainty.

"You sure you got this?"

Eldora nodded. "It's an old trick I used to do when younger."

What Eldora was proposing to do could wipe her out before she even made it through the door she opened. Mad respect.

And something more. Grief. She didn't *love* Eldora, but she'd started to like her, to look up to her. Paige was losing another person to look up to. "I'll take care of the rest."

Eldora smiled and closed her eyes.

A wind whipped through the area.

The other Blackman witches looked around. A few raised their voices in alarm.

A few DoDO agents shouted an alarm and ran their way.

Paige finally saw the Eastwoods. They fought with a fury and force she hadn't seen from them. Leslie swooped down with eagle claws and raked one of the agents, drawing blood for the Eastwoods to pull from. Paige raised her magick to defend. That's where *her* strength lay. Not in door magick. Not in spells.

In magickal fists.

But *only* if her magick decided to show up. Had she managed to rest up yet?

"We're going to need doors," Paige told Leah and Ollie. "Lots of them. When the Blackmans are free and the bindings of their magick are gone, tell them to open doors and get us all back home."

Leah nodded, her blue eyes wide.

Ollie stared at Eldora in confusion.

"One last thing," Eldora said softly, her voice somehow strong enough to be heard over the rush of her wind.

DoDO was almost on them. "Yeah?"

Eldora smiled. "Tell Merry to give them hell."

Paige didn't get another word of warning. Eldora's head fell back. The ropes that held her family fell away. The chair rose into the air toward a door that ripped open with a deafening roar.

The Blackmans scrambled away. Leah shouted something to Phoebe. Phoebe shouted to her family.

Paige was all fists and flying human feet against DoDO agents who came in without bullets, and thankfully the elements *did* heed Paige's call. The agents were focused on trying to recapture the Blackman witches.

A pulsing beep sounded through the chaos, sharp and distinct.

"We need to get out of here!"

Doors opened all around Paige, and her witches began disappearing.

A DoDO agent came at her, his hands filled with white lethal magick.

Paige advanced on him and caught his fist as it came down on her.

But instead of being hit with his power, it settled within her.

His eyes went wide.

She smiled fiercely and went in for the kill. Or maybe the massive wounding.

A hand grabbed her from behind and yanked her hard.

As she fell through the door, an explosion rocked her with the concussion.

The door she'd come through slammed shut.

And she landed hard on the floor.

Silence.

Cold floor.

Solid ceiling.

Paige lay there for a minute, the mage magick still flowing through her, and breathed.

Well, that could have gone worse.

23

Paige lay on the ground like a lump, willing the floor, the walls, the *planet* to stop moving. It wasn't that she was dizzy. It was simply that she had lost her sense of where *here* was.

Cool hands reached down and touched her.

Leah's magick. Her red-veined door magick settled around Paige like a weighted blanket.

But then, another set of hands found her, pressing down on her shoulders. Words were muttered into her ears that registered only as sounds. Speech was so *limiting*.

The All Mother's language filled her with knowledge of where and how and when and why, of life and death and acceptance of both, of... *so* much.

Eventually, her consciousness crammed itself into the boxes of words and her ability to understand *human* came back as though she were floating to the surface of the ocean.

She listened to those words, spoken by a female voice she didn't recognize, coming back to the human world. The world stopped rotating, and everything solidified.

She found herself staring up into Phoebe's black eyes.

Synapses fired as if the Blackman witch were downloading information into Paige's psyche. It wasn't that she *understood* what was being said, exactly. It felt more like a software update, where a necessary patch was being installed. Paige knew just enough about computers to understand that. She was the one who fixed everyone's computers when they stopped working. One would think that would be Tru, but no.

Phoebe's eyes and face left, and Paige just laid there, doing her best to keep the floor from leaving. Her only responsibility in that moment was to make sure the tile didn't float into the sky because... it could happen. Not really, but it made her feel like less of a schmuck for just lying there.

Why was she able to take the mage magick, and what was it doing to her? If she hadn't been pulled back, would she have made it? At the time, she'd felt so in control, but as soon as she'd been taken out of the battle, she'd lost herself.

This didn't make sense. She needed more information. What was happening with her magick? What was she becoming? Not a mage. She refused to believe she was becoming a mage on top of everything else because... no. Just... no. She was already a very powerful witch and shifter. If she had suddenly inherited a bunch of mage magick on top of all that, she was giving it back. She'd be giving *something* back.

But it certainly didn't feel like it was working. Her magick wasn't—It was hard to explain. But it just felt like it was out of sync with her. Like there were two different things trying to occupy the same space. She imagined this new magick was an asteroid, she a planet, and her original magick was a dinosaur waiting to be exterminated.

What would happen if this new magick killed her old magick?

Cawli growled low in the back of her mind. He gave her a mind a brush of comfort and disappeared again.

As Paige struggled to her feet, her ears started to function. Words weren't making any sense yet, but she comprehended meaning and other sounds. Shoes scuffed against the floor, people moaned in pain. Heavy sighs of frustration. That was certainly a step in the right direction.

Eventually, however, words did make sense. Merry had taken charge alongside Leslie and they were getting the Blackman witches and the wounded cared for.

How had the DoDO gotten in? That was the question. Whatever weakness they had found needed to be plugged.

However, it appeared as though that was exactly what Merry and Leslie were working on.

Irritation flared a bit that they hadn't talked to her about what to do with the wards, even though that wasn't rational. She'd been knocked out. What did she want? The world to stop until she was ready to take charge again?

No. And it wasn't as if those wards were singularly Paige's. Everyone had invested a little bit of themselves, which was the reason they were so strong. And now, with Merry and Eldora having a bit of input on the consciousness of the wards, they were almost just as much theirs as hers anyway. However, Paige had been the one to initiate them, and so she felt a sense of ownership? That probably shouldn't be what she felt, but she did.

Nobody *owned* the wards. That line of thinking went to a bad place. She had bigger things to handle and this moment just amplified that. A year ago, her top concern would have been the wards. She'd have been in Merry and

Leslie's place, trying to figure out how DoDO had gotten in to take the Blackmans.

So, what was *she* supposed to do? What was her job now? She was the "bigger problem" person. So, what was the bigger problem?

Well, they had a lot of those. Communication. Information, extraction, protection. How could they communicate with each other and the world? Who needed extraction? Who needed protection? Where would they set up protection hubs? How would they keep DoDO out?

What was the mage magick doing to her?

She really needed to make time to read those books, but... why did they have to be so *thick?*

Focusing on what she *could* handle, Paige took in a deep breath and gave Phoebe a nod of thanks.

The woman nodded back and continued her conversation with Merry.

Okay. Well, first, they needed to see if they could get networks set up so that when something like this happened, someone could help. Communication and extraction first. Set up the infrastructure. They couldn't afford to be this blind. *Reacting* would get them killed.

Paige turned to Leah. "I need you to work with Phoebe—" Who'd just lost someone in her family. Grandmother? Aunt? Paige needed to not be callous. She'd lost Alma recently, so she understood what that meant. "—to work together and see if you can make these doors a reality."

Leah's blue eyes shone with concern. "Are you okay?" she asked, her voice small. "Really okay?"

No, she wasn't. "I'll be fine, Bean. If we get word that someone needs us, we need to be able to get to them, but we may not get good location information all the time."

Leah took in a deep breath and visibly pushed her fear away.

Pride swelled in Paige's chest. She *hated* that her daughter was learning that skill, but she was so glad she was stepping up to the plate.

"Okay," Leah said. "But we need information."

Nice one. Paige held up her hand to give her daughter a high five.

Leah paused and then did a half-assed slap, confusion marring her expression.

One day, the girl might understand Paige's pride, but now she wouldn't. Probably. "I'll work on getting you information and locations. But right now, I just need to know what you can set up, how quickly you guys *can* get it set up, and what you can do to make it easier. Also, what you guys need. We might need a few doors or a lot. I don't know."

Leah nodded once and turned away to find Phoebe.

"What about me?" Ollie asked, stepping up, his hands clasped behind him.

This was so weird. "Your mom doesn't need you?"

"She might, but I think we need all door magick on deck. Don't you?"

"Probably." That certainly seemed to be the issue. "You've also got blood magick, though. You and Leah will become stronger as blood is spilled?"

Ollie nodded. "It's pretty handy in a war. We have plenty of prisoners to draw from." His normally warm eyes went cold. "That will help."

Paige didn't agree. "We're not the animals they are, so don't stoop to their level."

Ollie nodded but with a sigh that said he knew she was wrong and he was right.

"You can see how handy it's going to be setting up the

network but with your own first. You two might be taking point on difficult extractions."

Ollie's eyes softened as he silently acknowledged what Paige had done there.

Leah was her daughter, her *teenaged* daughter, and she'd just admitted to letting her to go to war.

"I'll teach her a few things about her blood magick." Ollie's voice softened. "And keep her safe."

"Please."

Troutdale could only be one hub. It could only be one destination. There had to be others.

Paige stepped out of the Eastwood magick workroom and saw *busy*. Everyone had something to do.

Everyone, that is, except for her smaller children.

Sometimes, being a mom was kind of a pain. She had bigger fish to fry, and she still needed to somehow keep track of her kids and find a way to save the world.

Leslie came up to her, both of her eyebrows raised in an expression of awe and excitement. "That was new."

It certainly had been. "Ley line magick. It affects me somehow, and I don't think I like it."

"Eldora really stayed behind?" Leslie turned toward the room, visually scanning the faces of the other Blackman witches.

Paige did the same. She recognized her half-brothers. Derrick, William, Ian, and Stephen were all accounted for and were assisting others. She didn't know any of them very well at all. They hadn't been raised together, and she had only discovered that they were even related recently. She hadn't tried to get to know them any better because Eldora had been kind of a deterrent. Paige had never trusted Eldora.

She just hoped that Phoebe would be a better coven

leader and would be someone Paige could trust because she had made Eldora a promise: treat them as she would her own.

She'd have to make good on that.

Leslie turned back to Paige. "I can take the kids from here."

Just the tone in Leslie's voice when she said that made Paige feel like she really was a horrible mom. "No. I need to figure this out. There has to be a way to do this and be a mom at the same time."

"If you were just going to work, it'd be impossible. But you're not. This is..." Leslie shook her head, her hand flopping to her side. "You don't have to be superhero mom."

Paige sighed. "If I don't, then I won't *be* a mom." Paige turned and gathered her younger children. Rai was sleeping in a medium-sized ball of fur and fluff. She made a really cute bear, but Paige found out quickly that even baby bears were heavy. She touched Rai's head and commanded her to change into something else.

She shifted into a baby fox. Kits were so much lighter.

Ember was in leopard form and pouncing on a much taller Bobby.

Bobby held his own pretty well, which should have surprised Paige, but he was almost as tall as Tyler now. Not —he really wasn't. He looked like a five-year-old maybe? A *tall* five-year-old, but he was definitely not a toddler anymore.

Whatever was going on with him was going to eventually bite her in the butt. She needed to be concerned and she was. But there were her kids and then there was the world. Which did she care for first?

Paige had to be glad the boy could carry himself.

Her stomach rumbled, reminding her she didn't

remember the last time she had actually eaten anything. She shoved her kids into the car—and realized that a five-year-old Bobby didn't *fit* into the car seat she had for him anymore, so he went without one and she just had to drive *super* carefully.

Paige took the kids back to the house—making a stop by the nearby thrift store for a car seat for Bobby—and fed them all, and then she put all three of them down for a nap. She wanted to nap as well, but she knew that was a bad idea. She didn't have the luxury.

So, instead, she called Michelle. "Have you been able to set up a communication network?"

"I'm on my way to you. Talk to you in a minute."

How long before the cell towers stopped working? Would it even matter? They didn't have power. How long before they didn't have juice to power their phones?

And, joy of joys, the Whiskey house had no water. They had a well, but it had an electric pump. And the food in her fridge was starting to get warm. They needed to find a way to save the food. Fast.

So, she called Suzanne while she still had power in her phone and asked the mayor to see what she could do about the refrigerated food. Suzanne assured her she was already on that and to have all food that needed cold storage brought to the high school.

She would give that fun chore to Margo, who would probably give it to her brother.

Paige wasn't certain what else she could do. She walked out to the back yard.

It was filled with people.

Paige wasn't certain why people sometimes gathered here, but they'd started to do so after Alma's funeral. For some reason, the Whiskey lands had become the town hub when things got bad.

She saw Danny Miller with new people and headed toward him.

He looked up at her with a frown that was quickly replaced with a slight smile. "Paige."

No time to waste on pleasantries. "How's the information network?"

Danny took in a deep breath and released it slowly. "It's not as easy as we'd like. The power is just one issue. Our internet is down all over. Cell coverage will likely be next."

That's what she'd thought. "Phones will run out of power first."

"Agreed. But even that's only a small problem. They've got—I don't know. They're deleting everything we post and share. They're erasing us from the net. The only voice being heard right now is the president's."

Fear froze in her. What... this should be impossible. They weren't in a dystopian novel. This was supposed to be *real* life. "That's not good."

"No. It's not."

"What about—" Paige hadn't always paid attention when Dexx went into his aluminum-hat tirades, but she did occasionally. "What about the dark net?"

"I'm looking into it."

Shit. That was *real?*

A mask slid over Danny's face. She recognized it all too well. When she'd been a detective, she'd had a mask of her own. "What are we doing?"

She knew he wasn't talking about the details. He wanted to know about the big idea. Were they succeeding? Were they going to war? "That hasn't been fully decided."

"And who's deciding this? You?"

Paige realized that she had to be careful what she told Danny. Yes, she trusted him. But how much of what she said could be taken out of context? She raised kids and a man, so she knew what that meant. She could *say* the words she meant out loud, but they'd be reported as they were *interpreted*, not as they were delivered. And how much did she want to admit? They had no idea what they were doing. That wasn't something the public really needed to hear.

"We're building a council of the top leaders. Leaders of each of the represented groups, paranormal and—" Oops. She needed to add the mayor or someone onto their council. "—human. And as more come in, I'm sure our counsel will grow. We want to make sure everyone's voice is heard."

"How far do you think this is going to go?"

Paige gave the reporter a frank look, the reality of their situation making her words harder. "Looks like pretty far."

Danny narrowed his eyes at her. "Well, we *have* been able to get *some* information gathered."

This was certainly news. "What do you have?"

Michelle came up to them and assessed Danny.

He barely acknowledged her. "The National Guard has been called. They've set up checkpoints along state borders. They're making sure refugees don't get past them. They're not just checking the highways. There're reports of refugees being captured everywhere. Out in the country, in fields. People are trying to shield and protect them. Those people are being rounded up *with* the paranormals."

This was bad. "Do we know where they're being taken?"

Danny shook his head.

Michelle nodded. "They're being rounded up and sent to prisons and camps, gulag style. It looks as though this has been in the works for a while. The infrastructure is already up. There were entire prisons emptied, and now they're being filled."

Paige had almost forgotten the best thing about having a dryad was that they had direct connections to trees everywhere.

She vaguely remembered hearing about private sector prisons. At the time, she really hadn't thought about it much. She'd had had bigger fish to fry like she always did.

At the time, the ruckus had been that the private sector prisons had quotas that needed to be filled. That if those quotas weren't met, the government had to pay these private owners lots of money. Millions of dollars. Trumped up charges. Stricter sentencing. People going to jail for things they didn't do, all because it was cheaper to imprison them than to let them pay taxes.

But now, they had an inrush of people being herded to these prisons.

At least that gave her a location. With the location, Paige could open a door, and they could get these people out, they could take them to safety.

That had to be something. "Do you happen to know of at least one of them?"

Michelle gave Paige a very hard look. She was pissed. "I have the locations of several. They don't know how to hide from us."

Danny frowned. "What are you?"

Right. He didn't know. "Dryad."

Danny's eyes flared. "How many of you are there?"

Michelle turned a cold hard gaze to Danny. "What are you trying to get?"

"I'm a reporter." He held up his hands. "And if we can use dryads to get the news out there, that could help us spread our network."

Michelle glanced over at Paige.

That might work better than the dark net. Paige had no idea how that worked, but if the government could control the internet, then chances were they could control the dark net too. "If you have someone you can spare, I think it's worth it."

Michelle slid her gaze elsewhere but nodded once. "I'll send someone over, but you won't sideline me."

She had addressed that last statement to Paige.

"I would never dream of it." Paige got the sense that Michelle wasn't just upset with the way the paranormals were being treated. She was also upset because her team had been hit by one of their own.

And that was something Paige was going to have to deal with as well. But, again, not right then. At that moment, they had a prison to break into. And that was exactly what Paige intended to do. But not before she handed off the baton. "Danny, talk to Tru. See if he can help get the technological infrastructure in. Then, set up with Michelle's contact. Build on what you've already got."

Danny took a step to turn away.

"And Danny?"

He stopped and turned back toward her, his expression filled with eagerness and excitement.

"Understand that what you're building here might be bigger than you anticipated." Paige wanted him to understand the full repercussions of what was going on. This wasn't just about the town of Troutdale. This wasn't just about trying to save paranormals from being abused or enslaved or incarcerated. "So, make sure the bones are good."

They were getting dangerously close to declaring war on an entire nation.

Or declaring they would enter the war that had been started for them.

The realization of their reality settled on Danny shoulders visibly. The eagerness and excitement disappeared and were replaced with cold resolve. He nodded once and left.

Paige had her own mission. She needed to see if they had the power and ability to retrieve their people. And if that was the case, then perhaps, they could take the power away from the president.

If they could do that, they might be able to blow out the fuse on this war-bomb before it exploded.

And *that* was something she was willing to do.

24

Paige invested some time reading her new books on ancient magicks. There were sooooooo many words. Wrangling children while reading wasn't helping. She also had to teach her twins that some of their favorite shapes—like the elephant—weren't necessarily great in small spaces like cars and living rooms. They'd nearly lost the TV and an entire couch.

The lamp was dead as were two side tables, and Dexx's favorite chair would never be the same again.

She had learned some "interesting" stuff about ley line magick and the creation of the three witch lines—more of them, actually. There were eight.

But more than that and all she could say was that the books were *thick,* and her twins were destructive. She still didn't know why she was able to absorb the ley line energy or why it wiped out her ability to shift.

It was time to make something happen in her drive to find a peaceful solution, which meant it was time to head into town and talk to people.

Paige had a call to make that would be better served in

person. If she was serious about getting wards around towns and communities, then she needed to speak to the Alaskan wood witches to see if they were interested in helping with the grounding trees which were pivotal to making the wards as strong as they could be.

Step one in her plan to take over the peace talks and keep the nation from imploding.

To do that, though, she needed a door, and to make that happen, she needed to make good on her promise to Eldora.

There was so much death, so many sacrifices, the "reality" was numbing. She *knew* she should be feeling something for Eldora's passing, that those emotions should be shaping her intentions and actions, but it was just one more thing on her laundry list of things to do.

Take care of Whiskey. Check.

Take care of town. Check.

Figure out what was wrong with her kids and their growing spurts. Not checked.

Find Dexx. Not checked.

Figure out how to overthrow DoDO. Super not checked.

Figure out what to make for dinner without a fridge or a stove. Not even worth a checkbox.

Take care of Blackmans. Check, check.

But she needed to make an effort and find a way *to* care, to overcome the numbness. *That* could kill those around her in a way they couldn't afford.

So, she and the kids walked past Pete's Garage in animal form with Bobby riding her horseback and was a little surprised to see all the bays open and four mechanics working. She had no idea what they were doing, but they seemed pretty excited about it.

Phoebe was doing a volunteer stint at the high school, so

that's where Paige was headed. The twins and Bobby loved it at the high school. She didn't know what it was, but they frolicked all the way up to the main office.

The receptionist just gave the twins a withering look. "No shifting outside of class."

Paige smiled at her. "They're two weeks old." Older? It seemed like one long Monday at this point.

"Hmm." The woman didn't seem receptive to changing her mind.

But Paige could understand that.

"I need to speak with Phoebe. Is she currently in a class?"

A drum sounded and a multitude of voices filled the hall.

So, without electricity and no bells, they used drums. Innovative and creative.

The twins scurried to their mother in cat form and Bobby looked around, intrigued.

Of course he did.

The receptionist told her what room Phoebe was in and then reminded her that her kids needed to be in human form if they were school.

Well, that wasn't likely to happen. Baby humans had to be carried. Baby kitties could walk.

So, Paige gave the twins an alpha warning to find a form, pick the form, and stick to it until they left the school.

They stared at each other, and then both picked baby elephants, which was great for Paige because they managed to clear a path through the meandering sea of teens.

The kids filling the hallway moved out of the way and exclaimed over the twins. A few knelt down to talk to them. They didn't have much to say to Paige except hello, but they liked the twins.

Everyone did, which was good.

She found Phoebe's classroom and waited outside. Most of the kids had cleared out, but there were two who had stayed behind discussing the class or homework.

Paige let the twins romp around, with Bobby keeping an eye on them to be sure they didn't pull a Dexx and destroy portions of the school, which was kinda weird. The boy had been two just the day before.

Phoebe looked up at Paige after the two students left. "I didn't expect you."

Time to start caring. "How are you doing?"

Phoebe frowned. "I didn't think you'd care."

"I do." Paige leaned against the chalkboard and folded her hands in front of her, careful not to fold her arms over her chest. That was the wrong impression. "I lost my grandmother a few weeks ago. I'm—" She couldn't *lie*. "You know? I'm just numb." She stared at the classroom, wondering what was *wrong* with her. Shouldn't a person like her *care*? "Grandma dying's hit me kinda hard. And—" She'd been allowed a *moment* to grieve. Maybe that's why she felt so numb. She was pushing down her fear and her grief and her worry over Dexx and her... when would she get a chance to *feel* again? "Eldora didn't realize it, but she'd started making that easier." Paige swallowed tears she didn't have time to shed. "I think."

Phoebe nodded once, her dark eyes distant. "She wasn't easy to let in."

That made Paige feel *marginally* better. "Are you a granddaughter?"

Phoebe shook her head. "I'm the strongest."

"Oh." Each coven was different. "Well, I *hope* we can build a relationship and a partnership."

"What did Eldora tell you?"

Paige met Phoebe's gaze. "To take care of you like you were my own."

"But we're not."

"Aren't you, though?" It was the truth and a heavy one at that. The Blackmans were family and a big one *and* one that belonged to her. With benefits, sure. But the weight of responsibility was greater. At least in that moment.

"You just want our door magick. You'd say anything to keep it."

They *did* need it. Paige raked her top lip with her teeth, trying to find the right words, not knowing what those might be. "I kept the Blackmans at a distance because Eldora threatened the life of my daughter and I hold grudges. She's gone and the grudge needs to go with it. You're valuable witches, but you're also family. Derrick and William and..." She suddenly forgot the names of the other two. "They're my brothers and at some point, I have to stop pretending they're not."

Phoebe sighed. "You didn't come here because you wanted to make nice."

"No. Doesn't mean I don't need to, though."

"Okay." Phoebe sat back in her chair and looked up at Paige, her expression wary, her arms open on the arms of the chair. "I'll give you a chance, but I can hold a grudge too."

"Noted. I need a favor." Paige pushed off the wall and gestured toward the door.

"With what?"

Paige knew that taking the leaders to run errands with her was a bad idea. They were needed here. But, like with Michelle, she could ask to borrow someone else. "I need a door and would prefer someone who's better at it than me."

Phoebe nodded with a deep breath. "Danger?"

"None. At least, there shouldn't be."

Phoebe grunted and held out her hand. A small door opened, and a young woman stepped through. "Angela, can you provide your Aunt Paige with a door this morning?"

Another niece. Paige shouldn't be surprised. "There and back."

"Where to?"

Paige had to take this girl in. She was a "niece" she'd never met. The girl looked a lot like Derrick, though, in the nose and eyes. At least Paige knew Derrick a little. "Cheechako, Alaska."

Angela opened her mouth in a silent "ah," and then held out her hand. "I'm going to need a pass from science lab," she said to Phoebe.

"I'll talk to Ms. Burnstein. Don't stay long. Science isn't your best subject."

The girl wrinkled her nose but nodded. She concentrated and drew the outline of an imaginary door. The portal opened and Angela motioned Paige through. "Thanks, Aunt Phoebe. Come on, let's go."

Amazingly, the twins and Bobby went through with no trouble and no wrangling.

The door closed behind Angela, and Paige was left with the stunning majesty of the Alaskan mountains and the tranquil silence of the cold, humid forest of pine and willow. They'd touched down in the parking lot that ran behind town. The park was in front of them and the back side of several of the shops were to their right. The air smelled amazing.

But the "town" was empty.

What was going on here? "So, you're Derrick's daughter?"

Angela nodded.

Good guess, but her attention was on the town. Was there danger? "Well, I'm sorry it took me so long to get to know you."

The look on Angela's face said she didn't care about Paige's "sorry."

Teenaged angst mixed with real wrongdoing was a mess Paige didn't feel like cleaning up just then. She had plenty enough on her plate. She had to assess if she'd just dumped the kids into a danger zone, but nothing set her alarms off. "This way."

She led them up a small embankment. On the way up, she talked about small stuff. How the twins were growing up and some of their escapades. And how Bobby'd nearly dumped a vase on Elder Yad's head the other day.

Angela didn't comment much, but she did seem to warm up.

A little.

Paige reminded herself that she didn't need every person—including teen people—to like her and led them to the town hall. She left them out front which was "more interesting than going inside." She just wanted the two elephants on the carless street.

Once inside, she headed to the back where Bertie's office was.

There was no one in here either.

Cheechako was a paranormal retreat. However, it was one DoDO knew about. What kind of danger were they in? Were their wards not working? She hadn't thought to check their ward tree in the park.

Bertie was in her office, though, and looked up with a smile, rolling out from behind her desk, her wheelchair gliding easily down the slight ramp. "Didn't expect to see you. Saw the big dustup at D.C. Thought you'd be busy."

"Here to check in on you, take a breather, and ask a favor."

"Sounds like a conversation best had over lunch." Bertie led the way out the building.

"The town's deserted."

"Is it, though?" Bertie wagged her dark eyebrows as she cut in front of Paige to roll down the ramp to the street. "Oh. These yours?"

Paige made quick work of introductions as they walked downhill to the diner. "The town's still operational?"

"We're in the middle of the Alaskan wilderness," Bertie said frankly. "You can bet your left tit we're operational."

That was good news.

Paige waited until they got their food and were tucking into their meal before broaching what she'd come for. "There are paranormals all over the States who need wards. And I've discovered a few things with them that could potentially help."

"Really?"

Paige filled her in on what they'd learned.

Bertie stopped eating and motioned with her bread, intrigued. "Never thought of doing that. But what do you want *us* to do?"

Paige quirked her mouth to the side, swallowing her bite of cornbread. "I want you and your coven to put up ward trees so that communities can build their own individual wards."

Bertie set her bread down. "And endanger my coven?"

Angela snorted. "We've already been kidnapped. So..."

Paige wished the girl had kept that to herself. "Can you sit this out and sleep tight at night?"

"Damn straight I can," Bertie snorted, but she dropped her thoughtful gaze to the table, her expression dark.

Saying that and meaning it were two different things, especially to someone who prided herself on protecting people. Paige knew that all too well.

It was time for full disclosure. "Look, Bertie, this isn't going to just blow over. The president's targeting us. Witches and shifters first, but *all* paranormals. She's holding our people in prisons. We know what's next. We've seen this in our history—pretty recent history at that. We're in trouble."

Bertie frowned, her expression closed.

Okay. She needed real stories. Paige had those. So, she shared them. She told Bertie about what had happened at the elven city and in Kansas. She told Bertie what the president had said and just how serious this was.

"I'm trying to find a peaceful way out of this, but I'm tired of wading through bodies. They're already waging war on us, and I can't sit by. Can you?" Being safe and pretending the world was okay were two different things.

Bertie raised her chin and then nodded once. "Well, we've known this was coming for a while." She blinked her dark gaze to the table and brought it back up to meet Paige's. "What's your plan?"

Paige used the rest of their lunch making arrangements to borrow Billie Black first and then maybe others as they got more locations. Bertie agreed, but she wasn't overly thrilled about it.

Angela had the kids under control, but she was getting antsy. "I can't miss math too. It's a big test. Science lab is one thing. Math's another. Mom will *kill* me if I mess that up."

Billie walked through the door with a rucksack slung over her shoulder, her dark hair braided out of her sharp face. "Hey. Thought I smelled fire in town."

"Funny." The last time she and Leslie had been there, DoDO had attacked and *their* little town had felt the Whiskey impact Troutdale was facing. Paige turned back to Bertie. "We need to head out, but I'll send someone with information when we have it. We're setting up a communication and extraction network. Since you have so much Alaskan wilderness, can we count you as a sanctuary point?"

"Let me think about it," Bertie said. "Keep us informed."

Paige promised to do so and prepared to leave. Angela didn't waste any time opening a door back to her high school. As soon as they were back, she disappeared to class.

It was time to hand Billie off to those who could formulate the plan.

Paige led Billie to the mayor's building, filling her in on what had happened in the short few weeks since she'd last been there.

"Damn! You've been busy," Billie said with surprise.

"You have no idea." They'd no more set foot in the door when Paige was pulled away by Bal, who had been waiting for her in the lobby.

Balnore was a Lilim, or a demigod, something Paige hadn't known in all her years growing up with him as the Giles to her Buffy. But now that she did know, things made a lot more sense.

"Hey, Bal," Paige said, already not wanting to hear why he was there. "You remember Billie, don't you?"

"I do," he said pleasantly, in a tone she knew all too well. "I am pleased to see you again."

"Same." Billie smiled pleasantly to him.

"Hold on just a sec, Bal. Got to take Billie to the mayor so they can hammer some logistics out."

She handed Billie off to Suzanne, who complained that she was the mayor of one town, not a leader of a revolution and herded the kids out.

"What's up?" Paige asked Bal, the rambunctious kids leading them down the street. They were starting to peter out and she wanted to get them home before they tanked. She didn't enjoy the idea of having to wait out their nap in town. She wanted to get back to the books and see if she might glean any other information. She needed to figure out how to make her shifting work while taking mage energy, while *everyone else* developed plans.

Balnore sighed and then touched her shoulder.

The trip back to the house felt like her stomach had been pulled through her nose and then shoved back down to her toes. She hated traveling by whatever method he used.

Rai sob-roared and Ember howl-trumpeted in discomfort.

Bobby just burped.

"Thanks, Bal." Paige tried to sound like she actually meant it.

He shrugged apologetically and then helped to get all three kids into bed.

When they were tucked in and mostly sleeping, Bal made them both tea. "The answer is that there is no answer."

Had Paige stepped into a half-finished conversation she hadn't started? "What are we talking about and what does that even mean?"

He glanced at the books with a raised eyebrow. "You'll find theories there, but no answers." He set a cup in front of her and sat down.

Someone she didn't know came running in through the

back door but wasn't interested in them at *all*. He just zoomed through house and then the bathroom door slammed shut.

"You wake the babies, you're taking them!"

"Sorry," the kid shouted back.

They were going to need to stock up on toilet paper.

Ew. And probably flush the septic.

Which—wait. They didn't have water without a pump, so how was the toilet working?

No. She didn't care. It *was* working and that's all that mattered. She just needed to accept it.

Right.

But toilet paper. She could add that to her worry list.

She was really interested to know how the—wait.

Balnore had just made tea.

With the stove.

She really *did* have electricity. She ran to her charge cord and plugged in her phone, not knowing how *long* the power would last. "Okay. Well, I need to know how to remain in the fight. We're headed toward war and whatever those mages use, it's affecting me."

"It's not—" Balnore licked his lips as the kid who'd ran to the bathroom came out.

He smiled apologetically and waved. "Hey."

Paige replied with her eyebrows.

Bal continued after the boy closed the sliding glass door. "You know that the original magick users blended the blood lines."

"I did read that." Though, it felt more like reading the *Book of Genesis*.

"Well, they were trying to create a witch powerful enough to wield both elemental and the ley line energies."

Fuck. No. "You're trying to tell me I can do that?"

"No. It can't be done unless you're... well, more than human. But I *am* telling you that you're the closest thing we've had to achieving that in a really long time."

That wasn't what Paige had wanted to hear.

"Let me give you a brief history of what happened in the previous attempts to blend the lines." Witches had gone crazy, and magick itself had seemed to "infect" the magick user. The things they'd done sounded like Doctor Moreau's Island.

"Infect?" He *had* to be kidding.

Balnore nodded, an apologetic twist to his lips as he continued. The world's history was filled with their attempts. Small disasters throughout the lands. Entire civilizations that just "disappeared" for no apparent reason.

"The two energies are not intended to mix."

She hadn't missed what he'd also said. *In humans.* "So, I can absorb the ley line energy."

"It appears so."

"But it affects my shift."

"Most likely because your shifter spirit is almost purely elemental."

"But if they're throwing it at me, what am I supposed to do?"

Balnore looked up at the ceiling as if in patience. "The previous witches capable of ley line absorption went insane. The last one devoured an entire town."

Wait. "Devoured?"

Balnore licked his lips. "There wasn't anything left of it. Ley line magicks are very powerful and very pure and are a direct connection to the earth. Mages can tap into it because they are disconnected from it, but a witch, an elemental witch, connects to the elements. The energies touch her soul. And that is what makes it so very dangerous."

So, in other words, in her attempt to save the world, she might very well...

Devour it.

Maybe the president *was* right to be afraid.

25

Paige invested the next few hours of relative peace and quiet while the kids slept to researching the books Elder Yad and Merry had brought, but Balnore was right. There were a lot of theories, but they hadn't gotten close enough to record any real facts.

But... if she could *connect* to the element earth and she could use its rawest of energy, shouldn't that be a good thing? Shouldn't she be able to use that to their advantage?

Her predecessors had gone insane and, according to their journal entries, they hadn't *thought* they were insane. So, maybe she was already suffering from something similar. What appeared like a good idea on the inside didn't from the outside.

Reading the accounts of what the witches said and how they acted sent chills down Paige's spine. She knew where those witches had been mentally. They were viewing the world —the human world—through the eyes of something much bigger, more powerful than humans could ever comprehend.

Their worries, their demands and commands, their

needs were all so small and insignificant to the wide world. These puny things were so destructive and so insignificant at the same time. The *world* didn't understand how something so minor could be so infective.

She also discovered an entry predicting how the world of humans would end, with each human devouring the masses in a continual plague of greed and hunger.

The zombie apocalypse.

She doubted seriously this was the reason the craze for zombies had spread. She figured it had something to do with the fact that people weren't stupid. They looked out at the sea of humanity and saw they generally had one thing in common—greed. And how would that greed win out? How would it play out?

An apocalypse.

Well, that was all rather riveting, but it just told her one thing.

She needed to keep *her* magick out of the ley lines. Plain and simple. Mages needed to be mages. Witches needed to be witches. And it would just be good practice not to mix the two.

Leslie came down the stairs with ruffled emotions. "Paige."

That single word shot out like a bullet. Paige got up, putting the books aside with a groan.

The great thing about living with a bunch of other people you didn't hate was that work got shared. Granted, it was bigger with all the people, but it was still done by more than one person. The sucky part of living with a bunch of people was that there were days when every little thing tended to irritate at least one person and that irritation cascaded through everyone else.

And lately, Paige had been doing a lot of little things to irritate Leslie.

Like not doing her own laundry. Or failing at dish duty. Or only making one meal a month. Little things.

Paige was due for a Leslie explosion, so she screwed on her concerned-yet-deflected face and greeted her sister.

Only to find Kammy walking behind Leslie, mostly naked.

Taller than the day before.

"What are your kids doing to mine?" Leslie stomped her booted foot from the last step and faced Paige full-on, her eyes filled with fury.

"Oh, crap." Whatever was going on with Bobby didn't stop at *just* Bobby. Her to-do list suddenly changed priorities at a high-alert level. "I don't know. I noticed it with Bobby, but we thought it was a prophet thing."

"A prophet thing?" Leslie's tone rose with both eyebrows. "The kid grows like a normal person for two years and then suddenly shoots up like a beanstalk with a giant, and you think this is a prophet thing?"

Paige didn't even understand how she'd been in the same house with Kammy and not noticed he'd grown so much in such a short time. "Did this just happen?"

"Yes."

Okay. So, if this was happening with the babies, what was going on with the other kids? She pulled out her phone and called the school. The receptionist was lovely as always —meaning she wasn't—and informed her that her kids were fine. Leslie's kids were fine. And no one was experiencing unusual growth spurts.

Okay. Well, there went that thought. "They were all sleeping together?"

Leslie nodded, her eye drooping with exhausted worry.

She turned to Kammy, having fun with the stairs he struggled with just the day before.

Paige herded the larger little boy up to the nursery.

Bobby was curled up in his toddler bed and was now almost the same size as Tyler, and the twins were the size of three-year-olds.

"This has to be proximity to the twins." A thread of terror rolled over Paige. What if there was something wrong with the twins? She'd blown it off earlier, hoping beyond hope they'd be fine, that this was just their normal. But *this* was not normal.

Leslie's angry worry melted into worry-worry. "We need to quarantine the twins."

Paige rubbed her head, not sure what to do or who to call. "I agree. The twins and I will..." Where would she take them? Where *could* she take them?

"Pea." Leslie took Paige's shoulders and thunked her forehead to Paige's. "You find a place where those two will be safe that's far away from other kids. Far away. Totally safe. And then you come back because we can't win this without you."

The full impact of the situation hit her. If she had to choose between leading a war and protecting her kids, she'd choose her kids.

Leslie knew that and was telling her she understood.

But at the same time, *her* kids wouldn't be safer if Paige hid with the twins. *Leslie* was asking her to choose her.

Fuck.

Leslie's body shook slightly. "I'll take care of Bobby and Leah."

Paige closed her eyes, trying to find the right solution to this. *Any* solution.

Leslie pulled back and gave Paige a look of solidarity.

But it really wasn't.

Paige worked on gathering the twins.

Bobby was a bundle of nerves and questions, but Leslie worked on wrestling him and Kammy into clothes from Tyler's room.

The twins were lethargic, which only fueled Paige's growing panic. She *didn't* know how to fix this. She had to carry them both around in human form. They wouldn't eat. They wouldn't help get themselves dressed. She stole clothes from Bobby and Kammy since the twins were now the same size the toddlers had been just a few days ago.

Who could she go to?

With them in human form, she needed to take a car. But her car was... she didn't know where. That was the problem with being part-time shifters. Sometimes, she needed a car to get to one place, and then she didn't on the way back.

She borrowed Leslie's and hoped they had enough gas.

She did.

She could go to the Blackmans, but they had kids.

She could to the Eastwoods, but... okay. She didn't *know* they had kids, but she was pretty sure they *probably* did. It was a big coven.

Shifters were out of the question. They *always* had kids. If they didn't have any of their own, they usually took in strays.

Dryads?

She didn't want to know if her kids would adversely affect other paranormals. Would they abnormally grow to the point that disease would infect the tree?

No. Where?

The Vaada Bhoomi. It'd be away from Paige, which she didn't like. Her emotions were so thick around the idea of "abandoning" her kids again thanks to what had happened to her before. Her mother had taken Leah for five years. The guilt was brutal, but it wasn't giving her the power of good decisions.

The best thing for her *twins* and her *other kids* was to take them where *they'd be safe,* which...*wasn't* with her. That didn't make her a bad mom.

It really didn't.

Paige continued to repeat that to herself as she drove to Cyn's house.

Cyn and Lynx came out to greet her.

Lynx was warm and inviting, his cat ears poking out with his black hair pulled back in a manbun. They exchanged pleasant smiles of greeting and then the two of them carried the twins into the massive house.

Cyn just kinda glared and held the door.

It wasn't that the woman was mean. She just really didn't like Paige.

She made a concerted effort to not "be an ass," which was the way some people saw her. She was a focused individual who sucked at small talk, but with some people, like Cyn, that was necessary.

So, in order to navigate Cyn to important things, they talked about events in town, even though each unfocused word grated on Paige's already stretched nerves.

She learned that Steve and Gary had rigged up a power system for the town and that there were sections open to the power grid. They'd already had a solar field and a wind farm nearby, but the locals had been reluctant to tie their city grid to it previously because of loopholes in legislation that no one really understood. But with those things out of the way, it was easy to get people talked into going green.

Lynx was better at dealing with Paige. He frowned at

her and interrupted Cyn with a hand on her thigh. "What's wrong?"

Paige filled them both in on what was going on with her twins.

Cyn's hand flew to her chest and her blue eyes rounded with alarm. "I'm not babysitting. I'm terrible with kids. Why bring them here?"

Paige had run this through in her mind on repeat, trying to find a solution—any solution. The only thing that made sense was to send the twins to the spirit animal plane.

She'd been warned these two were exceptionally powerful. What if the reason their little bodies were growing so much was because he animal spirits they contained were just too powerful for their tiny bodies? "I was wondering if your parents would be able to keep them in the Vaada Bhoomi until this blows over or I can find answers to what's going on."

Cyn frowned, with a different shade of alarm. "You want *my* parents to watch *your* kids in the *Vaada Bhoomi*?"

"Yes." No. Paige didn't have unfettered access to the spirit plane, so she'd have to *ask permission* to see her twins when she could spare time.

First, Dexx. Now, this?

Her heart hurt with emotions she *couldn't* allow to rule her. That, in and of itself, pissed her off. "They're half shape-shifter, so being over there with the other shifters might help stabilize their growth? Or maybe there's something in the library that might give us some information on what's going on with them."

A different kind of alarm crashed over Cyn's face. "You're afraid the growth won't stop?"

Paige stared in the face of the possible mortality of her newborn twins with uncertainty. "Yes."

Cyn slapped her palms against her thighs and stood up. "Well, that I can help with. I think. Let's see."

Cyn took Rai, who was still sleeping, and Lynx took Ember, who was blinkingly awake. They went to the bedroom and to the closet door, which served as a permanent portal. Cyn opened it and walked through like nothing.

Paige settled her resolve—she wasn't a bad mom. She wasn't—and went through.

Cyn and her dad greeted each other, and they talked about the things he'd discovered. He was busy cataloguing the many artifacts stored in this castle. The room had changed a lot since the last time Paige'd seen it. It was organized now. Things were labeled.

And it was a lot bigger, as if it grew with their needs.

They all walked through the castle to the library, which was huge. How were they going to find anyone in here?

Cyn and Arthur seemed to be well practiced at this, though. They didn't ring any bells or announce their arrival. They simply walked in and maneuvered through the stacks and stacks and stacks of books that rose toward the high ceiling and found her within minutes.

"You want us to..." Charlotte blinked her green eyes and shook her blonde head as if trying to clear the fog from her mind. "I don't understand."

"I just need to see if there's any information in here that would explain their rapid growth," Paige said as clearly as possible, her patience thin and growing thinner. "And the growth of the kids around them." She had to be with her twins, but she also needed to be with Leah and Bobby. "And to see if their lives are in danger."

"Just." Charlotte released a petulant sigh and tipped her

head with a frown at Arthur. "*And* you want us to keep the children here?"

No. Paige didn't want that at all. She wanted her twins with her. "We're at war. So, yes. Unless you think that taking them into battle would be safer while their lives and the lives of their siblings and cousins are already in danger because of this, then sure. Yeah. I'll take them with me."

Charlotte licked her lips and glanced away. "I'm sorry."

Paige gnashed her teeth together in frustration. "Sorry. I'm just—" She couldn't finish what she was about to say because the words were meaningless.

Charlotte nodded with a big breath, as if settling the weight of responsibility on her shoulders.

It was a lot for Paige to ask of practically a complete stranger. "I'm hoping they'll be safer here because of their shifter side. Their animal spirits are very strong."

"Thunderbird and rajasi," Arthur said.

"Yes." Maybe that had something to do with this? Their spirit animals needed to get their little bodies big enough to handle them? She didn't know.

I will remain here, Cawli's voice said inside her mind.

"Who is that?" Charlotte asked, spinning around.

Huh?

Paige turned, trying to figure out what Charlotte was hearing.

And saw a cat. The creature had very interesting markings, an array of dark stripes along its belly and odd spots along its back.

But those eyes? She knew those eyes. "Cawli?"

He nodded his little cat head. *I can stay here with the twins and help keep them in line.*

"Well, that would be..." Charlotte looked up at Arthur, her eyes wide. "...helpful."

"You're a cat?" Paige couldn't quite wrap her head around the fact that her big-feeling spirit animal who was so powerful was so... small. He was the same size as a large house cat.

I am. This is my first form.

Huh. Well, she could stand there and gape, or she could get on with the business of abandoning her kids.

She really had to stop saying it like that.

I agree. You are doing what is best for them. You are not abandoning them.

Arthur set Ember down and gave Paige an awkward hug.

She fought it for a moment and then accepted what he offered.

He pulled back. "We will watch over them and we keep them safe."

"And," Charlotte said, placing her hand on Paige's arm, her expression filled with caring, "we will look for an answer."

"Thank you," Paige whispered around the knot in her throat.

Then, she kissed each of her sleeping kids, tears threatening to spill out, sobs threatening to take over—

And walked away.

26

Anyone who says it's easy to walk away from their kids to go to work or save the world is a shamer. It took everything Paige had to keep on walking. Out of the castle, out of the bedroom, out of the house, and then to drive. Down the driveway. Down the road.

Back to her house.

But this *was* the best thing *for her kids*. Not for herself but for them.

Once home, she walked into a quiet house and her heart opened like a dam. She made it to her empty bedroom and sobbed like a broken thing, missing Dexx, missing her kids, missing her freakin' sister who lived in the same freakin' house but who was so busy—they both were—that they never really got to really see one another.

When was the last time they'd all just hung out?

Too long.

She came to the end of her tears and took a shower, recovering in the hot water, letting it take more than dirt and smell, allowing her sorrow to slide down the drain as well.

When she was done, she tested her shift. She felt mostly back to normal, so she chose the shape of an owl and flew to town, stopping to see Leslie. The shop was full and busy with patrons—more than was comfortable, actually—and Leslie looked pleasantly frazzled. Like this was the thing she enjoyed.

But when she looked up and saw Paige, her smile disappeared. "What happened?"

Paige shook her head and gave her sister a smile. "Nothing. I'm just stopping by to say hi."

Leslie knew better than that and her expression said so, but she didn't press the matter. "No twins."

"They're in the library."

Leslie frowned as she thought that one through and then nodded and tipped her head to the side. "I hadn't thought of that. That's probably a good way of... yeah."

Paige gestured to the store. "What are we using for currency?"

"Barter." Leslie shrugged. "When we don't have money..."

"But how are you going to get supplies?"

Leslie huffed a chuckle. "I'm going to go back to just making stuff. And by 'going back,' what I mean is doing things I've never done before."

Right? Alma might have known how to create soap from things she could make or provide herself, but Leslie had been raised by the internet. Why make or forage when she could get it with two-day free shipping?

"I have some wax coming in from the bee guy. There are eight of them here, by the way. And I'm getting some herbs from one of the plant people in town. There are a bunch of them. I'm getting blossoms from one of the orchards. I'm even getting rocks from one of the rock guys."

F.J. BLOODING

Paige hadn't realized any of those things were... things. "Sounds like this was the best thing—" She literally couldn't come up with a better word? No. "—to happen to our little town."

"Well, the special interests of people came out and became useful, that's for sure. We've also got a couple of sewing people, knitters, and crocheters, and we've got a few people who know how to *make* yarn. Spinners. They spin. And we've got someone who has sheep and some kind of ox thing that's super hairy. And we've had a request to get llamas or alpacas. I don't know what the difference between the two are, but there's a request to get some. And we have a supplier."

"Really?"

"I'm working with Phoebe on that one. Nice girl. Real sweetie." Leslie's drawl was soft and gentle. She was really in her element and having fun.

"Right? I was a little skeptical at first." It felt good to just be normal for a minute and forget.

"I don't think we'll have much of an issue letting her in." Leslie bobbed her head from side-to-side and made a circling motion with her finger to encompass the Whiskey clan? Paige was going to assume that, anyway.

"Or the brothers." Technically, they were Leslie's too, but in a step-step kind of way. They were Paige's father's *other* kids. When people were worried about breeding, sometimes the family tree looked like a jungle. Oh, what would judgy people think of them?

Judgy things. That's what.

"Riiiiight." Leslie drew the word out. "Love you?"

"Love you back." Paige gave her sister a hug.

Leslie held on a little longer. "I'm real sorry, baby sister."

"Yeah," Paige said around the tears she'd thought she'd left in the shower and melted into her sister for a moment, accepting the nonverbal support they both knew she needed.

"You gonna be okay?" Leslie asked in Paige's ear.

Paige nodded, swallowing the tears back. Where the hell was Dexx? And was he okay? Were the twins going to be fine without her? Was Bobby okay? Were these side-affects going to do him or Kammy any damage? "Always."

They parted ways and it was time to get to work.

Paige wasn't certain what was going on next, but Willow found her.

"I've coordinated the supply run. Here's the list of people who have volunteered for each."

Paige looked at the list as they walked down the middle of Main. She recognized a lot of the names. "And it's a normal supply run?"

"Yes. According to Chuck, there's minimal risk."

Said like a project manager. "Okay. When are they thinking of going?"

Willow gave her the rest of the details on that and a few other things. She got filled in again about the electricity. Things really did seem to be good there, though there were *still* a few loop holes they had to jump through, but Willow knew some contract law and a few contract lawyers and had called in a favor.

The mechanics at the garage were working on enhancing the cars so they wouldn't need gasoline since they weren't certain they could get any of that. Willow had been unable to trade for gas so far and she said it didn't look promising. She just didn't have the right contacts.

Which was okay. They'd survive.

They made it to the corner Paige needed to turn to head

to Red Star when Willow stopped her. "Chuck has information he wants to share with you."

That sounded serious.

Willow pursed her full lips and licked them with a frown. "I know you want to do something, but..." She paused, running her bottom teeth along her top as she thought. "Do what's *right,* not just what feels right."

"And what do *you* think that is?"

Willow sucked in her lips for a moment and shrugged. "You know, *this* we can manage. You do something..." Her lips worked as if forming words she shouldn't speak. She met Paige's gaze, her eyes filled with worry.

Paige nodded at her, silently telling her it was okay to voice her opinion.

Willow gave a oh-well-it's-not-like-I'm-getting-paid-anyway look. "He's found one of the prisons and they're planning to invade it."

That *sounded* like something Paige would *want* to do.

"But if you guys *do* that, then all of this? All that I'm doing? It's done. We'll be at *war* and I..." Willow quirked her lips and shrugged deeply. "I don't know I can save us through *that.*"

Paige took in a deep breath and looked away, chewing on Willow's opinion. It was sound council. "So, Chuck's, huh?"

Willow nodded, her expression softening slightly. "Mayor's office. You'll at least think about it?"

"Yeah," Paige said with a sigh. "Keep up the good work."

Paige walked into a town leadership meeting. She knew most everyone there, though there were a few new faces. Danny Miller and another young man who was introduced as a dryad, Harrison Walker. He didn't go by Harry.

Which... you know, was good information. He was *really* adamant about it.

The dryads *had* found one location where paranormals were being held, but their chances weren't good, and not everyone fully understood it. They'd watched a little too much TV.

"It's a prison," Paige said to the group. "This isn't like TV, where the inmates can just pop off the covers of their lights or bust into the plumbing of their toilets or sinks so they could make a witty escape. It's designed to keep people in, which also means it's designed to keep people out. This won't be easy, and if you get locked in, we might not be able to get you back out."

Chuck narrowed his pale blue eyes. "So, you believe we should sit this out?"

She really wished Willow *hadn't* sounded so damn realistic. "We just need to come up with more contingency plans because there are more ways this can go wrong than right."

Their plan relied heavily on the Blackman witches and Paige being able to do magick.

Which would go badly if they had magick suppressors like they'd had at the White House.

Right now, the plan was for Paige to go for the door controls and see if she could assist there, but she had no way of knowing the layout of this particular detention facility.

It was a *prison*, not a country club.

So, with all their plans and secondary plans in place, it was up to her if they were going in or not.

They'd put it to a vote, and it was split almost down the middle, with the winning side to go.

Going to the elven city was one thing. Standing up to an invading force in Kansas was one thing. But this?

They'd be the invaders. This would be a declaration of war and was a decision that couldn't be taken lightly.

As everyone talked amongst themselves, Paige tossed it around inside her head.

Chuck met her gaze from across the table, not offering judgement, just giving her support.

The *president* had authorized the invasion of cities. She'd allowed troops to storm homes and take families from their beds. She'd allowed agents to shoot *children* as they fled to safety.

The declaration of war had already been issued.

Finally, she nodded.

Chuck rapped his knuckles on the table and started issuing commands.

Those who weren't in favor weren't a hundred percent *against* it. They simply weren't comfortable with the consequences of these actions, and that was something Paige understood all too well.

With the plan in place, it was time to gather the troops, which really just meant that everyone went and said their good-byes.

Paige didn't.

Her people were either mired in the trenches of helping everyone or were goddess knew where because she didn't.

Chuck found her standing at the balcony of the mayor's office. It wasn't *much* of a balcony and probably wasn't designed for a *person* to stand on it. It was tiny, not even wide enough for a chair. She didn't understand it and didn't know why a *door* opened to it.

But she also didn't have anything else to do, and it was her one and only quiet moment for... well, since two days after the twins were born, when she and Dexx had been quietly napping on the couch.

She wasn't thinking, wasn't worrying, wasn't dreaming, or worrying, or anything else. She just let her mind... go.

Chuck stood silently beside her.

Which, of course, made her brain jump into high gear because maybe she was supposed to *be* thinking something at that moment. Like all the alternative plans for when things went wrong because things *were going* to go wrong. They were breaking into a *prison*.

Were they *insane?*

"You won't always have the answers."

She had a feeling he was trying to tell her things would be okay, that she wouldn't completely fuck this up as a leader. That statement did absolutely nothing for her.

"Trust in your instincts and in your people. As an alpha, you are only as strong as your pack."

Which was strange to hear because everyone seemed to have this opinion that alphas were only as strong as their dickish personality presented them to be. "Well, then, I'd say we're pretty strong." But strong enough?

She had to hope so. After all, they had ... she forgot how many actual people, but there were people in the plural who liked bees, plants, and rocks. And those were the odd ones. They also had amazingly discovered a way to bring power to a community that had been shut off from it. They had people who could and would get the news out when it was being suppressed. There were people able to take care of the kids while others fought and died. There were cooks and healers.

Really smart and talented people.

And some pretty powerful fighters. Yeah, they had those. And some incredibly powerful witches.

So, yeah. Hopefully, they were strong enough.

"This could be the tipping point."

Of what? Paige didn't know much about war. She'd never read Sun Tzu, never even really wanted to. She might have to, though. She didn't want to be the weakest link in their line of defense, and ignorance was *not* a strength, no matter what anyone chose to believe.

But she did know they were nowhere close to a tipping point. Things were just going to get worse from here on out.

What was her point? What was *she* looking for? When would *she* know they were getting close to a tipping point?

When she saw how far the president was willing to go.

Like with a child throwing a tantrum, Paige knew she had to push back. And when the toddler—the president of the frelling United States—pushed back, she'd have to push harder and harder and harder until she discovered where the president would stop. Where were *her* lines in the sand?

Only then would they have a definition to this war.

But more than that, she had to see how far her pack—all these paranormals who followed her—would go. What were *their* lines? How far would be too far for *them*?

Because that would define this war as well.

How far was *Paige* willing to go? Looking at Merry Eastwood and how Paige had been so upset and angry at her for freely walking the streets after murdering people for magick, and now Paige was okay with just working with her to the point she was actually growing a little respect for the woman? She had to question herself. She was changing. Her morals were bending. Too far?

They would find out soon enough. It wouldn't just be Paige who would know. Everyone who followed her would as well, and that terrified her.

What was she *thinking*?

"All true leaders worry."

Well, that one was helpful at least. "You don't show it."

"That does not mean I don't."

Those quiet words settled Paige's nerves a little. "Do you ever get scared?"

He nodded quietly and clasped his hands behind his back.

People were gathering in the street below them. It was time.

"Do you remember when your family came to us?"

She remembered Chuck's "welcome wagon" all too well. Dexx'd been driving. She'd been napping for the first time in, well, a while, and he'd lost control of his shift, only to be overrun by shifters. "Yeah."

"I was scared *then*."

She and Dexx had been two terrible unknowns at the time, new to the world of shapeshifters. Dexx was this powerful saber-toothed cat and no one knew what to make of Paige. "We were a danger you couldn't know."

"No." Chuck turned to her, his blue eyes hopeful, his lips pinched and frank. "I was scared of the world you two would open for us. I was scared of the change you would bring. Good or bad, the time of change is always the hardest, getting people to see the potential of how great or how bad a thing could become. Change is always met with fear and ferocity."

She'd been so naïve then. She almost wished she could go back. At least then, she had people she could look up to, people she could bring her problems to when they became too big.

"We will be okay." He gripped her shoulders firmly, giving her an alpha push. "And we *will* weather this."

This time, however, his alpha push wasn't as *her* high alpha. It was simply the push of a *fellow* alpha. She swallowed. "But will we weather it *well*?"

"No matter what you do today or tomorrow, no matter how you fail or succeed, those who survive will find a way to do so as well as they can."

"In jails?"

"If they must."

It wasn't great information, but it was helpful, staring into his blue eyes as they leveled the world of worry into a large and mostly flat playing field. People were survivors. At the end of the day, she could fall on that. "Thank you."

He nodded and released her, disappearing back into the mayor's office.

Paige took in one more deep breath and held it for a moment, surveying the town.

As a leader, she'd kinda failed to protect this town once.

But the people of this town had proven they were capable of surviving.

She went downstairs and into the street, locating her Blackman witch—Bonnie. Well, there were several, but Bonnie was the one who was leading the other Blackmans this time. "Let's see what we can do."

Bonnie didn't wait for further instructions. She opened a door, and Paige stepped through.

To just outside the walls of the prison.

There was nowhere to hide, and it was dusk, so, Paige threw up her hands and called on a small duststorm to hide them as that was really the only thing around—dust, pale dirt, and low shrubs. Great place for a prison.

The rest of the people came through and the door closed.

Paige had been able to pull up one picture of the place. Only one, from a high angle.

Three main cell blocks surrounded a central hub, but which ones contained paranormals?

She visually scanned to see if she could locate dampening fields.

None that she could immediately see.

It was time. "Can you get us into that cell block?"

Bonnie nodded.

Paige knew that, once inside, there wasn't going to be a place to hide. They'd appear right in the middle of the room —if they were lucky—and would be immediately exposed.

But that would tell her whether she was able to use her magick or not.

Bonnie opened the door, and she stepped through.

Into the "common room" of a large cell block. She powered up her witch hands.

And they answered. She stepped back through, and the door closed, everyone looking at her expectantly.

"I have magick."

That was all they needed. Doors opened up all around her.

The fight was on.

27

B reaking into or out of a prison isn't easy. They were
designed with hundreds of years of experience
taken into account. Doors wouldn't magically
open. Alarms would easily be set off. One wrong move
could be catastrophic.

Paige was the only one with law enforcement experience, though she did not have much detention center experience. She had never been on prisoner escort duty. She
couldn't even say if this was a normal prison facility or if it
had specifically been designed to house supernatural
people.

Paige and her team managed to gain entrance into cell-
block A, take control of the command area, and there were
no alarms raised.

However, they quickly found their first obstacle within
moments of having done so.

With the guards contained, Paige and her team went
into the actual cellblock. There, several of the incarcerated
supernatural people were already mingling, trying to figure

out what was going on and what they needed to do in order to assist.

One of the women came up to Paige, her expression grim. "The collars are set to explode as soon as we leave the premises. We cannot leave with these on."

Well, Paige had known this wouldn't be easy. DoDO had to know that Paige and her people would make an attempt to free the wrongly incarcerated supernatural people. However, they would have no idea which one she planned to hit.

She also knew that, after this, there would be new measures put into place to make it harder. So, they had to make this count. "My daughter was able to open the collars using her lightning ability."

"Great," someone said from further back in the cell-block. "Where is she?"

From his tone, Paige got the distinct impression he was irritated with her for not bringing the solution to their problem. She could understand that. However... "I decided to keep my newborn baby out of prison and away from battle." She wasn't going to allow people to get upset with her for protecting her children. "Anyone *else* with electrical abilities?"

Another woman pushed her way to the front of the crowd, her grey uniform ripped in several places. She sported a black eye and several other bruises and abrasions. "Lydia has lightning abilities."

That was great news. Paige really didn't want to open a door to the library and bring her daughter into the prison. "Where do we find her?"

She got a few different reports about a secret portion of the prison where the more powerful people had been taken.

There were rumors that these people were being experimented on and tortured.

Paige knew that it would be pretty easy to come up with these allegations. After all, they were incarcerated and were probably being treated poorly. By the looks of things, each of them had been beaten or tormented in their own way. Several looked as though they had lost considerable weight since they had been placed there.

Paige went up to the command center on the second floor—if one could call it a second floor. The ceilings were low, making the entire area feel constricted. However, from here, she had a full view of the entire cellblock without the benefit or necessity of any TVs and cameras.

One of the guards, Mike, offered to show her how to open the cell doors without raising the alarm.

"Traitor," one of the other guards spat.

Mike ignored him, pushed a button, and led them out of the command center. He took them down several wide, empty, uncluttered halls. They passed several double doors until they located one single door that had no name to distinguish it from the rest.

He turned to Paige. "Brace yourself. This is the only reason I'm helping you. I think we've gone too far."

Paige had some idea of what to expect. She wasn't completely dumb to this situation. She'd been in bad situations with terrible people before.

There was a big, open space with several beds that had been segregated off by blue rolling curtained walls. Each compartment contained a bed or a chair. Each of those held a person who was tied down.

Each person was also hooked up to several pieces of medical equipment, monitoring their vitals.

However, no scientists were currently there.

That was certainly a red flag. Paige knew it shouldn't be this easy. For all that they had experienced a few scuffles, things were going a little too smoothly for her comfort. Something was about to happen. She just needed to know what.

She turned to the woman who had given her Lydia's name. "Where is she?"

The woman searched, scanning each of the faces. She shook her head, her eyes filling with tears. "She isn't here."

Paige scanned the area for another door. "Do you know of another way out of here?" she asked Mike.

He shook his head. "Honestly, this is as far as I've ever come."

"Let's free these people and see if we can find another way out of here." Paige went to the person closest to her—a man tied to a chair with sticks poking out of his fingertips. That was a form of torture that made her stomach queasy. "Do you know of another way out of here?"

As soon as one of his hands was free, he worked to pull the sticks out of his fingers, his face filling with pain and the monitor raising a few alarms of their own. He jerked his head toward the back. "They have a bunker. Heard them talking about it. It's well-fortified, or so they say."

But how fortified? She had a lot at her disposal. A lot of power. A lot of people.

She went to the back and searched for the door. She located it fairly easily. It was, of course locked, but there were no magical protections around it. At least none that she could see. She switched to witch vision and then to shifter vision. But still, she could see nothing.

If this was merely a physical door, she should be able to take it down.

The tortured man stood beside her, his fingers bleeding,

but there were new things poking out of them. It looked a little like metallic claws. "I call dibs."

Great. They also had mutants. "Let's see if I can break in first."

She touched the door and felt it with her earth magick to see if there was anything special with the door. Just metal. She didn't even have to call on the other elements. She simply worked the hinges and the lock, humming them into different vibrations and frequencies, moving them the way she wanted. The pins of the hinges rose on the other side of the door, and the lock slipped out of place.

The door fell into the room.

Several people in lab coats jumped, releasing various sounds of startlement.

All of them except for one. He was cool as a cucumber, with the face of a snake, and he held a gun to a woman's head.

The woman was strapped to a chair, with iron cuffs and a metallic crown of thorns.

The woman who had alerted Paige about Lydia stepped into the room with a choked sob.

"Jill, don't," the crowned woman said.

Well, at least now Paige had a name to go with the woman's face. Not that she was likely to remember it for very long. "Let her go." Paige didn't release control of her magick. She kept it coiled within the center of her soul. She wasn't sure what she intended to do with it, but she did know that, whatever she attempted to do, she would not be faster than a speeding bullet, especially when the barrel was right next to the woman's head.

The man sneered his ugly face. "You played right into our hands. You gave us everything we needed."

A chill swept down her spine, but it *was* confirmation of

what she'd feared. "Care to share with the class what you have planned?"

"We're going to allow you to leave." The ugly man sneered. "Take the ones you already have and simply walk out."

"Okay." Paige clapped her hands and smiled happily at him. "Thank you so much."

He frowned.

That's right, motherfucker. "Yeah, I know. The collars go boom. That's the reason we're *here*. You know and I know that electricity is capable of disengaging the collar. And that's the reason you're holding Lydia hostage. Now, be a good villain and let her go so that you can live to see another day."

He gave her a disgusted look. "You think *I'm* the villain? *You're* the villains. You and these mutant powers. You threaten our every way of life."

"Oh, yeah. I can totally see that. We've been keeping you from going to work every day or buying your groceries or paying your rent or watching as much binge-worthy TV as you possibly can in one afternoon. We've been such an abominable threat for the past—oh, I don't know—thousands of years? We haven't been the ones killing people in the name of gods. We haven't been the ones dropping bombs on entire cities. We've just been sitting around licking our buttholes—because that's what shifters do in shifter form. They lick their buttholes—while living pretty unremarkable lives so we can stay under the radar so that people like you don't get afraid because we're living next to you."

He appeared taken off-guard.

Paige took a step closer as she spoke. She didn't know how she was going to get him to remove the gun from

Lydia's head. But this woman was their surest way of getting out of there. At least, their surest way of determining what the next trap would be. The first one was obviously the collars, but what did DoDO have planned after that? "You haven't had to live in fear of being raped or murdered. Maybe an occasional bite? Sure. But that's no different than the average human killer. It's not like we're taking our guns and shooting schools and grocery stores and churches. What exactly are *we* scared of?"

The man narrowed his eyes. "Don't come any further."

His hand shook on the pistol grip. And his finger was on the trigger. That wasn't good.

"Are you scared that we're going to eradicate humans from the face of the planet? Are you scared that we're going to imprison you? Or strip away your rights? Perhaps, we'll treat you like the cattle you apparently are. We'll have fields of humans ripe for the slaughter. For vampires or were-wolves who love human livers." She wasn't even sure if werewolves liked livers.

He pulled the gun away from Lydia's head and pointed it at Paige. "I said stop moving."

At least he had it pointed away from Lydia. That was something she could work with.

She raised her witch hand and knocked the gun away.

However, as soon as her magick hand began to move, he pulled the trigger. Time moved in slow motion. She saw the bullet coming toward her. In this small space, he really didn't have to aim. She tried to dodge, but she didn't have superhuman speed. The only reason she was able to slow this down was because she knew in that moment this was her last breath.

A dark cloud of smoke appeared in front of her and before it formed into a familiar face. The doctor was knocked to the ground and the bullet was shoved toward the ceiling.

Time sped back up again to the sound of people screaming. They weren't true screams. They were just short bursts of exclamation. Also, it was a little hard to hear over the ringing in her ears. Gunshots and small spaces were *loud*.

Bal looked at her like she was stupid and just shook his head. His lips moved, but she couldn't hear him over the ringing in her ears.

She and a few of the other people behind her moved to secure the scientists and free Lydia.

Jill came forward and knelt beside the crowned woman, removing the metallic devices.

Slowly, Paige regained her ability to hear what people were saying. She pushed her way out of the bunker with Balnore by her side. Her demigod protector was handy, but if they were being recorded, she didn't want the president knowing about him. She wanted him to be her secret weapon for as long as she could keep it that way. "We're being recorded."

"It's not being transmitted," he said, his low timber voice breaking through the ringing.

That was good news. "Then, we need to destroy the video. They can't know what we're capable of. If they do, we ruin any chance we have of saving anyone else."

Bal nodded, his eyes going icy. "I'll take care of it."

Paige herded everyone else into Cell Block B, which was apparently the largest of the three.

Lydia said she had enough charge to send a cascading lightning bolt through everyone's collars, disabling all of them.

And she did, but it was such an explosion that it also hit several of the people, including Paige.

The ringing in her ears wasn't the only thing she had to worry about now. One of the bolts of electricity had hit her squarely in her chest, and she was having a hard time breathing.

She turned to one of the Blackman witches and nodded. It was time, but she held up one finger. They needed to test drive this with one door and one person to see if there were any other booby traps.

The woman nodded and opened a door.

Paige reached for the first available person, not caring who it was. She asked him if he was okay going through.

He didn't answer. He just jumped through the door.

Paige sighed heavily, glad she was able to take in a deep breath, even though it hurt a little, and poked her head through. He seemed to be okay. "Make sure he's not bugged," she said to one of the people there.

One of the Eastwood witches stepped up and did a sweep with her hands while Tuck used a police-issued wand.

He nodded and mouthed something she couldn't read because his mustache and beard hid his lips.

"He's clean?"

He nodded again.

Great. She stepped back into the prison, raised a hand, and made a circling gesture. "We're clear."

With that, the Blackmans opened several doors, and the inmates streamed through.

The captured guards and scientists who were bound were led to the doors.

Paige stopped Margo. "What are we doing?"

"Taking them with us." Margo's words were like arrows piercing the ringing in Paige's ears. "We're not leaving them behind."

"Our resources are already stretched."

Margo shrugged, her scar pinching her eye. "I'm okay with killing them. Are you?"

Paige wasn't.

Margo raised a dark eyebrow and proceeded to guide her captured scientist through the door closest to her.

Bal appeared beside her. "We need to leave quickly."

"What did you do?"

He gave her an expectant look. "We're destroying the evidence."

"By?"

He gave her a grim smile and pushed her toward the closest door.

As explosions sounded.

"Quickly, now," he told the witches holding the door.

The door sealed behind the last witch as the jail exploded into a fiery ruin.

28

That had certainly gone better than Paige had expected. What did that say about this war? About the president? About her? Was the president weak? Were Paige and her people strong?

Paige's brain kicked into work mode by the time she made it back to town, and she was grateful she didn't have to worry about lugging the twins around, even though that didn't stop her from worrying about their excessive growth. She just had too much to do. There were a lot of people to check in on and to make sure were okay.

Paige needed to be frank with herself. She could *hope* they'd find a peaceful solution, but the fact of the matter was that the president was obviously not interested. Did Paige really need more proof?

No. She didn't. They *were* at war.

She helped get the ex-prisoners a place to stay. The town was running low on easy places to put people.

It wasn't that they were running out of houses or rooms to put them. They were running out of houses and apartments to give people without sharing. The newcomers didn't seem to mind, as long as it was a house and they had some semblance of freedom.

"Willow," Paige called from the mayor's conference room.

"Yeah?" Willow asked, walking in with a stack of paperwork.

"Can you see if we have a caseworker of some sort? We need someone who can help everyone assimilate the best, deal with things they need help with, show them resources."

"On it." Willow frowned and handed her one of the files. "We do have a bit of a situation, though. Some of the people you freed had kids who were taken from them."

Of course they did. How was Paige going to find them and get them returned?

The dryads? They'd been able to find the prisons. "Let me make a few calls."

Willow nodded and disappeared, leaving the folder with names and contact information—their new addresses because none of them had phones.

So, Paige devoted a considerable bit of time working with the dryads to see what they could do to find a location on a site that held the kids. Paige was a failed mother who'd had her daughter taken from her, and she knew that was one reason she reacted the way she did about her kids, why she'd ignored Dexx's request to leave the kids in Troutdale. As the person who'd lost her kids, she couldn't stand by and let these people lose theirs too.

The dryads were still working on that when Paige was hit with a wave of fatigue. She needed to go home and see her own kids.

Paige and Leslie spent the night with the kids, but there was a note of worry that ate at Paige and didn't let her sleep. She wanted to know how the twins were doing, and she knew that the newly freed parents were probably crazy with worry over their own kids' location and safety as well. She felt guilty being with Bobby and Leah while they still had no idea where the other kids were and if they were okay.

The next morning, Leah was full of ideas, and Paige couldn't get that girl to settle down or complete a thought, so she took her kids into town with her.

She shifted into a bear because Bobby said he wanted to ride a bear. Horses were faster, but she preferred the bear to the horse anyway. The eyes were in the right place.

Everyone was pretty used to seeing bears by now, so there weren't any freak-outs.

She made it to the mayor's building and shifted, letting both kids slide down her back. She was probably going to be a horse next time, to see if that worked better. She almost wished she could shift into a dragon. That would be neat, but try as she might, she couldn't quite make that one work. She could turn into dinosaurs, but not into a unicorn, Pegasus, or a dragon. Why was that?

There were only three parents inside the mayor's building when she arrived, and they seemed to be keeping their shit together pretty well.

Suzanne looked at her and smiled, standing up from her chair to greet her. "We have a lead on the missing children."

Oh, thank the Mother. "That's excellent news. Where? What do we need to do to get them back?"

Suzanne's smile widened, and her shoulders sagged with relief. "Let me fill you in."

The kids were being held at yet another detention facility. However, this one was in Portland.

Really. Had the president planned that?

Paige invested the next several hours discussing options to get them out. Their sources had mentioned a secret weapon, but they had no idea what that might be. Paige certainly wasn't looking forward to finding out.

They nearly had a plan of attack when Tuck showed up, a bit more ruffled than normal and looking concerned.

"What's wrong now?"

She couldn't see his lips as they hid behind his salt-and-pepper mustache and growing beard. But the rest of his face was pinched and nervous. "I just received word that the president is coming here."

Was this a win? "Any word as to why?" Paige knew why. "Dumb question. Sorry."

Tuck waved her off.

Paige turned to the mayor. "You're our leader."

Suzanne just shook her head wildly, her eyes wide. "Not on this, I'm not. That's you. I'll continue finding homes for everyone. But this mess is all yours." She clapped her hands as if that settled it.

Well, it kind of did.

"Come on, kid," Tuck said gruffly. "Let's get some things hammered out."

Paige followed Tuck to his old beat-up Ford truck and got in.

"Heard about Dexx."

Since Dexx worked for him, she certainly hoped he'd heard.

"I'm sure he'll be okay."

He *had* to be okay. "I hope so." But, frankly, no one was going to know that until he actually made it home. "After all, it *is* Dexx."

Tuck grunted as he turned right, heading toward the highway. "That won't necessarily make things any better for him."

Paige fully understood that Dexx was a stubborn man

and that, sometimes, his stubborn personality could seriously get the better of him. But she was still hopeful that his good sense would prevail and also his stubbornness would remain. She didn't understand how DoDO had managed to get him. One day, she was going to get her answers. She wasn't certain the world would remain standing when she did. "Where are we meeting her?"

"At the roadblock."

That seemed weird.

He gave her a sideways glance and then shook his head. "We're in a whole new world here, kid. She's treating us as if we're invaders." He gave her a helpless shrug. "I got *no* idea what to do here."

What did that even mean for them? Were there new rules that she needed to know? Things that would bite her in the butt later?

She was certain there were. The president wasn't doing things this way without a reason.

They spent the rest of their time discussing small things like the weather while they waited. Tuck wasn't much of a feelings guy, and Paige wasn't much of a small talker. So, their conversation was a little stilted. However, Tuck was still one of those people she enjoyed being around. His wealth of experience in most things law enforcement was a reassurance to her. In these areas, she didn't have to be the expert.

Was there a class in government she could take? With all the online classes available, she was sure there was, and she was going to invest some time to learn because she couldn't remain this dumb...or naïve or whatever term she wanted to use. If she was going to become a world leader—she nearly choked on her own spit with that thought—then she needed to know how the world worked. She needed to *be* an expert somewhere in this.

"The trick is," Tuck said, leaning against his truck with his arms folded in front of him, staring daggers at the DoDO agents on the other side of the exit sign, "most of us are doing the exact same thing—pretending we know what we're talkin' about and hoping no one catches on."

She realized he was trying to make her feel better. However, he didn't. What she wanted was for someone to have answers. And what he was saying was that no one did. "If the president wants to talk, we'll go to the Whiskey house."

Tuck nodded. "Good call."

It was the best way to keep the president away from downtown, so, Paige *hoped* it was a good idea. "Hopefully, she wants to talk."

Tuck grunted.

The president's motorcade came down the highway and pulled to the edge of the road as it reached the off-ramp. It was time to put this show on the road.

The president's vehicle came to a stop, and several security personnel poured out, with their sunglasses on and their earpieces in, making it quite clear that they were there to protect and serve.

Paige and Tuck stayed out of their way. It wasn't their intention to restrict their ability to do their job. They just wanted to protect their town and save as many paranormals as they could.

For the first time since this started, Paige was laser focused.

The president got out and walked down the off-ramp.

Paige and Tuck met her halfway.

The president raised her chin. "Do you have somewhere we could talk?"

"My place. I'm flying ahead to make sure we don't have any surprises."

"Like?" the president asked, her interest piqued. But not in a good way. It was like she was hoping to find ammunition to use in her campaign.

"Like kids, Madame President. They like to hang out, and I need to make sure we aren't going to be interrupted by a ton of freakin' kids."

"Who should be in school."

"Except that school has let out for the day." Which it had. Only just barely.

The president gave her a cool look. "Your phones work, don't they?"

The tone in the president's voice hinted at a rub-in, like she wanted to remind Paige they couldn't power up their phones. Of course, Paige could totally be misinterpreting that, but she felt it. "They do," Paige said, not wanting to give the president any room to ask her to join her on the ride. "But kids don't carry them. At least, not here. Most of us don't have that kind of money, especially now that all income has been cut off."

The president smiled. It was a flicker of one, like she was glad and then reminded herself not to show it.

"Just follow the sheriff." Paige didn't wait. She changed into an owl and launched herself into the sky.

But halfway through, she realized she needed to fly faster and give the townspeople the heads up. So, she shifted into a white-throated needletail, which flew considerably faster. She then changed into a peregrine falcon for the dive, shifting into human form as soon as her feet touched the small balcony.

Suzanne jumped as Paige appeared, interrupting another meeting with more distraught parents.

Bobby sat quietly in one of the extra chairs in the office.

"Paige, I thought—"

"No time. Just keep everyone here. I'll be back for the mission as soon as I can." And then she was off again before Suzanne could do much more than sputter. Paige did, however, blow a kiss to Bobby and told him to behave.

He shot her a grin and winked.

She didn't know him well enough to know if he was saying he'd be good or that he'd be good at finding trouble.

Tuck was driving the speed limit, thankfully, which bought her a little time. He'd probably done that to *give* her the time to warn people. But that also gave the president an opportunity to see what they were doing with the town, which wasn't exactly what Paige could call a bonus.

She made it to the house in time to clear everyone out, enlist the pack to keep an eye on the perimeter, and start the coffee pot—the big one, not the single serve—by the time the president arrived.

Secret service went through her house and did a quick sweep, coming up empty.

The president walked in as the coffee pot gurgled and glugged, saying it was done.

"Coffee? Cups are here. Sugar's here. Milk's in the fridge."

"Creamer?" the president asked, with a pleasant enough smile, setting herself to the task of making her own cup.

With that all squared away, Paige invited the president of the United States to sit at her kitchen table. "What do you want?"

"Right to the heart of it, I see." The president winced.

F.J. BLOODING

"Well, if you want it that way, I happen to know you broke into one of our camps and released several criminals."

The president's tone suggested that Paige was, indeed, in a lot of trouble and needed to be on the defensive. And if Paige and the paranormals were treated like citizens of the U.S., then, maybe she would, but Paige wasn't afraid of the repercussions because... they were already criminals. For having been born or turned or whatever. "I didn't release criminals. The paranormal in that facility were illegally detained."

The president's gaze was cool. "They resisted registration."

"Which isn't even legal. So, that's what we can expect? We've been living here just fine for generations, but now, all of a sudden, we'll be criminals if we don't volunteer to be collared?" Paige frowned at her, shaking her head. "Don't you see the parallels here? We're repeating history. It didn't work for Hitler and the Jews. It didn't work for the U.S. and the Japanese. It's not going to work here, either."

"Paranormals *are* the enemy."

"The only crime most of us have committed is having been born. Racism is the same, except now you're adding jail time."

"Except we're not talking about the color of your skin. We're talking about teeth and claws and magick."

"So, dentures, manicures, and mood swings."

The president tipped her head to the side, with a Mom-glare.

"I'm just trying to shine a light on the reality of your argument." Paige *understood* the fear but didn't want it to gain ground. It was still baseless. "Why the vendetta? What makes this personal to you? Something to do with your daughter?"

The president set her coffee cup down on the table, and her expression closed.

Well, that one hit close to home. "Was she bitten? Turned?"

"I was raped," the president blurted.

Not surprising. Paige worked law enforcement. She had a pretty good understanding of just how many women were raped in America. "By a paranormal?"

The president nodded. "A shapeshifter. When she was born, I didn't know what to do with her. I was ashamed, but I kept her. I loved her. But then she shifted."

This was a story Paige thought would be more common than it was, having the adopted kid shift in the middle of a birthday party or something.

"I took the matter to the pack, and my rapist wasn't brought before a court. Their leader 'dealt with it,' and then, when I made a big display about it, they filed to take my daughter. And won. I learned years later that they won because the judge was also a shifter."

That surprised Paige a little because, if that was the case, the two of them had a lot more in common. They'd both lost their daughter to people using connections against them. "Hmm. So, you want more justice? You think he got off easy?" She didn't get the feeling that the president was *too* broken up about having lost her daughter. It was more like she was upset over the *idea* of having lost her daughter, which just irritated Paige more.

"Your kind needs to operate inside the law."

Paige didn't know how best to verbally take this argument. "Well, I can tell you that the pack probably did handle it. They're usually pretty tough on rapists. And the alpha handled the situation so that the public didn't get wind of it and turn it into... this. So, I can't fault him for that."

The president narrowed her eyes.

"Look at it from our side, Madame President," Paige said, trying one more time to get through to her. "Your kind are really good only at being scared."

The president narrowed her eyes. "Be careful what you say next."

"Why? Because we might be declaring *more* war on each other? You might threaten to incarcerate *more* of our people, shut off *more* towns? And I'll threaten to *save* more of my people? I mean, come on. We could do this all day."

The president took in a deep breath. "I'm offering peace."

Well, now. Paige wanted to hear the details on what her version of "peace" looked like.

29

"What are we talkin'? Beyond forced registration."

The president folded her hands around her coffee mug. "There will need to be certain concessions. The people are scared."

"Because you created then fed their fear."

The president tipped her head to the side and lifted one shoulder in a shrug. "Did I really have to try hard? As far as campaigns go, this one was easy."

On one hand, at least she was being honest. On the other... "What about the kids who died due to your 'campaign'?"

The president went rigid. "I did not authorize that."

Paige didn't know if she believed that. "What about the kids who were separated from their incarcerated parents?"

The president's lips went thin, but then she opened a hand, palm up toward her. "They can be released."

"When?"

The president appeared upset as her nostrils flared.

Maybe Paige had managed to do more damage than

she'd thought. "And the other people you're holding prisoner?"

"They will be as well."

This was going a little *too* well. Paige was missing something. "To be returned home?"

"No."

There it was, the point where things got hard.

"But we can discuss reservations."

"Instead of prisons?"

The president gave a nonverbal acknowledgement.

This was insane. "Did that work out for the natives?"

"It did for us."

"But... did it work for the natives? Why would I agree to this? Also, what land would you 'give' us? There are no lands left."

"We would have to move a few assets around, but, be assured, we do have land available."

"Why wasn't this your first move? Why did you decide to use prisons instead? To treat us like prisoners?"

"Because you're criminals and terrorists."

"Convenient titles to slander people in order to get what you want."

The president clamped her lips shut and shook her head, glaring at Paige.

Finally, a reaction that wasn't smug. "We're *not* criminals or terrorists. We're people. We're parents. We're brothers and sisters, daughters and sons. We're wives and husbands."

"Some of you have multiple husbands and wives."

"Some of us are Wiccan too. Some worship Thor and the old gods. Are you going to hold that against us?"

The president ducked her head. "We will give you parcels of land in—"

"How big?"

"—order for you to build your cities."

"And will we be forced to wear the collars?"

The president paused. "No." She was upset, by the set of her lips, but her eyes promised something worse instead.

"What? Out with it."

"But there will be a chip."

Paige felt like she was pulling teeth from a mule. "And?"

"And," the president sipped her coffee and carefully set her mug down before meeting Paige's gaze, "there will be a perimeter. Controlled access. People can't just come strolling in when they want, and you can't leave. Even with your door magic. Anyone who leaves the boundary will die."

"By the chip."

The president smiled warmly.

"So, like a prison."

"But you can build it like a town, make it feel better."

"And the rules?"

"You will have to obey ours. We will provide a police force. They will monitor things, provide enforcement of the laws and curfews."

"Jobs?"

"Normal jobs. You can do whatever you want. You will need to create money, pay the taxes that will be invested in paying for your lands and protections."

This wasn't peace.

"As an offer of good faith, the children of the criminals you freed are already on a bus headed toward us as we speak."

"Where?"

Her gaze was cool. "They're three hours out."

"So, that's long enough for me to gather whatever councils we might have, discuss this, and give you our answer. And is their safe return contingent upon our answer?"

"Your surrender will be necessary." The president stood. "You can keep Troutdale as one of your homes, but the humans will need to be removed. If they do not come willingly, I will need you to assist us with removing them for their own safety."

Wait. "What?"

"We will be bringing all paranormals together, which will include those who drink their blood."

"Vampires."

"Yes. I noticed you have none here, but that will change. You will get vampires and many other paranormals here. I cannot risk humans' safety."

Paige clamped her mouth shut. Vampires and the Eastwoods couldn't survive together because of the blood magick. It stirred a blood lust in the vampire they couldn't control. Even the wards didn't protect them.

"The children in my care look forward to your answer." The president didn't offer her hand. She just left.

Paige stared daggers at the president's coffee cup, letting the information filter through her head.

Margo walked through the back. "Everything go okay?"

Not even close. "Anything happen?"

"Not a peep."

"Good. Stay on alert. I don't know what else she's going to throw at us, but I know she's not done."

"Understood." Margo slipped out the back door, sliding it closed behind her.

Tuck walked through the front door.

Paige met him in the hall. "We need to make sure they leave."

Tuck turned on his heel and left again.

Thankfully, he didn't ask any questions.

They needed a meeting but not just the normal leaders. Tuck needed to be there. The leader of the incarcerated paranormals needed to be there. All the other leaders were needed.

And she had to work fast.

She flew to the Blackmans. She was getting used to flying fast, though fast flight also meant bigger appetite. She needed to eat at each stop. She talked with Phoebe, who sent members of her covens to retrieve the other leaders, calling up doors and disappearing.

She then used the amulet Merry had given her and told her to meet at the mayor's office, which wasn't going to be big enough. They needed to go somewhere bigger.

The high school gymnasium.

She called every person she could think of. Chuck, Danny, Suzanne, Michelle—who wasn't taking her calls. So, she reached out to Harrison Walker instead.

And while she flew and talked and gathered, Paige thought about her opinion. What did she think about all this?

Her first concern when they'd started this was to find a peaceful solution, and she had one. It met the needs she'd set for herself. Protect this town and save as many paranormals as she could.

But this cost was too high, and the world was watching. If *she* folded now? The other paranormals didn't stand a chance.

She didn't want to accept the agreement. She wanted to find the bus the kids were on, take them, and tell the president what she could do with her "peace" agreement.

They all gathered at the high school, and with an hour

to spare, she had everyone she could think of there and represented.

She got up and spoke into the microphone. It looked like a mobile karaoke machine. It sounded like it too. "We have a peace offer from the president."

She then went into the details of it, spelling out what the president called peace.

"This isn't peace," one woman said with a growl.

Paige agreed. They needed to vent their frustration, to talk things out. But they also needed to know what was at stake here. She held up her hands for silence. "The people we freed from the prison are missing their kids. The president is offering to return them *if* we accept her offer. They're on a bus headed here right now. They're almost here."

Chuck stood, shaking his head, his blue eyes filled with disappointment. "You *want* us to accept these terms?"

Paige *knew* what she thought of this, but saying it out loud? She had to be honest with them. "No."

The crowd shifted, and the tension almost visibly released.

"But we need a plan to get those kids back to their parents and to safety. We need to figure out a way to release the rest of our people. Where are they going to go? Because we can't take any more refugees here. There will be traps at the prisons now. They *will be* expecting us, and we have to be ready."

Kendall rose to her feet, towering over those around her. "We are warriors."

"Some of us are warriors but not all of us." Paige looked around at the different types of paranormals and felt for the first time *why* she was the one standing before them. She was a shifter and a witch and talked to the same elements they all spoke to. She listened and she acted, weighing their concerns. She wasn't always right. She didn't profess to be. She wasn't any one of the other alphas. She was all of them.

And that knowledge made her feel more in control. "We need to remember that even our non-warriors have strengths."

Paige read the room, and they seemed... relieved.

Relieved that she was about to declare war on the United States of America.

Tuck stood up. "The president is on her way. She's being escorted now."

"Do not threaten her life," Paige told them. It would be too easy to take the president out right here and now.

"Why not?" someone shouted.

"Assassinate her now while she's weak," someone else yelled.

"That's a bell we can't un-ring," Paige roared, using her alpha will to back her words. "Do we have someone to take the president's place?"

"You."

"No." Absolutely not. "First of all, that's not how the government works. There is a chain of command here, and I'm nowhere on it. Nowhere. Secondly, I'm not fit to lead a nation. Thirdly, decide who *is* going to lead us. It won't be me. I'll run the protection side of things. I'll help with the war, but the leader? That needs to be someone who actually knows what they're fucking doing." Someone who didn't need to search for an online class on how the government worked.

The gym buzzed with this new update as Tuck disappeared.

"And besides that," Paige continued, "we're not making

a martyr out of her. Do *not* make a martyr out of that woman. Do you hear me?"

Kendall smirked.

A few people squirmed, but most everyone else opted to simply hold back.

Tuck came back with a team of men in black and the president of the United States.

They were about to do something they couldn't take back, and for the first time since the day she'd stood outside the courthouse fighting for her daughter, Paige felt like pissing herself.

The president came up to Paige and smiled at the gathered paranormals. "The children are just outside of town."

"Excellent." Paige kind of wanted to see how the president would react. She wanted to know what was at play here. What kind of woman was the president and just how far was she willing to go?

But was Paige willing to bet the lives of children? There was no guarantee the kids would be safe. "I need to know if you intend on returning our children."

Disappointment settled like a fine sheen of dust on the president's face. "You do know that, in refusing my offer, you'd be declaring war."

"We're declaring our rights. Rights we were born with, Madame President. We're declaring we don't deserve to be treated like criminals. What's wrong with that?"

"You're dangerous."

"As dangerous as you?" Paige turned to the president and squared off with her. "Will the children be safe? Will they be returned?"

The president narrowed her right eye, gnashing her teeth. "Yes."

"Are you sure?" Because there was something in her

expression, *something* that hinted the *only* reason the president was agreeing to return the kids was because she had something else up her sleeve.

The president ground her jaw. "Yes. *They* will be safe."

Paige didn't believe her.

Neither did a few of the others. "Where are they coming from?"

The president's eyes went frigid. "They're coming from Portland."

Chuck and a few others got up and left.

"I want to formally let you know that your offer of 'peace' is respectfully declined." A thick knot wrapped itself in Paige's chest as she said those words out loud. "We will not be herded onto your reservations. We will not be chipped and treated like cattle for the slaughter. We were born free American citizens, and that's how we're going to be treated."

"How do you think this is going to play out for you?" the president asked, turning to the gathered crowd. "I have armies. You have..." She sneered and gestured to the people. "Pets."

Paige knew just how much fire power was at the president's fingertips. She didn't worry about nuclear attacks but others? Missiles? Would their wards withstand a direct missile attack?

She'd have to make a few adjustments, if she even could. "We will not live like that, Madame President. We are free people and we *will* be treated like it."

The president took in a deep breath, straightening as she did so. Then she met Paige's gaze. "I had more faith in you."

"As I you." The full force of those words hit Paige like a hammer in that moment. Her entire world rocked in those three words. She'd had complete faith that the president of the United States would look after them, would see their best interest, and would eventually find a real solution.

Not this. She'd thought it, had aced it, but she hadn't *believed* it would go this far.

"You will wish you'd taken my offer," the president said as she and her security detail left.

"You'll wish you'd heeded mine."

They were now at war.

3 0

They managed to retrieve the kids safe and sound, but Paige knew something else was going on there. Something else was afoot. She didn't know what she'd read on the president's face, but the woman had been smug when she'd said the kids would return.

Paige had sent Margo and Clem to see what they could find, but they'd come back with nothing. She didn't want to stir up a bunch of trouble, not with the talks going on right then.

Paige knew something wasn't right.

For four days, the president didn't make another move on Troutdale. She didn't make another move on the other paranormal communities either. Danny and Tru had managed to get their own network up and running. Tru was still building on the network that Paige didn't understand. Danny's network of dryads and information made sense. Tru's network of jargon and "nets" didn't.

They had information. That was what mattered. They had information.

And information was good.

They had a reprieve, and while that *felt* like a good thing, it probably wasn't.

The gathered paranormals—with more arriving every day—voted that she would lead them through this war.

A *real* vote. With delegates and the whole nine. She didn't campaign, but she still won as the war effort commander and as their leader. Though, to be fair, there were only a couple of others who'd offered their names.

She needed experienced people around her, so she made Kendall her second-in-command.

She also built a cabinet of sorts after *taking* that online class on how the government worked. They were no longer ruled by some secret council. The Elders didn't even have a member on board. None of them had been voted in.

She stood in the corner of the room, watching this new Cabinet bicker in the conference room of the Red Star Division. Suzanne had said she'd give up her office, but Paige had insisted that wouldn't happen. The town still needed their mayor and her office. They'd become the beating heart for the town and that's how it needed to stay.

Originally, she'd let everyone meet at the Whiskey home, but Leslie had started showing signs of wear. Their home was no longer the sanctuary it had once been.

So, Paige had taken it to the only other place she could think: Red Star.

But this wasn't going to work either. Eventually, Dexx and his team—his *entire* freakin' team. Where in the hell were they?—would be back and they'd need their space back. But for now?

For now, they were collecting votes for secession and dividing the U.S.

"We have Montana," Rory said. He was a big, burly

dryad from a grove that was apparently bigger and more powerful than Troutdale's grove. "They're ready to vote."

Paige still didn't understand what exactly was going on here. They were making a bid to secede from the Union, an act that Paige was fairly certain had failed a couple of times before. Texas had attempted it once before and it'd failed.

So far, they had Texas, California, Oregon, Washington, Alaska, Hawaii, Idaho, Montana, Wyoming, the Dakotas, Colorado, and Nebraska. Then, there were the three odd ball ones: New Hampshire, Vermont, and Florida.

How was that supposed to work?

They had a lawyer, Nancy Niesgal. Paige remembered her name as "Nice Gal," even though that wasn't how it was pronounced. She had a lot of names and faces to remember and she had to somehow build relationships with all of them. This was... ridiculous.

Willow was helpful here as well. She'd been the one to come up with the pet names to help her remember.

"We file for the right to secede," Nancy repeated as everyone else bickered, squabbled, and threw out wild ideas. "That will buy us time."

Paige knew they weren't going to be able to buy a lot of time and they weren't wasting it. They'd set up locations for people to relocate to in the wilderness of Northern California, Montana, and Oregon. The president had offered camps or reservations. So far, the paranormals weren't offering much more than that. But their refuge camps wouldn't have killer chips.

Paige had also set up people to watch over supplies and others to help them build new homes, new power grids.

No fences, though. Anyone could come in and out as they wanted.

But each of these hubs would be protected with a ward tree and a Blackman and an Eastwood.

There weren't enough Whiskeys to share, though.

They hadn't invaded any other prisons yet. That would come next, but in this time of "peace," Paige was preparing those flocking to them.

She knew that others were setting up refugee camps elsewhere. There was a growing one in New Mexico that was making the news, but so far, New Mexico hadn't opted to join their bid to secede.

"How will this work?" Paige asked again. She'd heard the words. She just needed them repeated so they'd drive home and become reality.

"Legally," Nancy said, "the Union is indestructible."

This was the point Paige was having an issue with. "Which means the vote is a waste of time."

"No. If we secede, then other states might as well."

"Like?"

"The Confederate states. If the west pulls out and then the south follows, the north will be all that remains."

"But they'll still have the federal reserve, the power, and the military."

"Legally, yes."

There was no "legally" to it. Paige was sitting as a *leader* to a *nation* with no money, no military, no support. This was a nightmare. The president was going to win with that alone.

There were so many things she could do. She could withhold medicine and then all the people with chronic illnesses would die.

She could "allow" a supply shipment in and then poison the food.

She could bomb the shit out of one the refugee camps.

The president had all the power.

Though, Paige had been contacted by a couple of other countries that were interested in hearing her plans, mostly because they didn't want their own paranormal societies to rise up.

Paige was glad that other nations were figuring this out, but she wished hers could. "So, if they still legally have all the power, what are we hoping to gain?"

Nancy held her hands open with a pinched expression. "When we withdraw our state support, the federal government is weakened. Right now, the U.S. is a superpower, but that's with the resources and taxes from all the states."

"And weakened, the U.S. will have more than one war front."

"It's possible."

"So, you think a civil war will bring a world war."

Nancy was somber for a moment. "That's the threat we're leveraging."

Right. Politics. "Okay. You do what you have to, and I'm going to see what we can do to shore things up here."

Nancy nodded and left.

Paige wasn't going to be any more help here. They were talking about war plans, and that was great. But without other structures in place, they *would* lose. They needed planes, boats, and weapons. They needed medical supplies and food.

They needed infrastructures.

So, she located people, working with them, coming up with ideas—real ideas—and then implemented plans that would actually work.

Another two days spent.

It wasn't perfect, but it was a start.

When she checked back with the war room, as she

called it, they seemed to have a plan as well, and a rough Declaration of Independence.

Oh, how history repeated itself. This nation had been born from the bootheel of tyranny, and it was being destroyed by it as well.

Apparently, the Oregon senator had put together a call for a vote.

In most cases, the states were divided. However, they were divided on the side of secession, though only barely.

She remembered Nancy's words. They didn't think they'd actually succeed in breaking from the Union, maybe even with a civil war. They just wanted to strong arm the president into giving them a few of their own terms.

And, apparently, she was supposed to hand deliver those terms when the official declarations were issued.

Paige reviewed the terms that were handed to her. Arrangements had been made for her to arrive at the White House, provide the terms, and then come back to await the president's response.

This was a ballsy move that could potentially be rather empty if they didn't have the infrastructure in place. She just hoped that the ball she had started rolling would actually make a difference.

She put on her most professional outfit, which happened to be a pair of jeans, her cleanest and nicest button-up shirt, and a blue business jacket. She just wasn't a politician and didn't believe she was ready for this. She took her own reporter and her own dryad. She wanted someone she could trust to speak the truth as it had been said instead of trying to interpret it and put their own spin on it.

The door that was open spilled onto the White House lawn. Technically speaking, they could have made the attempt to open the door into the Oval Office, but Paige didn't want to be that forceful, nor did she want to invite the president into overreacting. The White House lawn was quite close enough. She also wasn't going to allow herself to be collared this time.

Security personnel reacted immediately.

She had already been prepared for that. She called up her magick and relieved everyone she saw of their weapons. "We are not here to fight," she said in as loud a voice as she could. "But I will be seeing the president now."

She did not make an advance on the White House. She didn't want it to look like she was storming the castle or attacking them. They were offering their terms and nothing more.

Eventually, the president came out, with a whole new set of Secret Service who were still armed. "I trust my agents are able to keep their weapons this time?"

"As long as they don't open fire."

"And what about you? I see you still have your magick." The president glanced at Paige's neck.

Paige wasn't about to tell the woman that those collars didn't affect her magick. "I've released it."

"I guess I will have to take your word for it."

"I suppose so. I won't waste your time. I am just here to deliver our terms."

"Your terms?" The president stood, her tone laced with condescending scorn.

Paige didn't know why the president was acting dumb. "Please don't. You put us in this situation. We are officially declaring our independence from the United States of America. We are seceding from the Union."

The president ran her tongue along her top teeth and snarled slightly before glancing at the cameras and straightening her face again. "You have to know that won't work."

"You have an opportunity here. You said you wanted peace. This gives you that. Instead of reservations, we're taking a few states. States with resources. This way, we're not draining the nation in order to 'support our people.'" Contempt she couldn't hide laced her words.

The president assessed Paige. "Do you have any idea how you would function? How vulnerable you will be without my protection? If you succeed in this—which you won't—other nations will attack."

"You." Paige wanted her to understand *their* full weight. "They'll be attacking you."

"I have armies."

"I have magick."

The president narrowed an eye.

"But it's not just that, is it? Each state has resources you need in order to make trades and buy your peace. So, I also understand how far you'll be willing to go to keep us. How many hundreds of thousands of us you will be willing to kill in order to keep our resources and your power. How many millions? When will enough be enough?"

Understanding dawned in the president's eyes. "You're quite serious."

"We are."

The president turned her gaze to the grass for a moment before raising it again. "What are your terms of peace?"

Paige outlined them as briefly as she could. "We remain free. We will not be treated as prisoners. We will not be incarcerated for being who we are. We will have our own legal systems. And we will protect everyone. Human and paranormal alike."

"But as your own nation."

Paige took a step toward her. "You're the one who took this too far. We could have had all of that. We still could.

You could pull back. You could save face. You could tell the nation that you had no idea what we are, that you reacted poorly to bad information and that you now understand that we're just people like everybody else. You could do that."

"That is not likely to happen."

Paige figured as much. "*You* are taking this to war. You think you have all the power. Maybe you do. You think you will smite us easily. You won't. I faced off with demons. You're only human."

The president said nothing, her expression merely stating she was listening.

"But understand this. The *world* is watching, waiting. We want peace. But we will not be treated like trash. As soon as you threaten our rights, we will stand up and fight, and we will not be easily suppressed."

The president took the list of terms and glanced at them. "I will consider these."

"That's all I can ask." Paige motioned to Bonnie to open the door. "But ask yourself how much innocent blood is too much? What price are you willing to pay? You swore an oath to protect us, the people of the United States of America. All of us. Not just the ones you wanted to protect. Remember that."

Paige didn't wait for a response. She stepped through the door and listened to it zip closed behind her. She hoped she hadn't just made the situation worse.

As far as big battles went, this one sucked the most. Everyone waited on pins and needles while the government officials discussed things beyond their control that would affect almost all of them.

Hours turned into days. Days felt like weeks or months.

The president called for stiff action to be taken against secessionist states. She called her militaries back.

Not all of them answered.

More than a few ships refused to leave their western harbors, something Paige knew wasn't supposed to be legal. She knew the men and women onboard might be court martialed and sent to the federal prison indefinitely. The federal government owned their souls until their contracts were up, and that meant answering the president's call.

Paige wanted to dive into her work and just disappear. She wanted the "politics" conversations to stop. She wanted the hate to stop.

But the idea that "politics" didn't affect her was over. She couldn't even pretend anymore. The politics of life was too heavy for her to ignore, too big for her to hide from. She couldn't simply ask people to stop talking about it so she could have a peaceful afternoon. She couldn't simply "unfollow" people and make their opinions go away when they caused her stress.

Which they were. They were all causing her a great deal of stress.

But this stress was brought on by her.

She'd been unwilling to stand down.

She'd been the one to invade a prison and free the inmates.

She'd been the one who had instigated this.

That wasn't to say that people were all sitting around and waiting. No. They prepared.

It gave her a little time to see how her twins were doing, though, and that was good.

The two raced through the castle halls, now rampaging around as the size of six-year-olds. One was a bear and the other was an elephant.

Cawli walked beside Paige in his small cat form, his large-for-his-frame paws silent. *They are doing well.*

"But are they slowing down?"

No. If anything, they are speeding up their growth cycle.

"But why?"

Cawli pounced to the side and caught something small and rodent-like.

Paige kept her attention focused on her kids. She didn't need to watch her spirit animal eat a mouse.

When he was done, he continued to walk. *I believe their bodies are growing in order to physically house the energy of their spirit animals.*

"But eventually, they will stop. Both of these spirits have been in the real world before."

Yes.

349

That brought up a question she'd meant to ask for a while. "Which one is the angel killer?"

Cawli pounced ahead and ignored her.

She waited.

Finally, he came back and gave her a very huffy cat face. *Ember*.

Really. That was interesting and maybe that was the reason there was so little writing about the rajasi. But at least she was starting to feel a little better. Hiding from stress did that. It gave the brain the ability to reset a little.

She was reading a lot of nonfiction in order to help her get smarter. There was a lot she needed to learn: government, psychology, management, and finances. She had to learn how to create a country, and the more she learned, the more she realized this could be possible. It'd be hard, but it was *possible*.

Aunt Paige, Kammy's voice called telepathically.

What was he doing there? Paige assumed that someone had brought him to Cyn's house to get her. Not everyone liked coming to the library because, apparently, *it* didn't *like* everyone, including Leslie. She'd come once.

Once.

That'd been enough.

Yeah, Kam.

Mom says, "Get her ass up here. But not like that, Kammy. You—"

Kammy was developing as a person and he'd taken to mimicking exactly what the other person said. It was uncanny, yet hilarious. *Tell her I'm on my way up.*

When am I going to be able to play again?

She heard his unspoken meaning. He wanted to play with the twins. *Soon.*

He sighed petulantly in her mind but left.

You're being called away, Cawli said as he padded beside her.

Yes. She didn't want to go. She enjoyed walking beside her spirit animal and being with her twins. However, it was time to reshape the world so her kids had a better place to live.

She went to the twins and forced them back into human form.

Rai's long, dark-blonde hair trailed down her back in waves as she studied her mom through eyes so like Dexx's, except hers coursed with sparking electricity.

"Be good."

She shrugged and gave Paige a hug.

It wasn't the hug of a kid who loved her mom, though. It was the hug of a kid hugging a stranger.

Okay. Well, after she fixed the world, she'd find a way to fix this.

Ember bounced up to her, tall and gangly and wearing a dress and a floppy hat. He grinned up at her with his dark chocolate eyes. "Be good." He threw himself at her.

She chuckled and wrapped him in her arms. He didn't need much to build a deeper emotional connection, unlike his sister, which was a surprise because when they'd been babies—just a day or two ago—it'd seemed to be a much different case.

Paige remained kneeling and stared at both her kids. "Things *will* be safe again, and we'll bring you back up again, I swear."

"And if you don't?" Rai asked, her five-year-old tone on point for her tiny body.

Paige didn't want to think about it because that would

mean she'd failed. "We'll move down here. Me, Leah, and Bobby." Paige paused, wondering where in the hell Dexx was. "Dad."

Rai blinked, her lips flat, as she nodded once.

Such a solemn kid.

"Don't blow up," Paige said as she stood.

She didn't wait any longer. She wasn't the type of person to stand around and say goodbye eighteen times before leaving. When she was done, she was done. Too many other things needed to be accomplished that day. She just didn't know exactly what those were.

Leslie waited for her in Cyn's bedroom. "We have a growing situation."

Paige had been waiting for this. She wasn't sure what the battle would look like. Would it be the full force of the United States military up against the citizens of Troutdale? Would it be a bunch of prison guards making Troutdale into a reservation of sorts?

Leslie gave her as much information as she could on the way, but it seemed as though most people had no idea, including Leslie.

DoDO had absolutely no qualms about keeping everyone in the dark. The only person they seem to want to speak with was Paige.

So, they drove to the entrance ramp and met Mario.

The National Guard had been stationed at the highway. Several Humvees and a few other troop transport vehicles blocked the highway. Obvious soldiers in camouflage moved with purpose, but none of them carried their rifles.

Mario twisted a little, with a crooked grin. "This is a pretty intimidating sight, I bet."

Yeah. It really was, but Paige wasn't backing down. She

was certain that if he was on this side, he wouldn't be nearly so flippant. "What are we doing here?"

He rubbed his chin for a moment and then looked around again. "I am here to formally invite you to the White House. You're being awarded the leader of the paranormal peoples."

The president was giving her a voice in the government. That was a move Merry and Yad had mentioned *could* happen, but Paige hadn't believed it.

Mario crossed his arms. "The leaders of your nation would like to discuss options."

"We already have the mandates and terms the president has provided." Paige narrowed her eyes a smidge. What was Mario getting at? "And she has our terms."

"And they need to be discussed. We cannot allow this to continue." He sounded like he'd memorized lines.

"We're fine."

"There are parties who aren't, people who are concerned your decision will not go our way." His lips twisted as he said that. "There are government officials who want to speak with you directly. This is not an invitation by the president."

Now, that was certainly a new development. "Give me their information and I'll make an appearance."

"We've already made the arrangements for your transportation."

She smiled at him. She wasn't about to allow him to take charge. "I'll make my own."

"I don't think you fully understand the situation."

Oh, but she really did. "I don't think you fully understand just how much I *fully* understand. Give me the names and I will make my own arrangements."

The smug look fell off Mario's face.

Five minutes later, she had the names and an address. It was time to see if they could bring some maturity to the situation. Paige really didn't want to be the person who broke the United States.

But if the president continued to threaten her family, that was exactly what Paige was going to do.

32

Paige and Leslie drove onto Main Street, and people were already there to meet with them, with Willow in the lead.

Within moments, Paige had a Blackman witch, a reporter, and a dryad.

Leslie held her go bag. "Don't worry about Bobby. I'll take care of him and Leah. Just be amazing. You got this."

"Willow, Leslie is my second-in-command. Help her the way you've been saving me."

Willow gave Paige a half-smile and snorted. "Sure."

Leslie and Willow turned to walk away. "How do I get a you?" Leslie asked as they headed toward her shop.

Leah bounded up on Paige, her backpack over her shoulder. "I'm going."

A week ago, Paige would have said yes in a heartbeat, her failed-mother mentality pushing her to keep her kids—especially the one she'd lost—close to her at all times, no matter the danger. But with all the battles she'd been in lately—D.C., the elven city, Kansas, here—she'd learned that being a mom meant sometimes leaving them in safety.

If only she'd listened to Dexx, he might be there with her where she needed him. "No, you're not. This could be a trap."

"Then, you shouldn't go."

The girl wasn't wrong. "I have to, but you're staying."

Leah glared, dropping her gaze to the ground.

"I need someone to protect Bobby."

"You need a babysitter," Leah grumbled.

"Sure. If you *prefer* to look at it that way, go ahead."

Leah released a petulant sigh and glared up at her mother.

"I love you." Paige cupped the back of Leah's head and kissed her forehead. "Don't break my town."

Leah gave her a mocking expression and walked away.

Oof. Daggers.

When Paige stepped through the Blackman door, she was met with three surprised faces and about a dozen others who were so engrossed in their discussion, they didn't even react. It was a large room with an ornate table in the middle, surrounded by green, boxy office chairs. The men and women in the room wore nice business suits, with their hair done well and their makeup perfect.

She'd stepped into a room of politicians. "Congresswoman Jacobs?" Paige hoped she hadn't gone to the wrong place.

Cameraman Mark stepped through and coughed.

Harrison followed and offered his hand for Bonnie, who closed the door behind her.

A few more of the people in the room turned to them.

But the heated argument dominating the space didn't even pause.

One woman came up to her with a smile and offered her hand.

Paige took it. "I was told we needed to talk. Paige Whiskey."

"Rachel," the woman said. "I'm Congresswoman Jacob's assistant. Please, come in. Do you need water? You can set your bags in the corner." She stabbed Cameraman Mark with a steely gaze. "No reporters. No cameras. You don't film in here."

Mark raised his hands in surrender.

Paige wasn't going to tell her that the *reporter* was Harrison, and he was already transmitting information. Or at least she assumed that was the reason he had a root connecting his hip to the potted plant beside him.

One of the people who hadn't been surprised by her sudden appearance stood. She flicked a look to Paige but continued speaking to her group. "—doesn't like it, then tell her she can piss up a tree. Got it?"

Paige might actually *like* this woman.

The four others didn't look happy at all, but one by one, they nodded. Once she made sure each had acknowledged her, she gave Paige her full attention. "Congresswoman Jacobs. Nice to meet you finally. Thank you for coming. And in such a timely fashion." She walked to the end of the long conference table and offered her hand. "Didn't like our escort?"

Paige stretched her witch senses to see if the congresswoman was any kind of paranormal. "Not really." This woman appeared to be one hundred percent human.

Congresswoman Jacobs winced. "Hadn't thought of that." The slight tick in her right eye said she had.

Interesting. Could this woman be trusted or not? Paige took the other woman's hand and gave it a good shake. "I have no idea what to expect."

"Good, then." Congresswoman Jacobs didn't appear to

want to mince words. "Neither do we, and we would love to get to the heart of this as quickly as possible." She led the way to her small group. "We find ourselves in a dire situation."

Paige had to agree with that. "The president is over-stepping her bounds."

"In short, yes. However, your actions are only helping her."

That wasn't exactly what Paige wanted to hear. "Tell me what the *real* situation is in as broad strokes as you can. And know this. I was a beat cop, a detective, and everything I know about how the government works came from an online class I took two days ago."

Congresswoman Jacobs outlined a few of the basics for her.

Number one, the president *did* have the authority to apprehend known terrorist cells. However, the proof she kept promising never appeared.

Number two, the president did *not* have the power to raise the U.S. Armed Forces against the paranormal citizens of the United States.

Number three, the president did *not* have the authority to blank out news sources or strip information access to any citizens of the United States. And according to the law, the paranormals were *still* citizens.

However, there was a growing movement led by the president to strip paranormals of those basic rights, stating they weren't human.

Groups of scientists were gathering information on their biological structure to state they were indeed human and so far, the data was good.

Right. For shifters, witches, and vampires. Sure. But what about the others? Like dryads and elves?

One battle at a time.

The biggest issue they were fighting currently, however, was that the paranormals were rising as insurgents that could lead to a revolutionary war. In that instance, the president was within her rights to apply the full force of the U.S. military against the paranormal forces.

"That would be bad." Paige wasn't an idiot. She recalled the battles in the elven city and in Kansas. Paranormals fell pretty easily to bullets.

"Indeed, it would." Congressman Allen said bluntly, stepping toward them. He was a white, portly man in a well-made grey suit. "There is a very real possibility that this could ramp up to civil war. And *that* is a weapon we can use."

This sounded a lot like chess. "How?"

"Let's say for a moment that you *did* take us to civil war," he said and then paused as if waiting for her to say something.

Like refute their intentions? No.

He raised a pale eyebrow and continued. "The power of the United States would not nearly be as great as the president seems to think."

"Agreed." Paige was glad the threat didn't go unnoticed. The threat of states leaving the Union was a *big* one.

According to the congressman, as soon as the states formally filed their intent to secede from the Union, they could then pull all of their resources.

Paige had done a lot of homework in her free time and knew what he was talking about. Exports. Market. Money. Taxes.

The real power of government.

According to their calculations, if most of the western states decided to secede—as they already had the votes to do

—then the exports would be removed from the federal government. Without those exports, the United States would have no financial backing for their debts. Without that, the United States would go bankrupt.

"*That* is how you win this war," Congressman Allen said. "Not with magick. Not with your political baby-kissing campaign. With the power of money."

That wasn't a game she had experience in, but she was willing to learn. "How do I use this?"

"You've already started it," Congresswoman Jacobs said. "You got votes to secede. You've got a lot of states, but no one has officially filed yet."

There wasn't actually a method for that, which was holding them up.

"The president," Congressman Allen said gruffly, "has been playing this game a long time. She's going after some of the states you won and she's trying to win them back."

"How?" Because, if the president was offering the states money, that was something Paige couldn't follow with. She struggled to pay her portion of the house mortgage, and it was divided by five pay checks.

This was where the conversation took a turn she was more than a little uncomfortable with.

"We're offering you a seat in the government as the representative of your people," Congressman Allen said.

Her people. Paige wanted to snort but refrained. "What does that mean?"

"You'd have a voice," Congresswoman Jacobs said. "The paranormals would be acknowledged."

"Uh-huh." Paige was waiting.

But instead of talking about registrations and collars and everything else the president had mandated, they turned the conversation to something that made her a little more uncomfortable.

She could then go to the senators and congressmen and the media as the *official* spokesperson and regain the ground she'd lost.

"Lost?"

"Utah is already backing out of the secession order," Congressman Allen said. "With Utah, there'll be others."

"But not Colorado," Congresswoman Jacobs said. "If you can keep Colorado, you've got a powerful play to make."

One of her assistants came up to her. "You'll want Colorado," he said, his voice pitched high, "California, Washington, and Montana. Also, if you could keep Alaska?" He winced and moved his head from side-to-side. "That one could be good too."

They were talking resources like oil and food. They didn't even *know* of the real resource Alaska had. "You'll want to keep Alaska."

Congressman Allen raised his face in the air as if scenting it, then smiled. "Of course. That's what we're proposing you focus on in the next several days, keeping and winning back the states you've lost and will lose as the president works to regain ground."

Paige'd come a long way from being a detective.

" All you're doing," Congressman Allen said, "is developing a credible threat that you are then going to hand over to the president and the media."

Paige could do that. "Who am I focusing on? The people? Or government people?"

A woman with shoulder-length dark hair and a maroon-colored business suit stood and walked toward them. "You need to address the world and the world leaders."

361

"Congresswoman Hernandez," Congresswoman Jacobs said, introducing the new woman.

Paige nodded and listened to what she had to say.

Congresswoman Hernandez gave her an appreciative smile. "The president needs to understand how much she could lose. We just need you to stir the other world leaders so that they *also* inform her of the tenuous position she's in."

Paige wasn't going to focus on the fact she was out of her element. "What's the end game? What are we hoping to achieve?"

Congresswoman Hernandez perched on the edge of the table and folded her arms over her slender form. "The president has already overstepped her power. We are voting for an impeachment investigation. However, there are several in the House who aren't sure which way to vote. So, what we're *really* hoping is that you clear the field to impeachment."

"Impeachment." Well, if the president were removed from her post, that could drop the threat entirely. Unless someone else picked it back up again.

"We need you," Congresswoman Jacob said evenly, "to show them how far she's willing to go and how willing she is to break her oath of office. But to do that, you need a voice that can't be silenced quite so easily."

"So, you want me to bait a trap."

"Yes." Congressman Allen stood. "We have already called the media. There will be several options for interviews. We highly recommend that you take them."

Paige reminded herself that they were running out of time. "I need to know how legal her terms are."

Congresswoman Jacobs straightened in her seat. "What terms?"

Paige spelled out for them what the president had

offered them. How they were being forced to register and how they would be forced to live on risk reservations and incarceration camps. She informed them that paranormals were already being gathered and thrown into prison against their will.

"So, that's what that was about." Congresswoman Hernandez shook her head, her expression filled with astonishment. "We'd heard there was an insurgent movement in one of the private prisons. But no one had any information. Now we know why. It was a cover-up."

A cover-up? That had to be good. "We can share that information."

Congresswoman Jacobs shook her head. "You need to be very careful about providing and sharing information. It not only shows that the president went too far, but it also shows that you did. You basically declared war as soon as you invaded that prison."

Paige pulled her phone from her pocket. It looked like it was going to be a long few days. "As far as traps go, this one is the furthest away from what I expected. I need to let my people know I'm okay and that I'll be busy for a while."

Congresswoman Jacobs nodded. "You should, yes. You're not out of the woods yet, though. There's more to it than a speech."

And then, for the next three hours, Paige and her entourage were shuffled from one location to the next while video cameras were put in her face as she talked delicately around explosive points.

She was officially sworn in as the Secretary of Paranormal Relations, which, as the news stories were blowing up, was a big deal. The president still had to officially appoint her, and her appointment had to be approved by the Senate, so the swearing in was a dog and pony show intended to force the hand of the president.

However, the question was whether or not she'd be invited to sit on the National Security Council, which... probably not. However, it would be a relatively good idea.

If she were awarded the appointment by the president and the Senate, she'd be on the Cabinet, would advise the president, and would be eighteenth in line of presidential succession.

Yeah. Paige...that. Fuck. It probably *wouldn't* happen.

Her acceptance speech was pretty simple. She'd had thirty minutes to alter what her speech writer, Aaron Rogers, had given her. She was given talking points for interviews that took up the next two days as just about every news program wanted to talk to her.

The reporters who had been with her during her first trip to D.C. were doing their utmost best to try to reconnect with her, to get her to divulge more information. She didn't burn any bridges, but she did let them know that, if they really wanted to build relationships, they'd help her not crash and burn in her first week on the job.

The president's reporters wanted verification of just how dangerous the paranormals were. The president had "proof," and Paige needed to provide some of her own that they were harmless. However, she had to be careful of what she shared because she hadn't been entirely in the right.

The elven city was off the list of conversation topics because the world didn't need to know about an alternate dimension. Imagine what some of the other countries would do if they found out they could invade elven lands? That sort of thing.

Kansas couldn't be talked about because while *her* access to the internet had been cut off, someone had captured the final moments of that battle, and they didn't want it to be publicly aired. They'd deal with the fallout if it happened, but it would be best if she didn't talk about it.

And she absolutely couldn't mention how she'd illegal broken into a prison and rescued illegally incarcerated paranormals. The question would be raised as to who the bigger criminal really was.

Her talking points were pretty limited.

By the end of two days, Paige was exhausted. She was more than grateful for her trial run with the twins. She'd have been lost otherwise, but she still wished she could punch a few of the reporters in the throat. However, she stayed to the script and kept things on an even keel.

Until one of the interviews was interrupted.

The producers and the reporter were quite upset and let the people watching know that this was unconstitutional.

However, it was the Secret Service, so they couldn't do much more than that. Paige was gathered, her entourage left to fend for themselves. She tried to take Bonnie with her, but that request had been firmly denied.

She wasn't going to let them know she also had the ability to open doors. Sometimes. Not regularly.

Paige followed them to the black SUV. "Where are we going?"

The lead security person just looked at her and said nothing.

Outside, Naomi was there to greet them in one of the black SUVs. She plastered on a smile, but it was a little thin.

"I hope you're okay." Paige wasn't certain what else to say to Naomi. The last time they had been together, Naomi had almost become a friend. But would she still be a friend? Would she still be *friendly*?

"Congratulations on your assignment."

"Thanks." Though Paige would like to know what the woman really thought of it.

Naomi focused her attention on Paige. "The president would like to have a word with you. I recommend going in there with an open mind."

Paige didn't have to ask for more information than that. She was about to receive new terms, and it probably would *not* be in her favor.

Time to see if she'd learned enough to negotiate better this time.

33

Paige didn't know what to expect this time, but she mentally prepared herself for the worst. She wasn't going to play nice or give the president the upper hand. They were already declaring war, so there was no reason to play to the president's tenderer side.

This time, when Paige walked into the Oval Office, the president was already waiting for her and in a full temper. "Secretary of Paranormal Relations? Really?"

As if it had been her idea. "We have a voice now. It'll be harder to snuff us out."

"I haven't appointed you."

"I'm aware."

"You don't *get* a voice unless I give it to you."

Paige pointed to the TV, where she was shown giving an interview. "I think you'll find it's harder to shut me up than you hoped."

The president rolled her eyes. "I thought when I offered the peace deal, you would at least think about it before taking it this far."

Paige understood this tactic, trying to put her on the

defensive. She wasn't taking the bait. She inhaled for a two count. "If it had really been a peace deal, we probably would have considered it. But I told you what we would and would not accept and you blatantly ignored me."

"You didn't even give me an opportunity to take your demands to Congress."

"You've had *days* and you've done *nothing*. This was nothing more than a false olive branch to say you *tried*. Everything you've done so far has been through executive orders. You aren't working with your government. You're acting *for* them, which could be seen as an abuse of power."

The president's eyes flared as she came around her desk. "Are you really threatening what I think you are?"

If the president thought Paige was flaunting impeachment, there was very little Paige could do to make that happen, but, "Yes," she'd be doing everything *in* her power to support that action.

The president was quiet for a jaw-clenching moment. "Do you have any idea the magnitude of responsibility of this office?"

Paige was now the governmental representative to the paranormal society, and while she hadn't been assigned an office yet or a full team to help her navigate the political waters, and while she hadn't been handed a laundry list of paranormal issues through governmental channels, she felt the weight of it. "You're abusing the powers you gave an oath to use to protect the citizens of your country. That's what I understand. And I also understand that you believe you're doing this to protect them because of what happened to *you*."

The president stopped several arms lengths away and gestured to Paige in irritation. "Why wouldn't you want to do what is *right*?"

"I *am* doing what's right. I think you need to figure out your definition of *right* a bit better."

The president pulled back as though she had been slapped. "You're trying to tell me I'm wrong. That trying to go after a rapist is *wrong*."

"You're killing *children* to go after *one man* who's been *dealt with* because it wasn't 'handled' the way you wanted." Paige stared at this woman hard, wondering *how* she'd be able to advise her if she was given the real appointment in the Cabinet. "No. You don't get to use that as a justification for this."

"You go too far."

"I don't think so." What would *too far* look like, though? "Do you really think that you're right?"

"Yes." There was no room in her tone that said she had any doubt.

Paige wanted to leave right then and there. However, she knew that this was a fight she had to win. No magick. No bullets. Just her intellect and the power of words. "Why? Because we have teeth and claws?"

The president curled her upper lip slightly. "Yes."

"Why? Because we have magick?"

"Yes." The president was getting more defensive. She crossed her arms over her chest and blinked.

"How do you think we have survived this long without being discovered?"

The president shook her head and looked around. "You kill those who get too close to the truth or you turn them."

"Do you have proof of this?"

"You have magick. You can make people forget."

If only it worked that way. "You think you know a lot when you have no idea. It doesn't work that way."

"Except that's exactly what your grandmother did to you."

Alma had made Paige forget she'd had a daughter after Rachel had taken her because Paige had reacted emotionally and had summoned a demon to handle the situation.

The president smirked. "We have it on record that this type of magick *does* exist and that it *is* used. How many times has it been used to bury situations? Or to make things disappear? Or to make people forget they even had kids? We won't ever know. Not until we eradicate the world of your kind."

Paige wasn't certain who was feeding her this nonsense, but it was just rational enough to have basis.

It was time to shift the negotiation. She had to remember that was what this was. Negotiation. "You bring actual cases to me, and we'll investigate. We'll gather evidence. We'll put together trials. But you cannot incarcerate an entire population based on the suspicion that a handful of people have committed crimes."

"If we can't get to the truth any other way, then that is exactly what needs to happen."

"By that reason, we should incarcerate all humans because you personally have proven beyond a shadow of a doubt that humans are capable of incredible evil. *You* should be eradicated."

The president's eyes twitched.

That hit. "Who's to say that being bitten or turned or finding out you have magick *doesn't* save them from the evilness of being a mundane? After all, look at what you've done. *You* have killed, Madame President. You've killed *children*. All in the name of protecting *yourself*. Did those *toddlers* do something to you?"

Doubt entered the president's colored eyes. "I didn't authorize kids to be killed."

Paige pulled out her phone. Technically, she wasn't supposed to have it, but this last time, she had managed to get in with it. She wasn't certain how. She only knew that it shouldn't be possible and that someone was probably going to get fired.

The president narrowed her gaze at it as if thinking the exact same thought.

Paige went to her documents folder and pulled up the video. She had saved it in case she needed to use it in the interviews or for media coverage, which, of course, she now wasn't allowed to use.

She pulled it up and hit play, handing it over to the president. "That was the attack on the elven city. DoDO invaded with the force you authorized and killed indiscriminately. Anyone who resisted. It didn't matter how young or how old. And you see that right there?"

The sounds told Paige where the president was in the video playback. "That's a pile of children who were killed with bullets you authorized. Why? Because the president of the United States discovered that elves were real and decided to eradicate them because one shifter raped her thirty years ago. Who did these elves kill? Who did those *child* elves rape?"

The president watched the video to the end and then stood there.

The room was wrapped in silence.

Had Paige just made an impact? Was the president now realizing that perhaps she had gone too far? Or was she just having a moment of reckoning where she discovered that this was now on video and it could go to the media? Paige couldn't tell. She tried sniffing the air to see if she could smell the president's emotions. The only thing she could discern was that the president was shocked. Though, for what reason?

The president handed back the phone. "You're threatening to take us to civil war."

Paige licked her lips and stashed her phone. She wasn't certain she could still do that if she was sworn in to protect the nation, but the president would have to be the one to officially give her the office appointment. "If the president of the United States is willing to kill children in order to prove a point, then you're damn straight I'm threatening civil war. This is not the nation I'm protecting."

The president met her gaze. "I was told that the casualties were few."

Paige met the president's quiet tone with the solemnity of her own. "On *your* side. The elves lost *thousands* of people. And they have a city they can't return to. When DoDO hit, they infected the lands and the water. The elves will never be able to return to that land again."

The president walked slowly over to the striped couch and sank into it.

Paige decided to push forward a little harder. "Madame President, that city wasn't even on American soil. DoDO invaded another dimension in order to destroy it. You need to understand. That was an act of war and the elves, by rights, can strike back with their full force."

"You attacked and invaded a federal prison."

"*After* you invaded a town and took paranormals by force. I was in Lawrence, Madame President. I saw what you did. I have video of that too. You had your private military invade your own country. That too was an act of war. The only difference here is that you decided to attack a group of people who were actively capable of building their own armies to rise up against you. And that is the reason you are so scared right now."

The president met her gaze.

"We are... tribal. For the most part. We have covens and packs and groups. We're not united." That wasn't entirely true. "Well, we weren't."

Something shifted in the president's eyes. More than doubt. Fear.

"The only thing you managed to do was to unite us under a common banner. You thought you could take this opportunity and bring us out into the light and destroy us."

The president listened quietly, her fingers lightly scratching at her pant legs.

"But what you did was attack women and children and *families*. And that is what the people of the United States will remember."

Silence dominated the room for several long moments, giving Paige plenty of time to think about what she should say next. However, she felt she'd said what was needed and now she just had to wait to see what the response would be.

Paige understood full well that she might win this battle and ultimately lose the war because of what she said here. This conversation was a field of mines.

But there were congressmen and congresswomen who were behind her. There were people who wanted peace and were willing to back her.

No. They weren't willing to back her. They were willing to back peace.

"The western states are seceding." Paige needed to push her advantage. "When they do, you will lose those resources, those monetary exports. Without those monetary exports, this nation loses its value and will go bankrupt. Imagine what the world will look like when the United States is no

longer the superpower. How many nations have you personally pissed off just in your term alone? How many attacks
will we have because the world knows you're unable to
oppress them anymore? Or to even defend yourselves?"

The president stared hard at Paige. "Do you understand
what you are threatening?"

"If you push this, *you* will be the one responsible for
breaking the United States of America."

"Aren't you a patriot? Don't you want to protect our
nation?"

"Against you? Yes. Against a nation that voted you into
power? Yes. Do I think we will do any better on our own?"
No. Because the government was complicated, and she was
quickly beginning to understand that there were no right
answers. Politics was this big game of making as many *better*
choices as they could, knowing that none of them would be
good enough. "I have to hope."

"You have to know that if you succeed in secession—
which you will not—then those very same nations you think
will come after me will come after you."

"It all depends, doesn't it? On what kind of relationships
I build. You forget, there are paranormals all over this
world. They're not just in your back yard. We're everywhere. And you have no idea what kind of partnerships we
already have in play."

The president balled her hands into fists. She looked
ready to say something, but the door opened instead.

"Madame President?" A man in uniform filled the doorway. "You are needed."

The president stood and gestured with her arm for
Paige to leave first. "I will consider what you have said."

"I hope so."

Paige was then shuffled back to the SUV where Naomi waited.

Had she won?

Naomi filled the silence with chatter on their way. Paige wasn't paying attention to where they were headed, but they stopped at the congressional office buildings. Aaron met her out front and escorted her back to the set of rooms they'd been temporarily using, peppering her with questions.

Everyone was abuzz. The only thing Paige got was that something major was happening. So, as soon as she saw a face she knew, she asked what was going on.

"I don't know what you said in there," Congresswoman Jacobs said evenly, "but the president has officially requested a peace resolution with paranormals."

That was good. "And my demands?" She needed to sound like she wasn't quaking her boots.

"Have they been entered into the agreement?"

Congressman Alan hung up his phone and set it down carefully, surprise filling his expression. He looked up at the congressmen around him. "The House is putting the president under investigation for impeachment."

Paige's heart stopped. They'd won. For now. It was a slight reprieve but a reprieve nonetheless.

Paige was going to take it.

34

No word on if Paige was going to get to keep a voice in the government which... she was now wanting, which surprised her. "Will this stop the civil war?"

Congresswoman Jacobs stood stunned. "Perhaps?" She didn't sound sure. "Though, I'm sure it would never have actually come down to that in the first place."

Paige breathed a sigh of relief. This was a solution she never would've thought of on her own. Impeaching the president. She'd abused her powers. She'd gone above and beyond to bring war to the United States.

Paige just had to hope this would work and that they could all find some semblance of stability again. America needed to understand that they could live in peace with their neighbors, no matter how sharp their teeth were.

She looked up, bracing herself. "What do you need from us?"

Congresswoman Hernandez smiled. "Quite a bit."

Paige stayed there for another four hours, giving these congressmen and women and a few of the aides that came trickling in and out what they needed. She gave them video proof of what had happened in Lawrence and in the elven city. She gave them information on the conditions at the prison.

But she did not give them names of everyone. She informed them that the Registration Act had to be stopped. They could add paranormal information to the census and people could volunteer that information if they wanted to.

But forcing people to register was a bad idea, especially since they now knew what the people in power were willing to do with it. Paige didn't know how many other cities and towns had been invaded. But she did know that others had, but the people who had wrongfully been taken *had to be* released and their children returned to them.

When she left, she was given the promise that these people would do everything in their power to ensure their safety.

"We ask that you stand down," Congresswoman Jacobs said evenly as Paige and her people got ready to leave. "We need to see that you and your people are indeed willing for a peaceful solution."

Paige was going to have to work at *that* because her people had been *ready* for war. However, she would be stupid to sit around and do nothing in the months it would take them to do anything about this president. "I will take this information to our people. If you restore electricity and communication, if you restore the social media profiles and everything else, that will go a long way toward rebuilding what was destroyed. However, you need to know that we now understand just how serious the situation is, and we will not be idly sitting on our hands doing nothing. We are going to work toward a future that protects us."

Congresswoman Hernandez came up to her and shook

her hand. "The Senate is pushing for your instatement to secretary."

Paige wouldn't hold her breath on getting that title, but she understood what the congresswoman was saying. If they could get her officially sworn in, it would be harder for her to lead a war.

Which was probably why they'd orchestrated the swearing in on national TV, even without the president's appointment.

Bonnie opened a portal behind Paige. "Let me know if it works"

"Before you leave," Congresswoman Jacobs said, handing her several folders. "You're going to need a staff, and we recommend finding knowledgeable people."

Paige didn't disagree, but were these people she could trust?

"You'll have some time but look over these. Maybe talk to a few?"

"I will. Thank you." Paige stepped through the icy barrier and back home.

Main Street in Troutdale was filled with people. News had traveled quickly. She wasn't entirely certain what news they had received, but there was a celebration going on.

Tuck found her in the throng. He handed her a cup of cider. "National Guard's gone. So's DoDO."

What a relief. That'd actually worked and not a single bullet or magick blast.

"Dexx is still missing."

Paige's heart twitched and turned. Should she have included his location in her demands? No. Her husband was one man. "Have we had any word?"

Tuck shook his head. "I'm sure he's fine."

He had better be. If he wasn't, Paige was now free to go save his ass if she needed to.

"I'll give you a few before we start talking about his replacement. The Red Star Division is necessary now more than ever."

Paige agreed. However, she needed a moment to sit around with her family and just make sure that everything really was okay. She still had this thread of anxiety coursing through her, twisting her mind and distorting her views of reality. She needed to sink into the sense that her family was safe.

She thanked Tuck for everything he had done and went in search of Leslie.

There, she was surprised to see two young kids she barely recognized—the twins.

Ember came up to her and wrapped his arms around her, giving her a good squeeze. He looked to be about the same age as Leah and Mandy, if not a little older.

Rai came up to her a little more subdued.

Paige gave her daughter a one-armed hug and held her close, pressing a kiss into the top of her head, though Rai was just barely shorter than she was. "I think we had a win today."

Leslie pushed her way in and gave her sister a hug. "Madame Secretary," she said with a snort.

"It's not official and probably won't be," Paige said, returning the hug gratefully.

Leslie held on for a long moment. "You did real good, baby sister."

Leslie's quiet voice thrummed through Paige's ear, filling her with warmth. She pulled away slightly. "That was the scariest thing I have ever done in my entire life."

Leslie chuckled. "You've done some pretty scary shit."

"You're not wrong." Paige looked around the nearly empty store. "You need help making more stuff?"

Leslie just shook her head. "We're out of supplies. So, there's nothing we can do right now. Except go out there and enjoy the win."

Paige located Bobby, who was still the same age as when she left. Thank the goddess for that. She was tired of watching her children grow beyond their years faster than she understood. On one hand, this was good. With the fact that they were still possibly heading toward her, she needed everyone in the Whiskey clan to be strong, capable fighters.

But these were years she would never get back.

She stayed close to her kids, all four of them. They didn't appreciate how she wanted to keep them all herded together, but they also didn't fight her much either. Rai kind of did. Paige wished she had been able to help temper that but knew that she still had time to do so. It would just be a little harder now.

Danny came running up to her, waving his phone in excitement. "The communication bans have been lifted. News is flooding in. I have a *lot* of missed calls."

A cry went up through the crowd. A large jolt of noise reverberated around them and then the streetlights all kicked on.

They also had power back.

Those were both good signs.

Paige turned to Danny. "What do we know?"

The Registration Act was in the process of being overturned. That didn't mean it was going to stop. It just meant that Congress had taken up the call and was trying to get it stopped. They were stating it was unconstitutional and that their enactment had been based on false information.

Paige now had a little bit more faith in the system than she had just moments before.

There was also news that the paranormals who had been incarcerated were being allowed to return back to their homes. There were videos from prisons across the nation of paranormals being released. Their loved ones greeted them. Some of them were just being released out into the wild.

There were dozens of these videos peppering the net.

Which just went to show how far the president had reached. She had very nearly won.

And with all of this, there was talk of impeachment. The major news outlets were using these videos as the reasons behind it.

Already, the party lines were drawn. There were many who stated the president was indeed correct in how she'd handled the situation and that anyone who said otherwise was on the wrong side of history.

But Paige knew exactly which side she was on.

The side that needed to win.

But at what cost?

They had skirted the idea of civil war. Looking around at all of these faces, recalling the turmoil she had witnessed in Lawrence and in the elven city, she knew it had to be the *very* last resort.

In the meantime, she needed to ensure that the paranormals who were now living in the open showed the mundanes and the world they could be trusted.

It was a whole new world with a much different set of rules.

But she was a lot more hopeful that this was one they'd be able to win. The American people truly did want peace.

They truly did want the safety of knowing that their friends and neighbors were people they could trust.

She just had to show them how.

Hugging Rai close to her and tucking her head under her chin, Paige watched and soaked in the noise of celebration. They would figure out how. And they would do it. The world was watching.

She *would* show them.

SNEAK PEAK AT LONDON BRIDGE DOWN

Ooooh, paperwork! Actually, the paperwork was a bit more toward *eww*. Dexx slid the paper to the done stack and pulled another one off the too tall stack.

Maybe Paige and Tony weren't all that wrong. "'Bo," Dexx called through the door.

A few seconds later, Rainbow Blue stuck her head through the door. Her afro came in first, followed by beautiful brown skin and childlike enthusiasm. "Yes, boss?" Her deep brown eyes twinkled.

He wasn't angry per se, but Rainbow had been told—asked to take a *little* more time and fill out more of the blanks on her reports. "Could you, oh I don't know, put a bit more description on a few of these?"

"I filled all the blanks, didn't I?"

Dexx suppressed a laugh somewhere between true humor and actual exasperation. "*Coloring* in the boxes isn't really filling it out. Words and stuff. I can't decipher colors."

"Isn't that what you said? White is yours, gold is Tuck's, and pink is—"

This time Dexx really did chuckle. "That's the 'in triplicate' part of the paperwork. You know, carbon copy without all the *carbon paper*."

"What's that?" Rainbow pushed the door further open and entered the office.

Dexx pressed his lips together and counted. "You're special. Short-bus special with a twist. Okay. I need you to *actually* write words. With a subject, predicate, noun, and verbs. You know, to add more *actual* color."

"That's it." Rainbow poked a finger toward Dexx excitedly. "You said add more color."

Was she only listening to the words she wanted? "Yup. Words paint pictures so I know what you did. So on this report, on Tuesday the twenty-fourth, you *red* at location—I'm calling it periwinkle—and green *detailed description*. Is that how it happened? Exactly *as* it happened?"

A grin split Rainbow's face.

"You could face an internal investigation if you left out any of the *brown*, but don't forget grey. I know red is still important, though."

Rainbow sat in the chair across from the desk. "These don't matter. How many times did you say we weren't really bound by the mundane's laws?"

Dexx nodded. That was before he had the hot seat. "You're right. We have a different set of laws, but it's *inside* the mundane law." Wait. That sounded familiar. Hadn't Paige said something like that?

Hattie, nodded. *Yes, cub. She told you almost exactly in those words.* His spirit animal was bored out of her skull, and not happy about it.

Well, shit. *Who asked you anyway?*

Hattie returned to her boredom, her spirit form rolling over and batting at imaginary butterflies.

Life had decidedly become less exciting since he had

the reins. Why had Paige and Tony had to leave? Oh yeah, they either moved on or were forced out.

"Come on, Bo. Please, for the sake of my sanity and your safety, use complete sentences and descriptions. You don't have to write an encyclopedia but make a complete statement."

Rainbow sat in her chair with her hands pressed between her knees and just smiled expectantly.

He tilted his head. "Something you want to add?" He waited for something, anything, but Rainbow just smiled. "'Bo?"

Nothing.

"Hey." He rapped his knuckles on the desk.

Rainbow jumped a little and blinked rapidly as though waking up. "Huh, what happened?"

Dexx let his head fall. Sometimes, it was like talking to a child. "Can you please start using words on your reports? Personally, I don't care if you use different ink to make it mean more to *you* but write words. Real words."

Rainbow nodded vigorously with that smile plastered to her face. "Sure, boss. Full assimilation."

"Are you... okay?" Dexx couldn't have Rainbow flaking. She was the little sister of the whole department. And she was the best detective they had. Better than Michelle, or Tarik. If she flaked, they would all suffer.

"Oh, I'm fine. I just got lost in your eyes."

Dexx couldn't tell if she was exaggerating or serious. "Sometimes I just want to throttle you."

"Why?" She looked as vacant as a deer in the headlights.

"So I can use your neck to warm my hands up."

"Actually, if they're cold you can just stick them in your

pits. It's really okay if you shower. They won't stink or anything."

Dexx dropped his head. "I'm going to kill whoever you learned that from."

Wide-eyed innocence answered. "Learned what from?"

"'Bo, go back to your desk before you leave on a stretcher."

"'Kay, boss. Anything else I can help you with?"

"Find a store with all the color pens, then buy them."

"I bet I can do that before you can."

"It's a race." Dexx showed teeth. She'd probably think he smiled.

Rainbow popped out of her chair and flung the door open, then jumped back with a squeak when she saw a person with a hand raised to knock.

She slipped past Mario Kester, his nearly white hair smoothed back, his bright blue eyes piercing.

Fuck. What did that *asshat* want? Sounded good in his head, so... "What the fuck do you want, asshat?"

Mario didn't even flinch. "Charming as ever, Colt," he said with his slight English accent. "I came by to see how things are going."

"Things are going smashingly. That's how you say that, right? Smashingly?"

"I think the word you're looking for is bollocks. It's a steaming pile of bollocks, and you've got to take a big bite from it." Mario took the seat Rainbow vacated, but he leaned back, almost lounging.

He didn't even ask. Limey bastich. "I'm pretty sure it might be closer to 'You've bollocksed up my day.'"

Mario's eye tightened a fraction. "Too right. But I didn't come out here for a lesson in language usage."

"And there goes the rest of the day." Dexx collected the

pile of papers and tapped them together in a neat stack, turning the top page over so Mario couldn't read it. Not that he'd get much, since Rainbow had only colored in boxes. Mario didn't need to know that, though.

"I come with an offer. No games, no hidden hooks. That's how you say it, right?"

What was he talking about? "I'm sure there's plenty of fine print you'll forget to share."

"Clean offer. My people were very impressed with your performance under my leadership when you helped us. We'd like you to come be an apprentice seeker."

They'd teamed up to take down a very large foe. One time. It'd been a one-time deal. Also, he hadn't been working for Mario. Dixx'd been saving that man's life. "Seeker?" Dexx leaned back, tapping his lip with a pen. "Apprentice? You fish and chip turds are the *apprentices* if anyone is."

"Over here, you call yourselves *hunters*. Not really the best descriptor since you don't eat what you kill."

This guy really knew how to get under Dexx's skin. He didn't know what it was about him. The sleezy tone, the calm as fuck body language, or that sneer. Dexx just wanted to punch him in his smug face. "But *seeker* is so much better? Find, but don't kill? I think I like *hunter* better."

"Call it what you will. Hunter, seeker, doesn't matter. We want you to work for us. Oh, I'm sure this place will be here to check in on in between missions."

This guy really wanted Dexx—a shifter—to work for DoDO who looked down on his kind? "Have you looked around lately? Things between my people— *our people* and you are a bit strained."

"What if they didn't have to be? If you remember, one call from me can make things quite warm for you." Mario shrugged with a hand. "Or they can be comfortable. We have a surprising amount of pull with your president."

"This is your *clean offer*? Innuendo and veiled threats? You've really got to read more books about selling yourself. 'Cause what you're doing here—" Dexx swirled his hand in the air, "—isn't the way to do it." He stood and leaned on his knuckles. "Counteroffer. You get the hell out of my office and keep going until you get of town, or I'm going to let Hattie eat what she kills."

Mario stood, staring Dexx in the eyes, and slipped his hand into his jacket pocket. He pulled a card out and slid it across the desk.

Dexx didn't twitch. He leaned on his desk and brought Hattie out a bit, enough to change his features and turn his eyes a flame green.

"Charming." Mario didn't rush from the office, but he didn't take his time either. He shut the door behind him.

Dexx pushed Hattie back and slumped in his chair. How did Paige get everyone to do what she wanted without threatening?

Apprenticing? As though he didn't have more experience than the whole DoDo house combined?

Mario had a point, though. If they had a line to the President, then things could be pretty hostile for any paranormal that didn't have protection. Like having powerful wards around their town or a paranormal police force like Red Star.

Dexx ran his hands through his hair and blew out his cheeks and scratched his head. One stack of papers to review, and another, much shorter, that was done.

"Enough of this shit. Let's go out."

Hattie turned over, her ears flicked forward in excitement. Days, weeks of sitting in the chair and doing nothing wasn't her idea of fun. Hunting demons and other bad guys, with liberal doses of play. *We cannot stay strong if we lay down to hunt.*

Damn straight. Dexx flipped his jacket from the hook and left the office.

The bullpen was *alive.* Well, when compared to the office.

Michelle entertained Tarik and Frey. Something was apparently worthwhile on the computer screen, but when they saw Dexx they filtered back to their desks and sat.

Rainbow furiously tapped at her own computer.

Ethel sat on a taller stool and watched.

Dexx's desk, which had been Quinn Winters' before it'd been his, was empty. The thing was cursed. However, it *had* managed to survive an all-inclusive department bashing from the lizard wizard and his gang.

"Who wants to go and see if we can find something to break?" Dexx gave the bullpen a mischievous sidelong look.

Blank stares met his.

"Nobody?"

Michelle used her pencil to point at her keyboard nonverbally stating she was busy. Paperwork. And computer work.

Tarik didn't move.

Frey crossed her arms.

"Hey, I'm not the bad guy. Let's go break some shit. 'Bo? You want to see what we can scare up?"

"Can't. I'm trying to snipe this two hundred color painter's pen set."

"What?"

Rainbow already had her attention back on her screen.

Fuck it. *Let's go, cat.*

We can patrol the border.

Maybe. We could go work on Jackie, too.

Hattie didn't think that was as fun.

Once outside, Dexx opened the door on Leah's '72 Ranchero and plopped into the seat.

The motor started almost as well as Jackie had before her accident. The exhaust burbled robust without crackles or pops. Caballo, as Leah had named him, had come a long way since his junkyard refugee days.

He and Leah had given him a Krylon makeover to make him a single color. Road warrior black in satin. He looked pretty menacing now, with chrome highlights.

Where should he go? Hattie's vote was to patrol the border, his own was to work on Jackie, but he couldn't do either.

Paige had told him to stay away from the border and had given him *explicit* orders to not get caught on camera. Psh. Those didn't mean anything.

They were lucky that the cameras only had blurred images of him in the fight with Sven. Through the entire battle with the demons, the shots of him were fuzzy to the point of unusable.

Paige giving birth on the blacktop? Clear as HD could make it. Until the crowd blocked the view. But Dexx? Amazingly free of airtime.

Dexx sat there in the parking space.

Paralyzed.

Indecisive.

The urge to *do something* pulled at him. Responsibility tugged in another direction.

When was the last time that had happened? Sometime in his high school career maybe. What was wrong?

He put his head on the steering wheel and when he

looked up, he was at the police department. The mundane department.

Chief Tuck's old beat up truck added a spot of happy orange color in the black and white lot. Rust and orange.

Dexx shut the car off and pulled the keys, wondering how in the hell he'd gotten there. He reached for the door handle and hesitated. Why would he come here?

Why did Paige have to go to D.C. now? She'd taken Leah and the twins, and now Dexx felt like part, or more than a part of him was missing. Did he feel the need to talk to Tuck? Was that why he was there? He couldn't think of anyone else to talk to?

No. He was there to tell Tuck what to do with his job.

Right?

Dexx opened the door but still didn't get out. Things didn't feel right.

He smelled a person coming up from the back of the car.

"You just going to sit there, or come in?" Officer Shirley and Dexx had a *not quite* adversarial relationship.

The few times they'd met, Dexx'd come out looking stupid.

"Hey. I was just..." Dexx rolled his wrist trying to think of something. "Looking for the boss." That sounded lame even to him.

"Then you're in the right place. You coming?"

No.

Yes.

No.

Maybe.

Shit.

Crap. Dixx got out and headed into the sheriff's station.

Chief Tuck had a largish office with a pressed texture walls and glass halfway up with slatted blinds for privacy.

Dexx stopped, rehearsing what he wanted to say. What *did* he want to say? That he didn't like the big chair, or he *did* like the big chair, but not all the responsibilities that came with it? He inhaled deeply, and let it go slowly.

Before he was ready, he tapped on the door. Shit. Why was he there?

"What's up, Colt?" The most interesting man in the world crossed with Sam Elliot looked up from a stack of papers. Damn, he looked *competent* behind the desk, shuffling papers.

"Gotta minute?" Dexx felt himself say. Had Hattie taken over somehow?

"No, but since you're here, I'll push the mayor back a little." The corner of mouth went up in a smirk.

"Ha, ha. You funny guy." Cop humor. He didn't get it. Or was he really pushing the mayor back? Didn't matter anyway since the city was walled off from the world.

"What's on your mind, Dexx? I hope it's not to tell me you're planning on breaking more of the city, because you and Sven did a pretty good job of it already. The good news is there's less to break now."

Dexx had never *once* intentionally destroyed *any* part of the city. *That* had always been bad people doing bad shit. "Always got to get another dig in, don't ya?"

Tuck smiled broad, without teeth. "If I didn't, how would you know you're alive?"

"Pea and Les keep me on my toes often enough." Did they? Why was he here, again?

"How are things on your side of town?"

Leave it to Tuck to hit the nail so hard it went *through* the wood. "I don't know. I'm the boss now, *really* the boss..."

"And you don't know if you're cut out for it? Maybe you thought you'd have more tee times, and less papers to finish? I thought that too, but it goes away after a while."

It did? At least he'd have a number to write on the calendar. "How long does that last?"

"Not long. Say, a day or two after you die." Tuck grinned at him again. The mentor teasing the apprentice.

"Hm." Situation normal, all fucked up. "So I have *that* to look forward to. Can't we get rid of the never-ending rain of paper? We're on our own now."

"Look, Dexx. I want to say it's all fun and games and you'll be out with your guys crackin' heads and blasting demons, and the truth is, you have a hell of a team, but they need your guidance. I know you want to lead from the front, but sometimes you have to push from the rear. The best Generals of all time lead the charge. The other best Generals lead from smoke-filled rooms. You may be one of them best. You'll have an easier time of it if you find the balance of pushing and pulling."

"How do *you* do it?" Tuck seemed the most level-headed man he'd ever known.

"I trust my guys. I give them the discipline I need in them and trust that they'll do the right thing."

That sounded good, but there was always the desk in front of him. That sucked royally. "I hate paperwork."

"At the end of every good job is paperwork." His face pulled up in another smirk.

The end of every good job? "The shitty kind, right?"

"Yeah, that kind." Tuck managed through a chuckle. "Dexx, I want you to know I'm here for you when you need help. Sometimes I have doubts too, but don't let your people know. The face you show them is the strength they'll take out there." He waved a hand toward the walls. *Past* the walls.

That felt right.

Hattie nodded at the truth of it.

"Go home. Relax. Recharge and come at it again tomorrow. It gets easier even if it doesn't get any more exciting."

Dexx stood up and half turned. "You sound a lot like Alma but without swearing or cookies."

Tuck barked a laugh. "She was an amazing woman."

"Yes, yes she was." Dexx missed her more than he thought he should.

Dexx left the office and drove home to recharge. He had an idea of what might help, but Hattie might not like it.

Jackie had a real shot at firing up tonight.

But only if the world didn't blow up first. What were his chances?

What's Next?

Join us as my husband takes you to England in *London Bridge Down*. Dexx is kidnapped and his memories are wiped. Why? Because his original enemy is back and ready to settle the score once and for all.

Dexx just has to remember who and what he's fighting for before it's too late!

Preorder *London Bridge Down* now!
https://www.fjblooding.com/pre-order-wwmr-book-2

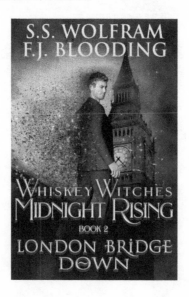

Don't forget to leave reviews! Let us know what you think!

Pre-order now at: https://www.fjblooding.com/preorder

Other Books in the Whiskey-Verse

Shifting Heart Romances

by Hattie Hunt & F.J. Blooding

Bear Moon

Grizzly Attraction

Here's the reading order to make it even easier to catch up!

https://www.fjblooding.com/reading-order

Other Books by F.J. Blooding

Devices of War Trilogy

Fall of Sky City

Sky Games

Whispers of the Skyborne

Discover more, sign up for updates and gifts, and join the forum discussions at www.fjblooding.com.

WHISKEY MAGICK & MENTAL HEALTH

S ign up to learn more about our books and receive this free e-zine about Whiskey Magick and Mental Health.

https://www.fjblooding.com/books-lp

ABOUT THE AUTHOR

F.J. Blooding lives in hard-as-nails Alaska growing grey hair in the midnight sun with Shane, her writing partner and husband, his two part-time kids, his BrotherTwin, Sista-Witch, TeenMan, and SnarkGirl, along with a small menagerie of animals which includes several cats, an army of chickens, a rabbit or two, but only one dog.

She enjoys writing and creating with her wonderful husband and dreaming about sleeping. She's dated vampires, werewolves, sorcerers, weapons smugglers, U.S. Government assassins, and slingshot terrorists. No. She is *not* kidding. She even married one of them.

Sign up for her newsletter, get free books, and join the discussions on the forums when you visit her website at FJBlooding.com.